gorgeous

A COMMANDER IN BRIEFS NOVEL

KRISTY MARIE

Editing and Proofing: Great Imaginations Editing
Cover Design: RBA Designs
Front Cover Photography: Lauryn Alvarez Photography
Cover Model: Joshua Butler
Formatting by: Champagne Book Design

For Jessica

You thought you hid it amongst the shadows, but I've always been able to see your light.

Brilliant and beautiful, you shine above all the rest.

My past has a face.
It's not bloody and riddled with scars.
It's not filled with pain and regret.
Instead, it's the light among the dark.
Beauty among the ugly.
Laughter among the cries.
Freedom from the chains.
The key to forgiveness.
My truth.
My demise.

prologue

Breck

"**B**rannon, is your family religious? Because your sister is the answer to my prayers."

"Shut up before she hears you."

"I'm serious, Brannon. Is your dad a terrorist? Cause your sister is the bomb."

"Captain Jameson, sir. She will hear you."

"Hey, Brannon's sister that's looking hot as fuck in the *Spiderman* tank top. Are we in a museum? Because you're a work of art."

"Drew! Stop it with the lame pick-up lines before your brother kicks your ass for hitting on Brannon's sister."

"Lewis, Cade is too busy entertaining himself elsewhere to worry about what I'm doing. Shut up and go annoy someone else. Brannon and I need to chat with his sister."

The video on my laptop is blurry and slow to load, but the pick-up lines come through loud and clear, and I turn the volume down so I don't wake up Jess in the next room. She's a night owl and considers the sun a devil. I don't know how we're best friends despite being total opposites. The only thing we have in common is our love of movies; superhero movies to be specific.

"Really? He's not here? Move so I can look. I can't see over the enormous beaver you call a head."

"Suck my nuts, Lewis. My head is not shaped like a pussy."

With all the shit talking and pick-up lines on the other end of my laptop, my small bedroom feels much like a bar right before closing.

I'm ready to fire back at the obviously bored Marines when my brother's big brown eyes and his even bigger smile fill my laptop screen. Lopsided and curious, Bennett's grin reminds me why I look forward to every Tuesday. At nineteen years old, Bennett Brannon has become my tribe. My slaymate. My weirdo. My bubba. My annoying big brother. He's the only good that has come out of the Brannon family besides yours truly, of course.

Best friends seems cliché for what Bennett and I have, but that's exactly what we are. Only a year and a half apart, we complement each other in the strangest of ways. He's lied for me. He's fought for me. And he won't ever admit it, but he's cried with me, too. The goofball is all the family I have, and the throb in my chest proves how much I've missed him these past six months while he's been deployed.

"B!" His bottom lip pulls to one side, showcasing the subtle chip in his front tooth —a teenage injury from when he hoped to be a pro skateboarder (insert extreme laughter here). The slight flaw is all that limits his smile from being labeled as perfect. I'm grinning back like a total weirdo when said smile drops into a frown, his eyes narrowing at the camera. "You've been working too much," he accuses me from the other side of the world; pushing back at a fatigue-clad leg whose face I can't see. "You're in college. Aren't college freshmen supposed to be partying? Have fun, B. You deserve it." He hesitates, staring behind him at something I can't see before he whispers, "Have you been getting the money I've been sending?"

I swallow hard and sell him a feigned smile that will convince him everything is peachy. I don't need him worrying about me when his company demands his focus. The military doesn't allow him to reveal where he is or what missions he goes on every day but

I recognize the misery in his eyes when he struggles to crack a joke about how badass he and the other Marines are and that I shouldn't worry my pretty little head about him.

"I'm—"

"Hook me up, dude," someone whines behind him.

My eyes widen before I'm full-on grinning.

These idiots make me laugh so hard.

"Who is that?" I ask Bennett, my head tilted to the side like it will help me see around his enormous head which practically covers the whole screen.

"Captain Drew Jameson, the major's brother," he explains, gathering up the cords to the laptop he's using to Skype me. "It's been a long few weeks, and he's getting out of hand."

Light flashes on the screen and it goes quiet. "Ben? You still there?"

His once pale face fills the screen looking tanner than I've ever seen it. "Yeah, I'm here. Sorry. I only have so much room with the cords." A door closes behind him and he turns the screen, leaning his back against something hard, giving me a view of his face and something like an alley between their military tents. "Okay, sorry. Is that better? Can you hear me better out here?"

I take in his tired, worn face and give him a smile. Damn I've missed him.

"I can hear you much better," I confirm softly. "How've you been? Are you guys still playing softball in your downtime?"

Bennett has always had a ton of friends, unlike me, who prefers to keep to herself. I have one friend from school I've hung on to for the past several years named Jess. Then I have Milos, an online friend. And that's it for my limited social circle. It's not that I can't make friends. I'm just overly selective. I'm not a person who can handle fake bitches.

Bennett, however, could make friends with a rock. A social person just like our mother, he makes friends wherever he goes which, if I'm being honest here, makes me a little jealous. Joining the military was a dream Bennett had as a child. He was determined not to inherit a position in our father's corrupt business. Once he turned eighteen, he gave my father the proverbial finger and enlisted against his wishes. *The Jacob Brannon* worked so hard to raise ruthless heirs to his poisonous throne, and we let him down by being decent humans. After Bennett made it through basic training and my father realized he was never coming home, he cut off every accommodation —including care packages —while Ben was overseas.

He's a royal asshole.

Bennett was a hero in my mind. He pursued his dream and let no one or nothing stop him. I admired the hell out of him and I wanted to be just like him. So, on my eighteenth birthday, I moved out of my parents' house, too. I wasn't going to college for business when I had my heart set on culinary arts. And I needed to give my father a colossal fuck you for abandoning Bennett when he joined the military.

I haven't seen or spoken to them in a year. Bennett continues to send me money every month to use for student loans and housing, but I don't. Instead, I've been saving it for when he returns home, if he ever does. I spend five days a week working at a coffee shop, paying my own way. Bennett has sacrificed enough for me. I wanna be sure he fulfills his dreams, too. It's the least I can do for him.

"Hell yeah, we've been playing softball," he tells me excitedly. "I hit a homer the other day." He swings his arms in front of the camera, making this "ahhhhh" sound like fans shouting for him. It makes me laugh.

"You're such a dork."

He frowns but isn't upset. If one of us didn't insult each other every call, then he would think something was up. It's how we show affection.

"You're a dork," he argues. "How is Jess? Has she asked about me?"

Ugh. My brother and my best friend; not going to happen. Can you say awkward?

"She asked if you were still lame and …" Something moves behind Ben, catching my attention. Is that…

"And? You were saying? Come on, B. Don't leave me hanging."

Farther down the alley, a guy in fatigues is leaning back against a tent. His pants… Oh God. His pants are caught around his boots, his massive thighs straining and flexing while he holds a head of hair in his fist, slamming a woman's face in between his legs. She's … she's blowing the shit out of him and my dumbass brother hasn't even noticed.

"I mean seriously, B. Has she asked about me? She writes to me and we flirt, but do you—"

"Ben, shut up. There's—"

"I feel like I should Skype her one day. Would that be weird? I mean, she's your best friend and all."

Bennett rambles on, insecure about his and Jess' feelings for one another as I stare at the spot behind him. The giant of a man seems like he's staring at me as he crushes the poor girl's face onto his shaft. There's no way he can see me from that far away, right? It has to be like ten or twelve feet. Maybe he can see the laptop but not me. Because if he can, he would see the flush creeping up my neck, my eyes wide at watching him take what he needs from this girl who clearly is doing what many women wish they could do.

He's gorgeous.

All tall and built like a tank. I bet he has zero fat on his body. I can't see his hair since it's hidden by a military-issued hat. But his eyes … deep and soulful as they watch me, watching him, seem so haunted.

"B? Yoo-hoo." Ben lets out whistle and I refocus on my brother and not on the fine piece of ass behind him.

"Just call her, dweeb. She'll talk to you. Unless you're being weird like you are now."

He makes a face and flips me off. "I'm not being weird. I just …" The guy behind him reaches behind his head, grabbing the back of his shirt, and removes it, draping it over the girl's head as if he's trying to keep her from view. His … let's count them. One … two … four … six … eight packs of abs! Holy alien babies, the dude is shredded. Each block of muscle flexes and clenches as his companion works him into a euphoric state.

I'm watching this free porn with the same intensity that Jess and I had when we staked out her ex-boyfriend. He, too, was caught with some cheap floosy with his pants down around his ankles. Not that this girl is a floosy. She could be his girlfriend for all I know.

All I know is he's hot as hell and I'm replacing the woman in my mind with a vision of me. The guy whose arms look like he spends more time in the gym than I would in a lifetime lets his head fall back against the tent. Holy shit! Is he coming? The woman's hands grip his hips, sticking out from beneath his shirt while his dog tags bounce against his sweaty chest as he watches … me. Not her.

I'm going to hell.

Seriously, why can't I stop watching him? Why can't I focus on my dumb brother who is still going on about Jess?

"So you think I should? Call her, I mean?" The sexy guy behind Ben pulls the girl up to her feet, and she dusts off her knees, handing him his shirt. She trails a nail down his bare chest before grabbing his dog tags and pulling him in for a kiss. He pulls his pants up, smacks her ass, and sends her off in the opposite direction. When she's gone, he strides forward, heading toward Ben.

Oh shit. Oh shit. Oh shit.

Be cool, B. No way he knew you were watching him.

He was too far away. But yet, I saw him.

Ugh. This is not good.

"Who do you have here, Brannon?"

Bennett jumps at the hottie's raspy voice behind him. He turns the camera, finally seeing we were not alone in the alley. The webcam refocuses as Bennett shuffles around awkwardly, and holy mother of all that is holy … the dark stubble blanketing the stranger's face … the sharp cut jawline … the square chin … and his emeralds eyes have me …

Bam! I'm pregnant.

The man is freaking angelic. He doesn't look human as he bends down in the focus of the camera. Bennett smiles awkwardly, clearing his throat. "I'm sorry; I didn't realize you were out here, sir." The guy shrugs in response as if those bulky shoulders are saying, *it happens*. "This is my sister B. B; this is my commanding officer, Major Jameson."

The Major Jameson.

Bennett raves about his commanding officer. When he first enlisted, he was a wee bit of a pussy. Bennett was a privileged kid and had zero common sense. He claims he was hazed like a mofo, and things turned around for him after he was assigned to Jameson's unit. He became confident and more knowledgeable in all things adult-like. Bennett claimed major took him under his wing and molded him into the man he is today. My brother respects the hell out of Cade. This fall, he will have served under Major Jameson for a year.

I try for a smile and pull it together. "Hi—"

Major Jameson cuts off my reciprocating greeting, nudging Bennett in the side. "Sister, huh? Might want to Skype her somewhere else so the guys don't see." He shakes his head, catching my eyes before looking away. "They won't hesitate to get off on the sound of her voice."

Kind of like he just did.

My mouth drops open. Was that supposed to be a compliment? I'm not sure, but I catch the slight twitch of Cade's lip, flashing me a playful wink as he disappears out of camera range, taking his phenomenal ass with him.

Bennett glances behind him at Cade's departure and mutters out, "Yes, sir," before turning back to me.

"Did you know he was out here?"

I will spare my brother the awkward and go with, "No. I had no idea."

Bennett and I speak a little longer before he has to go. I tell him that I miss him and that I love him even if he is weirder than the lady with twenty cats down the road. We share a smile and then a laugh. He promises to call me next week but he never does.

That call was the last time I saw either of them.

Bennett died two days later.

Major Jameson was never heard from again.

chapter one

Breck

Dear B,

I have to make this email short. I'm in desperate need of some shut-eye. I've been waking earlier than the platoon to condition with Major Jameson. I've been falling behind in our physical fitness assessments. Some days I think I've made a huge mistake enlisting in the Marines. What was I thinking, B?

By the way, I saw your review of Kick-Ass. Perfectly written. #yourestillaloserthough

Private Bennett Brannon

★ ★ ★

"Are you sure you want to do this, B? I mean, I doubt he'll even recognize you. It's been four years since you've last seen him."

I pause, dropping the yellow sundress into my suitcase. Actually, it's been three years and eleven months, but I don't want to argue with Jess and defend my actions, yet again, that moving from New York City to Georgia without a job, to check up on a man who may or may not remember me, is a good idea.

I will admit, it sounded better in my head a few days ago.

"What happened to all that nonsense about living like we're twenty-two?" I smirk at Jess until I realize my mistake. "Wait, no," I blurt out but Jess is already smiling like she's got me exactly where she wants me. "T-Swift sings *dancing like she's twenty-two*, not living, goober. Besides, you act like you're in your fifties and did not just turn twenty-two, so technically that phrase doesn't apply to you."

"Oh, well. What's done is done," I admit with a shrug, wadding up my discarded dress and shoving it into my suitcase. The fact is, I made my decision and I'm sticking with it. Even if it is a terrible one. A stubborn bitch to a fault, I will fall on my sword before I admit to Jess that I might be questioning this decision a bit. She'll "I told you so," me for days.

With an exaggerated and highly dramatic sigh, I meet Jess' pinched expression. "I need to do this," I say with an air of confidence, my voice not nearly as shaky as when I chanted it last night into the bathroom mirror like I was doing some kind of Bloody Mary ritual. "He needs help, Jess. I can't leave him out there all alone." I shrug my shoulders like this is all the explanation she needs to understand my rationale. I may not be a psychologist or anything, but I think I can find this man—a hero in my eyes—a place to stay, even if I might not have one myself.

Jess doesn't agree, and like gum underneath the disgusting desks at our old high school, she's hardened and not letting go of the subject until I see her point. And right now, her point is simple: She thinks I'm being an idiot.

I'll agree I'm being a bit irrational, but I've already decided.

I'm doing this shit.

Jess tries again, this time softening her normally sharp tone by reminding me, "He has a family, Breck. He doesn't need you to come save him."

Ugh.

"I know he does, Jess." It's like I'm talking to my grandma when I slow my words down so she can fully comprehend what I'm saying without having to repeat it a bazillion times. "But you didn't see him," I say, snatching the newspaper article from my bag—the only way I can think of to get her to understand the gravity of his situation. The paper's edges are crumpled from pulling it out, crying for the man my brother used to rave about being so full of life but now only existing.

I'll never forget his eyes. Haunting, yet sharp and aware. A jawline that is all straight lines and good bone structure from his Irish heritage.

No, I could never forget Major Cade Jameson as I blinked back tears and mourned the once strong and fearless leader my brother looked up to. There, in black and white, was a man in tattered rags, slumped in an alley, his head down as he ate something that looked like soup from a can.

My heart spasmed in a painful beat as I looked on, reading the article about not enough space or resources to get the homeless off the street. Tears spattered the thin paper as I cried for my brother's hero. I cried for a man who gave everything for his country and was left hollow and empty inside.

I tried for a couple years after Bennett's death to find Cade but never could track his whereabouts. His parents hadn't seen him in years. It was like he disappeared until I found him by chance, in the Madison Times, a freak happening I can only describe as fate. I received an email, meant for my father, about the possibility of buying up property in the small town of Madison, Georgia.

I intended on forwarding it. I really did. But something about the headline stopped me. I had been searching for him and he was there the whole time.

He was homeless.

And that's when I knew what I had to do.

I owed it to Bennett.

I owed it to Cade.

I would give up my life here in New York and help Cade find a chance at a new one.

Because Bennett would want me to.

Glancing down at the newspaper clipping in my hand, I read it one more time because I'm a straight-up masochist, and I feed on the hurt that looking at this image makes me feel.

Poverty on the rise in Madison. Many investors turning away from restoring the historic downtown due to a high volume of break-ins. Are the homeless to blame?

The headline judges me, night after night, as I lay awake with a roof over my head and clean clothes on my back. Not that I live lavishly or anything. Jess and I share a squatty two-bedroom apartment in New York City, no thanks to any of my family. My father, fuck his soul, is a greedy piece of shit and keeps his money for himself and my mother. Ever since Bennett and I moved out, Bennett going into the military, and me going to college for culinary arts, they abandoned us like the trash they thought we had become. "Brannons don't join the military. Brannons go to Georgetown like their ancestors and become wealthy businessmen and fuck people over at every opportunity." Okay, he didn't say the last part, but that still doesn't make it any less true. Even after Bennett's death, my parents still ignored me like both of their children died from that bomb.

Jess' sigh pulls my head up from the article. Her tortured expression breaks my heart. I don't want to leave her. She's the only family I have left. I've worked so hard here at the Culinary Institute of America to make something of myself. Top of my class, I scored the coveted internship at À Votre Goût after I graduated, working with head chef Philipe Christianson. It's my dream come true and I'm giving it up. I know Jess thinks I'm crazy, and maybe I am, but I feel it deep in my heart that this is what I am being called to do.

"Can you just wish me safe travels?" I beg her, as tears clog my throat. My best friend sniffles, folding my Batman socks and placing them silently in my suitcase. Reaching across the mound of clothes, I pull her hand into my lap. "And call me every day? I can't do this without you."

Jess' chest heaves and silent teardrops trail down her face, taking the mascara she applied perfectly this morning with them. "I love you, dumbass," she sobs, pulling us together atop the mound of clothes. We lay there, crying in each other's arms until the tears dry and Jess says,

"Come on, let's go look in my closet for something for you to wear that doesn't look like you came from Comic Con."

Laughing, I lift off her chest, noticing the remnants of our cry-fest on her silk shirt. "My clothes are fine," I argue, but she waves me off, already up and headed to her room across the hall.

"B, if you want to score a piece of ass like Jameson, you're gonna have to up your game."

I don't tell her I'm not going to fuck him. I want to help him. But it makes no difference to Jess. Help him or fuck him, either way, you dress with the intent of seduction. Wiping the last of my tears, I tuck the newspaper clipping in my pocket and follow her to her bedroom where we inevitably cry again while promising to grow our small movie blog. Along with our online friend Milos, our blog, The Three Musketeers, has been with us through everything. It's important that we keep it going.

It's not long after our cry-fest that Jess drives me to the bus station and refuses to tell me goodbye. I kiss her on the cheek anyway and wave at her from the window of the bus.

She flips me off.

Text me back, bitch!

Breck!

I swear, I will come find your ass!

I'm getting really scared, B. Please call me.

My phone buzzes with hateful love messages from Jess, but I can't bear to answer her right now. All I can do is watch them. He's healthy and vibrant, laughing at something she says from across the table.

I'm too late.

I should feel grateful that someone found Cade and got him off the street, but I don't. Something like jealousy burns in my throat and tastes bitter as I swallow it back down. I know I said I came out here for Bennett, but the damn romantic in me dreamed up all these scenarios on the twenty-hour bus ride here of Cade and me living together and helping each other cope with our losses.

But's that's not what I found when I finally made it to Madison, Georgia.

What I found was a small town buzzing about a local physician named Anniston McCallister taking in six homeless veterans. The locals at the diner I stopped in were all in agreement that her boyfriend, a pro baseball player, was not happy about her recent life change, and they were all placing bets on when he would lose his shit publicly and bring the media to their small, quiet town.

I knew it was Cade when the older lady swooned, talking about the handsome fella with the enchanting green eyes. You don't forget eyes like his. Or an ass like his—not that granny mentioned his ass, but she had to be thinking it. I listened to their tales of Anniston and her defiant nature until they changed topics and started arguing over politics. That's when I paid my tab and bummed a ride from a friendly guy—okay, he was a little sketchy, but they don't have cabs in Madison. I was desperate to get out of there and find Cade.

I told Frank, the sketchy guy, about Anniston, and he knew exactly who I was talking about. After several uncomfortable minutes of him talking about how hot she is, he agreed to drop me off in the square, at the Farmers' Market, claiming Anniston frequented it almost daily. Which is where I currently sit, hiding in the trees like a total stalker watching her lightly punch Major Jameson in the arm as they dine outside at a rickety picnic table.

I can't hear exactly what they're saying but it's obvious Cade is listening intently as his eyes focus on nothing but her. My stomach roils as I realize he's found a home and he looks … happy. Something tight squeezes my chest but I refuse to cry over this. My mission was simple: find Cade and help him get back on his feet.

Anniston beat me to it.

And, unlike me, she's incredibly beautiful. Jess was right; I am crazy for doing this. Now I've lost my internship and probably the only opportunity I would have had to establish my name in the culinary industry. I'll have to start over, probably at a fast-food joint. It won't be with Philipe, but whatever, as long as I'm in the kitchen, I'll be happy.

I think.

After a few more seconds of spying, I pull out my phone and brace for the *I told you so* and type out a text to Jess.

Cade's fine. He's with some doctor who found him. She's beautiful.

I'm just about to type *I'm coming home* when I hear Anniston's voice much closer than it was before.

"Yes, Theo, we're on our way home. We stopped for lunch." She pauses and then huffs out, "Don't be an ass. I said I would pick you up. How was I supposed to know your flight would be early?"

Anniston paces around the grassy area, rolling her eyes and smiling into the phone when she says, "Keep talking like that, Von Bremen, and I'll make sure that's the last time you speak for the day." She laughs hard, holding the phone away from her ear while Theo yells through the speaker. "I'll tell you what, Theo. If you can refrain from being a total asshole in the car, I'll give you a blowie when we get home."

I don't know if he agrees or what because she winks at Cade who looks as though he could vomit any second. She hangs up the phone and asks, "Want me to drop you off at the house, Gorgeous?" Cade quickly nods his head in relief.

I watch as Cade holds the door open to the SUV parked along the street, and helps Anniston in. As she passes, she strokes his face with her fingertips, and I tense up with … I don't know what. Cade isn't mine. Just because I've sacrificed my potential career for him and left behind everything I have ever known doesn't make him belong to me. My stomach is just upset from the move and all.

That has to be it.

Cade and I share something special, something no one will ever understand but the two of us. Without even knowing each other, Cade and I are bonded.

We both loved and cared for Bennett Brannon.

And his death broke both of our hearts.

I realize two things in that moment. One: My stomach really is revolting against the greasy diner food. Two: Cade isn't homeless anymore and doesn't need me to intervene and save him like I thought. Bennett's letter flashes in my mind.

You don't leave the brotherhood.

Call it insanity.

Call it fate.

Call it curiosity.

Call it me being a stubborn ass, but the promise I made to my brother roots me to the ground. I delete my previous text message to Jess and go with, *Found him! He's even more gorgeous than I remember. He's living with a local doctor. I want to be sure he's okay before I come home. I miss your face. I'll call you when I check into a hotel, and we'll work on the Avengers review.* I end the text with a string of heart emojis and hit send.

Two minutes later I get, *You better, whore. Sneak a pic of him and send it to me. I want to know what the face of your demise looks like.* She also sends emojis after her text, but they vary between hearts and the middle finger. It makes me smile.

With a renewed outlook, I take a deep breath and look up at the heavens.

I'm doing this.

One way or another, I'm going to get to know Bennett's mentor; the person who held his hand as he took his last breath.

I don't respond to Jess but instead wander over to the Farmers' Market. I need a job and a place to stay, but other than that, I have nothing better to do than browse all the fresh grown produce and handmade trinkets. If I didn't have to conserve my money, I would buy a ton of this stuff. All the homemade jellies and sauces intrigue me.

"Can I show you anything?"

I'm shaking my head when I look up and meet the eyes of a woman who has the sweetest expression, reminding me of home. Reminding me of Jess.

"I'm sorry," I start, eyeing the jam, considering splurging on one jar when I see a handwritten sign propped against the table of jams.

Help Wanted.

chapter two

Cade

One year later

"**F**ifty bucks says I can get that chick's number." *Drew's eyes dare me to take the bet.*

I've never been a man to turn down easy money, or girls for that matter, so instead of agreeing, I up the ante, countering Drew's bet with one of my own. "A hundred says I get her number and her friend's." I tip the neck of the beer in the direction of the two girls at the high-top table we've been eyeing all night.

The cute blonde is my type. Long ringlets of soft hair spiral down her back, ending at the edge of a tiny white crop top that showcases her flat, tanned stomach. Her friend, although not what I typically go for, is just as appetizing with her chestnut hair pulled tight into a sleek ponytail.

Someone is getting laid tonight.

And that someone is me.

Drew's hazel eyes narrow, silently weighing his odds. "You're drunk. No way are you getting both their numbers."

Oh ye of little faith.

The dinky wooden chair slides across the tile from the force of my weight as I stand, situating my already thickening length. Just the thought of this challenge is getting my dick hard. Throwing back the last of my beer, I flash Drew a cocksure smile that clearly reflects my confidence in this matter. "You in, or are you out, bitch?"

He drags in an exaggerated breath and frowns. "I'm in."

I'm feeling all kinds of cocky, and I square my shoulders, slamming down my empty bottle of Corona before engaging my swagger toward the poor, lonely girls. My approach seems almost expected when I stop at the empty chair at their table. Both girls smile, bat their eyes seductively, and track over the muscles flexing under my shirt. All that mascara will look phenomenal when it's streaked down their faces in two hours.

Oh yes, these girls are going to be a lot of fun.

Eighteen months, stuck in the asshole of the world, I'm ready to indulge. And these pretty ladies look exactly like my flavor.

"Ladies." The Georgia accent is thick when I drawl out the word. Women love the twang. I can't remember the last time it failed me.

The dark-haired girl giggles, whispering into her friend's ear. I can't hear what she's saying but the blonde one licks her lip before biting down. I'm certain I'm about to be a hundred bucks richer. The brunette invites me to sit with a wave of her hand. "I'm Laura, and this is Candece." I flash them the "Jameson smile," and they giggle.

"I'm Cade." I hold out my hand and Candece, the blonde one, wastes no time grabbing it. I kiss the top of her hand, dragging my lips across the smooth skin as slowly as I possibly can, making sure my eyes remain on her baby blue ones. She giggles.

Not surprising at all.

I reach forward, extending both hands to catch Laura's, and repeat the same greeting. They look at one another, then at me.

Moment of truth. Let's see those lady-balls, girls.

"How 'bout we get out of here?" I suggest, making sure my lips mouth the words against their hands.

Eager eyes stare back at me and ... blink. And blink again.

Come on, ladies.

Okay. Obviously, they need more incentive. My tongue—always my ace in the hole—snakes out, licking Laura's finger, inching down until the tip of her manicured nail is at my lips. I slip their hands together, and their eyes grow wide. Since I'm a betting man, I wager they're not even breathing.

It's go time.

With what I hope to be a sexy smile, I lean down and suck their fingers into my awaiting mouth.

Together.

Hard. Soft. Swirling of the tongue... I'm sucking on their middle fingers like I can already taste the sweet flavor of their clits. Back and forth, I switch speeds until Candece moans.

Bingo.

Lifting up, I let go, licking my lips like I would if they had come all over my face.

"Whad'ya say, ladies? Curious?"

Laura speaks first, with no hesitation this time. "I'm in."

I smile, letting her know wordlessly how much I appreciate her willingness to play and then arch my brows at Candece. I'll take just Laura, but I would much rather double my pleasure. Afghanistan was a lonely-ass time. There's nothing better than this welcome home present right here.

A one-night stand.

Even my mom's homemade apple pie isn't going to taste this good.

I'm shifting in my seat, my dick raging against the seam of my fatigues. Just imagining myself balls-deep in hot, wet pussy has my dick leaking into the fabric.

Please, Candece. Please make my motherfucking night.

I turn on the charm and poke out my lip like I'm fucking pouting and ... she giggles. "Okay. I'm in. But I don't do anal."

What a shame.

I look at Laura. Her returning smile says everything I need to know—she absolutely does anal.

I swear my dick tries to high five me, jumping in my pants with celebratory glee.

Staying cool, I stand, offering my elbows. The girls each take a side—giggling of course—and we head for the back exit of the bar. The wink I flash Drew as I pass has him scowling. "Don't wait up, honey. This might last all night." Laughing, I push past the other patrons with my new company in tow.

"Cade! Wait."

I turn around, ready to negotiate the terms if Drew wants to join us, but when I face him, his hands are dripping blood, pooling onto the dirty tile of the bar.

"What the fuck, dude? What happened?"

Did he cut his hand on a bottle?

I'm pushing through the crowd, trying to get to him, when his words stop me.

"Why did you do this?"

Every ounce of blood drains from my face when I look at him again. I barely recognize him. His body is mangled, his arm nearly detached. Blood is fucking everywhere. Even his eye is hanging by tendons, almost resting on his cheek.

"You did this," he whispers, a single tear falling to the floor.

"I'm … I'm sor—"

I jerk awake, the bamboo sheets tangled around my legs, the taste of copper lingering on my tongue. The memory attacks each time my eyes drift closed.

I can't fight the demons in my dreams. I can't run from the horror. I can only pound it out on the pavement. I'm helpless as they consume me in my subconscious, forcing me to watch my brother die over and over again.

I'm prepared when the door pushes open with a creak. Waking Ans and the guys with my screams at night is a common occurrence. Most of the time, they let me work through it on my own, but when the nightmares turn violent, one of them—usually Ans—will come and distract me with various activities until I'm tired enough to go back to sleep. I call out before anyone enters, my voice gruff, "I'm all right. Go back to bed."

"It's a good thing I don't give a shit."

The sarcastic tone doesn't startle me like it used to when he first came in here. For the past few months, instead of my angel, the devil himself appears in the doorway when I wake the house with screams. This time, as the clock glows 4:09 a.m., Theo pushes through the door, uninvited like every morning, dressed in running gear and carrying two cups of coffee.

"Anniston is still asleep," he mumbles.

Total bullshit. She's not asleep. She pretends to be so Theo and I can run every morning before anyone rises. I'm almost positive she threatens the guys to silence because they wouldn't hesitate to rag our asses about the newfound bromance we have going on. Everyone pretends not to notice.

It's insane, I know. Me and Theo—friends.

Who would have thought?

After that fateful day in the barn when Theo jumped in front of Anniston, sparing her from a bullet to the chest by taking one himself, I have mad respect for the guy. I almost lost her that day. The day she foolishly helped Lawson, one of our veterans, hunt down a girl he had been following for months, trying to rescue her from the clutches of our local human trafficker. The guilt of my delayed reaction still weighs heavy on my shoulders almost daily. I didn't jump in front of her, and I was closer to her than Theo was. No, I remained frozen while Lou, the asshole human trafficker in our town, fired off a shot, intending to kill Ans. If it weren't for Hayes' quick trigger finger, I doubt I would have fired my weapon in defense.

I failed my family.

Again.

"Who's Andrew and why do you have his dog tags?"

I snap to attention at the mention of Drew's name. Theo's rifling around in my stuff, which is common, winding the beaded chain around his fingers. Dammit. How could I be so careless? I always keep them tucked underneath the mattress where prying eyes can't see, but

I was in a bad way last night. It was his birthday. Thirty-first birthday, only six months younger than me.

I kick off the sheets, ignoring Theo's question, and make my way over to him, adjusting my length underneath the waistband of my boxer briefs. Theo catches the movement and curls his lips into a look of disgust.

"Is that mine?" I ask, taking the coffee from atop the dresser.

"Yeah," he says.

I nod my thanks and take a small sip. "So, you nervous?" I grin over the top of the travel mug, nearly gagging on the cold-ass coffee. He's been awake for hours.

Theo glares at me, tossing the dog tags. I catch them in mid-air before they hit the ground, securing them in my palm before giving him an I-know-the-truth wink. "You can tell me. I can keep a secret."

Theo chugs the rest of his coffee and slams his cup down on the dresser. I chuckle at his deflection, which only pisses him off more. "I don't get nervous, Jameson. Stop being such a girl. It's just a fucking wedding."

I'm grinning so hard right now that my cheeks hurt. I love pushing his buttons, especially on mornings like this. It's a great reprieve from the hellish nightmare I endured.

"Just a wedding, huh?" I flick his baseball hat with my finger. "Did the commander finally agree to let you wear the hat?" He shoves me hard, my lower back stinging from the hit I take against the dresser.

"Are we running or talking fashion wear? It's a wedding. I'm showing up. I'll say, 'I do' and then I will rip the ridiculously expensive dress off her body and fuck her until she doesn't give a shit what's on my head."

I belt out a laugh when he storms off, throwing open the door leading out into the hallway. "I'm going to run with Killer," he calls over his shoulder. "She's less of a vagina than you are today."

I'm desperately trying to rein in my laughter before he gets really pissed. "Don't be so sensitive," I garble out. "Let me throw on some shorts and I'll meet you downstairs. Here," I say, extending my coffee to him. "Heat this up while you're in the kitchen."

He grumbles something low I don't catch and lumbers forward and snatches it from my hand. "Put on a shirt while you're at it. I get sick of watching your massive man tits bounce around while we're running."

I flex my pecs up and down with a smile. "Von Bremen, have you been checking me out? I'm flattered—" Theo slams the door before I can get out the rest of my jab, muttering something about me being a cocky motherfucker.

My mood has brightened tremendously in the last fifteen minutes. I was sure I would wake up depressed. As much as I would like to lie and tell you I am completely cool about today, I'm not.

My angel is getting married.

In six hours I will walk her down the aisle and give her away *to* Theo.

My nemesis.

My friend.

My brother.

After everything we've been through, from hating the sight of each other to joining forces to protect her, I've grown to respect him. Underneath all the asshole comments, the lewd and taunting behavior, is a man who loves a woman so unconditionally that he is willing to do anything for her. Even die for her. I can't deny that kind of devotion.

"Jameson! Get your ass moving!"

Theo's patience has expired.

Throwing on a pair of athletic shorts—I skip the shirt on principle—I grab my socks and shoes and hustle out the door before he can shout again.

"Cade!"

Too late.

"It's four in the morning, assholes!"

I bang on Hayes' door as I pass, answering his dickish, yet warranted remark. "We're going. You may want to tell what's-her-name to truck it out of here before Ans wakes up. Otherwise, the commander will take out all those pre-wedding jitters on you."

I jog down the steps with a grin after I hear a thump and several swear words, and meet an annoyed Theo, holding my recently warmed coffee in his hand.

"Don't even say it."

I waggle my eyebrows devilishly, and with a stupid smile, I say it anyway.

"Thanks, biotch."

★ ★ ☆

Our run turns into a sprint. Theo is not having any jogging today which clearly shows that I was right. He's nervous. "I thought you weren't nervous," I tease, walking around to cool off. My chest could literally be a Slip 'N Slide with the amount of sweat running down into my shorts.

"Jameson, do not even try to lump me in with your awkward ass by saying I'm nervous. I'm not fucking nervous." He paces in front of the freshly painted barn, chugging his water and spitting the majority back out. I make an amused scoff, and he whips around to face me. "Seriously, Jameson. Nervous is what you do when you're stalking the jelly girl at the Farmers' Market. This" —he points at his bare chest, having tossed off his shirt two miles ago—"never gets nervous. Anniston and I have been together since middle school. I always knew this day would come."

Apart from the annoying comment about me stalking the jelly girl, a.k.a. Breck, the brunette who works the Farmers' Market booth on the weekends, his comment makes me laugh. "You did not *always* know this day would come. Just over a year ago you were frantic, trying to drive me away from your 'middle school sweetheart.' Don't fucking lie, Von Bremen. You were scared she would send your ass packing. You should thank me."

He scoffs, spitting his water in my direction. "Thank you? For what? Being a pain in my ass for the last eighteen months?"

I shrug, walking toward the barn doors, checking the locks. "My presence made you act on your feelings for Anniston."

Truth.

Theo had been such an asshole trying to get rid of me. He made sure he rubbed my face in his relationship with Anniston. He wanted to make sure I knew she was his. Back then, I had a thing for her and could have done without him in her life. Obviously, times have changed.

Theo throws his head back, his fake laughter echoing in the open pastures. "You are such a chick, Jameson." Another laugh. "Fucking feelings … how 'bout you take your feelings and fucking act on them and ask the jelly girl out?"

My mouth snaps shut, my jaw going tight. He knows why I can't ask Breck out. No matter how appealing she is, I can't. I made a promise to myself to stay away from women.

"Her name is Breck, not the jelly girl," I correct, which only makes Theo laugh even harder.

"I bet you know her bra size, too."

Not technically, but I guess she is a solid C cup. She's always wearing these ridiculous superhero t-shirts that hug the fuck out of her ample chest. A chest that would fit perfectly in my hands to squeeze.

Fuck, it's like she tries drawing attention to them.

Even her cut-off shorts and Converse tennis shoes dredge up fantasies of jerking off onto her tits. Her nerdy style screams *I work in a comic book store*, but she doesn't. Instead, she works all day at the local orchard making jellies and pies. Just thinking about her bent over a stove, my hands wrapping around her hair, twisting it in my fist so the back of her neck cools down … pushing her chest against the island …

Water splashes my chest and I jump back. "What the fuck, dude?" I swipe Theo's backwashed water off my chest, wiping my hands on my shorts. They're damp when I pull them back, and I feel my eyes narrowing into a glare, but Theo doesn't care. He's ridding his nerves by getting on mine.

"You were thinking about fucking her, weren't you? Are you planning on using all the hot water again this morning so you can whack off to your jelly girl?" His eyebrows jump up and down like the moron he is.

Me jerking off in the shower is a running joke in the house.

Not that it isn't accurate.

It's the only way I can get off anymore, but the lack of privacy in this house is egregious. A man should be able to fantasize without some asshole hitting his stopwatch every time he hears the shower turn on. I guess that's the only downside of living at a foundation with five other guys and a commander, the only woman in the house.

Theo doesn't stop there when I flip him off. "Does the orchard girl know you barely eat any of the jam you buy from her every weekend?"

I wonder if Anniston will be upset if he walks down the aisle with a black eye.

"Anniston loves the jam," I argue with the extra annoying idiot today. "And I eat it. Sometimes."

I turn, heading up the hill to the house, done with this conversation. I need to get ready. Soon there will be a fuck-ton of people coming onto the property for the wedding and I want to be sure I'm there to inspect each one of them. Nothing is going to ruin Anniston … and Theo's big day.

"Whatever you tell the demons in your head, Jameson." Theo's stupid face appears next to me. "But you and I both know Anniston eats carbs literally once a day, and she certainly doesn't waste them on jam."

I don't need to look at him to know he is grinning at me with all the smugness he can muster up.

"And we all know Mr. Fourteen-Percent-Body-Fat doesn't either. Admit it—it's my wedding day—you want to fuck the jelly girl."

I sigh, trudging up the hill in the blistering heat. "You're not going to let this go, are you?"

The man that has become as close as a brother knocks into my shoulder. "Not a chance. Now, tell Daddy if we need to have a talk about the birds and the bees."

I punch him with all thirteen-point-five percent of my body fat and make a promise to apologize to Anniston later.

She'll understand.

He had it coming.

chapter three

Breck

Dear B,

I fucking did it! I made Private First Class. Major Jameson is taking us all out to a bar to celebrate. I feel like I'm the baddest motherfucker in the platoon. I gotta go. They're calling for me. #pleasehookmeupwithjess

Love,

The awesomest brother you have

"OMG, Jess! You will not freaking believe the way they decorated this place. It looks like all four florists in the county dumped every flower they had onto this plantation."

Snooping around and calling Jess while Sue, my boss, waits in the van for me to instruct her where to bring the three dozen pies we baked for the wedding might not be the most professional thing I could do right now. But how often does an opportunity to sniff around the coveted McCallister Jameson Foundation come around?

Never.

The closest I get to Cade Jameson is when he comes by the booth every weekend and purchases six jars of jam. Sometimes he says hi. Sometimes he grunts out a thank you and turns around and leaves looking pissed off. He's a strange one, and this is as close as I'll ever get to Cade in his comfort zone. I must seize the opportunity and do some recon. Okay, fine, I'm just a nosy bitch, but I'm beyond curious about what goes on behind these doors. Just judge me now because I have no hope I will come to my senses soon.

My quest to get to know Major Jameson has a way of bringing out the foolish college girl in me versus the new, twenty-three-year-old aspiring baker who has not seen a real penis in three damn years. You can feel sorry for me here. This girl needs a man.

"B, are you seriously sneaking around? They invited you, dumbass. Just be normal."

I make a face but still hold my crouch, peering through the back fence, getting my first look at the pale pink flowers combined with white lilies scattered down a makeshift aisle between dozens of white wooden chairs. "Psht. I am being so normal it would impress you."

"I doubt that. With the way you're gasping for air it's probably obvious to everyone around you that the most walking you've done has been back and forth to the oven."

"Milos!" Jess scolds but it has no bite because she is fucking laughing. They can both suck a nut. Just because I only run if I'm being chased does not mean I'm that out of shape.

"Who invited you in on this call, Milos? Isn't it like dark-thirty over there in Croatia?"

He laughs at my total ignorance of time zones. "As a matter of fact, you interrupted our work call about the review." His tone turns a little stern as he continues to half-ass scold me for bailing on the call last night.

I was busy. Cooking. Shaving. Trying to pluck this stubborn devil hair from my eyebrow. I had to miss the call. I had real emergencies to deal with.

"Don't start. You know what this means to me. I have penetrated their fortress!"

Milos and Jess both laugh at my choice of words. The three of us are so juvenile sometimes. "B. Go do your damn job and keep your hands to yourself. The last thing I need is to have to lie to my parents about why I need money to bail you out for groping all those hot Marines. Remember, self-control." Jess' warning is ridiculous. I wouldn't grope *all* of them. I only have eyes for one.

"Ten-four." They both groan at my military terminology. "Gah, both of you are total buzzkills this morning."

"We're working. The Ragnarok review needs finishing before tonight and we're hung up on whether we like Hemsworth's comedic role with Mark Ruffalo."

"How could y'all?" I whisper-yell into the phone. "He was perfect. This movie was his best yet! Five stars all the way. Y'all better not downgrade him because Mark was off his game." Sighing, they stay silent knowing how I feel about Chris. The man turns my panties into a rain jacket. He could be on screen and fart and I would still think he was golden. Debating his comedic acting … they're crazy.

"Go to work, B. We'll talk later tonight."

Right. I have work to do. Like, maybe "accidentally" running into Cade Jameson.

"Okay. Love you, both of you, even if your opinions on Ragnarok suck."

"Bye, B. Behave yourself." They snicker and hang up.

Pocketing my phone, I straighten to my full height, acting like I belong here. *Be cool, B. You got this shit.*

I round the front of the house, noticing several caterers filing through the front door of the beautiful white plantation house. I'm guessing this entrance is the best place to ask someone where to put these pies. I bound up the creaking steps and notice the front porch is freshly painted, the banisters wrapped in tiny white lights for the wedding. Pink flowers are nestled into planters every few feet, creating an old country elegance. It's simple and beautiful.

Sigh. I want a wedding. I mean, I need a man first but what's the harm in a dry run sans the man? Weddings make me feel magical, like

I'm a princess—

"Excuse me." I startle at the deep voice in front of me. "Can I help you?"

Black dress shoes are where my eyes start. Then they drift up muscular legs that bulge at the seam of his dress pants, letting you know he loves to do leg presses. Farther up his beautiful body, a lean torso is hugged by a white button-down shirt, left open, drawing attention to a deep tan. His eyes, my God … they're almost golden in color. And his mouth is … frowning. At me.

Right. He asked me a question and I'm standing here like I'm star struck.

Get it together, Breck.

I plaster on a smile and extend my hand, which unfortunately is stained an ugly shade of purple from smashing up blueberries all day yesterday. "I'm Breck. I have pies."

O.M.G. Did I seriously just say I have pies?

"I mean—" He stares at my outstretched hand and takes it after a beat of awkward silence. "Can I start over?" I plead, trying to bury my head in my collarbone. My first big job ever and I blow it. Sue will never forgive me if I ruin any future business for her.

The McCallister Jameson Foundation hosts huge fundraisers, and it would be nice if we could do more business with them, but my nerves at being in Cade's house betray me. That's it; I'm destined to be a waitress for the rest of my life. My hand trembles and I look up to see the handsome stranger who opened the door is laughing.

"Come on, Breck, who has pies." Oh, great, a new nickname. "I'll show you to the kitchen."

A sigh escapes with my smile of appreciation. "Thank you."

He leads the way and I'm happy to report that his ass looks just as good as the rest of him.

"I'm Mason, by the way."

I jerk to attention, praying he didn't just catch me checking out his rear end.

"Hi, Mason. It's nice to meet you," I recover smoothly even though my voice sounds timid as I follow him through the halls, heading for what I hope will be the kitchen.

The interior of the house is just as precious as the outside, with light colors and family photos making up most of the decor on the walls. I guess when your foundation comprises of six men, you learn to keep it simple.

"Here we are."

I take in the clean kitchen with stainless steel appliances. But what grabs my attention is the two guys at the breakfast table with a bottle of Jack between them.

"One pussy for the rest of your life, man," the blond teases the dark headed stranger with magnificent blue eyes who I happen to know is Theo Von Bremen, the retired two-time Cy Young winning pitcher. I may or may not stalk his Instagram page.

And, no, the whole reason is not because he has an ass I could bounce a quarter off of. Bennett liked his team. That's the truth, somewhat.

Theo doesn't answer his friend. Instead, he slams back a shot and then does his friend's shot too.

"Ah, shit." Mason touches my shoulder with a groan. "Wait here. I'll be back in a minute."

I nod, entranced by the two at the table, and secretly admire the forearm porn going on as they slam back another round of Jack.

"The same tired blow job for eternity."

Theo, who apparently will have the same tired mouth and pink taco until death do him part, takes another shot while the other hot-ass laughs, continuing to taunt him with fucked up wedding comments.

"What the fuck?"

I jump in response to the familiar voice.

Cade Jameson has entered the building, and holy alien babies, he's wearing a motherfucking tank top with his dress shirt hanging open. Those delicious pecs toy with my emotions as they flex underneath the snug fabric, taunting me with ridiculous requests like: Bite me, Breck.

Crazy, right?

But Cade has some serious voodoo going on because I take an unintended step in his direction when he snaps, "Are you seriously getting him drunk, Hayes?" Cade charges over to the two drunks and snatches the bottle of liquor from the table before turning and pouring it down the sink.

"Aw! Come on, Major. I was just having a little fun with him. He had some nerves."

Cade mumbles something low that sounds a lot like *stupid motherfuckers*.

"Cade." Theo's glassy eyes meet mine like he just realized I was here. And then he smirks at me. "Jameson," he mutters.

"Don't talk to me right now, Von Bremen. Commander is going to be fucking pissed that you're drunk two hours before the wedding."

"Jameson."

Shoulders hunched, Cade sighs at the sink before straightening and walking to the table, sliding a glass of water in front of Theo. "Drink all of it."

Theo laughs at the glass of water and tries to lay his head down on the table. "No, no, no. Stay upright," Cade scolds, his tone laced with exasperation, pulling him up in the chair by his shoulders and then glaring at Hayes. "This is your mess. Sober his ass up right now."

"Jameson."

Cade loses his temper, yelling into the kitchen with the voice of a Marine. "What, Theo?"

Silence.

You could hear a mouse burp in China. That's how quiet it is in this kitchen until Theo snorts and points to me.

"Your jelly girl is behind you."

Jelly girl? What the hell is with these people and nicknames? First I'm Breck who has pies and now I'm jelly girl? Should I be insulted or flattered that they take notice of me enough to give me a nickname?

I'm going with flattered because I'm an optimist.

And well, the fact that Theo made it sound like it was Cade's nick-name for me—however terrible—makes me feel pretty fucking amazing.

Until Cade whips around and faces me with hardened eyes like the last thing he wants is for his jelly girl to be here.

I blink back at his scowl and swallow. Except, it seems like I've swallowed a tennis ball, so I try swallowing one more time before I offer him a hesitant smile.

Mason comes in and places his hand on my shoulder, completely out of breath. "Good. You found them," he says to Cade. "And Breck." He smiles at me with a glint in his eye that I'm not sure what to make of until he says, "She has pies."

Theo, and who I assume to be Hayes, doubles over laughing. I'll admit, it was a super dumb thing to say, but damn Mason, could you not have kept my little blubber to yourself, you walking orgasm?

I'm about to apologize to Cade when I notice he's smiling too. He wipes any evidence of a smile off his face, clearing his throat and addressing me for the first time since I've been standing here.

"Breck."

"Hi." *Hi? Really? Where is your inner hot girl? Your inner cool kid?*

"Hi," he says, his voice full of gravel.

Did I bring a change of panties? If I didn't, these will have to come off. Major Jameson is going to dehydrate my lady parts with that broody look and sexy voice. *Damn it. You are a professional, Breck.*

"I, uh, I didn't know what Anniston wanted me to do with all the pies. We have thirty in the back of the van."

Cade's eyebrows shoot up. "Thirty?"

I nod and clasp my hands in front of me to keep from jumping his fine ass.

He turns around after a beat and motions with his index finger for me to follow him up the staircase. "I didn't know we ordered pies. You'll need to ask Anniston."

"I don't want to bother her," I start, but he shakes his head and continues up the steps. "Don't worry about it. I need to ask her about some things myself."

The last part of his sentence sounds like he's pissed. Surely, it's not about me being here. Maybe there have been other issues? I'm going with that theory.

"Fifty bucks says he takes another thirty-minute shower today."

The two guys left behind in the kitchen drunk-laugh. I don't understand it, but I gather Cade does when his shoulders tense right before he hollers back at them, "Sober up, Theo. Or I'll run you until you puke it all out."

It's assault if I push him down on these steps and tear open his suit pants like an animal, right? I'm asking for a friend, not that I want to do such a thing. But if I was, I blame it on that damn commanding voice he used. I can't help that it went straight to my clit and vibrated around a little.

"Through here," he says, directing me through a bedroom door, only rapping once.

Anniston calls out almost immediately, claiming she is decent. Cade pushes through and I trail behind, feeling very out of place in the moment.

"How do I look?"

Anniston twirls around, and I hear Cade suck in a breath before he clears his throat and rasps out, "Like an angel."

It's not jealousy swirling around, making me feel like I want to shove him out the door so he can't stare at her strapless, gossamer gown. She does look like an angel, but is it awful that I want Cade to think she looks like a troll? I'm a bitch for thinking it but he certainly didn't look at me like that when I walked in. Granted, this sexy chef's jacket hides my best assets, but still, my makeup is on point and my hair is pinned into the cutest French twist that took me over an hour to learn how to do from watching YouTube tutorials. And here Cade is, complimenting her perfect curls and tight body. Okay, so he said she looked like an angel, not that he wanted to dry hump her against the doorframe, but—

"Hi, Breck! You look beautiful!" Anniston swishes toward me, bypassing a scowling Cade. She squeezes me in a tight hug before lightly touching my hair. "Your hair is exquisite. Did you do it yourself?"

And now I feel like a turd. I've only met Anniston a few times at the market. She mostly deals with Sue or sends Cade. I like when she sends Cade.

"Doesn't she look gorgeous, Cade?"

Okay, now I fucking love her. With a confident glance at Cade, I hike up a brow and wait for my compliment. He coughs, eyeing my hair and then trailing down the rest of me at a lazy pace before he licks his lips and admits, "She does."

Score!

I don't even care that he had to be prompted. But then he continues and the high I was riding is quickly sucked out of the room. "Not that I mind another beautiful lady in the house, but what exactly is she doing here?" He openly glares at Anniston and they stay silent, locked in each other's stare as they silently communicate.

"Theo wanted pie," Anniston finally says, breaking the tension-filled silence.

Cade scoffs. "Theo hates pies. He wanted cookies."

Anniston shrugs and taps me on the shoulder as she goes back to sit at her vanity. "Well, he got pies. Any other questions, Major Jameson?"

Her no-bullshit tone halts any further arguments from Cade. The only indication he's still pissed is the twitch of his jaw, but he grinds out one last question. "Do you want her to leave them in the kitchen?"

Anniston turns to face Cade, her eyes going wide. "No," she states, waging a silent war with Cade. "I want her to serve them at the reception like Sue and I agreed upon."

I almost expect Cade to stomp his foot, but he doesn't. He squares his shoulders and inhales a ragged breath before tipping his chin once in understanding.

"Thanks so much for doing this, Breck," Anniston continues like she and Cade weren't just silently feuding with each other. "The guys are excited to gorge on your famous pies." While Cade is glaring holes in her face, Anniston continues to praise me for baking all the different pies so each of the guys could get their favorites. I don't tell her we made twice as many as she ordered. She and Theo are big names in this town, so we thought she may have more guests than expected and wanted to come prepared.

"It's not a problem. I'm glad we could help." I move toward the door when she glares back at Cade. Obviously, they are about to have words. "We'll get set up in the kitchen. Thank you for this opportunity, Ms. McCallister." I turn the knob to let myself out, and Anniston acknowledges me with a big smile.

"The pleasure is all mine, Breck. I plan on doing much more business with you and Sue in the near future."

I swear Cade chokes. But I don't stay and confirm it because Anniston swings back around to face him and they lock eyes in another epic stare-down.

For some reason, I envisioned Cade and Anniston's relationship functioning very differently. I may enjoy this wedding a lot more than I originally thought.

chapter four

Cade

"**Y**ou did this on purpose. Asking Breck to cater the desserts. You know how I feel about her." My tone is accusing and Anniston damn well knows it. I am beyond pissed. "Thirty pies, Anniston? Are you fucking kidding me?"

She ignores me, touching a strand of hair and smiling at me like she has a fucking secret. "I don't understand what you mean. How do you feel about her?"

The low rumble in my chest feels volcanic. I'm two seconds from exploding with rage. I don't want Breck here. She makes my body react in ways I finished warding off several years ago.

"I feel like she's annoying," I lie to Anniston, my arms folded across my chest to ease the tension in my body.

Anniston laughs out an amused sound. "Really? Shit, I had no idea. Maybe we should order the hundreds of jars of jam online then. I thought you liked her brand of wholesome ingredients."

I cut her a look of death and then amend it with a sigh. "You're being worse than Theo this morning." A look of pride comes over her face at the mention of her soon-to-be husband.

"Zip me up, will you?" she asks, thankfully changing the subject.

I almost say no and keep with my attitude about Breck being here, but I know resolve when I see it in the hard set of her jaw. Whatever secret Anniston has, she won't share it with me anytime soon. She has a plan, and whether I like it or not, she's going through with it. It's like I'm back in Afghanistan, butt clenched as I take cautious steps into enemy territory, waiting for the inevitable click of a landmine that will change my life forever.

I admit that's a little dramatic, but after enduring another nightmare and this damn wedding, I'm feeling a bit mopey and a whole lot of pent-up. The shower I had after my run with Theo this morning did nothing to quell my overactive imagination of Breck with those innocent gray eyes and kissable lips. My dick is like Theo when he sneaks carbs and sugar—hyper as fuck. Hard. Soft. Hard. Soft. The front of my briefs has left my skin raw from the amount of pre-cum saturating the cotton material and rubbing up against me. And Anniston fucking invites her under my nose to hang around for the whole damn day?

This can't be happening.

"Cade?"

Right, her dress.

With a sigh that rivals all the epic sighs of the world, I move behind her, clasping the tiny zipper between my fingers. I screw my lips up in a sneer and glare at her in the mirror, but my heart isn't in it because she blows me a kiss and I chuckle.

"I hate you sometimes," I lie, lifting the zipper along her soft curves before releasing.

Anniston turns, fully aware that I don't mean what I said, clutching my cheeks in her hands as we stand face to face in silence. Her eyes, full of love and acceptance, seem to reach right down into my cold, dead heart and warm it from the inside out. I know what she's going to say before she says it. "You deserve to be happy, Cade."

Same argument, different day.

"I *am* happy," I repeat for the millionth time.

Anniston pulls me in for a hug. I oblige and hug her back. I know she means well and I don't want to fight with her on her big day. Anniston doesn't agree with my "no women" philosophy. Probably because she and Theo think sex solves just about anything. But sex ruined my life.

Sex killed my brother.

I killed my team because of a woman.

And after Anniston changed my life by forcing me out of the ditch and shoving food down my throat, I vowed to never let down the second chance family I've gained through her. I don't need any distractions. Apart from what Theo says, sex does not clear the demons from my head. Well, it's been so long I can't remember, but I don't think it will.

Anniston pushes back and places a soft kiss on my cheek. "Theo wants to hire a stripper for your birthday." I snort and she continues, lightening the mood. "I voted for a hooker but Hayes said he had girls he could get to do it for free." She shrugs her shoulders, turning to the vanity and applying a little more gloss to her lips. "You know we like to save money around here."

After sliding her finger in her mouth, she smacks her lips, verifying no gloss is on her teeth. Theo says the move is total bullshit— the sliding the finger in their mouths to get off the extra lipstick—he thinks they do it to make us think about blowjobs. Had Theo seen that, he would have offered to slide something else between her lips. Trust me, I've seen it. He's not shy about unzipping his pants in front of an audience.

"I appreciate the birthday plans, but a quiet evening at home sounds perfect."

She rolls her eyes.

Do I know they'll all do what they want for my birthday? Yep. But there's no harm in expressing my opinion even if they don't give a shit.

"Is it time to go?" she asks.

Checking the fitness watch on my arm, I nod solemnly. "It's time. Are you ready to marry the pain in the ass?"

Anniston smiles big, buttoning up my shirt. "I am," she says sweetly. I finish tucking it in, foregoing the jacket since Anniston didn't want anyone formal apart from Theo—I'm sure she has a kinky reason for it—and offer my elbow to my commander of the past year and a half. She doesn't waste time looping her arm through mine as we head out into the hallway. "I'll need you to make sure the reception goes smoothly. I might be indisposed for a little while," she instructs me.

This time it's me who rolls their eyes. "Of course, Commander."

Hayes and I have a bet going on how long they'll last before they disappear. Hayes thinks Anniston and Theo will disappear after they say I do. I wager they will have a little more class and at least wait an hour into the reception. But after hearing Anniston, I think Hayes might be the winner tonight.

"Thad and his girlfriend Audrey are coming. Theo claims she's knocked up."

"Why does he think that?"

Anniston tries to mask her chuckle when she says, "Because he says no woman would stay with Thad this long unless she had to."

Good lord. Just when I think he's acting like a decent human he says some bullshit like this. "I feel sorry that Thad shares the exact genetic makeup as Theo."

Theo and Thad are identical twins. They may look exactly the same, but they could not be more different. Where Theo is aloof and rude, Thad is caring and polite. They have a weird relationship that I still don't quite understand.

Anniston laughs. "He's only teasing. He's secretly happy for him, but he would never say something so sentimental and make Thad think he was going soft."

This I know. Theo shows affection through crude and crass remarks.

We take the steps slow so Anniston doesn't fall over her dress, and when we reach the bottom, she turns, grabbing my upper arms so I face her. "Are you going to be okay?" she asks.

The answer to this question has everyone tiptoeing around me.

They think I will lose it when Ans marries Theo, but times have changed.

Do I love her? Absolutely.

Do I think Theo deserves her? Grudgingly, yes.

Will my life change after she's married? We'll see, won't we?

"You'll always be my commander," I say instead.

My answer makes her smile. "That's right. We're a team."

A family.

The only people that matter to me.

I shake off the emotions, grabbing her hand. "Let's go get you married so we can dip into Theo's millions."

We laugh along the way to the backyard where we pause at the flower-lined aisle stretched across the field. Theo is pacing at the front until Hayes pulls him to a stop, forcing him to turn and look at his bride.

For once in his ADHD life, Theo stands frozen, not moving a muscle as the music starts and Anniston takes a step forward without me. Apparently, she's ready to get to her man. I pick up the pace, trying to slow her down to the beat of the march, but she doesn't care. She moves at a steady clip until we reach the podium and the preacher asks, "Who gives this woman's hand in marriage?"

Anniston turns to me, waiting. Clearing my throat—I should have grabbed a mint—I announce clearly, "I do."

And then I place her hand in Theo's.

★ ☆ ★

"Sir. Sir. Can you open your eyes for me?"

I probably could but I don't want to. I want the woman, with the voice of an angel, to keep talking to me, the beautiful cadence of her voice lulling me into a deeper trance. I feel her presence move closer, the heat from her body warming the frostbitten skin over my arms where the blanket didn't quite reach throughout the night. Soft fingers, filled with warmth, press against my neck, her unsteady breaths grazing across my ear, sending shivers down my spine.

No sooner than she touches me, she pulls her fingers back and places them on my forehead. I want to close my eyes and relax into her touch, but the beeping of her phone pulls me back to the land of the living. Unfortunately, I'm still alive, and the last thing I need right now is a trespassing charge. "I'll move. Don't call the police," I grumble out, my voice sounding as if I've been smoking since puberty.

Blinking a couple of times, I try to clear the grit and dryness from my eyes, and my God ... those wide, mesmerizing blue eyes stare back at me curiously. Blonde tendrils escape the gray beanie pulled over her ears, accentuating the flush of crimson along her cheekbones. Ethereal beauty is the only way I can describe it. I'm staring at an angel in the flesh.

An angel who is about to call the police.

I blink back at the swollen lips pursed between wanting to speak and being in shock at seeing a vagrant on her property, and then allow my eyes to wander as far as they can in an effort to get a look at the hand still resting on my forehead. She pulls back quickly and stumbles.

"You're freezing. I think you're hypothermic," she explains, her cheeks blushing even more from the wind.

I frown, making a weird noise in response to her concern, and attempt to sit up.

"I'm fine," I lie, waving off her concern, but it sounds like "Ifiiime." My words slur together and I feel like it's time to get the hell out of here before I scare her even more. I attempt to put pressure on my stiff legs, but a searing pain shoots through them, and I groan. With reluctance, I lay back down on the hard ground and just wait. This is going to take me a minute.

"You're not fine," the angel admonishes, giving me a look as though it's pointless to argue with her.

Lying down feels so good.

If she would just give me a few more minutes, I could rest up enough and have the energy to endure another few miles in the cold. My eyes drift closed just as she startles me awake by yelling, "Do not fall asleep!"

I can't deal with this right now. I'm so tired. Dragging my heavy arm over my eyes, blocking out the sun and her beautiful face, I act like a complete asshole. "Leave me alone, lady."

"I'm calling an ambulance," she argues.

Damn it. Do the people in this town really have nothing better to do than to chase off the homeless?

"No," I mumble against my arm, clarifying, just in case the "no" wasn't clear enough. "I won't go."

I lower my arm from my face and force open an eye just in time to see her roll hers, giving me a look that I'm sure makes men bow at her feet. Lucky for her, I don't care.

"I'm not leaving you here to die," she explains, growing more agitated with my blunt answers.

I try not to show my emotions. It's a matter of life or death in the military, but for some reason, this woman makes me want to argue. Who does she think she is ordering me around? I'm not a Marine anymore. I'm a civilian, and not even a contributing one at that. I narrow my eyes and meet the defiant set of her jaw.

She's stubborn, I'll give her that, but so am I.

"Go away," I repeat as firmly as I can, but it comes out slower than usual and more muffled.

With a resigned huff, she rolls her eyes at me and reaches for my arm, wrapping her tiny hands around me. "Come on, dude. Let me get you warmed up, then I promise to let you go so you can die another day."

Am I in the twilight zone? Is this chick for real? Is she really trying to manhandle me up and help me?

For a moment all I can do is just stare at her, my gaze tracking back and forth from her hand on my forearm to her determined eyes. And then she pulls as hard as she can. She doesn't even jostle me. I may be boxing below my class right now, but at six-foot-two, I'm no lightweight. And this angel here, as determined as she might be, isn't going to move me from this spot unless I allow her.

"We can do this my way or the hard way. Either way, You. Will. Do. It. Now. Come on!"

If I wasn't nearly hypothermic, I think that bossy statement would have made my dick hard. *A few years ago, I would have loved to break a little firecracker like her, but that's not who I am anymore.* The angel, adorned in running gear, gives me another pull, and against my better judgement, I let her pull me up. My legs feel like jelly when I finally struggle to my feet, and she quickly nudges her body under my shoulder, supporting my weight as best as she can, and we start taking slow steps. I try really hard to keep from leaning on her since the smell of coconut seeps out from her pores as she struggles to walk with me. *It's obvious this girl has no self-preservation. Helping a stranger out of a ditch ... where is her husband? Or boyfriend? Someone should be looking out for this crazy, selfless girl.*

One foot in front of the other, I drag my frozen feet across the grass, unconsciously deciding that I'll indulge her and see her home safely before leaving. *Fuck! My gear. I'll have to go back and get it. Not that I had much, but I definitely need my blanket. It's not often you find one of those.*

We stumble several more times before finding a good rhythm and balance to our weighted steps.

"What's your name?" She tries to make conversation as our steps crunch along the frozen ground.

Maybe I'm tired of being rude or maybe I feel guilty for not using my manners—*my mama would be horrified*—but I decide to indulge her curiosity and tell her my name. It comes out broken like I have a stutter. "C-C-Cade."

My guardian angel, who has no sense at all, takes a sharp breath and holds it a few seconds before looking me straight in the eye, like whatever is in that beautiful head of hers is now decided.

"It's nice to meet you, Cade. I'm Anniston McCallister."

My life changed forever on that freezing February morning. Anniston McCallister took a scrawny, half-dead man who didn't care whether he lived or died in that ditch, brought him to her house, forced food down his throat, and commanded him to be the man he is today. There isn't a single day that goes by that I don't try to be the man she believes me to be. She's made sacrifices for me and the guys to have a second chance at life, and I want to make her proud.

"Come dance with me, Gorgeous!" The beauty in a dress that enhances her angelic nature waves me over, shoving a scowling Theo to the side.

I wave her off and shake my head. I'm not dealing with a grumpy Theo this evening.

"She won't stop until you do it." Thad, Theo's twin brother and former manager, quietly tells me what I already know. I know she'll come pull me out of the chair if I don't come dance with her. But I try to keep my newfound friendship with Von Bremen intact by keeping my hands off his woman. It's taken us a while to get to this point so I have to make sure he sees that Anniston is forcing me to dance.

Never looking at Thad, I say over the top of my beer, "I know, but your brother looks about ready to explode. I don't need his drama right now."

Thad chuckles, confirming that I'm accurate in my assessment of his brother's state of mind. "You're right. He's liable to cut you."

Anniston frowns at me and I try holding a smile so she knows I'm not upset. If she thinks something is wrong, she'll shoo all of her friends and family out of here and we'll end up in a deep conversation. But instead, she whispers something to Theo and he nods, rolling his eyes at me before stalking to the table.

"Congratulations, bro," Thad starts but Theo waves him off, pinning me with an annoyed look. "Go dance with her so I can fuck her. I'm tired of waiting." I can't help but grin when he snatches my beer and downs it in one go.

"Hurry, Jameson, before I change my mind."

Most women would be appalled at what he just admitted, but if I know Anniston, that's exactly what she whispered in his ear to get him to come over here. I don't let her angelic nature confuse me. She's just as wild as Theo.

Shaking my head, I stand and let Theo plop down in my seat. "I would hate to come between you and pussy." He nods; agreeing that depriving him after Ans held out on him last night would be detrimental to his physical well-being.

"Stop talking and go make me laugh at your terrible rhythm," he mutters, shooing me with his hands.

I ignore his remark and tell Thad and his girlfriend Audrey goodbye before I turn and head toward a smiling Anniston.

"Gorgeous," she drawls, extending her hand to me.

Interlacing our fingers, I pull her close, hip against hip.

"Commander."

Her eyes sparkle under the extra lighting we had installed exclusively for the wedding. She pulls her hand from mine, touching my face with her palm, asking me the same question she always does when she's not sure where my head is at.

"You still with me?"

I nod and spin her around, making her laugh. "I'm always with you, Anniston."

chapter five

Breck

B,

Has your ass ever been tired? Like, literally tired? Well, Major Jameson has worked me so hard that even my balls cried this morning. Cried, I tell you! I know you're probably laughing right now but seriously, every inch of me hurts. The kind of hurt you know will stay with you for weeks. All I can hope is that Jess will be impressed with my new bod. Yeah, I said bod. Make sure Jess is home when we Skype this week. *wink wink* And no, I don't only want to see her. Don't be emotional.

I miss you, loser.

#thefoodheresucks #pleasesendcookies

Private Brannon

"Here you go," I say for the millionth and two times to the nice man in a black suit.

"This looks wonderful, thank you."

I smile, accepting his praise and trying like hell not to watch *them*. He's dancing with *her*.

Cade is dancing with Anniston.

I know it's not logical that I feel jealous at seeing them sway and dip, laughing about who knows what. I know it's crazy. But I can't help feeling a little butthurt about watching them together. Maybe it's because that should be me with him. Had I found him first, maybe it would have been.

That's not what happened though.

I was too late.

"Where are the cookies?" I tear my gaze from the dancing Gods to find Theo, raking his eyes up and down the dessert table.

"Did she seriously order Cade's pies and no cookies for me?" Theo huffs over the cherry pie, running his finger along the outer edge of the pan. "She is getting punished tonight. This is bullshit."

"I can make you some," I offer. Sue would be proud. Making the biggest celebrity in our small town happy is no easy feat. He ponders my suggestion for a moment and then waves me off. "Don't worry about it. I'll get some cookie tonight."

"Are you being disgusting to a lady again?" The other guy at the table with Theo this morning—Hayes, I think—interrupts, nudging Theo's shoulder.

"Did you know she didn't order cookies?" Theo asks him, still not letting the cookie thing go.

Hayes ignores the question and gives me a megawatt smile that I'm sure drops panties every time he lets it loose. "Let me apologize for my rude friend and properly introduce myself. I'm Connor Hayes, but everyone calls me Hayes." He extends his hand over the table and I have to remove my glove to shake it.

"I'm Breck," I return, but he knows that since Mason already announced it in the kitchen earlier.

"You have pies," he says with a chuckle. It seems he remembers my newfound tagline.

There's no sense in denying my awkward. "Yep. That's me."

Hayes hums and eyes the pies spread across the white linen tablecloth.

"How long are they going to dance? I'm ready to leave. The wedding is over, right?" Theo says aloud to no one in particular.

"Can I taste that pie?" Hayes asks, pointing to the one apple pie that remains untouched.

I nod, tearing my eyes away from Cade once again, "Sure. How big of a taste?"

The cockiest smile I have ever seen spreads across his face. "The size of your fingertip."

Heat floods my face as I let his words sink in. Does he really want to take the bite off my finger?

Theo snorts, not looking at us. "You have a death wish."

Hayes laughs him off and nods to the pie. "Can I get a little taste, Breck, who has pies?" His question is laced with underlying meaning, and I pick up on it loud and clear as my vagina, God rest her soul, fist bumps me.

"Uh."

Don't be a coward, B. He just wants to suck it off your finger.

It's a totally normal thing to do at work.

If you're a stripper, maybe.

What do I do? It's not like he's ugly. He has pale blue eyes and juicy lips that should never be given to a man. I bet they would feel fantastic suck—I clear the hormones from my head and decide that I'm taking one for the team. Sue would appreciate that I made our client happy.

"Okay."

See, I got this.

I almost trip getting to the pie and Hayes smiles instead of laughing.

"Do you want me to, uh?" I don't know what I'm asking here. Do I shove my finger in it and pull out his bite, or do I cut a piece like a professional and spoon some onto my finger? I don't get to clarify, because Hayes, the charmer he is, knows exactly what I'm asking, his eyes already narrowing, his tongue snaking out over the plump pillows he's using as lips.

"Stick two fingers in really" —he demonstrates with his index and middle finger, dipping them low as if he has a pie in front of him, making a "come hither" motion back and forth—"really slow."

I gulp and Theo mutters out, "I'm taking all your clients when he beats you into a wheelchair."

"Do you want to leave or not?" Hayes says to Theo, his eyes never leaving my fingers which are poised over the pie. "Go ahead, darlin. Give me a taste."

God help me, I do it like he asks, making the motion with my two fingers back and forth just like he showed me, in and out of the warm pie. He groans, placing a hand on the table for support. "That's my girl. Now, ease them in."

Hayes leans forward and parts his mouth slightly at my fingers which are dripping apple bits and sugar all over the table.

Holy shitballs.

I wonder if Sue will still think this is me taking one for the team?

I'm thinking it's a no but I'm not a quitter, so I push at Hayes' lips and … fuck me. They feel so soft, softer than mine. I wonder what brand of lip balm he uses or if he's lucky and never has a dryness problem. That would be totally unfair.

"Incoming," Theo warns, but I don't know what it means as Hayes wraps his hand around my wrist and guides my fingers past his lips.

And then he's gone, leaving my fingers dangling awkwardly in the air.

"You're getting on my nerves," Cade growls at him, shoving a laughing Hayes away from the table.

"I just wanted to taste your favorite pie since you think so highly of it," Hayes responds, but how he says it seems like code.

Cade lunges for Hayes but Theo steps in between them and adds fuel to Cade's fire. "Better be careful, Jameson, or someone may sample *all* of Breck's pies. They're looking mighty delicious tonight." Theo licks his lips and Cade shoves him into the table, causing it to rattle the utensils.

"Don't start with me, Von Bremen."

Geez. Is the testosterone high in here or what?

"These look delicious, Breck. Can I have some of the strawberry one?" Anniston pushes through the three scowling men and grabs a plate. I wipe the remnants of the apple pie off my hands and cut her a small piece. "Oh no, cut me a big piece," she says.

An amused noise escapes me. I can appreciate a fellow foodie, even though she'll probably run it all off later.

"No problem."

I add another slice, and she slides some of the pies over and takes a seat on the table. "Mmm…this is sooo good," she drawls, grabbing the guys' attention. "You can lick it off my finger, handsome."

Theo rolls his eyes and Hayes only laughs.

"Another time, Commander. Your husband and I have to work together. I would hate to show him up with my oral skills and steal you away." The three of them laugh, lightening the testosterone-fueled mood. I chance a look at Cade to see if he's smiling, but he's not. In fact, if looks could kill, he would incinerate me where I stand.

I scowl back at him, and he looks shocked for a second before he turns away.

Asshole.

What have I ever done to him except smile and try to make small talk?

"So, B…" Anniston starts and ignores Theo who whines about wanting to leave already. "Do you cook anything other than desserts?"

Cade makes a weird noise in his throat that I don't understand.

"Uh, yeah. I do."

Anniston turns around on the table, tugging her dress out of the way. "Really?"

I nod as someone approaches the table. "Can I get you anything?" I ask politely to the redhead who only has eyes on one thing and it isn't my pies.

"No thanks," she tells me, tugging one of Cade's hands from his pocket. "Major Jameson owes me a dance."

Cade grimaces but lets her pull him away from the table.

I hope she falls on her five-inch hooker heels and lands face first in cow shit. Not that there is cow shit, but since I'm wishing and all, may as well go for broke.

"Who invited that whore?"

"Theo," Anniston scolds. "Nicole came with Lawson. She's not hitting on Cade."

Theo scoffs. "Sure she isn't."

I don't know who this Nicole is, but I'm relieved to know she came here with a date and it wasn't Cade. And the fact that Cade seems to be miserable on the dance floor makes me feel a little better, too.

Not that I have a right to be jealous, but hormones are a crazy thing.

"Back to what I was saying." Anniston pulls my attention from Nicole and Cade. "Would you be interested in maybe staying at the house while Theo and I are away on our honeymoon and teaching the guys some cooking skills?"

I must look shocked because she hurries along, getting to the point. "Most of them have basic skills and we rotate cooking nights. Vic is exceptionally terrible." Hayes and Theo both nod, confirming they agree with Anniston's assessment. "I think it would be good for the guys to learn the craft. It will definitely score them more pussy, and I think they will have no problem getting on board with the idea."

Hayes chokes down a laugh and I stare at Anniston McCallister with rapt fascination. Does she really care if they get laid? It's almost like she knows I'm assessing and possibly judging her, but she smiles and pats my shoulder. "Don't worry. You'll get used to me. Just think of me like one of the guys."

Theo rolls his eyes at her comment—clearly, she's not one of the guys to him—but he keeps any comments to himself as he turns back to scowling at Nicole who is still dancing with Cade.

"I'm going to get Jameson," he blurts out to Anniston.

Anniston shoos him and Hayes away in agreement and frowns when she observes Cade's tense shoulders under Nicole's hands. He sways on the dance floor as far away from her as he can get, but she keeps plastering herself to his chest, closing the distance. Cade's eyes scan the crowd as if he's looking for an exit or someone to save him from his current predicament. It's a heartbreaking sight. Knowing Theo spotted it and came to his rescue cements him as a friend in my book.

"He doesn't enjoy female companionship," Anniston tells me as we both watch Theo pull Cade away without acknowledging Nicole at all. Hayes steps in and dances with her, making another sultry smile appear on her face.

I wonder what the story is with her and the guys?

"I didn't know that," I admit after Theo and Cade disappear out the door.

Anniston sighs, taking a bite of pie. "He needs time." It's almost like she's warning me, but that's crazy. Why would I need a warning?

"Thank you for the offer," I say, ready to let her down about teaching the guys some culinary skills, "but I work at the orchard during the day and I wouldn't have time for anything else." With waking up at five o'clock, picking fruit off the trees before sun-up, and then spending the rest of the day in the kitchen with Sue making pies and jam and any other requests we get, my ass is tired. I barely have time to watch my superhero films and keep up my reviews with Jess and Milos. Taking on another job? Uhh … something would definitely have to give and I would feel bad bailing on Sue after everything she's done for me this past year.

Anniston stands and smooths her dress down. "How 'bout we talk to Sue about it?" Her tone is not asking. She's telling me with a subtle smile that she is determined to get what she wants. Well, if Sue doesn't care, then who am I to argue about teaching five hot dudes how to cook?

"Sounds like a plan."

The party is winding down when one of Theo's friends yells across the barn to where Theo is tugging Anniston through the crowd, intent on leaving. "Where are you going? You have to throw the garter!"

Theo stops, turning to look at Anniston, and asks the room, "What the fuck is a garter?"

Hayes belts out a laugh next to me and mutters, "This ought to be good." Almost like everyone expects an explosion from him, the crowd goes silent, waiting for someone to answer Theo's question. Finally, Thad speaks up and informs him it's the elastic belt around Anniston's thigh.

"And I'm supposed to throw it to you assholes?" he asks, clearly amused.

Thad sighs but nods his head. "To all the single men."

Theo pulls Anniston back into the crowd, mischief dancing in his eyes as he approaches Thad. "And what do you do with it?"

Thad rolls his eyes and takes a deep breath before responding. "It's tradition."

Theo scoffs and turns around to meet a smirking Anniston. "You knew about this shit?"

She smothers a laugh and nods. "Come take it off of me, Von Bremen, so we can get out of here."

Theo looks around at his audience and shrugs. "Whatever you losers want."

Someone brings a chair over and Anniston sits, extending her leg out from the sheer layers of her skirt. "Get on your knees, Teddy." Her tone is playful as Theo shakes his head and drops to one knee.

"I'm just supposed to pull it off and throw it to these motherfuckers?" he asks Anniston again, making sure he's clear on the process.

Anniston holds back a smile and props her heel on his thigh. "Yep."

With a chuckle, Theo lifts up her dress, pulls her low in the chair, and buries his head underneath, pinning Anniston's legs with his hands. She squeals out half-assed objections and Cade groans while Hayes' body shakes beside me. Anniston's face flushes and she becomes incredibly wiggly on the chair.

After a couple of minutes of everyone holding their breath in probable anticipation, Theo emerges from under the silk with something white hanging from his mouth.

He looks around and flashes Cade a wink before spitting out the item in his hand and admitting, "Shit. This isn't it." He stuffs what is clearly Anniston's thong in his pocket before turning and snatching her body once again. "Hang on, I'm going back in."

Groans and soft snickers echo in the crowded barn. Apparently, everyone has grown to expect these kind of shenanigans from Theo. Cade shakes his head as Anniston squeaks and tries to stifle a moan under Theo's torture. "I almost have it," he yells from underneath the dress, keeping us updated on his progress.

Anniston's head falls back, and she tries reining him in by calling his name, but he keeps going until the crowd shuffles around, feeling slightly awkward by watching this insane garter throwing ordeal.

"Theo!" Cade shouts out his warning, and immediately Theo pops his head out, his face glistening under the lights.

Holy shit.

No way was he doing what I think he was doing.

Right?

Theo wipes his face along his sleeve and helps up a shaky—and not embarrassed—Anniston. Then with a wicked gleam, he launches the garter at Cade like a slingshot. Cade catches it easily and balls it up before stuffing it in his pocket like it's no big deal.

"Everyone happy now?" Theo teases. The surrounding crowd seems to all laugh except for his parents. His mom looks like she would beat him if she didn't have so many witnesses. His dad just glares. "Well, if that's all, Ans and I are going to make use of this videographer and have her film something more worthwhile." He nods at Hayes directly next to me and says, "Find something to do, boys … unless you want to watch."

Theo's mom explodes. "Theodore! Stop being so crass! Your grandparents are here for God's sake."

Hayes buries his head in my shoulder, smothering his reaction to Theo's scolding, and I try not to act weird about having a hot guy's face in my neck.

"Good to see ya, Ma." Theo pulls himself and Anniston from the crowd, never apologizing for his behavior. "Grandma. Grandpa." He nods at Cade, and reluctantly Cade smiles and nods back, shaking his head as Theo and Anniston nearly sprint from the barn. The only thing that can be heard in the stark silence is, "Fucking finally! How long does it take for me to fuck you, McCallister?"

chapter six

Cade

I'm in some kind of horror movie. She cannot be serious.

"Come again?" My request comes out a little growly, but it doesn't faze Anniston in the slightest. She keeps on shoving clothes—and several sex toys I don't acknowledge—into her already full suitcase.

If this is where she is going to wait me out with silence in hopes I'll let this tidbit of information go, then she is mistaken. She cannot drop this on me and just assume I won't have an opinion. I'm sure she expected my reaction, and this silence is her strategy to get her way.

We've come so far in our relationship in the eighteen months I've been living with her. Even though she's still the commander and controls almost everything, she respects my opinions and allows my authority since I've proven I can be her partner in this foundation instead of her charge. Don't get me wrong, she still kicks my ass in training and tells me when I'm being a broody asshole, but otherwise we're more on equal ground now.

"Ignoring me will not make me go away, Anniston." I try one more time to appeal to her sensible side before I unleash the fury that's building under the surface. Finally, she lifts her face and meets my stare head-on and ... smiles. Mischief and sisterly love smirk back at me.

"Don't smile at me like that," I scold her. I am in no mood for her games. Her smile grows, plumping her rosy cheeks in the process.

"I can smile at you however I want to, Major Jameson. You're just so darn cute when you're pissed." She drops the sundress in her hand and approaches me, dragging her hand along my cheek as she's done from day one. It's her way of showing affection.

"This little frown line right here" —her index finger pokes at a spot close to my lips—"is so incredibly sexy. You have no idea. You could have the entire county of women—hell, even the men, too—on their knees in seconds, fighting for the chance to suck you off."

There it is. The real Anniston I've grown to love, crude mouth and all. I grab the hand poking at my face and cut her a look. I know what she's doing. "You're trying to distract me. It won't work."

She sighs and pulls away. "Fine. I asked Breck to come by and check on things while Theo and I are gone." She shrugs her tiny little shoulders at me and grins. "No biggie."

Yes, biggie. I don't need any help, and I sure as hell don't need Breck, with her distracting ass, lurking around the house, causing all the guys to have wandering eyes. I nearly beat Hayes into an early death last night when he tried licking the pie off her fingers. I don't think I've ever been so jealous in my entire life, watching Breck in her Chef's jacket, a blush staining her cheeks from the steady stream of compliments and phone numbers being thrown her way.

Having her so close, the smell of apples radiating from her hair, had me hard all night. I've never been so miserable in my life and I've lived through some horrible shit in the military. Last night's torture doesn't end there, though. Oh no. Anniston had to strike a business deal to keep my walking fantasy in the house for two weeks. Hayes' shenanigans last night will be nothing compared to what they'll do to me with her living here. It's not a secret I find her attractive. And ... that I jerk off to her in the shower occasionally, but I can't have her, so what's the point in dangling my addiction in front of me?

Two weeks with her is going to be fucking brutal.

"That's very thoughtful of you, Commander, but I think I can handle it. This isn't the first time you've left us for a few days."

She and Theo have left several times before. Granted, it's not been for two weeks, but still … how hard can it be? We have a routine. Most of the guys work, so why the need for Breck unless Anniston is playing some kind of matchmaker game, which is what I suspect.

"Thank you, Major. I thought so, too." She's being formal to piss me off, and she is not going to let this go. I can see it in her eyes. "I also asked Breck to cook meals. The guys love her pies and she told me she used to be an aspiring chef before she left her hometown." She shrugs again, shoving a pair of handcuffs in her suitcase. Looks like their honeymoon of visiting all the ballparks in the US will be from the hotel window. With the amount of toys and restraints packed in her suitcase, they won't get in much sightseeing.

I scoff. "I see. So, is she going to bring the food over or cook it here?" The thought of Breck damp from the heat of slaving in the kitchen immediately has me adjusting myself so Anniston doesn't see. I love food, and I love it even more when I don't have to cook it. Add a feisty brunette with a body of an angel and I'm done. I'll get a blister with the amount of jerking off I'll have to do to stay sane.

"I told her she could fix them here and stay in Lawson's old room."

I choke. "For two weeks?"

"Yes."

"Commander!"

She's enjoying this. Her laugh gives her away.

"With Lawson and Nicole moved out, we have an extra room. Breck doesn't have a car, and the orchard is half an hour away. I don't see the reason behind your tantrum this morning." She cuts me a look before delivering the killing blow. "You don't want her on the streets at night, trying to walk to the orchard, do you? Because you know she won't take a handout."

I hate when Anniston is right.

I hate that she knows exactly what to say to shut me up.

"What about her job at the orchard? Won't she be needed there?" It's worth a shot. One last argument to keep Breck half an hour away and out of my fantasies.

This time, Anniston rolls her eyes, like how dare I doubt her powers of persuasion. "I—and, I really mean Theo here—spent so much money with the orchard for the wedding that Sue graciously offered up Breck and her services."

Does that statement make me hard? Offering her and her services … no, not at all. I'm a reformed player. I don't engage in sexual activities—unless with my hand—anymore. I am getting my life right and I won't have a woman distract me ever again. The last time that happened, I lost everything.

"What about, Breck? Does she even want to do it?" My stomach clenches at the thought Breck will be here under protest. Why does it bother me that she wouldn't want to be here? There's no way I actually want her to *want* to be here, right? That's crazy thinking.

"She was the one who suggested it. Not the whole staying here part" —she waves away the statement—"that was my idea. She only suggested bringing over some healthy meals in case you Neanderthals resort to pizza and cereal to avoid cleaning the kitchen."

The thought had crossed my mind, but I'll never admit it.

"Ugh. You're killing me. Why can't you just let me handle it?"

I flop down on her bed, jostling her suitcase in the process. Her face turns serious when she steps over to me and turns my face to hers and whispers, "Because I love you and I will always take care of my boys."

Fuck me.

"That's a low blow," I accuse, pulling back so I can look at her. "Tossing around the love word is our kryptonite and you know it."

With a kiss to my jaw, she goes back to packing. "When have you known me to play fair?"

She has a point. What Anniston wants, Anniston gets. I blame Theo for making her this way, but realistically, it's just in her DNA.

She loves hard and judges no one. Every decision Anniston makes, she believes, is for the greater good. She means no disrespect or harm by forcing you to do something you'd rather not. She sees it as giving you that little push to do what she knows is good for you.

Translation: I'm fighting a losing battle here.

But I give it one more college try. "I'll take her home every night," I promise. Why didn't I think of that earlier?

"I already told her she could stay. It's rude to uninvite people, Cade."

Is it technically uninviting her? I'm thinking it's alternative hospitality. But regardless, Anniston and Theo are going to load up the rental car that's parked out front and be gone for two solid weeks. What Anniston doesn't know won't hurt her. I'll simply make Breck miserable so she'll beg for a ride home every evening.

Five men in a house … she hasn't seen shit.

I almost let out the evil laugh brewing inside me but manage to smother it down. "You're right. Where are my manners?"

Her bright, answering grin kind of makes me feel like a jerk for plotting Breck's demise at Foundation De La Asshole.

"There's my southern gentleman. I knew you would see it my way."

Sure I do. I fake smile and nod to her suitcase. "Are you planning to let Theo dress at any point in this calendared fuckfest?"

Her laughter fills her—and now Theo's—bedroom, which currently looks like a warzone. She and Theo definitely consummated the marriage last night. I wish I could say they kept it contained to this room only, but I can't. The kitchen, living room, and the gym (who the fuck knows what went down in there) all look just as bad. And before you think we all sat around watching 4-D porn, we didn't. We packed it up and went to the bar, staying until last call. Hayes figured they would wear themselves out by then, and he was right.

"I'll let him dress at game time. I read the ballparks have some kind of weird dress code. Something about wearing socks and shoes or some shit. So maybe I'll let him put on socks and shoes."

Smartass.

"As long as you feed and walk him at some point," I say with a chuckle, getting up and heading to the bedroom door.

"Come hug Mommy and Daddy goodbye."

I ignore him. It's the only way to deal with this type of taunting from Theo. I've learned this over the past year and a half. Most days, we all take it in stride and pop off with something equally demeaning, but since Breck's arrival an hour ago, I'm on edge and need the physical release. Instead of a nasty remark, I punch Theo's arm as hard as I fucking can.

"Now is that any way to show your feelings, Jameson? If you're going to act out about it" —he rubs his upper arm, a shitty grin still wide on his asshole face—"I'll let you kiss me on the cheek."

Before I can rush him and throw his ass down on the gravel, Anniston steps in front of me. "Don't let them burn the place down, okay?" On her tiptoes, she places a feather kiss to my cheek. I chance a look at Breck who's been standing off to the side watching this shit-show transpire. She looks away quickly but I catch her glaring at Anniston before she does.

That's interesting.

Anniston makes her rounds, hugging each of the guys and spouting off last minute orders. I watch Breck the entire time. She never takes her eyes off the ground.

"Okay, time to get on the road, Ans. All your goodbyes are getting my dick hard," Theo says, knocking into my shoulder, pulling my attention away from Breck. "Fuck her. For the whole two weeks," he whispers into my ear.

I glance at Breck to see if she heard his crude suggestion, but she's still finding something highly interesting on her shoes. Theo continues, "Get her out of your system, man. Screw that whole celibacy shit right into her pussy. Fuck her and chuck her."

Sighing, I ignore his comment. "Try not to be too big of a dick while you're away, Theo. Commander packed enough restraints to keep you immobile for days." He scoffs but I continue, "That's if you're conscious after she plows you from behind with the strap-on I saw stashed in her suitcase."

It's total bullshit, but by the way his brows lower and his asshole grin morphs into a frown, I feel pretty proud of myself. I clap him on the shoulder, "Enjoy the honeymoon. Drive carefully."

I walk away with a chuckle catching a low "Uh huh" from Theo.

"All right. Come on, Ans. You better go before we all get diabetes from your sweet goodbyes."

Anniston pulls away from Hayes, tears evident in her eyes, and launches at me hard, wrapping her arms around my neck. I hold on to her easily but then she whispers, "I love you. You know that, right?" I nearly lose my grip as a weird noise bubbles in my throat and my stomach clenches with something like cramps.

"I … I know. I love you, too," I say, sounding like a chain smoker.

Anniston's smile is wide, displaying her perfect teeth. She gives me a kiss on the cheek before Theo yanks her from me. "Goddammit, Ans. One more second and I'm gonna come in my pants. Let's go! It's tradition to blow the groom in the rental car, and I'm tired of waiting."

He swats her ass and tosses her over his shoulder, intent on putting her in the car with no more interruptions, except to holler one more parting asshole remark. "Behave, boys. And keep it wrapped. We're too young to be grandparents."

I can't stop the laugh that bubbles out.

This motherfucker. I might actually miss his ass.

Nah.

I flip him off and wave at Ans buckled into the passenger seat until the car disappears out of the driveway. Then I turn to Breck and politely ask, "Can I offer you a ride home?" Her mouth falls open as if she's shocked that I would ask such a thing thirty seconds after Theo drove away with the commander.

It's best if Breck realizes I'm an asshole now. I'm giving her the option to leave before she thinks any less of me. I almost want her to stay with her pouty bottom lip that has me ready to snatch the back of her hair and bring her face to mine just so I can bite it back into a smile.

But I can't.

I'm not a man that deserves her attention.

It's best if she leaves, for my sake and hers.

When I realize Breck has still not answered my question and it's grown quiet amongst all of us, I chance a look at Vic who just shrugs at me. He's no help. I let out a sigh, suck in my resolve, and raise an eyebrow into my don't-fuck-with-me face, and repeat, "Can I offer you a ride home, Breck?"

From here it looks as though she's on the verge of tears, but I can't be sure because she flips me off, turns on her heel, and storms inside. The only sound as the five of us stand here is the screen door bouncing off the frame.

"That was harsh, dude."

I glare at Hayes who has no business giving me etiquette advice. How many times has he made women cry by leaving them before he tossed the condom in the trash?

"Aren't you late for work? I thought I heard Theo say you were scouting a local high school prospect today."

Theo and Hayes started up a professional baseball scouting agency when Theo retired from the big leagues. The new job keeps Theo in the game but not away from Ans for very long like they both wanted. With Theo and Hayes staying busy, Ans and I have had time to grow our foundation the way we've always envisioned, including the new barracks to house additional veterans. We're trying to grab high-risk guys recently discharged from the military and build skills they need to transition into civilian life before they end up on the street. It's a brilliant system and we're anxiously awaiting the new space.

Hayes nods his head in agreement and chuckles. "I sure do, boss. See you bitches later." He claps Mason on the shoulder as he makes his way to the porch. "Make sure major gets his shower time." He makes a jerk-off motion with his hand and then cuts me a grin over his shoulder. "Otherwise, you' ll have one hell of a day."

Seriously? How many assholes do we have in this house?

"You're working my nerves, Hayes."

He laughs and bounds up the stairs. "That's not all you're going to be working tonight, Major."

Everyone is a fucking comedian. You take a long shower occasionally and they all think you're in there whacking off. There is absolutely no anonymity in this house.

Mason comes over as I stare at the fucking screen door that still hasn't latched. I am going to fix that—today. "It's just two weeks. Don't forget who you are." He taps me on the chest and walks away, instantly making me feel guilty for hurting Breck's feelings.

Screaming *fuck* into the open pasture does nothing but cause Tim and Vic to look at each other with wide eyes. "I'm fine," I reassure them. "I just need a run. I'll be back."

They both nod wordlessly, and I take off into a sprint before I can do or say anything else. Two weeks with Breck is going to be a disaster.

chapter seven

Breck

B,

I got your package yesterday. You and Jess are too sweet to me. *Classic Batman DVDs? Where did you even find the vintage covers? Christmas in the desert hasn't been too bad. Major Jameson asked me and Captain Jameson if they could have some beers with me and watch the Batman DVDs. I'm pretty trashed from all the beers but at least the homesickness is fading and I had a nice time. I hope you and Jess are having a great Christmas. Tell Jess she can always send me nudes to perk me up.*

#thenewxmensucked #yougavethemtoomanystars #merrychristmasbrat

Private Brannon

Head pounding, I tiptoe down the stairs of the plantation. I couldn't sleep after Cade woke me, screaming out, "No, Drew!" The gut-wrenching sounds as he struggled to pull himself from the nightmare tore at my heartstrings. Sounds of pure anguish poured out into the hallway for almost twenty minutes before I got up to go check on him.

Just because he was a dick and ignored me for the rest of the day yesterday doesn't mean I want him to suffer. Well, maybe he can suffer a little, but not like that. I didn't have to concern myself though, because by the time I put my hand on his door, Hayes stopped me and said he had him.

For two hours, I laid there listening to the rhythmic pounding of the treadmill before it finally stopped. I don't know if he went back to bed or went outside. Honestly, I was too nervous to check. He sounded like he was in so much pain, and I know from experience, that with pain comes anger. And I'm no one's punching bag. So I pulled out my laptop and messaged Jess.

Being an insomniac herself, she's always up late at night. Like a best friend, she didn't ask me what was wrong or why I was up at the ass-crack of dawn. She just let me vent about the new sucky Netflix series we had high hopes for.

After a couple hours of working on our latest review of the new Marvel movie, she crashed and I decided I may as well get up and prepare the guys breakfast. Anniston said they get up at five-thirty, but she thought they might take the opportunity and sleep in with her being away. Either way, I'll have their breakfast ready for whenever they decide to come down.

The kitchen is spotless and smells of cleaner when I finally manage to get to it after falling down a couple missed steps on the staircase. Note to self: Fuzzy socks and hardwood stairs do not mix.

The plantation is old, but the inside has been totally updated, and it's gorgeous. I reach out, running my hand along the smooth butcher block island, a double oven with six burners, basically, every chef's dream kitchen. Hot damn, B is doing some cooking today! But first, I need some Tylenol. This throbbing headache behind my eyes is bringing me down like a bad hangover.

Before she left, Anniston gave me a tour of the house. Located downstairs is a fully stocked medical office where she treats the guys for minor injuries and illnesses. But surely, as a physician, she keeps regular meds somewhere close by. I believe the exam room stays locked and only one person has a key, and I'll bet that one person is Cade. No way am I breaking down and asking him where I can find the pain reliever. I'll suffer before I ask that asshole.

I start with the cabinets, going through each one and coming up empty-handed until I see the two small upper cabinets above the refrigerator. Who the hell can reach that? Well, I guess the guys can pretty easily since most of them are at least six feet. My five-foot-six frame will not cut it though. I grab one of the bar stools and drag it to the counter. Before I put all my weight on the granite countertop, I test one foot. I'm not a beluga whale by any means but I like to eat, so a stick I am not.

The counter doesn't creak or splinter in cracks with my Superman socked foot bearing down on it so I risk it and put my full weight down, reaching over to the cabinet. It's still difficult with the refrigerator in the way, but I manage to get the door open and spot meds. I stretch as far as I can, one leg lifting behind me to keep me balanced. Almost … I can just barely get my fingers on the—

"What the fuck are you doing?"

The hateful-ass voice startles me and the bottle of precious Tylenol goes flying to the floor, knocking the lid off and scattering all the tiny miracles of pain relief.

"Damn it! Look what you made me do," I yell at Cade who is standing in the doorway, sweaty and sexy—wait, no, I mean sweaty and asshole. He crosses his arms, and the look of disgust on his face makes me want to throw the rest of the shit in this cabinet at him.

"Look what *I* made *you* do?" he repeats back in a huff. Disbelief clouds his features as he takes a hesitant step in my direction.

You will not look at his bulging arms, I tell myself. You will not— fuck it. They are so damn delicious.

His forearm flexes as if he's forcefully keeping his arms together. The movement has me spellbound as I envision swiping the tip of my tongue along its ridges.

"What the fuck are you doing, Breck?"

His clipped tone pulls me from my fantasy, and I snap to attention, a hand on my hip. "Why do you keep the damn pain relievers up so high? I mean, it's not like—"

A very excited voice interrupts my rant. "Holy fucking shit. My fantasy has come true."

I turn around to see a smiling Hayes licking his lips while his eyes make a slow trail down the length of my legs. "I call dibs," he taunts at Cade with a playful bounce on his heels.

"Get down from there," Cade barks at me way too loud for this hour in the morning. Mason appears behind them, wearing a knowing smile.

Embarrassed and feeling like I'm the kid caught sneaking candy before dinner, I push away from the cabinets and carefully inch back to my stool to get down. Now is not the time to argue with Major Pain in the Ass. I'll just get my two Tylenol from the floor and swallow them down like a lady and make these assholes some breakfast. Cade can kiss my ass with his—fuck! My socks slip on the granite and I nearly take a swan dive off the counter, but I'm a ninja and totally save myself by grabbing the cabinet knobs.

"Dammit!"

I feel him before I see him. Cade swipes me from the countertop and sets me on the floor like I weigh nothing. If it had been in a different setting, I would have felt like a princess being swept off her feet. But alas, it's just me in a kitchen full of Marines, one who wants me gone, and the only thing that will serve as a memory is the sweat of being in his arms for just a second, lingering on my skin. If I admit that I sniffed him, will you judge me? It's been a long time. Give me this one moment.

Almost in a trance from the sweet smell of his deodorant, I mutter, "You're sweaty."

Cade scoffs and pushes away from me. "Go put some fucking clothes on! It's not appropriate for you to be in socks and a fucking t-shirt. Men live here!"

I almost laugh in his face and call him on his bullshit. Anniston has never come to the market in a conservative outfit. It may look like I don't have shorts on under this USMC t-shirt, but I do. So he can take his nun-like attitude and save it for someone who gives a rat's ass. But I'm a professional, so I take a step forward, cross my legs, and curtsy right in front of him. "Yes, sir," I say.

The kitchen goes silent until Hayes lets out a snort and doubles over in laughter. A grin tugs at my lips but I keep it contained out of self-preservation. Cade, a face red with fury, is not laughing. Maybe taunting him after a rough night was a bad idea.

"Go. Put. Some. Fucking. Clothes. On." Each word is gritted out through clenched teeth, and it has the intended effect. Humiliation crawls across my face and I push through Mason and Hayes without letting a single tear fall. I make it all the way to the guest room before the first of many wet splatters hit my shirt.

Fuck him.

How dare he embarrass me like that in front of the guys. I'm dressed. I have on shorts for fuck's sake!

I rip off my clothing and decide to chill out under the spray of the comforting shower. I'm angry, and yes, my feelings are hurt. Part of me wants to go back to the orchard and call Anniston and tell her I'm sorry. I can't do this. Cade is not who I thought he would be, and I think that's what bothers me the most. Bennett got to see a different side of him, and it makes me wonder if it's just me or if this is who he really is now.

Out of the shower, wrapped only in a towel, I flop down onto the bed, my tears finally gone. I'm going home. I'm going to go downstairs and make them breakfast, and then I'm calling Sue. I didn't sign up for this sort of treatment. I bring up my email, settled in my decision about leaving, and type in Anniston's email address. Before I talk myself out of it, I type out my resignation.

Anniston,
As much as I hate to do this after only twenty-four hours, I feel like

it's in the best interest of all parties involved for me to resign from giving the guys any further cooking lessons. They seem to do well on their own, and at this point you would waste money by having me here. I appreciate the opportunity and hope you'll keep us in mind for any future needs you may have.

Sincerely,

Brecklyn

I hit send, and within a couple of minutes, I get a text back from Anniston. *What did he do?* The fact that she knows it was Cade causing trouble makes me feel better. For some reason, I thought she may think it was me causing a scene here.

I try to type out a professional and objective response. *He's being a dick. A BIG one.* So much for being professional.

Anniston sends a string of laughing emojis and then, *He can be. Don't quit yet. Give him another day to come around. If you still feel like leaving after that, I won't stand in your way.*

Ugh. Why does she have to make me feel bad about it? *Okay. Any advice to help me deal with him?*

Her response is quick and to the point. *Push back.*

Hmm. I can do that.

I send her a text back thanking her for the advice then pull out my bag and rifle through the clothes Jess packed for me.

Game on, Major Dick.

Vic and Mason are waiting at the breakfast table by the time I make it back to the kitchen. Showered and changed, I breeze past them and toss them a smile that says what happened earlier means nothing. Clumsy or not, I am not letting Cade's attitude dampen my morning teaching the two men—who are watching me rather curiously—how to make pancakes.

"Gentleman."

Mason grins first. "Breck," he drawls, dragging his finger across the bow of his lips, his eyes dancing with playfulness. At the sink, I wash my hands and say over my shoulder, "I thought we could make pancakes this morning."

Someone chokes but I don't look back to see who it is because Mason answers, "Sounds good."

For the first time since I arrived, I feel a real smile emerge. I love cooking. Just the thought of it brings a wave of calm over me. Cooking has always been my happy place and to be in my element in this extraordinary kitchen is like home. Jess and I would always wake up Sunday morning grumbling over the top of coffee until I was caffeinated enough to mix batter. Magically, Jess' bad mood would dissipate, and before we knew it, we were moaning and humming over a stack of buttery goodness.

Straightening, I turn to the guys, "Are the others coming?"

Vic stares at Mason and they exchange a look before Mason addresses me, claiming, "They went for a run with the major."

A run? Didn't he run enough last night? I don't ask Mason though because that would make it seem like I care what Cade is doing.

And I don't.

"Oh. Okay, well, let's get to cooking. I'm starving," I say instead.

I show my new students how to sift the flour. How to measure the right amount of buttermilk and the proper technique to pouring the perfect circle on the skillet. Both guys work in silence, absorbing my instructions, and I feel all kinds of proud when Mason plops a perfect golden pancake onto a plate.

"Nailed it," he says smugly, his lips twitching with a smile. I hover over his shoulder and stare at his masterpiece. "Can I eat it?" he asks me, already picking it up and shoving half into his mouth. I slap his shoulder and move to his right to take a peek at how Vic is doing with his pancake since they have deemed him the worst cook of the bunch.

I'm not prepared, and I can't stop the sharp inhale that I suck down the wrong way. I erupt into a coughing fit.

Mason asks, "Is that Mickey Mouse?"

Vic throws the pan and the perfect Mickey Mouse pancake into the sink and storms out of the house.

Mason and I stand in the middle of a silent kitchen, watching as the screen door bounces against the hinges where Vic slammed it on his way out.

"I'm sorry," I stutter out to Mason. I don't know what I'm apologizing for, but I can take a guess that Vic is not as cooking challenged as they thought but rather *chooses* not to cook.

Mason makes a soft noise beside me and puts his arm around me, offering comfort. "We didn't know," he admits. With a few pats to my back, he turns off the stove and gives me a pained look. "I need to call Anniston."

I nod, knowing this is a big deal and they need Anniston's advice on how to handle the situation. "I'll be back to help you clean this up."

I wave him off, about to tell him that I can take care of it when Hayes and Tim come in with matching concerned expressions.

"What's up with Vic?" Hayes asks.

Mason shakes his head and pushes past him. "Ask B. I gotta go call Ans."

Hayes grabs a bottled water from the fridge and tosses one to Tim who catches it and takes a seat on one of the bar stools. Hayes takes a look around at the mess that is now all over the kitchen counters and asks the same thing Mason did. "Is that—"

I cut him off, answering before he can go any further. "Yep, Mickey Mouse."

An audible gasp floats through the air and Hayes breaks it with a tortured sigh and mutters, "Holy shit."

I don't understand the significance of all of this, but I can *feel* it. Whatever I just discovered about Vic is huge. Hayes does something on his phone and keeps muttering that he *can't believe it*. Needing something to do, I grab a cloth off the counter and wipe up the spilled flour along the floor.

"What happened?"

I freeze at the sound of Cade's raspy voice. "And what the fuck do you have on? I told you to put some fucking clothes on, not take more off."

Anniston's text flashes in my head as the thought of throwing this flour-crusted rag at Cade's beautiful face overwhelms me.

Push back.

Standing, I toss the rag into the sink and not at his face like I want to, and turn to face him. Cade stands in the doorway, dripping with sweat, his shirt clinging to his pectoral muscles like a second skin. His nipples are hard as they strain against the fabric of his t-shirt. Hair that is wet and ravaged from the combination of his sweat and hands sticks up in the sexiest way as if someone yanked him down to his knees by those chestnut locks and he fucking enjoyed it. The urge to run my fingers through those waves is borderline insane, but when Cade grunts out a distasteful sound, I get my horny self together and respond properly. "I have *fucking* clothes on," I challenge the mountain of a man glaring at me like if he had Cyclops' powers he would burn me where I stand.

"Those are not clothes, Brecklyn."

Oh, it's like that, is it? How does he even know my full first name? Did Anniston tell him? Oh God. What if she told him my last name? Will he remember it? It's been five years so hopefully he won't. And hopefully Anniston didn't feel the need to disclose it.

Cade waits for my response, hands on his hips like I fucking owe him an explanation.

Push back.

"It's called a romper, *Major Jameson.* I suggest you *Google* it if you're confused on the current fashion trends." I want to add *dick* to the end of my statement but I refrain. I also refrain from admitting that I chose the shortest romper that my ass likes to eat, and that I personally would have rather kept my shorts and t-shirt on, but I don't.

Because he deserves it.

And he started it.

Cade doesn't answer me, and I'm not sure I want him to since I can literally hear his teeth grinding as a muscle in his jaw works, flexing back and forth in censored rage. With my head held high, I match his hard stare, my arms crossed. I'm not about to show weakness to this man.

"Okay, children, let's not argue fashion decisions." Hayes breaks our standoff, stepping in between us and giving Cade a slight shove through the door. "We need to talk," he tells Cade, who still hasn't torn his eyes from mine.

Hayes pushes at his chest again, trying to get his attention. "Major?"

Cade still has his hate glare locked on me, and well … I'm fucking tired of his shit this morning.

I flip him off and mouth *asshole* at him.

I swear he growls and tries to push past Hayes, who now realizes his major is about to lose his calm, and orders a red-faced Cade, "Your office. Now."

I try hard not to smile and stick my tongue out like a child when Hayes yanks on his arm, pulling him from the doorway.

I fail.

★ ★ ★

Cade and Hayes have been locked in his office for twenty minutes. The kitchen is clean, no thanks to Mason and his empty promise. He's been MIA since he ran out of here claiming he needed to call Anniston.

The whole house is eerily quiet.

I don't like the silence or the tension I feel like I created. I wish I would have known cooking was Vic's trigger, but from the reactions of the guys, they didn't know either.

Killer, Mason's dog, whines at the back door to be let out, and I open it when no one else comes out. I've seen Mason let her run loose in the pastures so I'm sure it's okay. The question is: Where is Mason? Shouldn't he be around?

I step outside with Killer, watching her dart around and chase a random squirrel. The air is thick with moisture but the sun beating down on my back feels heavenly. You know what the McCallister Jameson Foundation needs?

A pool.

A humongous pool where I could lounge in a chair and watch five chiseled bodies do the breaststroke the entire length of said pool. What is Anniston thinking not having a pool?

Killer barks, darting for the pond down the hill, and I take off after her not wanting anything to happen to her. Not that she isn't capable of taking care of herself. She's a trained military dog, for goodness' sake. Death and battle are her specialty. She's probably killed a man or two. Make sure nothing happens to her ... yeah, right. She should make sure nothing happens to me.

I'm panting, sweat running down my forehead when a beautiful sight pulls me to a stop.

Skipping rocks, along the edge of the pond, is Vic.

A military green t-shirt stretches along his back, his tan cargo pants stuffed into his boots. Vic is the man you see on all the billboards enticing you to join the Marines. He was bred for the military, with his short hair, strong jaw, and unforgiving eyes. Along the water's edge, he stands tall, his towering body looking larger than the trees in the distance.

Killer plants herself beside him, watching the rocks skim along the water's surface. He reaches down at her arrival and grazes his hand along her head, between her ears. I slow, taking measured steps until I come to a stop on the other side of Vic. Bending at the knees, I lower myself to the ground and draw my knees to my chest.

Side by side, we stare out into the horizon, Vic skipping rocks, Killer snapping at the dragonflies, in comfortable silence until Vic breaks it with his raspy confession.

"He was six."

This feels remarkable. Something that will forever be a memory for me.

I don't respond, and Vic keeps going. "He was such a picky eater. My wife and I tried everything." Vic pauses, watching the water ripple. "We were taking him to Disney World that summer, and I told him that if he didn't eat, he wouldn't be big enough to ride the rides." With a faraway gaze as if he's locked in a memory, Vic chuckles to himself.

"We started making everything into Mickey Mouse to encourage him to eat. Fruit. Vegetables. Even his sandwiches were in the shape of Mickey ears."

A tear falls onto my hand and I want to tell Vic that I don't want to hear the rest of his story. My heart already feels as if it's been wounded and he hasn't even gotten to the climax of his story yet. But something tells me he needs to purge, and he's chosen me to confide in. So I suck up my feelings and stay strong for him even if my chest squeezes painfully.

"They deployed me two months before we were set to leave." A shaky breath vibrates out of Vic and then he clears his throat, dropping the bomb I'm not prepared for. "Kai, my son, was killed a week later in a house fire. He gained six pounds that summer. He was big enough to ride most of the rides but I never got the chance to tell him."

His throat works as he swallows down the emotion he's keeping contained in his massive chest but not even staring at the water stops the silent heaves that rack through his body. "They think I can't cook." He turns, giving me his eyes which are bloodshot and watery. "I can. I just don't have a reason to anymore."

I nod, wiping at the tears that drip down my cheeks. My hands shake, and I want to reach out to this broken man. This father who can't bear to cook because it reminds him of his dead son. My voice quivers. "You don't have to," I promise, barely getting it out. And I mean it. Vic makes a low sound in his throat and then picks up another rock, launching it into the water.

He sighs. "Yeah, I do. It's time."

He tosses another rock and I sit quietly next to him absorbing everything he's admitted. I came here under the notion that I was teaching guys who didn't know how to cook some basic skills. Now I realize it's so much more than that. Vic just admitted that he knows how to cook but that it pains him to do so, and with a desperate plea in his voice, he knows he needs to do this to move on. I don't know if I can handle that type of responsibility, but for Vic, I'm going to try.

After a while, Vic breaks the silence and shocks me again. "Let me teach you *my* recipe for buttermilk pancakes," he challenges me with a smile. His face is strained when he extends his hand and offers me not only a hoist up but an agreement.

A pact.

Between me and him. Helping him through this painful transition.

It will be my honor.

My privilege.

And ultimately, a bond that will never be broken.

I clasp my hand with his and let him haul me to my feet, and with a voice more confident than I feel, I challenge him back. "Let's see what you got."

chapter eight

Cade

I can't tear my eyes away as she stands on her toes and wraps her arms around Vic's neck. They stay that way, locked together, and I know she's not going anywhere now. Whatever happened in the kitchen this morning probably had something to do with Vic's past. But by the way Vic curls into her, taking her comfort, I am certain she knows what caused his outburst this morning.

Bonds like those are unbreakable.

I should know. It's what anchors me to Anniston. No one understands my faults and my demons like she does, and no matter what happens, I will never let our friendship go.

Breck and Vic separate, and I notice Breck wipes at her eyes. Is she crying? I'm curious about what they were talking about, but I won't ask. I can respect Vic's privacy. When he wants to share with me, he will.

"You think he's alright?" Mason takes the spot next to me and gazes out the back door, watching Vic and Breck throw a ball to Killer.

I don't know if he's okay or not, so rather than answer him, I ask what I need to know. "What did Anniston say?"

In my peripheral, I see him shrug his shoulder. "She said she would call him later." Knowing Anniston will call him makes me feel a little better. I won't be surprised if she comes home early to be with him.

"Do you think we should still shoot today?"

I debate Mason's question for a minute and then decide that keeping our routine will be consistent, and I know firsthand that when your life seems to be spiraling out of control, having consistency is like a life raft that you can hang on to.

"Yeah, we'll give him a few minutes and then go."

But Vic doesn't need a few minutes. He and Breck are walking toward the house and Mason and I immediately scatter like two chicks eavesdropping in the bathroom stalls. Mason darts up the stairs, and I round the corner and slide into my office, taking a seat at the desk like that was my intent all along.

Laughter filters through the house as Breck's sweet chuckle glides across my skin and goes straight to my dick.

"Are you saying my pies were dry?"

"No, I'm just saying they could have used a little more butter to flake the top."

Vic? A flaky top? What in the ever-loving fuck does he know about cooking? He burns cereal.

A hearty, throaty sound rings closer to the kitchen and I imagine Breck's head thrown back, her sparkling gray eyes twinkling with amusement.

"Well, Chef Vic—wait, is Vic short for anything?"

There's hesitation from Vic, like he's deciding if he wants to let Breck in, to let her get to know the real him, or keep some of his secrets and his distance from her.

A throat clears and then, "It's Vincent."

Breck, unaware of such a monumental disclosure continues on with her annoyingly happy tone. "Well, Chef Vincent, I'm eager to learn your secrets. Please enlighten me on the art of the perfect pie crust."

Vic's chuckle fades, and I feel sure they turned for the kitchen. I fiddle with my phone, no longer able to hear what they are saying from my position in the office. I'm stunned. Vic knows how to cook? Why hasn't he been cooking? Why have we been choking down shit that looks like something Killer barfed up? Was it all a joke? And what did Breck do to change his mind?

So many fucking questions and I can't get any answers because I've been hateful and avoiding Breck. As mean as I've been to her, I doubt she'll even grace me with an explanation, let alone a secret she shares with Vic.

I pull up Theo's number and type out a quick text.

Vic knows how to cook.

In my haste to purge the long-standing charade Vic had going, I fail to anticipate the response I get out of Theo with that text. He doesn't disappoint.

Have you been taking Anniston's birth control pills again?

It was one time!

Anniston gave one to me, claiming it was anti-anxiety medicine to calm me down before I threw out the first pitch at the Atlanta Stadium for a Memorial Day baseball game. Instead of Xanax, it was one of the sugar pills in her monthly pill pack. Either way, Theo won't ever let me live it down.

I'm serious, I respond.

So am I. You sound like a chick. Who gives a fuck if he cooks?

I'm at a loss and let my head bang against the desk, laughing. Von Bremen has a way of making you feel like an idiot.

Because he never has before, I argue, booting up my laptop.

Well, you haven't had sex in a million years either but I doubt we'll gasp and send out a group text when some no name finally pops your cherry.

Before I can respond, another text from him comes through.

I take that back. We'll probably throw a party for the poor girl. She'll need some comforting after that major flop of an experience.

You're an asshole is all I respond with.

And you're hormonal. Get laid and stop fussing over Vic and his cooking skills. He's allowed to have secrets, Jameson.

In a way, Theo is right. Not that I need to get laid, but that Vic is entitled to his secrets. I certainly have mine and appreciate that none of the guys try to weasel them out of me. Thankfully, Theo isn't one for a heart-to-heart chat so he never asks or acts like he gives a fuck.

I send Theo the finger emoji which he returns with a GIF of two girls kissing that I may have saved to my phone for later. I get to work on my computer, catching up the budgets for the foundation. I don't want to seem obvious hovering around the kitchen to see what Vic and Breck are up to.

Before long, two hours go by and the kink in my neck is all the convincing I need to call it a day. I stand, stretching the muscles in my back and arms before I lumber out into the hallway.

The house is quiet.

I poke my head around the corner, chancing a look into the kitchen. The counters have been wiped down, and the dishwasher is humming. No food is left out and I find that rather disappointing. Not that I would ever mention it to Breck. If I'm hungry, I can make myself something to eat. I don't need her to do it.

I wander through the halls, looking for any sign of the guys, when faint singing stops me. It's coming from the gym. I creep closer, the humming getting louder. I peek through the crack where Breck has left the door ajar, and my mouth fucking waters at the sight before me.

With a cloth between her fingers, Breck is singing a song about a lollipop. Full and plump, her lips mouth the words into the mirror, her tongue snaking out, licking and caressing the softness there. I find myself biting down on my own lips, containing almost a whine of neediness when Breck pops her hips out to a certain part of the song. The scrap of fabric she calls a romper is inching higher with each shake of her rounded, voluptuous ass.

Oh my God? Is she trying to twerk?

Breck arches her back, engrossed in the music, and pops her hips in and out, thrusting slowly like she's riding—*get a grip, Cade.*

I manage to tear my eyes from her ass when she straightens, the music fading. She scrubs at a spot on the wall of mirrors and I laugh silently when her brows lower, her mouth pulled tight in concentration as she works the rag, trying to clean a nuisance spot.

When she tries scratching it with her fingernail, I make my appearance known. "I wouldn't touch that mirror without gloves."

Breck startles, her head whipping around, and then very carefully, she tugs the hem of her "romper" down. Fashion my ass. She looks like she would rather be wearing anything but the teasing wardrobe choice only meant to piss me off. I know her game, and I'm not biting.

"Why? What's wrong with touching it?"

I pull my gaze from the laced hem of her shorts to her curious eyes and push further into the gym, coming to stand behind her.

I don't know why I like to make her uncomfortable. She fidgets, watching me watching her in the mirror. Slowly, I drag the pad of my finger along her hand, up her arm, stopping at her bare shoulder. She shivers, and a smile tugs at my lips before I lean in, inhaling her sweet scent. "Because that mirror has seen more dicks than a brothel."

A sharp inhale is her only reaction.

I chuckle, placing both hands on her delicate shoulders which fit perfectly in my palms. "This is Theo and Ans' favorite place." I nod to a spot near the bench that no one uses except for them and possibly Hayes. He has no shame. I'm sure he's christened nearly all the equipment.

Breck swallows. "What about you? Is this *your* favorite place?"

The shower is my favorite place as of late but I wouldn't dare admit to gripping myself with enough force to kill a man, envisioning yanking Breck's head back by her hair while she screams out my name as I impale her from behind. Nah. I think I'll keep that to myself.

"I don't know." I breathe my answer along her neck, my lips almost grazing her ear. "I haven't had anyone to try it out on."

Breck blinks nervously.

Why the fuck did I tell her that? *Great, Cade. You look like a damn loser.*

I push away, a scowl already forming on my face. With a couple of steps back, safely away from the alluring smell of apples, my voice—and sense—goes back to normal.

"I … uh," I start, tongue-tied at what I need to say versus what I want to say. I want to ask Breck what Vic said to her outside. I want to ask what she said to have him back in the kitchen with laughter in his voice.

But I don't ask her any of those things. Instead, my gaze drops to the floor. "Whatever you said to Vic …" I swallow and meet her eyes that now shine with … unshed tears? "Thank you." I hurry out the rest, afraid if she keeps looking at me like she wants to touch me, I may let her. "It's hard for us to talk about things sometimes. The fact that Vic confided in you is …" I shake my head, still shocked that he confided in Breck instead of me or Anniston. "Unbelievable. He must really trust you."

Translation: You must be more amazing than I imagined.

A smile tugs at the corner of Breck's lip. "So, you wanna grab a rag and help me wipe off the dried jizz on this mirror to thank me?"

Low laughter spills out between my fingers as I attempt to mask the amusement at her quick change of topics. She smiles, proud of her comeback, and extends the cloth out to me. I back up, already shaking my head. "Fuck no. Why are *you* even cleaning it?"

She's here to cook, not clean. Anniston made sure we knew that before she left. Commander didn't want us being lazy asses and allowing sweet Breck to volunteer for all the household duties.

Breck shrugs. "I was bored, and I thought I might as well be useful."

I roll my eyes at her generosity and snatch the rag from her hand. "It's Hayes' turn to clean. There is a schedule posted on the door." I point to the laminated calendar taped there. "Besides, most of the" — my brows lift when I quote her—"'*jizz*' is probably his."

Her face scrunches up like she tasted something sour.

"Gross," she says simply, backing away from the mirror.

With a smile, I head towards the door. "Come on, we're going out back to skeet shoot."

In her defense, she only looks slightly scared for a second.

In my defense, her innocence makes me weak as fuck and I asked her before my brain caught up to my actions.

"B!"

Mason shouts to Breck from the bed of my truck, reaching over the side for her hand. She squeals and takes off in the worst run I've ever seen. She could use some lessons on proper spine alignment. I hold back a smile as Hayes lifts her over the edge, grabbing his back in a moan when he sets her down in the bed with him, Mason, and Killer.

She slaps his shoulder as Hayes winces. "What did you eat this morning? Lead?" Breck shoves him, and he grabs her hands, pulling her into him for a hug. "I'm just teasing, darlin." Still in his arms, Hayes winks at me over her head. I keep my cool, walking over to the driver's side and opening the door.

"Hey, Major?" Groaning, I push back from the door and peer into the back where Hayes has finally let go of Breck. "You planning on teaching her to shoot?"

I shrug a shoulder and remain indifferent even though my dick just jumped at the idea of wrapping my arms around Breck, my hands on hers, breathing calmly into her ear and telling her when to pull.

"If she wants to," I say to the way too eager sniper who is still far too close to Breck for my liking. But he knows he is, and that's exactly why he's staying so close. He loves to push my fucking buttons. Not much gets under my skin … except this girl.

My jelly girl.

The brunette that annoys me and intrigues me.

The first woman in five years to get a reaction out of my dick.

"Whad'ya say, honey? Want the best sharp shooter in the southeast to teach you how to beat the major in skeet shooting?"

I make a face when he winks over her head while she blabbers about not being sure if she wants to or not.

I'm not going to stand in his way if he really wants to teach her. Hayes' eagerness to pick up a shotgun is nothing short of a miracle. Eighteen months ago, he couldn't look at a gun without having an anxiety attack. It wasn't until he had to fire a shot into Lou, to save Anniston, that he overcame most of his issues. He still doesn't practice sniping, as was his profession in the military, but he will shoot skeets with us and practice with targets occasionally.

Anniston and I consider anything gun related a win.

"We need to get moving. It will only get hotter," I say, rethinking this whole idea when I see that Breck's romper is already sticking to her breasts. Her neck is damp and the hair at her ears is starting to curl. "Breck, get in the cab with Tim. Vic can ride in the back."

Breck glares at me, her chin tipped down and her smile bearing way too much confidence. "I'm good here, thanks."

Hayes wastes no time jumping in. "I'll take care of her, Major. Come on, beautiful. You can sit in my lap so I can keep my arms around you." The walking erection flops down in the bed and pats his lap for a grinning Breck. "Safety first, B. Ain't that right, Major?"

He wants me to beat the fuck out of him.

He's literally daring me to punch the cocky smirk right off his face.

I play it cool, tamping down the urge to snatch him out of my truck and take a cheap shot at his pretty-boy face. "Right. Safety first. Let's go." I tap the edge of the truck and get in, feeling petty when I see Hayes' smile drop. Another confirmation he's not into Breck and only doing these things to piss me off.

After putting the truck in gear, I turn up the country song about a body like a back road, reminding me of Breck's delightful curves.

"Ooh! Turn it up!" she yells into the open back window.

"Sit down," I scold her when she stands up against the back glass, her hips already moving to the music.

"I promise, I'll hang on," she screams over the wind. Vic tosses me an amused grin as he watches Breck dance in the bed of my pickup. I slow down, careful not to jostle her since she's stubborn as fuck, and find my eyes darting to the review mirror more than they should.

Her hands drum on the hood as the chorus kicks up and I have to fight the urge to slam on the brakes just to take it all in. Her rhythmic hips sway behind the glass, matching the melody of the song that seems to have been written just for her.

But I don't stop.

I don't take it all in.

Instead, I tap the brakes and bark out, "Keep your hands on the hood!"

She laughs, unfazed. "Yes, sir," she says, but she doesn't put her hands down. She reaches up even farther, pissing me off more when the shorts of her romper lift up higher, exposing a small birthmark on her inner thigh. Tim masks a laugh and Vic looks out his window to hide his own smile.

I sigh. "The fucking women in this house…"

Vic chuckles and raps his knuckles against the door. "It's best if you realize it now."

"Realize what?"

Vic stares longingly out at the hills as the new barracks we're building come into view. "That you're already done for."

"I don't understand," I tell him. Really. He might as well be speaking Mandarin right now.

Vic blows out a breath and smiles. "You'll know soon enough."

I slow to a stop and Hayes bails out the side, helping Breck down. Vic hops out with Tim right behind him and I don't have time to ask him exactly what he meant about knowing soon enough. Sounds like voodoo to me.

Everyone has already gone around to the back of the barracks and set up by the time I arrive. Hayes is going through the basics of gun safety with B. "This is the safety here." He demonstrates how to flip it off and on and then explains how to track the skeet and brace the shotgun against your shoulder. Breck nods and worries a piece of hair between her fingers.

"Will the kickback hurt?"

Mason makes an amused sound low in his throat before answering. "We're just using a twenty gauge."

Breck casts a worried look at me and I explain. "The smaller the gauge, the less of a kick it has." I walk over and pick one up, running my hand over the barrel. "You'll be fine."

Breck takes a deep breath and bobs her head up and down like she's trying to will the confidence into herself. "Yeah. I'm 'bout to smoke y'all bitches."

I choke on a laugh when the guys all join in a cacophony of laughter.

"Come on, Annie Oakley, let's see what you got." I tug Breck by the arm to the designated spot and Mason mans the skeet shooter, ready for B's command. Hayes passes me the cocked and loaded gun, and I place it into Breck's shaking hands. "You're okay," I soothe, coming up behind her, my fantasy coming true as I place my hands on top of hers. "Breathe with me," I tell her, my voice deep and raspy as I struggle to hear it over the intense pounding of my pulse.

In and out, Breck breathes in time with me until her hands have stopped shaking. "We'll do this first one together, okay?" She whimpers out a noncommittal noise and I take that as an answer. "When you're ready, yell *pull*."

We breathe another few breaths together and then she yells into the open pasture, "Pull!"

The machine raps out a springing type sound and my eyes track the discs' movement in the sky. I pull on Breck's arms and she follows my movement fluidly. My index finger presses harder on hers. "Squeeze," I whisper into her ear, pressing down on her finger. She does, and a loud pop sounds right before the clay disc explodes.

"I did it!" she shouts, handing me the gun so she can jump up and down. I hand it over to a grinning Hayes as we both watch her silly victory dab. "I really did it," she cries out, her voice growing louder right before she rushes me, jumping up for a hug. I catch her in midair, the momentum making me take a step back. She's excited, her uneven breaths blowing the tiny hairs along the back of my neck.

"I did it," she mumbles, squeezing my shoulders in a hold I'm sure she considers tight.

"You did," I repeat, basking in the sweet smell of honey from her hair. Breck's body molds to mine, and fuck if I want to put her down.

The old Cade wouldn't have.

The old Cade would take her back to one of the empty rooms and celebrate the victory with her.

Instead, the new Cade sets her down on her feet and asks, "Can I offer you a ride home?"

chapter nine

Breck

Dear Dork,

You cannot imagine the smell of five guys who have not showered in a week. Holy shit. We call it the FAN smell. Feet, Ass, and Nuts. I think they should add armpits, too. The smell of Lewis' should come with its own biohazard warning. #youthoughtmygymclotheswerebad #jesshasnttextedme #doesshehaveaboyfriend?

Your big bro.

After a thorough scouring of the pantry, I've decided that there just isn't enough food in here to make another meal. It's been three days since Anniston and Theo left on their honeymoon and I didn't think to ask Anniston about how I was supposed to get groceries. It's not like I do this all the time—being a personal chef to five Marines—to have some sort of procedure down pat. So as much as it pains me to do so, I'm going to have to ask *him*.

I frown a little as I pass by Tim who is adjusting something on the screen door. "Do you know where Cade is?" I ask him hesitantly. Tim doesn't turn from the door.

And then it occurs to me. I'm such a dumbass.

Tim doesn't hear well, and for the most part, only reads lips. But he speaks, albeit brokenly, which confuses me on how long his hearing loss has been an issue. Getting closer, I place a hand on his shoulder and grab his attention. He turns from his work on the hinge and graces me with a brilliant, toothy smile. With slow enunciation I ask again, "Do you know where Cade is?"

Tim points to the room next to the stairs. Cade's office.

"Oh." I eye the door like some kind of serial killer waits behind it. Damn it. Why couldn't he have been in the gym or something?

Tim chuckles and stands. He turns me around to face the door and then he whispers ever so lightly in my ear, "You'll be fine."

I'm already shaking my head when he pushes me toward the door and knocks twice for me. "I wasn't ready!" I whisper, but he's already heading back to his post.

So much for his support.

"I'm busy," comes the response to the knock.

Great. Cade's in a fantastic mood. This should go over beautifully.

"I'm sorry. I just have one question," I say to the still closed door. Something crashes in his office and I take a step back just in case I need a head start to run.

A burst of air rushes from the door as Cade swings it open with force. "What?"

Did he fucking growl at me?

I blink.

One. Two. Three times before I respond to his rude remark. A muscle in his jaw twitches as he waits me out. "Um …"

His brow cocks up and I know, without a doubt, I am annoying the shit out of him. "Um …" he repeats, almost like he's insulting me.

This asshole.

"We need groceries," I tell him, looking down at his bare feet. That's interesting.

"And?" He prompts me for more of an explanation instead of the crystal clear one I just gave him.

"And … Anniston said to ask you when I needed something for the meals."

Cade sighs and turns on his bare heel, heading back into his office without answering me. This motherfu—

"I need a half hour and then we'll go."

We'll go?

I thought maybe he would ask for a list or give Tim the card to take me. "I hate to disturb you. Can Tim take me?"

Cade looks up from his desk after picking something up off the floor—a paperweight—and levels me with a look that I feel certain brings grown men to their knees. "I said" —he grits out with a nasty frown on his face—"that I needed half an hour. Since I've had to re-peat myself, I need an additional three minutes."

His words feel like a slap to the face. Instead of throwing my flip-flop at him, I opt for a more mature route and slam his office door closed, muttering, "You can take those thirty-three minutes and shove 'em, dick."

I'm feeling pretty euphoric when the door swings open and Major-Pain-in-My-Ass stands there, a beautiful angry God, his big hand clutching the doorframe. "Get in here. Now!"

His tone only scares me slightly.

I look to Tim. His eyes are wide with shock. Not a good sign.

"Why?"

Both of Cade's eyebrows climb his forehead in disbelief at my backtalk. What did he think, I was just going to say, "Yes, sir?"

Cade and I stay locked in an epic staredown until he lunges for me, snagging me by the upper part of my arm. I cry out. He's not hurting me, just scaring the shit out of me. Cade pushes me inside his darkened office and points to a chair. "Sit."

I hope he sees my what-the-fuck expression and interprets it appropriately.

He must, because he sighs, and then amends his demand with, "Please."

Since his southern accent makes my nipples tingle, I sit down, but not without huffing so he knows it killed me to do so.

Cade takes a seat behind his desk and gets back to internet shopping or whatever he's doing on his laptop. Am I really just going to sit here until he's finished? All because he's mad at hearing me tell him to shove his thirty-three minutes?

Give me a break.

"Can I go now?" I ask and then lean over to pick up a piece of paper on his desk, inspecting it.

He snatches the paper from my grip. "No, you can't."

This is bullshit right here.

"I'm sorry, okay? You pissed me off and I shouldn't have told you where to shove your timeframe." I try for respectful and businesslike.

His lip twitches.

"I promise, I'll mind my tongue when I'm in front of the guys." If I wasn't staring at him so hard I would have missed the almost smile he nearly lets get away from him. "Major Jameson."

That gets his attention. He leans back in his chair, his eyes dilated with something I can't place. "Since you insist on talking and distracting me, why don't you pull your chair over here and help me so I can take you to the store faster?"

"Help you with what? I know nothing about the military." A lie. The six-foot-something gorgeous specimen of a man gets up and pulls my chair—with me in it—next to his, leaving tracks in the rug.

"You went to college, right?" I nod cautiously as he turns the laptop to face me. "Help me understand the concept of Macroeconomics." He tugs at his dark locks and literally collapses on the desk. "I'm trying to obtain my Master's Degree and I can't seem to grasp the subtleties of economics," he mutters, not looking at me at all.

I pick up the computer and place it in my lap. "I don't know how much I'll know. I only have a bachelor's degree in culinary arts, but I can try and help you," I offer.

Relieved is not the word I would use to describe what Cade looks like as he scoots his chair closer to mine. Fucking ecstatic is how I interpret the smile when he breathes out, "Thank you."

We take over an hour to figure out the gibberish that is economics, but we get his work completed for the day and now we're driving into town for the groceries I need. The list I wrote out is clutched in my hand, and I pray the sweat doesn't make the ink bleed. That's all I need is to not know what the hell I came to the store for after making such a stink about it.

Cade has yet to speak again other than telling me to put my seatbelt on. The country music he has turned up loud is a clear indicator he doesn't want me to talk. Whatever. He can sit over there and brood. I'm going to act like his attitude doesn't bother me even if it's killing me inside.

Why doesn't he like me?

Why doesn't he want to talk or get to know me?

The other guys have no problem cutting up with me, but not Cade. He's been standoffish since I arrived. I guess it doesn't matter anyway. Helping him is a moot point since Anniston already has. I don't even know why I'm still here and not back in New York with Jess.

I'm still broke.

I work for a room in Sue's house.

I'm not a chef at a five-star restaurant like I had planned.

I'm nothing.

I'm just a girl who thought she was doing the right thing for someone and now her pride won't allow her to go back home and admit defeat. Or maybe, I kind of like it here. The scenery is hot at least.

"We're here," Cade says in a low voice, pulling me from my minor meltdown in the passenger seat of his truck. Unclipping my seatbelt, I thank him for driving and reach for the handle. "Wait," he says, opening his door first. I look around at the full parking lot and notice nothing out of the ordinary that would require me to wait in the truck. But then Cade comes around to the passenger side and opens my door for me.

Why God?

Why must I be attracted to this man that wants nothing to do with me?

Cade waits patiently as I slide off the seat. I stand in front of him, awaiting further instructions. He doesn't disappoint. "Walk to the inside of me." He pulls me to his right side and then lets go of me just as quickly as he grabbed me.

We walk through the parking lot before curiosity gets the better of me. "Why do I have to walk on the inside?"

I look up just in time to see him roll his eyes. He remains mute on the subject and I finally just can't take it anymore. I draw to a stop and go around him to his left side. Cade looks shocked for a moment but he yanks me across his front, placing me back at his right side. This time, securing me with his hand around my wrist.

Sighing, I let him pull me towards the front of the store, but then he shocks the hell out of me by answering my question. "I don't want you getting run over by the idiots charging through the parking lot."

I make a show of looking around for the said speed racers before I ask another question and get another eyeroll. "What if they back over me?"

"They won't back over you."

"How do you know?"

Cade pulls to a stop and rakes a frustrated hand through his hair. "I won't let them back over you. Now, please stop asking me so many questions."

My heart tripled its beats.

Did Cade Jameson just admit that he would protect me and not let a car back over me?

He sure did.

And for that reason, I make a zipping motion against my lips, offering him my silence for the rest of the walk into the store.

He rolls his eyes again.

The local market in Madison is super small. Like really, really small, maybe about ten aisles total. Getting everything you need generally comes from visiting several stores within the county, but to keep Major Grumpy happy, I'm going to substitute where I can so I don't have to ask to go to another store.

We split up, Cade taking the cart since he said he needed to get bottled drinks. I weave through the crowded market and grab as many things as I can, folding up my t-shirt and using it as a bag. When I can't possibly hold anything else without flashing my boobs from the weighted groceries, I seek out Cade to empty my finds into his cart.

I spot his big head easily since he is by far the biggest man in the entire store. He's towering over the produce section, some girl giggling with her hand on his chest. Pausing, I watch the scene unfold a little more before I approach them. The last thing I want to do is interrupt homegirl's game and ruin Cade's potential booty call, but then Cade flinches and his entire body goes rigid. Whatever the girl just said, she made him uncomfortable.

Damn it.

What am I supposed to do?

Does he want me to help him?

Or do I go back to the cereal aisle and pretend I didn't see them?

Fuck, I can't leave him like that.

I start toward him, a million questions running through my head. What if he barks at me and embarrasses me for interrupting him?

The girl talking to Cade runs her fingers through his hair, and the look on his face breaks my fucking heart. I know exactly what I need to do.

I saw Theo do it at the wedding.

I have to get this girl away from him.

Pronto.

I hurry toward Cade, but before I reach them, I say loudly, grabbing their attention, "Babe. They didn't have that low-fat crap you wanted, but I figured you could splurge. A little fat won't kill you."

I reach them and dump all the stuff from my shirt into Cade's cart. Then I turn and wedge myself right up next to him, looping an arm around his waist, staking my claim. His body is unforgiving with all the hard muscles against my … well, not so hard muscles. No love handles on this man.

He's so solid.

He's … stiff.

I realize my proximity has made Cade uncomfortable so I take a step back.

Oops. I was so worried about the crazy girl in front of him that I forgot about the crazy girl inside me.

I offer an awkward smile, and after a couple of seconds, Cade reaches around and pulls me closer to his side. "I think I can indulge you tonight," he returns after a beat, shocking the shit out of me.

I try not to swoon over the fact he's playing along. The way he said indulge felt more like an innuendo instead of calorie counts but I know he didn't mean it. This is all a ruse, but it puts a stupid smile on my face when I glace up at the chick hitting on my major.

"Hi," I say with fake cheer before standing on my tippy toes and speaking loud enough so dumb-dumb gets the message. "Since we're indulging, did you want wine with dinner?"

Cade grins and nods his head slowly. "Nothing dry. I'm in the mood for something sweet tonight."

I return his knowing smile and squeeze his side. And bless the dumbass hitting on him because he fucking squeezes me back.

"It was good seeing you, Samantha," he says, taking a step back. I play along and send Samantha on her way with a cocky grin of my own.

She smiles at Cade, confusion clear on her face. "You too, Cade." Then she scampers off without a backwards glance, and I let go of Cade quickly.

"Uh …" I take a step back. "I still have a few more things to get."

He nods. "I'll come with you."

We finish shopping and check out with a cart full of groceries. Cade never thanks me or even acknowledges what we did in front of

Samantha back in the produce section. Instead, he loads the bags into the cart and tells me to put my feet on the bottom rack. Then, he jogs down the parking lot before jumping on behind me, sandwiching me between his hard chest and the cart's handle. We race down the rows of cars, and it's so exhilarating that I throw my hands up like I'm on some kind of roller coaster.

And the craziest thing happens.

Cade laughs.

And it's the most precious sound in the entire world.

★ ★ ★

"I'm ready to go upstairs." His gruff admission pulls my attention from the notebook resting on my lap. I was almost finished with the new X-Men review before he interrupted me.

I set the pencil down in the spine and feel myself smile at him for saying goodnight. Maybe he is warming up to me after all. But when I get a good look at his face in the glow of the porch light, he's frowning. Frowning isn't necessarily a bad sign with Cade. He tends to do it a lot. I like to call it his lazy smile.

"Okay, goodnight," I respond cheerfully, hoping he'll grace me with a real smile.

It doesn't work.

He huffs out a breath instead and turns to face the backyard so I can't see his face any longer. "No. I mean, I want to go upstairs but I can't until you're inside, and I've locked up."

Oh.

He wasn't just being nice and telling me goodnight. I pick up my pencil, slightly disappointed that he wasn't being sweet, and go back to my review. "Oh," I say, focused on my sloppy handwriting. "I'll lock up. I want to finish this review, and it's peaceful out here."

I take a peek at Cade. His head hangs low in defeat. When he says nothing, I go back to writing and try my best to ignore that he's pouting at the edge of the patio.

A noise, almost a groan, snaps my head up as I catch Cade raking a hand through his hair. I watch as he takes several deep breaths and turns, facing me with that fucking frown again. Without a word, and six—yes, I count—sighs later, he comes over, grabbing the lounger beside me and pulling it a few feet away, throwing himself down into it.

"Are you planning to wait on me?"

Cade leans back in the chair and looks up at the stars above. "Yes."

Okay. That's not what I was expecting.

"You don't have to wait. I promise, I know how to lock a door."

"Finish your review, B."

He called me B. Does calling someone by a nickname mean they are getting comfortable around you?

I'm going with yes.

The grin I'm donning is brighter than the stars he's staring at but I keep my head down and focus on this review so Jess doesn't cuss me out in the morning for not having it ready.

Mystique, although misguided in this film, delivers, once again, a flawless performance of how women superheroes are stealing the spotlight away from their male counterparts.

"What movie are you reviewing?"

Oh, hell. He's making small talk with me. I can do this. We can do this. It's just talking. Who cares if it's awkward?

"*X-Men: Days of Future Past.*"

Silence.

Men are taking the roles as sidekicks to these exceptional women—

"What did you think of it?"

"I … uh." I set my pencil down and close my notebook, clearing my throat. "I loved it. I'm digging the women superheroes these days. It's very refreshing." Cade tips his chin at the stars like they answered instead of me. "What about you? Do you like superhero movies?"

He snorts. "No."

He doesn't elaborate on his statement and the silence feels constricting. "Oh," is all I manage to get out.

Cade sighs and his chair creaks beneath his weight. "Heroes

don't exist. No one is selfless. Everyone lies and everyone takes. I find watching inaccurate portrayals of heroes annoying."

I swallow down the pain and disappointment that rises from deep within me. Cade has no hope. No faith that people are good and honest. How can he feel that way? *He's* a hero.

"I like the idea of hope," I confess quietly. "That when all feels lost, someone is out there for you, waiting to pick you up and fight your wars."

Cade's head whips around and he sits up straight, turning sideways in his chair to look at me. "You live in a fantasy," he grits out, his eyes turning cold and dark under the moon.

I shrug. "It's better than living in hell."

Cade stands, his chair sliding back. "Let's go. You're obviously done, and I'm tired."

In the three days I've been staying here, I've yet to see him retire before midnight, but his glare and the twitch of his cheek tells me he's not asking my opinion. I've hit a nerve, and he wants the hell away from me, but a true hero looks after his people even when he doesn't want to. Like, making sure they are behind locked doors before he can rest.

I ease off my chair, tucking my notebook under my arm.

"Goodnight, Major Jameson."

When I'm through the door, he stops me. "B?"

I turn around, a stupid smile tugging at my lips. "Yeah?"

Cade's frown turns up at the corners and a slow smile takes its place instead. I find myself grinning back at him until he scratches at his cheek like he's a little nervous.

I've finally made progress with him. Internally I fist bump myself until he says, "Can I offer you a ride home?"

He chuckles as if it's almost a joke at this point.

Fucker.

My eyes roll as far as they can without looking like the exorcist. I straighten up, turn on my heel, and walk through the door.

And lock it.

It's the first time I've seen Major Jameson look thoroughly shocked. His mouth falls open and his eyes go wide before he rushes the door, checking the handle.

"Open the door," he says with an air of authority.

I give him a one-finger wave, blow him a kiss, and return, "Goodnight, Major," before heading up the stairs to my room.

One of the guys can let Mr. Annoying in.

chapter ten

Breck

B!!!!!

Guess who I got a package from? Yep, your crazy best friend sent me a package with a letter that said, "To build up your forearms." It was a box of porn magazines! Drew wants to propose to her right now. Ha!

And yes, I appreciate your package just as much. The major ate all the cookies you sent, though. Please send more.

Sometimes I love you.

#jessismysoulmate #thinkaboutit #youcouldbesistersforever #please-letmedateher

Bennett

Four days later, after what will be referred to as the greatest feeding frenzy in history, I'm beached out on a log, allowing my stomach to curse me for all the lasagna I packed in. Why am I on a log you ask? Well, the guys—obviously, not Cade—harassed me after dinner to join them outside for beers and a bonfire. What they failed to mention was that they needed a referee to judge their archaic caveman skills of who could start the fire—without a lighter—the fastest.

I'll admit, I had my doubts any of them could do it, but when they asked me to count down, I knew they were serious and my panties were headed for the hamper early. It wasn't the confidence and hilarious taunts they threw back and forth at each other while they were ground level, holding half of their chiseled bodies up with one arm. Or even the way their forearms strained under the evening sky.

Nope. It was none of those things.

Don't get me wrong, those were a bonus, but the real show was Connor Hayes. This ham laid down in front of me, blowing on the kindling he had gathered, describing in great detail how starting fires was like warming up a woman.

"Firm strokes," he crooned, rubbing the two twigs together, one vertical, the other horizontal. "And when she is burning up…" He flashes those cerulean eyes to mine and lightly blows at the center of the joined sticks. "You give the core what it needs to explode." I couldn't even answer the son of a bitch when he licked his lips, my throat and clit throbbing as I watched him hollow out his cheeks, blowing ever so lightly until the wood (and my temperature) went up in flames.

"You alright, darlin? You look a little warm."

You will not wipe your forehead. You will sit on this log, get one good look at this devil of a man, and then you will never think of it again.

The corners of my lip tip up into something resembling smug. "You lost," I declare, hiding behind my smile, praying no drool pools at the corners, stealing the effect.

Hayes tilts his head to the side, his mouth slightly open, and his eyes narrowed.

"Come again?"

I glance back at the other three guys huddled around the giant campfire, their grins egging me on. "I said… you lost. While you were being the fire whisperer, the guys had their fire roaring and even got the s'mores from the house."

Lips that no man should ever have, fall into the cutest pout I've ever seen. I push up from the log and pull Hayes behind me, toward the guys. "Come on, *darlin*. I'll make you a s'more to cheer you up."

Hayes snorts out the laugh he was holding and pulls me close to him in a bear hug. "I think you're picking up bad habits living with us." My eyes narrow, trying to figure out just what he means by his statement, when he chuckles. "All I'm saying, B, is that a week ago you would've sat all wide-eyed and quiet." He shakes me when I throw him a you're-getting-a-laxative-in-your-breakfast-smoothie-tomorrow look. "Now you give just as good as you receive."

Is it possible to feel like you just got voted prom queen at twenty-three?

Hayes kisses the top of my head and fields the jabs from the other guys. Midnight falls over the world, but in the glow of the flame, I gaze out to the four Marines laughing and tossing marshmallows to each other.

It starts in my feet. Bubbling and tingling, the sensation travels up my thighs, across my six-pack abs—fine—my zero-pack abs, swirling and digesting until it settles in my chest.

One week is all it took for me to fall in love.

One week to figure out what my brother used to rave about.

One week to find a home.

★ ★ ★

"Okay, Okay. B, give us your best pick-up line."

The guys and I are several beers in and the conversation has only taken a turn for the worse. Mason insisted that I drink with them, and who am I to turn down a man with eyes the color of gold that melt the bra right off you? Yeah, I took the damn beer, and the subsequent three.

I wave off Hayes' asinine request. "No. Women don't need pick-up lines. We have vaginas."

Vic smothers a noise in the neck of his beer. "Not the kind Hayes takes home," he mumbles, intending on insulting Hayes, but Hayes gives Mason a high five. He's the opposite of insulted.

I hold my breath to keep from laughing at the two idiots and nod to Tim who's been the quietest of the bunch. "How about you, Tim? Show me how you woo a woman."

The group goes scary silent and I worry I made a colossal mistake. I know Tim has issues with speaking, but that doesn't mean he can't participate. But again, I don't know. I'm the new kid. This could be a total no-no.

"I mean, if you want. You don't have to," I clarify before it gets any more awkward.

You can literally only hear the crickets and the crackling of the fire.

Mason breaks first, clearing his throat. I bet he's going to tell me I'm not allowed in their circle anymore and to go back to the house. "I—"

Tim stands, handing over his beer with a smile. Shocked as hell, I blink several times, hoping that I didn't upset him or embarrass him by asking him to fake hit on me when he has such a hard time communicating.

Tim claps Mason on the back and heads toward my chair with a wicked smirk that tells me I have no idea what I've just done. He stops in front of me, his deep brown eyes sparkling under the firelight. "Fuck me, huh?" I joke, this ridiculous laugh tagging onto the last of my sentence like a schoolgirl.

A twitch of a grin attempts to bust through Tim's façade, but he holds it back, squatting down in front of me, his earthy smell of firewood and soap washing all over me. Hands the size of plates lock down on my knees. Breathing seems like a bad idea at the moment.

Someone crunches a graham cracker, the noise making me jump. Probably Hayes. His horny ass is probably enjoying the hell out of this.

Tim's body pushes through my legs and I let out an "eep!" He shushes me, trailing a long finger up the curve of my hips, along my ribs, cresting to a stop on my shoulder. My pulse pounds to an unsteady rhythm with each stroke of his steady hand.

Oh God. I hope he doesn't feel me sweating.

Whose idea was this again?

Oh, right. I wanted Tim to feel included.

He definitely seems comfortable.

Great idea, B.

Tim's hands are on the move again, kneading the muscles along my shoulders. I've never had a massage before but if I had, I'm positive this would top any of those experiences. The condensation from the beer I have clutched in a death grip drips onto my hand and I freaking jump again. I'm in sensation overload with Tim in my face. Breathing. Closer. Until we're nose to nose. My traitorous body betrays me when his warm breath feathers along my cheeks, his palm caressing the curve of my neck before coming to a stop at the base of my throat.

I freaking shiver in his arms.

His fingers spread wide, taking up nearly the entirety of my neck. The only movement is his thumb rubbing soft circles over the hollow of my throat.

Dear God.

This man hasn't said a fucking word and I already would go home with him.

He moves closer to my ear, his breath ghosting every part of me until he stops, drawing out the torture. I can't tell if it's the buzz of the beer or the high of being in Tim's proximity, but I feel lethargic. Fluid like a puddle.

"Brecklyn." The cadence is smooth when he whispers my name along the edge of my ear. His fingers squeeze my neck, not choking but preparing me for something great. And then he does the unthinkable. He squeezes harder, his tone rougher than I've ever heard as he grates out each word separately. "Beg. Me."

To all the women in the world: You are not prepared for this man.

I have to tear my eyes from the fire so they can roll back in my head. The sound. The broken fucking sound of his voice has me in a trance as my head flops back against the lounge chair.

"Holy fucking shit!" Hayes hollers from his seat. "I think I just came."

Tim pulls back and rolls his eyes, gracing me with a smile before swiping his thumb across my cheekbone in a sweet gesture.

"What the fuck, man? You could have been going with me to bars and scoring pussy left and right. What—" With a burnt marshmallow on the top of his stick—a real one, not the one in his pants—Hayes motions wildly at Tim when he stands. "You are a beast," he exclaims, waving the marshmallow around like he has some kind of sword. "Seriously, dude. You are coming out with me this weekend."

Tim shakes his head, taking his beer back from Mason and chugging it.

"Oh no. You are not telling me no after this shit. B orgasmed on the spot!" Hayes yells.

Before I can deny his ludicrous statement, something hits me on the side of the head and an audible gasp echoes around the fire. "Oops. Sorry, B."

I glare at Hayes, feeling along the side of my head where gooey, sticky marshmallow clings to a large chunk of my hair.

"Hayes!" I spring out of the chair, goo sticking to my fingers. "You suck," I yell at him with my sticky ass hands on my hips. One by one, they all start snickering until they are full-blown howling.

"I-I'm sorry, B." Laughter breaks apart his sweet offer. "I'll help you get it out."

I wave off the charming blond and turn to head into the house. "I got it. You boys finish up."

In their defense, they hold in the worst of their laughter until I get to the door.

Bent over at an awkward angle under the kitchen faucet, I try to get the side of my head under the running water. It's harder than it seems to keep it from running down the back of my neck, but maybe I'm just that uncoordinated. The latter could be the case.

The marshmallow is damn near glued to my head and all I keep doing is pulling out strands of hair instead of the sticky gunk.

"Fuck," I mutter, losing another long strand to the marshmallow Gods.

"What are you doing?"

I freeze when the heat of Cade's breath flutters along my neck. I've learned he likes to get close and make me uncomfortable. Why? I have no clue but I don't exactly hate it.

"Hayes threw a marshmallow in my hair." I hold the clump of matted hair up for him to see. "And it's stuck."

He raises his eyebrows, the corner of his lip tipping up in an almost smile. "He threw it at you?"

"No." I shake my head and put it back under the water. "He just got excited when Tim choked me."

Cade makes a strangled noise.

"Oh no! He didn't choke me, choke me," I rush out to explain as Cade's face reddens, the lines on his forehead extremely prominent. "I told him to hit on me and …" Cade eyes widen, and I realize for my and Tim's sake, I need to shut up.

Cade's fist clenches at his side as he stares at the wad of hair that looks as if it's been came in, now that I think about it. He doesn't say anything when I pump the dish detergent on my fingers and attempt to work out some of the sticky marshmallow. He just watches me, his shoulders tense as he eyes me with suspicion.

Finally, he sighs and turns off the water.

"Hey!" I protest, but he ignores me and hands me a dish towel.

"Come on, you will never get it out that way."

Water is dripping down the front of my shirt, the hand towel no match for my thick mane, when Cade tracks a droplet that darts over the swell of my breast. He swallows, his Adams apple bobbing with the movement.

"You need a comb," he tells me, his voice strained and raspy.

I move the towel and try to catch the fleeing droplets when he pivots, clearing his throat and ordering me to follow him.

Here's the thing: I'm an ass girl.

Firm and in the perfect half-moon at the bottom … I want to grab it and squeeze. Hard.

So, when Cade leads the way to his room, that perfect ass of his flexing as he takes each step, I get needy.

Real fucking needy.

I wonder if he would let me grab it just this one time. Like a perk of being employed at the McCallister Jameson Foundation. One squeeze per cheek at the end of the day.

"Breck."

Lost in rewriting the employee handbook, I tear my gaze away from Cade's ass and find him grinning at me over his shoulder. "Do you need a minute?"

Oh, he's got jokes.

"There's something on the back of your pants," I say, unaffected by his smile.

He nods, letting out a chuckle. "I get that a lot."

"Arrogance is a terrible quality," I reply without a filter.

His smile drops to a frown and I think I've hurt his feelings, but then it tips back up before he spits, "So is desperation."

I'm speechless that he assumes I'm desperate. He disappears into his bedroom without acknowledging my butthurt expression, heading for the en-suite bathroom with a purpose. "Hurry up. I don't have all night," is all he calls out.

Did he hurt my feelings just now?

I think he did.

I am not desperate. Just because I appreciate the hours he spends in the gym does not mean I want to ride him like one of those mechanical bulls.

Eh, maybe I do a little. I do have a neglected vajayjay, but shame on him for noticing. You don't call a girl out.

Cade shouts "Breck!" over the running water in the bathroom

and I call him a bastard in my head before sighing and dragging my ridiculous mess of hair inside his room. God help me, it smells like him. My sense of smell is overpowered with scents of cinnamon, cedar, and soap.

This is not a good idea. If he thinks I was desperate on the stairs …

With slow steps, I peek into his bathroom and find him perched on the edge of his shower. His legs are stretched out straight and a bowl is sitting beside him.

"What are you doing?" I ask, only sounding a little terrified.

Cade rolls his eyes and motions between his legs with the comb. "Sit down so I can comb this mess out of your hair."

Is it your right arm or your left arm that hurts when you're having a heart attack?

"Come again?"

Cade sighs and looks to the ceiling. "Don't make this weird."

Don't make it weird. Right. Got it. We're just boss and employee, sitting in each other's lap, combing marshmallow out of my hair. Just another day at the office.

I ease forward, my pulse pounding in my ears as Cade spreads his legs for me to wedge myself in between them.

"You will have to lie back and put your head in my lap," he instructs me clinically.

What he really needs to say is that I'm going to lie on his dick. But he doesn't because he's a gentleman.

I nod and swallow, squatting down in front of him. I turn and face the bathroom door and slowly lower until I hear him groan out of frustration. Cade pulls me the rest of the way down, my shoulders resting comfortably between two massive thighs.

"I'm sorry it has to be in the bathroom," he mutters, clearing his throat, working my hair out from behind my shoulders, and laying it across his lap. "We can't do it in my bedroom."

The way he says it is almost like he's telling himself. Either way, I say, "Okay. Thanks for helping me."

He grunts out a noise and I hear the squirt of something before his hands go to my hair, applying conditioner from root to tip. It smells of herbs and a hint of spice. Hand over hand, Cade works the conditioner into my hair, and I find my eyes closing from the simple act of him threading his fingers through my locks.

His thighs flex and I wonder if I'm getting too heavy. I try shifting but he pins my shoulder. "You're fine," he scolds, swiping the comb through my hair for the first time. I moan and immediately feel like I have a fever coming on.

"I'm sorry," I say. "It feels so good when someone plays with my hair."

Cade chuckles, his stone abs flexing against the crown of my head when he tries for another angle. He tugs through a matted piece and I wince. "Sorry," he mutters.

"It's okay. When I was little my mom used to yank the hairbrush through my hair and threaten me with a pop on the hand if I cried. I'm used to it."

Cade's thighs tense up under my shoulders. Why did I tell him that?

"All I'm saying is that I'm not tender headed. Do your worst."

Cade still doesn't relax after I explain so I try to stay still and not flinch as he works the marshmallow out bit by bit, only pausing to rinse the comb in the bowl beside him.

"Are you and your mom close?" he asks me out of the blue.

"Uh … no." This conversation could go south if I disclose too much about my past to Cade. But I want to know him and I want him to know the *real* me. "I moved out as soon as I could. It's just me now."

"Your parents are dead?" he asks me quietly, pain in his voice.

"No. My parents are just assholes. We don't keep in touch."

"Do you have any siblings?"

Ah, shit.

I swallow as a hundred different lies float through my head. Ultimately, I go with the truth.

"A brother. He died a few years ago."

Cade's hands stop their ministrations.

"What about you," I ask, readjusting on his thighs as he starts up again.

"My parents are alive," he says quickly. "We haven't spoken since my brother passed."

I'm shocked he disclosed that much given most days he barely graces me with a glare. I want him to talk more about Drew, his brother, who was Bennett's captain. He was killed in the explosion with Ben. Bennett said he was a good leader, that he and Cade were the best the Marines had. I'm sure he was exaggerating, but he respected them both, claiming they were old school warriors. Rebels without a cause. The perfect duo.

You see, Cade and I are bonded like no one else.

We lost everything that night.

We're orphans in our own lives, neither one of us knowing how to move on from the aftermath of losing our brothers.

I'm searching for hope, and someone to fight alongside me, but Cade is choosing to fight alone. He's given up on making peace with his past. He's moving on without the closure.

"All done," he says, patting my shoulder. "You'll probably want to shampoo my conditioner out of your hair so you don't smell like a man."

I sit up and feel his hands on my back, helping me. "Thank you," I say with sincerity. Cade tips his chin and stands. I have to scramble up so I don't fall down.

"You're welcome."

The front of his sweats are soaking wet, and there is a monster dick imprint where his boxers strain to keep the beast contained along his thigh. Where was that thing when I was on his thigh?

Cade catches my focus and pushes me out of the bathroom.

I stumble but quickly right myself and turn around. With a smile, and not looking at his hard cock again, I say, "Thanks again."

Cade grunts and I head toward my room when he calls out, "Hey B." I look over my shoulder with a smile. He grins. "Can I offer you a ride home?"

My smile drops and I slam his bedroom door as hard as I can, but even the noise doesn't mask his laughter.

And it makes me fucking smile.

That night, I don't wash my hair. I fall asleep surrounded by the smell of Cade.

chapter eleven

Breck

B,

    Knock knock. Who's there? Mustache. Mustache who? I mustache you a question, but I'll shave it for later. Ha! Beat that one! Guess who got caught masturbating into a grapefruit last night? Lewis! Captain Jameson, aka major's brother, Drew, woke up to a noise, pulled his weapon, and apparently scared him and Lewis both. Major tried asking what happened but he could barely get the words out from laughing so hard which only made Drew and Lewis redder. We all are ready to come home for one reason or another. Which reminds me, is Jess seeing someone? She's been distant.

    #dontevensayit #shessooooooohot #findanotherfriendandletmehaveher #ikillbugsforyou

    Private Brannon

"Hurry, B! The movie is starting."

Three bottles of soda and two bags of popcorn are sliding through my arms as I yell, "I'm coming" to Hayes from the kitchen. If I only had another hand, I wouldn't have to make another trip back for the licorice. Or if one of the four lazy asses would get up to help me this also would not be an issue. After I stare at the lone bag on the counter for a beat, I decide that making the extra trip would only cause grumbling. Especially if I asked them to pause the movie. Manners be damned, I bend my knees and hover over the bag until I can get a good purchase with my teeth.

I sprint for the family room in all my greedy glory, stepping over Vic's feet and dropping one soda in his lap. "Thanks," he mumbles, catching the drink in his massive hands, never looking away from the TV as the credits fade from the opening scene.

"Damn, darlin. You could have asked for some help."

God love Hayes and the concerned pout on his lips. He looks offended that I didn't ask him to help me carry all this stuff. I spit the bag of licorice into his lap and give him a reassuring smile. "I thought we could use snacks."

Opening the bag, Hayes takes out a stick of the stringy, red snack and sucks it in between his plump lips before sliding further to the arm of the sofa, creating a small opening between him and Mason. "I could always use a snack," he agrees, taking the bags of popcorn and handing them off to Mason while he maneuvers the remaining drinks from under both my arms.

The food is passed around, and I take a moment to look at the guys and make sure they all have something to munch on during the movie. Tim is in the recliner, soda in hand, eyes fixated on the screen, while Mason stretches his legs against the ottoman. Everyone seems to be settled and ready to watch the horror flick Mason bootlegged off the internet.

Except Cade.

He refused to watch the movie with us, insisting he had work to do in his office. I tried to sweet talk him but he only grunted out a firm, "No," and slammed the door in my face. I let his sour attitude go, but part of me wants to storm back into his office and tell him he should come have some fun. A defeated sigh turns into a squeal as

Hayes yanks me down into the small hole he created between him and Mason. "Watch the movie, darlin. He's fine."

I nestle under the throw blanket Hayes offers and snuggle up next to him. He's probably right. Cade is fine. He doesn't need me to worry over him. Obviously, he needs space from everything. I just wish he would talk instead of closing himself off from the guys. They can't help it I'm here causing him grief. At least I only have a week before Anniston returns home.

When Mason turns the lamp off and plunges us all into darkness, I feel a pinch at my side. I whip around, not able to see the knowing smirk on Hayes' face, but I can almost feel the smile spreading all the way up to his cheeks. Instead of slapping his hand away, I snatch the licorice out of his mouth and cram what's left into mine.

"Somebody is being naughty," he rumbles under a low laugh.

Somebody could make a girl's panties go up in flames with that one sentence.

"Somebody better keep his hands to himself and watch the fucking movie."

Hayes and I both startle at the sound of his command before he turns on the light and reveals his pissed-off expression. Jaw tight, his forearms strain at his side as his eyes bore a hole into Hayes. "Am I clear, Sergeant Hayes?"

Hayes' body shakes from holding back his laughter as he salutes Cade almost comically, "Yes, sir."

With a hate-glare aimed right at me, Cade turns and heads up the stairs without another word.

"Look what you did, B. Now we'll have to run an extra mile tomorrow all because you can't control yourself around me."

Mason groans beside me and I look at them all incredulously. "What are you talking about?"

Tim casts an apologetic look in my direction but doesn't answer me. It's Vic who finally explodes, standing from his seat on the floor and punching Hayes in the leg. "Stop fucking taunting him."

Taunting him?

Like making Cade jealous?

I tip my chin back to Hayes and he grins boyishly. "Don't worry. It's good for him."

Mason turns off the lamp. I want to ask Hayes to elaborate, but he covers my mouth, shushing me and pointing at the screen as the first victim screams.

★ ★ ★

It's after one in the morning and I still can't fall asleep. Visions of a masked man hiding in the closet have me on edge. And by on edge I really mean scared shitless. Where did Mason find such a gruesome movie? It's all I can think about when I close my eyes—me waking to a man plunging his rusty knife in my throat and laughing evilly as he gets his rocks off by watching the life fade from my eyes.

No superhero saved the girl in the movie.

Everyone died.

The killer lived.

What kind of bullshit is that? I watch scary movies occasionally, but I want the good guys to win. Everyone wants a happily ever after, right? Sweat clings to my Optimus Prime t-shirt like I've run ten miles uphill. Ugh. This is going to be the longest night in history. See if I let the guys talk me into another horror movie again.

Turning over and groaning into my pillow, I try thinking good thoughts, like Cade's muscular ass this morning when he asked me to hold the ladder so he could clean out the gutters. Calves that looked like they were carved from stone flexed below the hemline of his shorts, taunting me to graze my hand against the soft hair covering them.

Click.

Click.

A noise outside my window has my head off the pillow in two seconds flat. I stare through the darkness, my gaze focused on the sheer paneled curtains. They don't move, and I can't see if a man is standing behind them.

You're safe, I tell myself.

But it doesn't make me feel any better because I hear another noise. This time it sounds like something is scratching the screen.

Fuck this.

I spring from the bed, racing through my door to Hayes' room. I rap lightly, hoping not to wake everyone with my crazy. "Hayes, open the door."

No answer.

I'm tempted to just open it and crawl into bed with him. He probably won't even notice. I bet it's normal for him to wake up next to a woman he doesn't remember getting into bed with.

I'm just going to do it. The worst thing that could happen is that he's naked. I can live with that image burned into my brain.

Inching the door open, I peek inside before a warm hand wraps around my arm. I try to scream but a hand clamps over my mouth, smothering the sound.

"What are you doing?"

Cade.

Oh God, it's just Cade.

My heart beats wildly, slamming against my ribs, no thanks to Cade scaring the shit out of me.

I push away and he lets me go but not before spinning me around to face him.

Emerald eyes watch me cautiously under the glow of the night-light illuminating the hallway from a nearby outlet. "You nearly made me wet my pants," I admit in a harsh whisper.

Cade's eyes drift past the hem of my shirt, past my bare legs, before stopping at my blue painted toes. "You're not wearing any pants," he says rather all-knowingly. It annoys me that he's being so literal and judging my choice of words when he just about gave me a freaking heart attack. I open my mouth to argue but he continues his assessment of me and asks, "What's wrong?"

I turn and give Hayes' door another glance, hoping he'll step out, but Cade answers my unspoken question. "He's out."

Great. He convinces me to watch a scary movie and then trots off to a booty call, leaving me defenseless. What a friend.

"Breck." Cade saying my name stops me cold. My name sounds sacred when he lets it float in the air between us. When all I do is stare, he tries again. "What's wrong, Brecklyn?"

I mentally bank the way he seems concerned and nurturing right now and make a note to analyze it later with Jess. She's good at reading underlying meanings with the opposite sex. Cade grazes his knuckles across my bare arm and causes a fit of shivers along my skin, a subtle hint to answer his question.

"I, uh … something is outside my window," I admit with shame.

Cade's forehead scrunches as he weighs out what I'm saying. "How do you know?"

How do I say that I don't really, but that watching some horror movie has me a little paranoid?

You don't, is the answer.

In no way do you look in the eyes of this hulk of a man—which may be a little amused at the moment—and admit weakness.

So I exaggerate a bit.

"Something is clawing at my window, trying to get in."

Cade's hand swipes across his lips as he tries to hide his smile. "On the second floor?"

Did I mention he annoys me? I stand a little taller and narrow my eyes at the cute fucking grin peeking out. "Maybe it's a vampire," I argue.

It's completely possible.

A weird noise—almost like a laugh—seeps between Cade's fingers before he straightens up and says, "I could always offer you a ride home. That way the vampires will stay here and pick us off one by one while you're safe at the orchard."

Smartass can be so sexy.

But not at one in the morning.

My hand inches up my side, about to flip him the bird, when he grins, looking ten years younger.

Heart, are you beating?

Did this annoying man's smile just kill you?

I'm still alive when Cade's hand snags mine, smothering the finger that itches to flip him off. "Stay here. I'll go check it out."

He shakes his head and gives me his back, taking the stairs to the first floor. And because I don't want him to go alone, I slip on a pair of flip-flops and trail behind him for moral support. Not because I'm scared.

"What are you doing?" he asks when he takes a turn into his office.

"I'm coming with you. You may need backup."

Cade squats behind his desk and arches a brow, his forehead wrinkling with the motion. "I don't need backup."

I shrug like I don't care either way. I'm still going. Cade rolls his eyes and opens the desk drawer, taking out a handgun. He points it toward the floor and stands, placing the magazine in his hand. Inspecting it, he pushes it into the handle of the gun, the motion making a locking sound.

With a deep inhale, Cade slowly drags his eyes from the gun until they land on me. I blink back at his intent stare and swallow. He's so sexy with his plaid pajama pants hanging low on his hips, his white t-shirt nearly ripping at the seam of his arms. Messy and sticking up in the back, Cade's hair is the definition of bedhead. He looks soft and boyish apart from the lethal weapon clutched in his hand, and I want to reach out and hug him.

"Let's go kill this vamp, *Buffy.*" Cade cocks the gun and my pussy clenches.

Yeah, it was that fucking sexy.

And he made a joke.

A fucking joke!

I'm falling for this man and it's not fair.

Why can't he be emotionally available?

Cade chuckles and pushes past me. "Stay behind me and don't talk or you can't come."

I nod my agreement and follow behind him. He grabs a flashlight from the kitchen and turns it on before opening the back door. The air is still and muggy when we step out onto the patio. Cade points the light above us, centering it on my window. He doesn't speak but raises his gun and takes quiet steps around the perimeter of the house.

A croaking noise sounds at my feet and I rush Cade, high stepping to prevent whatever lurks in the dark from scampering across the top of my foot. What I didn't expect was losing my flip-flop and falling into Cade, the only thing preventing my plummet to the ground being his pants.

Yep.

Clumsy strikes again.

Cade jumps and curses, not able to grab his pants as they plunge toward his knees with my momentum. "What the fuck, B?"

Finally, I'm able to right myself, slightly disappointed that Cade has on boxers. Too bad I didn't get a face full of ass. "I'm sorry," I wheeze out into the night air. "I thought something ran across my foot."

Cade gives me a disbelieving look and hands me the flashlight, pulling up his pants. "So, is it a vampire or a mutant frog that's scaring you tonight?"

I swipe the beam of light around me, hunting for said devil frog, and come up empty. My lips purse, and when Cade has his pants settled, I hand him back the light. "I think you scared off the master vamp with your terrible sense of humor. Maybe he'll lurk at your window now."

Cade scoffs like he dares a vampire to lurk at his window and live to tell about it. I hate to admit it, but his confidence turns me the hell on.

"Let's go. There's nothing out here."

I nod reluctantly and head into the house. Cade locks the door behind him, retreating back to his office to secure his weapon. When he returns, he pours a glass of water and offers it to me. Without shaking, I take the glass from his strong hands and flash him a smile in thanks.

"You okay now?" he asks, his butt leaning against the counter. Lucky counter. I bet it sees more ass than the showers around here.

I pick at my hands, the skin dry from all the hand washing I do. "I guess." I'm not going to say, *hell no. Something was scratching at my window and there might be a serial killer lurking in my closet.* Cade would think I've lost it.

"Want to watch TV for a little while?" My head snaps up and Cade darts his gaze to the living room and shrugs. "Watching TV works for me sometimes when I have nightmares."

Do I want to rush him and squeeze those eight-pack abs until he begs for mercy?

You bet your ass I do.

"Are you offering to hang out with me tonight, Major Jameson?"

Cade's eyes go crossed, and he pushes past me on the way to the dimly lit living room, calling over his shoulder, "Goodnight, B."

I stand in the kitchen with a ridiculous grin on my face as Cade turns on the TV and settles on the sofa.

He's warming up to me.

I let Cade get comfortable before I join him in the living room. A fleece throw is draped over the arm of the sofa, and I grab it, bundling up into a cocoon on the other side of Cade. He doesn't look over, scrolling through the channels before stopping on *Transformers*.

Bumble Bee comes on the screen and my ribs feel tight as I think of Bennett and this movie. It was his favorite.

I yawn, absently admitting, "I love this movie."

Cade turns and cocks his head to the side. "I thought you only liked hero movies?"

How 'bout that? He pays attention.

"This is a hero movie," I correct him, slouching into the cushions, the adrenaline of hunting a mythical creature earlier wearing off.

"How so?"

Cade honestly seems curious as his gaze flicks back and forth from the screen to my face.

I give him a tired smile, yawning once again. "Apart from the military and the alien beings, the true hero is the awkward high school kid." My head lolls to the side, inching closer to Cade's shoulder. "Sam gave awkward kids like me and my brother hope that one day we would find purpose. A place amongst the heroes."

"Huh," is all Cade responds with, turning back to the movie. Bumble Bee attempts to hide behind the flower pot and I feel my eyes closing, my body drifting down as if strong hands are pulling me into a lap, my face colliding with the softest flannel. I snuggle down with a content hum when my scalp tingles under his touch. I feel the safest I've ever been when I hear, "Go to sleep, baby. I won't let anything happen to you."

chapter twelve

Breck

B,

Eight weeks! We're coming home in eight weeks. I hope. You never know, but it's soooo close I can almost taste it. I miss you, loser. Oh! I almost forgot. I heard one of the guys say his daughter has a VLOG. Maybe you, Jess, and Milos should look into it? Kind of goes with your movie review … you still suck though.

#butsomeonehastoloveyou #weneedmorecookies #majoreatsthemall

Bennett Brannon

✯ ✯ ✯

Washing dishes sucks about as much as a menstrual cycle. Anniston said the guys would wash them, but after seeing how hard they work all day with their jobs and workouts, I feel a little guilty staying home and watching them scrub pots and pans after a long day.

I only offered once, and they jumped on the idea like I was selling Girl Scout cookies—the caramel ones.

Vic dashes past me, throwing, "See ya later, B," at me before I can respond. He's obviously running late. Mason clomps down the stairs about five minutes later, dropping the F bomb as he hurries past, snagging a protein bar off the counter, Killer right behind him. "We overslept," he tells me, shoving half the protein bar in his mouth and dropping a piece to Killer, who doesn't even chew it.

Come to think of it, I didn't hear them going for their morning run. I've gotten so used to the early morning noise that I've learned to sleep through the grumbling hotties. "Where's Cade?" I holler at Mason's back as he runs for the back door.

"Don't know. Gotta go."

Something feels off, and it's not because I fell asleep on Cade last night and woke up tucked into my bed this morning like that's where I fell asleep all along.

Something feels *really* off.

Maybe it's that their routine is broken or maybe because it's silent in the house. I assumed everyone was outside. Turning off the water and wiping my hands on the towel, I head upstairs, checking Tim's room first. It's not locked. I knock, and he opens the door, looking out of sorts. His sandy hair is sticking up, giving him that freshly fucked look. I know that's not the case, the empty room confirms it, but still ... how unfair. Hair that naturally looks good when you wake up should only be saved for women. Men don't deserve freshly fucked hair.

"Everything okay?" I ask with a smile, trying not to look at those yankable golden locks.

He nods and rasps out a broken, "Woke up late."

I tip my chin in acknowledgement and elaborate on what I know about the situation. "Cade didn't get up in time to wake everyone up."

Not that Tim has anywhere to go. He stays with Cade most days and helps around the plantation. No one has confirmed it for me, but I think he struggles with his hearing loss.

Tim looks behind me and then mutters that he'll be out soon. I nod and move to the next door in line. Hayes. I knock, but no one answers. Pushing open the door, I brace for an eye full of nakedness, but he isn't in there.

What the hell is going on around here?

I pull my phone out of the waistband of my shorts—yeah, I'm classy like that—and text Hayes.

Are you okay?

He responds immediately with a selfie of himself sandwiched between two women. The caption under the picture says, *Very much okay, B.*

He's incorrigible but seriously adorable.

I type out a response while heading to Cade's room.

Cade didn't get the guys up this morning. I haven't seen him.

Hayes calls me instead of texting back. Obviously, he's just as concerned about Cade missing his routine as I am.

"Hey," I breathe shakily into the phone.

"Have you checked his room?" Hayes doesn't even bother to greet me. "On my way now," I return, rapping lightly on Cade's bedroom door.

When Cade doesn't come to the door, I grow even more concerned. "He's not answering. Maybe he's out in the barn? I haven't been outside yet."

"Is his door locked?"

I try the handle. "Yes, it's locked."

"Fuck!"

Hayes' response sends a shooting pain straight to my chest. "What do I do?" I plead, trying the handle again like it might somehow magically open now when it didn't a second ago. I hear keys jingle on the other end of the line. "I'm on the way, but in the meantime, go to Anniston's room. She keeps a set of keys in her bedside table."

I'm already sprinting down the hall to Anniston's master bedroom. Her door is unlocked and I'm digging through her nightstand before Hayes can give me further directions. "I have them," I say, out of breath, already heading back to Cade's room.

"Good girl. Now, B—" Hayes takes a deep breath and what comes out of his mouth next nearly drops me to the floor. "Whatever you find in there, know it's not your fault. You couldn't have stopped him."

My fingers falter and I nearly drop the key. "What are you saying?"

Hayes sighs, the engine of his car nearly masking the sound. "I'm saying we aren't supposed to lock the doors. The fact that it's nine o'clock and Cade hasn't been up and has his door locked … it's not good, B. I want to prepare you. Suicide is always a concern for guys like us. It's hard for us to adjust to the normality of everyday life. Especially with the demons Cade has."

I don't know when I started crying, but here I am, scared shitless to open this door, with tears pouring down my face. All I can say in response is, "No." Cade cannot be dead. We were making progress. He was happy.

Wasn't he?

"I'll call you back," I tell Hayes against his protests, and hang up.

Whatever you find, B. It was not your fault.

But for some reason, I feel like it is. How did I miss that he wasn't up this morning? Maybe if I had noticed earlier, we wouldn't be in this situation.

Slowly, I push open Cade's door. It's dark, his blackout curtains pulled closed. The good news is, blood isn't splattered on the wall and he's not hanging from the ceiling fan, but he's probably a considerate jerk and slit his wrists in the tub so Anniston wouldn't have to do a whole lot of cleaning.

Oh God.

His bathroom door is closed. Bile rises in my throat, and I feel about ninety-nine percent sure I'm about to puke on the carpet.

"Cade," I whisper in the dark. Why am I in the damn dark? I pull out my phone, pressing the icon for the built-in flashlight. The only thing awry in his pristine room is his bed. It's not made like he usually keeps it. The sheets are in knots and hanging off the bed, pooling onto the floor.

A groan pulls me from my inspection of his bed. "Cade," I rush out, opening the bathroom door without knocking.

What I find will forever haunt me.

Cade is curled up on the tiled floor, his arms wrapped around his head as if he's trying to crush it between his hands.

"Cade." I approach him slowly since I'm not sure what's going on. Is he sick? Is he having an episode? I don't know. I feel out of my element here. Maybe I should call Hayes or better yet, Anniston.

"Go away," he groans, his face twisted in obvious pain.

My chest feels heavy as I ignore his rude-ass response and inch closer. "I can't do that."

His body spasms and he lunges for the toilet, dry heaving. In between bouts of nausea he growls at me to leave again. I act like I don't hear him and turn on the faucet, grabbing a rag from the cabinet and running it under the cool water. When he crumples to the floor in a ball of pain, I make my move and press the rag against his neck.

"Please go away, B," he whines, but I barely register it. All that is going through my head is that he's not dead. He didn't want to die. I feel like I lost twenty pounds of worry as I watch him writhe on the floor.

"What's going on?" I ask him, already assessing as much of him as I can see. "Do you have the flu?"

He groans but manages to get out, "My. Head. Hurts. So. Bad."

His head?

He moans, curling in on himself again. It's a pitiful sight that makes me want to put my arms around him and take away every bit of pain he's feeling, but I know he wouldn't appreciate the gesture. Cade is not a man that wants to appear weak. Sometimes though, even heroes need saving.

"I'll call Anniston," I tell him quietly, already dialing her number.

"No," he grits out after another wave of pain takes him. I ignore him and step out of the bathroom.

"Breck? Everything okay?" Like Hayes, Anniston spares me no pleasantries, so I do her the same.

"Something is wrong with Cade," I blurt out.

In hindsight, that was probably the wrong way to start the conversation because she damn near shouts at me to explain, and I quote, "Very fucking quickly."

"I mean, I think he's sick."

That settles her down a little and I continue to tell her about his condition.

"Check and see if he has a fever," she instructs me. I enter the bathroom and Cade is where I left him, on the floor, a beautiful, broken mess.

"Cade." Why am I acting like I'm approaching a wild animal? "Anniston wants me to check for a fever." If I wasn't watching for a reaction, I would have missed the slight shake of his head. Too bad.

"Put me on speaker," Anniston demands.

I do, and Cade clutches his ears. "Turn it down," he begs me.

I do, and Anniston speaks quieter and less aggressive than she did with me. "Cade, let B check if you have a fever."

He grunts out a "No" like the stubborn ass he is.

Anniston sighs, obviously wishing she was here to handle the situation herself. "Tell me what's going on, Gorgeous, and then B and I will leave you alone."

We will?

Cade mutters that he's nauseous and his vision keeps getting blurry, and paired with the headache from hell, he's not in the mood to argue with us. Even sick, he's keeping his asshole attitude intact.

"B, take me off speaker."

I whisper to Cade that I'll be right back. He may have mumbled a *thank you* or *go away*. I couldn't tell.

"B, I think he has a migraine," Anniston says.

"Does he get them often?" I ask. I'm curious because, well, I'm a sponge with anything concerning Major Jameson. I soak up any info they have to offer.

"No. Never. Has he been sleeping?"

I think through the past week with him occasionally falling asleep on the sofa, the guys insisting on not waking him. But I don't know if he fell asleep with me last night. I'm guessing no. But I can't speak for the majority of nights, so I'm going to go with optimism. "I think so," I report to Anniston. I mean, I don't sit up all night and watch him. Okay, just that one time. It was only for like an hour and he was in a common area. That's a free pass.

"So, no dreams?"

"Maybe a few," I amend.

She sighs and then inhales a big breath. "Okay, Breck. I'm calling in a prescription to the pharmacy. Send one of the guys to get it and then figure out a way to get Cade to take it. He'll fight with you because it will knock him out, but make him get it down."

I absorb her instructions like I'm about to disarm a bomb in a few minutes. "Okay. What do I do in the meantime?"

"Turn the air down and get the room colder. See if he'll shower and drink a cup of black coffee. The steam and caffeine will dilate the blood vessels in his head. Pull the curtains closed and keep it dark and quiet. Maybe he'll fall asleep …" She hums for a second and then says, "You can always try to massage his pressure points. Do you know how to do that?"

Not really, but I can Google.

"Yeah, I think I can manage."

Anniston sighs, and I hear Theo say, "We're not going home. Breck can handle him."

Have I mentioned that I love Theo?

"You're right," she tells Theo before addressing me. "You got this, B. I'm calling in his prescription now. Have Hayes or Tim go get it. Call me back if you have questions."

I hear Cade groan. "I will, I promise."

Theo whispers for Anniston to, "Wrap it up." His voice sounds kind, like he knows how hard it is for her now that she's worried.

"I am," she says to Theo and then whispers, "Text me when you have him settled," before hanging up.

I want to say no as the jealousy bubbles up, but I don't. She's so used to taking care of Cade that I can understand it's hard to let go and allow someone else to do it.

I find the thermostat in the hallway and turn it down to sixty-five before knocking on Tim's door. He answers, damp from a recent shower.

"Cade has a migraine. Anniston called in some meds to the pharmacy. Can you pick them up for me?"

He nods, leaving the door to grab his keys from his nightstand. He steps out wordlessly and kisses me on top of the head before trotting down the steps. The love this family has for each other gives me all the feels which will make it harder for me when I have to leave in a week.

With a last-minute call to Hayes, I head back to the bathroom and kneel next to Cade, ignoring the "Leave me alone," he garbles out.

"Anniston called in something for your head. She said you need to take a hot shower to help dilate the blood vessels."

He moans, squeezing his head again, and I realize he's going to need a little nudge. I turn on the hot water in the shower, the steam filling up the small bathroom.

"Let me help you into the shower," I beg, my voice a soft plea. He turns and swallows, grimacing in pain. "You're not going to leave, are you?"

This man and his persistence. "I'm afraid not."

He tries rolling his eyes but it must hurt because he sucks in a sharp breath and closes them. "Turn out the light," he moans.

I do what he says save for the canned light in the shower. I can't have him falling, can I?

"If I let go of my head, it feels like it will explode."

I nod like I understand what he's feeling, but I don't. I've never had a migraine before. "What do you need me to do?"

"I …" It's like he gags at the thought of what he's about to say but maybe it's the nausea. He tries again. "I need help to get my clothes off."

Oh.

To say I'm not eager to strip this man down, even in his weakened state, would be total bullshit. I will take what I can get, and if this is the only time I see Cade Jameson naked, then I will live on the memory for years to come.

"Okay. I can help you with that." I refrain from adding, "*With my teeth.*" I feel like he wouldn't appreciate the humor in our current situation. He pulls his tired body up into a seated position, his eyes pinched closed, his hands fisted at his temples. "Let's get your shirt off first," I suggest with a whisper.

He folds over on his knees in obvious pain and mutters out, "I'll just shower with my clothes on."

Since he's being ridiculous, I do what any girl in my position would do. I grasp the hem of his t-shirt and lift it up his back, not even paying attention to the scars that discolor his skin. Without acknowledging what I'm doing, Cade pulls his hands from his temples so I can pop his head through his shirt.

"Do you think you can stand?"

He makes a noncommittal noise I take as a yes. I stand first and check the water temperature before I slide under his arm and help him ungracefully to his feet. We stumble but are finally able to lean against the wall for some extra support. Cade is trembling from what I assume is pain and I pray I never experience a migraine of this magnitude.

"I think I can get my pants," he says. I wait as he tries removing a hand to slide his pajama pants over his hips and stops, sucking a painful breath through his teeth. Without asking, I place my hands on each side of his hips, letting him know my intentions. When he doesn't protest, I slide the elastic band over the slight curve of his hip before cresting over his delicious behind. It's even better than I imagined. Smooth and rounded, and perfectly sculpted by hours of hard work. I pick up the pace so he doesn't think I'm the kind of girl who takes advantage of a horrible situation.

When he's standing bare, his front unfortunately facing the shower, I clear my throat and ask, "Can you do the rest?" I wouldn't be opposed to helping him wash his hair or scrub the hard to reach places if need be.

"Yeah. Thanks," he mutters.

It was worth a shot.

"I'm gonna go make you some coffee. I'll be back. Don't lock the door."

I fly down the stairs and use the single serving coffee maker, cussing at it the whole time about being a slow ass. It's barely beeped that it's finished when I snatch the cup and run up the stairs, spilling burning drops of liquid over my hands. It's as cold as Frosty's asshole when I enter Cade's darkened vampire lair. I place the cup of coffee on his nightstand and knock on the bathroom door. The shower is off.

"Cade. Do you need help?"

He opens the door in only a towel, and I stare. Sue me. His body is a glorious work of art, all scars and honor. I'll tell you one thing, my blood vessels are pumping just fine … to my vagina.

I guide Cade by the hardened bicep to his bed through the darkened room until his legs hit the mattress. "Sit," I order in a raspy tone. He does, and I hand him the cup of coffee. "You need to drink some of this. I'm sure it tastes like straight-up ass but Anniston says you need to."

He lifts a brow and manages, "You've tasted ass before?"

He's fine.

If he can crack a joke, he's okay, but he's in a towel, and damp, so I'll stick around and make sure. Just in case he needs help to get dressed. Yes, I'm courteous like that.

"You're so funny. Drink it."

He takes a few sips and makes a face. "I told you. Tastes like ass, doesn't it?" He hands me the cup and closes his eyes, breathing deep.

The door cracks and I turn and see Tim with a bag.

His medicine.

I mouth *thank you* to Tim before taking the bag and closing the door, already opening the bottle. Hovering under the bathroom light to read the label, I see he only needs one pill every four hours. I fill a glass of water and take it to him.

Immediately he says, "No."

"You need it," I argue with the idiot who's doubled over in pain.

"It'll put me to sleep."

"Which is exactly what you need."

He disagrees and tries to stand. "Please," I beg, stopping him by putting my hand on his bare thigh. "Please don't make me watch you writhe in pain anymore. I can't take it."

I fully expect him to tell me to leave then, but he hesitates, eyeing the pill in my hand and then my face. "Please," I plead one more time. It's hard to watch someone you care about in pain. He sighs and takes the pill from my hand, swallowing it dry. I hand him the water and he takes a small sip then hands it back.

Placing it on the table, I motion for him to lie back. Cade's hands go back to his head and he folds over his knees again. "Stay with me?" he begs into his lap.

Say what?

Did he just ask *me*, of all people, to stay with him? The man who asks me if he can give me a ride home every day? The man who just told me to go away about a billion times wants *me* to stay?

Holy shit.

A self-respecting woman would tell him no. I helped him and now he needs to rest, but like I said, even heroes need saving sometimes, and I just put my cape on.

"Are you sure?" I need confirmation he actually asked and it wasn't the pain talking.

"Please don't make me ask again."

Humility will get you everywhere. Especially in my panties. "I'll stay," is all I'm able to get out.

He mumbles out a quiet, "Thank you," before folding his almost naked body into the bed. He's shivering, and I wonder if it's truly a migraine, but then I remember it's like below zero in here and he's damp and in a towel. I lift his comforter up off the floor where he kicked it earlier, and pull it up to his shoulders. I slide in next to him awkwardly. I'm not sure what the hell I plan on doing while he rests. I can't turn on the TV or play on my phone because of the light and noise. Cade groans into his pillow. "My head is fucking pounding."

I remember Anniston saying something about pressure points but I don't want Cade to know I'd have to *Google* it in order to try and do it. Kind of lessens the faith. "I can massage your shoulders," I offer. "I don't know much about pressure points but maybe it'll help until the medicine kicks in."

I do know how to massage some damn shoulders. I'm not totally worthless.

Cade doesn't jump at my offer and I don't take it personally. He's not thinking clearly with the pain and all.

"That would be nice. Thank you," he finally rasps out.

Two *thank yous* in less than ten minutes. Times are changing, folks!

"You're welcome," I say.

Oh my word. You're welcome? I am such a loser.

Instead of commenting, Cade rolls flat onto his stomach and holds his pillow over his head.

Easing the comforter off his shoulders, I start in the middle of his back, kneading and pinching slow circles as deep as I can into his tense muscles. He never says if it feels good or if it's annoying the shit out of him but I keep going because for once he doesn't seem to be in as much pain as before. Hours pass—okay, it's about fifteen minutes, but my fingers ache and my shoulders hurt from the awkward angle of trying to massage Cade's back from the side of the bed. It would have been much better if I could have sat on his butt. What? It's more ergonomic.

Slowing my circles, I pop the fingers in my hand, rolling my wrist in a stretch. When Cade doesn't protest, I look closer and notice that his arms are limp and not flexed at his head like before. His breathing is slow and even.

He's asleep.

I pull the blanket up to his shoulders and ease the pillow off his head, taking a minute to just stare at him. It's rare that I get a chance to just all-out gawk at him, so I take this minute as a reward for dealing with his shit all week and not poisoning his food like he deserved.

His face, dusted in dark hair, seems peaceful, and I hope that means he's not stuck in a horrific nightmare. Watching his back rise and fall with every breath, I realize that under the hard exterior is a man who will one day change the world.

chapter thirteen

Cade

There's a breeze drifting across my ass crack, gentle and rhythmic, like breathing.

Flat on my stomach, in bed, the room still dark as night, I can't decipher what time it is. How long have I been asleep? And why can't I roll over?

It hits me just as another breeze grazes across me.

I fell asleep with Breck's soft hands kneading my back, easing the pain of the most horrific headache I have ever felt. I don't know what brought it on or when I felt like death would have been a viable option, but stubborn Breck and Anniston couldn't let me die in peace.

Especially Breck.

Fucking sliding the pants off my hips like it was a profession. Had I not been about to detonate from the inside out, I think I could have been tempted to touch her. Just one single, solitary touch. To know if she feels just as good as I imagine she does. But no. Pain ripped through me, punishing me for my sins, and I was weak before her.

It pissed me off.

I don't know why. She's so stubborn, always pushing me past my limits. Constantly trying to talk to me.

Constantly being cute.

"Oh no." The hiss Breck lets out shoots right over my ass, coincidentally going straight to my dick.

"I'm sorry," she stammers out, pushing off of my butt where she was resting, her cheek against my bare cheek. At some point I lost the towel, and the blankets failed me.

Breck sits up on the side of the bed, blushing profusely. "I did not mean to fall asleep on your…" She motions to my backside where I'm still sprawled out.

Reaching for the headboard, I stretch the muscles in my arms and flash her a smile. "Sure you didn't."

My cocky statement sobers her quickly, and her face turns serious as she scolds me with a hand on her hip. "You're not as gorgeous as everyone tells you," she spits at me, totally lying to me and herself.

With a playful wink, I say, "That's not what the drool running down the crack of my ass says."

Her eyes go wider and her cheeks get redder than I've ever seen them, and she stands, gasping in horror. "I did not drool down your butt." I make a show of reaching back and checking, and she makes a pained noise. "Fine!" she whisper-shouts. "I may have slobbered on your butt a little."

This time I groan, thinking of her slobbering on something else of mine.

"Thank you," I tell her solemnly. "I …" I turn my face and look at her watching me cautiously. "I should have told you I wasn't feeling well. I didn't handle the situation correctly."

There. I said thank you and apologized for making her worry. I won't ever forget her begging me not to make her watch me writhe in pain. Those words cut deep, and as much as I wanted her to leave, I didn't want to make her hurt, too.

"You're welcome," she says, the pink fading from her cheeks already. "Do you still have a headache?"

I nod and decide to be honest with her when usually I would lie and blow off her concern. "A little, but it's a dull ache I can handle." I certainly don't want another one of those pills. I slept the best I have in weeks, and I know you're thinking, "And? What's wrong with that?" Well, I'm what Anniston calls a martyr. I feel like I don't deserve a peaceful night's sleep from the horror and nightmares when my brothers, my team, will never sleep and dream about women and wake up with morning wood. They'll never marry. Never have children. Never teach their sons to fish. Their daughters to shoot a gun.

They are dead, and I'm to blame.

This is my penance.

Rest and sweet dreams are not what I deserve for killing my team.

I deserve every single nightmare that plagues me.

"Cade?"

Breck's worried tone pulls me from the memories of my fallen family. "Yeah?"

Breck moves closer to the bed, a towel in her hand. She hands it over with a timid smile. "Do you want another pill?"

I shake her off and mutter out a quiet, "Thanks but no thanks," and grab the towel.

"Okay, well I'll make you something to eat. I'm sure you're hungry."

Now that she mentions it, I am pretty hungry.

"Thank you."

She smiles and heads to the door, pulling it closed behind her, giving me the space I need. I check my phone first and see dozens of messages from Anniston, checking up on me. I decide to just call her since I know that's the only way she'll believe me when I tell her I'm okay.

She answers on the second ring. "Cade." Her voice sounds pinched like it's all she can do to restrain herself from bombarding me with questions.

"I'm feeling much better," I say, putting her out of her misery first thing.

She breathes out a sigh of relief on the other end of the country, and it makes me smile. "I've been so worried," she admits, rustling something into the phone.

"I'm sorry. I was going to call, but it got too bad, and then …" I trail off, not wanting to relive the bathroom incident with her and Breck teaming up against me.

"What brought it on?" she asks, knowing to change the course of the conversation.

"I don't know. It started in the middle of the night, and by morning, it was a full-on raging inferno." It started after I carried Breck to bed and sat in her room all night watching her sleep. I tried to lie down around four but couldn't and then the headache started and that was that.

"Huh. Well, take it easy today and drink lots of water." She pauses and I know she's about to fuss at me. "Don't wait so long the next time to take something. You scared the shit out of me." I grunt back a noncommittal response that she takes as my agreement. "You scared B, too."

I groan into the phone, sitting up and placing my feet on the carpet. "Don't start. I know, okay?"

Anniston masks a laugh before telling me, "Theo wants to talk to you. Hold on."

I make a show of groaning into the phone in annoyance, but a grin already tugs at my face. I know he's about to make fun of me, and honestly, I'm looking forward to it.

"Jameson," he starts, coming on the line, not even bothering to ask how I'm feeling, "The demons need a release! Your head won't almost explode if you get laid occasionally. Pussy is good for you. How many times must I tell you this?"

I laugh and regret it when the pressure in my head builds again. "Fuck you," I tell him jokingly.

He hits right back, not missing a beat. "Fuck me? No, Jameson. *You* need to be fucked. Long and hard. Damn it. I have raised a failure." He laughs at his own joke, and I shake my head, standing up and testing out my balance for the first time since it left me this morning.

"I hope Anniston makes you beg for a release tonight."

He scoffs, offended. "Jameson, for the one billionth time, Ans is not my fucking commander. In fact, I am *her* commander. Do not take me for an obedient little shit like you are."

I hear, "Oh really?" in the background, and it sends a shock of pain through my chest. I hate to admit that I actually miss Theo, but I miss these two and their crazy a whole lot. Being here without them feels empty.

Theo whispers into the phone, "Now look what you've done. I'm going to have to use my expert skills to get us out of this mess." I laugh at his usage of the word *us*. *We* didn't get into anything.

He did.

And I hope Anniston makes him pay for it.

"Be sweet, Von Bremen. Maybe she'll go easy on you." I laugh when I hear him growl his protest into the phone.

"Bye, Gorgeous!" Anniston yells so I can hear. "Take it easy today."

I promise I will, and hang up when I hear Theo say, "Don't look at me like that."

I'm smiling for the second time in an hour, slipping on some boxers and cargo pants. I look around at my clean bathroom and take a guess that Breck cleaned it at some point while I was asleep. Brushing my teeth and swiping on some deodorant, I pull on a t-shirt and head down the stairs. The smell of peppers and something tangy reaches my stomach and almost tears me in two with a growl.

"Imagine my surprise when I peeked in your room this morning …" I stop three steps from the bottom, not looking back as Hayes clomps down the steps behind me.

"Thanks for checking on me," I lie, trying to deflect.

Hayes laughs, bumping into my shoulder. "Did she lick up the center?"

"Shut the fuck up," I tell him with authority. I do not need this kind of rumor flying around the house. From the shock on Breck's face this morning, she honestly did not mean to fall asleep on my ass. The thought of the drool, slipping between my cheeks, tugs at my dick again. "Drop it. It was a rough morning."

Hayes pushes past me with a chuckle before throwing back, "I wish all my mornings started out that rough."

Sometimes I fucking hate him. I glower at Hayes when I step into the kitchen, his chin on Breck's shoulder, begging for her to slip a bite of food in his mouth.

"Please, B. I'm starving!" Breck snickers and grabs something I can't make out and pushes it between Hayes' lips.

He moans.

My chair scrapes the floor and Hayes backs up with a laugh. "Yell for me when it's ready, darlin'." He winks at me, licking the remnants of flavor off his lips.

I flip him off and look at the clock. It's after one. I need to go by the barracks and check out the progress. The construction has been slow, and the forecast calls for rain tomorrow. I need to be sure the crew is getting as much done as possible.

"I need to check on the construction crew," I tell Breck for some strange reason. She turns from the stove, her brows furrowed.

"Okay. Do you want me to put your food in the fridge?"

Ugh. I deserve that.

"I thought maybe you would want to come with me and check it out before I give you a ride home?"

Wide gray eyes nearly take up her whole face. I've shocked her speechless.

Fucking finally. Is that all I had to do to shut her up?

But then she narrows her eyes and shocks me by throwing a handful of scrambled eggs at my face.

My dick is hard, and it's all Breck's fault.

Our conversation started out simple. I wanted to get to know her a little better and atone for my dickish behavior over the past few days. It was an innocent and friendly conversation.

And now I'm rock hard, trying to be discreet by rolling to my stomach so she can't witness the teenage-like fail of my dick tenting my jeans.

After checking over the new construction and giving Breck a tour of all the rooms, and gushing about our future plans for the foundation, we decided to sit on a blanket next to the pond and enjoy the sunshine.

"But why is Thor your favorite? Why not Superman?" I've been asking her random questions regarding her love of superheroes. She's adorable to watch, eager and excited when she sits up on her knees, her hands motioning as she goes on about each of their qualities.

She winks at me. "You mean other than the fact that Thor has a big hammer and speaks with an Australian accent?"

And that's why I'm groaning and resting on my stomach like a fourteen-year-old boy.

Fuck if I don't want to show her how I use my hammer. My dick could probably destroy shit too with the amount of steel I'm feeling. I roll my eyes, keeping my front firmly pressed to the throw blanket. "So basically a pretty face is what you like?"

Her silly smile drops and she looks slightly wounded. "No, not just a pretty face."

I'm amused, arching my brows, daring her to come up with other qualities other than his big hammer that sets him apart from the other heroes. I see how she ranks her heroes. By the size of their hammer.

"Thor is my favorite for a multitude of reasons." She takes a breath like this is some kind of huge conversation we're having instead of a friendly chat.

"I'm teasing," I start, but she slaps a hand over my mouth.

"Let me finish. You asked me a question, and I intend on answering you, Major Jameson."

Again with the Major Jameson.

My cheek twitches with her manhandling me, and I remove her hand from my face, clutching it between my two hands and securing it against my chest. Breck eyes our hands, but doesn't pull away, and I try not to analyze why the fuck I did it in the first place.

"Please continue," I encourage with a playful grin.

Her lips purse and she tries to look annoyed with me. "Thank you. As I was saying, Thor is my favorite for a multitude of reasons. One is that he is selfless."

"Aren't all superheroes selfless?" I counter.

Her hand, still captured in mine, twitches. "No. They aren't all selfless but the majority are. You are correct in your assumption."

I nod, not really giving a shit if I'm correct. I disagree on all accounts. No one is selfless. Even the made-up douches are selfish. She'll never convince me otherwise.

"But Thor…" She blows out a breath and looks to the sky. The clouds are drifting at a lazy pace, their forms puffy and soft, appearing closer than they are. "Everyone in Thor's family betrays him." She pulls her gaze from the clouds and stares at me hard as if she is willing me to hear and absorb everything she's about to tell me. "And yet, he still fights for what is right. He still loves." This is deeper than I care to discuss. "He still forgives his family and tries again."

Now I'm certain I don't want this conversation to continue. He forgives and still tries again? Uh, yeah. That hits a little too close to home and I'm not in the mood.

"Thor's an idiot."

Breck doesn't look offended that I insulted her hero. Instead, she gives me a sad smile. "I like to believe that even though I may have been betrayed or made mistakes, I'm still capable of forgiving myself and others. Thor is my favorite because although he is the God of Thunder, he's just as human as the rest of us. He hurts and feels but he still picks himself up and tries again. He never backs down even when he is scared."

The food she made earlier is rolling around in my gut, churning at the hidden meaning of her words. I'm not Thor. I'm not selfless. And unlike Thor, I *am* scared to open the door and forgive. I don't deserve to forgive myself. I don't deserve to start over and be happy. I deserve to feel dead inside.

I don't deserve a second chance.

"And he has a nice ass."

I choke when she blurts out that last statement and pulls her hand from mine, patting me on the back. "Don't take it personally, Major. Not everyone can have an ass and a big hammer like Thor."

I flash her an annoyed glare and roll over, my erection long gone after that conversation. "Thor is a made-up character," I say, yawning at the end. "His ass and his hammer have been immortalized through legends over the years. If he were human, he'd be an asshole like the rest of us mortals."

Pain throbs behind my eyes, the migraine I'm nursing coming back to haunt me.

"Is your head hurting again?"

A terse chin jerk is all I can manage when another sharp stab of pain zings through the top of my head. Please don't let me get nauseated again. I'm groaning into the fabric of the blanket, sucking in sharp breaths when I feel her hands tug at my arm. Cracking one eye open, I see the concern in Breck's frown.

"Let me help?"

She's asking me this time. Not demanding. Not commanding. The decision is mine. Are we friends or not? What's funny is that I don't even have to think about it for very long. Being with Breck feels so natural. So simple. And I crave her skin on mine like I had a mere few hours ago.

My voice sounds gritty when I tilt my chin in a pathetic nod and give in. "Okay."

Breck's eyes widen before a ghost of a smile tugs at her lips. She stretches her tanned legs out in front, her arm supporting her from behind. "Come here." She pats her thigh, insinuating I should lay my head down on her. Let me be crystal clear when I say that if I follow through with this bad decision, my head will be inches from her pussy. I'll be able to smell it. Feel the heat from it.

My dick is hard again.

The pain is what pulls me from my side of the blanket, crawling on my hands and knees to her. It's not the need for her that coaxes my head down into her lap, my chest resting on the soft fabric of the blanket. And it certainly isn't the feel of her hands in my hair as she makes soothing sweeps that have me groaning and closing my eyes.

Breck stays quiet, stroking through my hair, slowly working her way to my back. The breeze cools the heat coursing through me, and I feel sweat bead along my neck. Breck is so in tune with my needs because she strokes up my back, pulling my shirt with it. I shiver when her fingertips graze the skin there.

The scars there.

It doesn't bother me like I thought it would. She's seen them before, yes. But she isn't repulsed by them. More like she's in awe, immortalizing them like badges of honor.

Or maybe she's just good at disguising her facial expressions.

The jury is still out, but either way, I let her look. I let her touch. I let her *see* me. The real me. No asshole. No Major Jameson. Just … Cade.

I turn and meet her eyes. She's watching me. Waiting for my reaction to her touch. For pushing at my boundaries. The fight wanes and I don't have the heart to stop her. I don't want to stop her.

So I give her a sad smile.

She doesn't smile back or say anything. Instead, she drags her fingers from my forehead, over my eyes. They drift closed out of instinct, but I keep them closed, looping my hand under her thigh, holding her close. We stay under the sun, listening to the birds chirp and the fish surface from the pond for what seems like hours, the pain in my head waning with each caress of her fingers as she traces random shapes and letters along my back. And I swear she spells out *mine*.

chapter fourteen

Cade

"**M**ajor Jameson." Breck pops her head in my office a week later, being a total tease by calling me Major Jameson. The sound of her addressing me as major does things to my dick. Things my dick should not be doing right now. Like getting hard under my desk.

"There's a man out here. He says he has an appointment with you." She relays the message, the scent of roses wafting in from the lotion I know she uses every single day.

"He says his name is Kane. That's a cool name …" She trails off, staring at one of the books on my bookcase. I track her eyes and see she's staring at my newly acquired comic book of Thor. I don't know what possessed me to buy it. I don't read comic books, and frankly, I don't know if I agree that Thor is the best superhero like she does, but I was curious and had already paid for it by the time I stopped and processed what I was doing.

Breck smiles, turning back. "He's kind of hot, too."

You have got to be kidding me. Why must all the women in this house be so damn aggravating?

"The potential recruit?" I confirm that the hot man we are talking about is the one out in the foyer.

She nods, flashing me a secret smirk before slipping her finger between her teeth.

In another life I would demand she come over here and fix the situation she's teasing in my pants. A slow, aggressive blow job underneath my desk would definitely be better than thinking thoughts of my grandma in a bikini to solve the tenting going on right now.

"He seems pissed."

Wait, what?

"Who seems pissed?"

She tips her head, indicating the person in the hallway. "Kane."

Right. Kane Kurtzman. A new recruit Anniston scouted in New York during a Mavericks baseball game. Recently wounded and honorably discharged from the United States Marine Corps three months ago. Anniston said he was having a hard time adjusting to civilian life and thought we could help him.

Her text asked me to feel him out and see if I thought he would be a good fit for the family. Apparently, he intrigued her enough for her to hand him a bus ticket to the plantation. Normally, we like to take guys from our own community. God knows we have enough homeless veterans in this small town to last us a lifetime, but we have to be selective since we aren't able to take veterans with too many psychological needs. Anniston sends all of us to a psychologist occasionally but we don't have one here on staff.

Theo's text went a little differently. His said, "What an asswipe. I hope you hate him as much as I do."

Although Kane's file is impeccable—he's a highly decorated marine and had just become a Gunnery Sergeant before he was injured—there are several memorandums by his superiors, most of which are for not following orders and being aggressive with his teammates. I like to give everyone the benefit of the doubt, like Anniston, but after Theo's text and reviewing this guy's file, I'm not sure he's right for us.

"Tell him I'll be with him in a minute," I tell Breck, trying not to look at the cheerleader shorts she has on today.

"Okay, I'll let him know." She closes the door behind her and I hear her relaying my message.

I flip through his file one more time before raking my hands through my hair and willing myself to focus. I'm trying not to think about Breck dancing in the kitchen this morning, humming out some rap song she didn't even know the words to. She kept inserting the word *watermelon* when she didn't know the exact phrasing. I don't know why I find it so endearing but I do. I stood there like a total stalker, watching her sway her hips before dropping into a squat and popping her butt in and out in those goddamned gym shorts that make me think inappropriate thoughts.

I wanted to stand behind her. I wanted her to grind on me and stop the ache in my jeans. I wanted her to build friction until I came inside my pants. But I did none of those things. I watched her until the song ended and she took a bow to the stove, stirring the grits she was making, then I bolted to my bedroom and jerked my dick twice to the image of me sliding in between those delicious cheeks that hung out of those tiny pink shorts of hers.

I'm going to hell.

And now my dick is hard again, a constant reminder that Breck is still here and not at the orchard where she belongs.

Giggling pulls me from my self-loathing and I stand, heading for the door. This motherfucker better keep his hands to himself. We have a strict policy on women in this house. It's not upheld most of the time, but we still have one, damn it. Kane hasn't even been accepted, and he's already on my shit list. Maybe Theo is right this time. I think I already hate him for making Breck laugh.

Get a grip, Cade. He made her laugh, he didn't fuck her against the coat rack.

I wrench open the door anyway, already annoyed. "Gunnery Sergeant Kurtzman, you can come in now."

My first impression of Kane as he pulls his head back from Breck is: No.

No, he will not mesh well with us.

No, he will not be around Anniston and Breck, or just Anniston when Breck goes home for good.

He's trouble, the cigarette behind his ear and the angry glare he sends my way all but spelling it out for me. Never mind that his entire body, save for his face, is decorated in tattoos. He looks like special forces but I don't recall seeing that in his file.

"It was nice meeting you, B," he says, winking playfully at her like they share a bond or something in the five minutes they spent together. Breck fucking giggles when he takes her hand and kisses it.

Oh, hell no.

"That will be all, Brecklyn." I dismiss her like I'm the master and she's my submissive.

Stop thinking sexy shit, Jameson!

The sharp intake of breath and the hurt in her eyes makes me instantly feel like a jackass. Why did I say that? She's not my secretary or my servant. She's become my friend, and I let jealousy really fuck up the progress we've made.

Breck gives Kane a sweet smile before curtsying and spewing sarcasm back at me. "Yes, sir. As you wish."

Why does it feel like I've been shot?

I open my mouth to apologize, but she turns away and sprints off without another word. Kane, on the other hand, looks as though he could punch me in the face and not feel bad about it at all.

"You Major Jameson?" he spits, sizing me up with a cold look.

"I am," I say, not sparing him another look but instead opening my office door wider, inviting him in. His steps are slow, and his face contorts in pain as he takes a few measured strides before stopping and taking a labored breath.

"Do you need assistance?"

Not that I really want to help him. I feel like the tension is high, and after the scene with B, I can already tell he doesn't like me. But I've been in his shoes before, and the days following discharge when you have no schedule, no orders, can be hard to manage. You're angry at everyone and everything. That's why what we have here at the McCallister Jameson Foundation can be a lifesaver for veterans.

"No," he grits out between breaths. "I don't need your fucking help."

I shrug like I don't give a shit either way and have a seat at my desk, waiting for him to take the last remaining steps into my office before taking the seat across from me in one of the wingback chairs.

"What's the extent of your injuries?" I ask, not looking at his file but rather the pain etched on his face.

He belts out a laugh that borders on evil. "My injury, Major Dick, is that I only have one leg."

"Do you suffer from phantom pain?" It says in his file he was caught in gunfire and could not get to the extraction point for two days. The muscles in his leg deteriorated from the lack of blood flow and the doctors had no other option but to remove it. His story—and the fact he called me a dick—has me staring at his right leg as he massages his knee where I assume a prosthetic is attached.

Fucking Anniston. No wonder she was enchanted. Not only does she have a thing for assholes but rehabilitation is her specialty.

"No," he lies, meeting me in a defiant glare.

I think we can add *denial* to his file.

"I see," I mutter, chewing on the end of the pencil I was using for notes.

Kane makes an exaggerated sigh that makes me want to toss the baseball paperweight at him, aiming straight for the sneer on his face. "Let's get one thing straight, Sergeant Kurtzman. You will address me as Major Jameson. Not Cade. Not dick."

Kane's eyes draw up slowly as he evens me with another look of contempt, but I keep going. If there is one thing I know how to do, it's earn respect. No one, and I mean no one, will talk down to me.

"Even if I no longer serve in the Corps," I drawl, glaring at the ass in front of me, "I am still a Marine and I *will* be respected." Kane narrows his eyes and I continue, "We have a hierarchy here. Those who fail to respect it will be terminated from our program."

Kane scoffs and mumbles, "Whatever," under his breath.

I stand up, looming over my desk, restraining myself from jumping over it and taking this asshole by the throat. In a voice calmer than I feel, I ask professionally, "Did Anniston tell you about the program here?"

The mention of Anniston's name softens him a bit. "She said" — he chuckles a little—"that she could help me as long as I submit." He smiles at the memory, and I groan. Of course she phrased it that way. No wonder Theo already hates him.

I straighten and smooth down my shirt. "What she meant by submission is by following the rules of our program and submitting to her training regime. If you can't do that, then you will not be admitted to the program. So far," I droll on, watching as he kneads his thigh. I'm not even sure he's aware he's doing it. "You don't seem to be very receptive to following rules."

His glare reminds me of that damn X-Men movie Breck was watching last night where the guy shot red beams from his eyes. Fuck. Her superhero shit is wearing off on me.

"Listen, douche." He stands awkwardly in front of the chair. "If dealing with assholes like you on a daily basis is part of the plan, I think I'll pass. I was doing your commander a favor by indulging her. She was quite insistent that I come speak with you, but clearly she thinks more of you than she should."

I clench the desk before I do something crazy like beat the fuck out of him and bloody my nice chair. Kane laughs, perceptive that he's managed to get under my skin.

"I'll show myself out. Thank your fine-ass commander for me." The growl that comes from my own chest fills the small office with a promise of a fight if he keeps running his fucking mouth. He only chuckles and opens the door. "Tell her thanks but no thanks. I'm nobody's bitch."

By the grace of God, I let him walk out of the house in one piece and immediately text Theo.

You're right. He is an asshole.

I quickly get a response back. *Told you. Do I need to send acid to dispose of his remains or did you do the right thing again?*

His ridiculous text makes me laugh. *I let him leave voluntarily. Please keep Anniston busy so she doesn't send more of his type down here.*

Will do, Major Pain-in-the Ass. Have you gotten your dick wet yet?

Immediately, I'm brought back to the reality of being mean to Breck moments ago. *Goodbye, Theo.*

You can say you miss me. I won't screenshot it and post it on Twitter.

Sure he wouldn't. Not that I ever would admit to such a crazy thing.

You can thank me on your knees when you get home. Your position as reigning asshole king is still intact. You're welcome.

I knew you loved me.

I don't respond after that. I have apologies to dole out and I'm starting with the pissed off brunette who is tossing dishes extra hard into the sink.

★ ★ ★

I ease behind Breck, careful to stand to the side so that my balls are out of the way in case she feels the need to take me down a notch. I'll admit, addressing her like hired help was an asshole move. I've only ever been jealous once in my life and that was over Anniston. The old Cade had no problem sampling women like an appetizer tray. There was never a need to order the entrée when you could get full on the appetizers alone. Being jealous is a fairly new concept to me.

And I don't care for it.

"I'm sorry," I drawl out slowly, allowing the southern twang to coat my words. "I shouldn't have spoken to you that way."

Breck slaps the faucet handle with her palm and whips around to face me. "No, you shouldn't have. You acted like a major dick."

My temple throbs with the start of a headache. Dealing with Kane and now Breck is taking its toll. I wish she would sit down so I could close my eyes and nap for a bit. Sleeping next to her has been heaven and hell. I still dream, but I feel her soothing presence fighting along-side me. She is a warrior. A hero like she obsesses over. But I'll never tell her that because I'm a coward.

"You're right. It was a dick move," I tell her, carefully placing my hands on her shoulders. "Let me make it up to you," I plead, rubbing up and down her upper arms. I don't want her to be mad at me. "I'll do anything you want to do."

Breck pulls back to look up at me. "Anything?"

My word vomit is coming around to bite me in the ass. My eyes narrow, my lips pursing as I rack my brain for a way out of this with-out hurting her feelings again. "Let me amend my offer," I say with a smile, hoping to soften the blow. "I'll do anything within reason."

There. Maybe she will take the implied no sex or any nakedness, even though my dick wants to.

"I want to play a game." She's excited and bouncing under my palms, her smoke colored eyes alight with eagerness. I groan because I hate playing fucking games. Unless it's a sport. The guys and I routine-ly have football and baseball games when we're all here. Sports are one thing we all can agree on.

But Breck is a free spirit and I'm guessing she doesn't want to play a game of touch football. "What kind of game do you have in mind?"

Her top lip curls into a cocky smirk and I know I'm going to re-gret this moment forever. "*Madden*. On the Xbox. Mano y mano." She taps her chest like some kind of barbarian and I can't help but laugh at her ridiculous proposition.

"You want to play against me on the Xbox?" I chuckle ever so lightly, "Football?"

Breck grins, her head bobbing with each question. "Are you scared, Major?"

This girl.

A grin tugs at the corner of my lips and I quickly raise my hand to cover it, biting my knuckles to keep from laughing out loud. "You're on," I agree under my hand. "Care to up the ante and make it interesting?"

Her head tilts to the side as she studies me. "Okay."

Okay? That was easy. I eye her and roll my wrist, encouraging her to speak her terms.

"If I win, you stop asking to take me home every night," she proposes softly.

Really? Out of everything she could ask for she wants me to stop being a prick and offering her a ride home?

Amateur.

"And if you win—"

I cut her off. "No, sweetheart, that's not how betting works. You don't get to pick what I get if I win."

Breck rolls her eyes. "Can I finish?"

I wave her on and she clears her throat, looking oddly nervous. "If you win, I'll take you up on that ride home."

It feels like I've been shot.

My lungs freeze and I can't breathe.

I stand in the kitchen, frozen and speechless when she puts me on the spot. "Do we have a deal, Major Jameson?"

My brain is fist pumping me and screaming out, "Fuck yeah." But my gut … my gut and maybe my chest feels like I'm about to puke. I know I ask her every day if I can offer her a ride home, but at this point, it's more like a running joke. I've grown used to her dancing and annoying little quips. Honestly, I look forward to annoying her every morning when I come down for breakfast.

"Do we have a deal, Major?"

Her stare is challenging and I know this is monumental. This bet is her subtle way of seeing if we've called a truce and are friends. And really, I think we have. But there's still that pesky hope in her eyes and I can't afford to have a clinger.

So I take one for team Jameson.

It's going to hurt, but it's for our own good. I don't need a woman in my life, ever again.

"You have a deal."

I extend my hand for Breck to shake and I have the awful

privilege of watching her face fall with my acceptance. She wanted me to counter.

I failed her, and if that doesn't make me feel like the biggest piece of shit on the planet then I don't know what else will.

With a deep breath and a forced smile, Breck takes my hand and shakes it. "We have a deal, then."

We sure do. And it fucking sucks.

"Suck on that, Major!" she yells, bouncing up and down next to me.

"Touchdown!"

Breck is a beast on the Xbox. A far cry from what I had expected from a girl. Anniston plays with us sometimes but she never wins. But Breck is kicking my fucking ass six ways from Sunday without even trying hard. Someone hustled me.

"Sit down," I scold her, pulling on her tight as shit shorts. "I can't see with you jumping around in front of me. Video games were meant to be played sitting down."

Breck pulls against my hold and remains standing, tossing me a cocky look over her shoulder. "Don't be a spoilsport, Major."

Is she serious?

Me? A spoilsport? Eh, maybe. But fuck!

Can her ass not look so fucking edible while she swishes it in front of my face as her guy rushes the next forty? No wonder I'm fucking losing. I'm distracted as hell.

"I'm not being a spoilsport," I say, pulling her down again. This time she sits on the edge of the couch, next to me, and huffs out a breath. I cock a brow in response to her attitude and she laughs. "I seriously can't see the TV," I tell her.

"You seriously are down fourteen points. Your QB has eaten more grass than Killer."

How do I argue with that? Especially when she widens her eyes and flashes me a genuine smile that deepens the perfect dimple in her cheek.

"You talk a lot of smack for someone who falls down the stairs on a daily basis."

The smile she was sporting plummets and I almost feel bad for saying it. Yeah, I hear that catastrophe every morning when she stumbles down the stairs. Why she doesn't take her socks off, I'll never know.

"Well, you suck at hand-eye coordination. What rank were you again?"

Obviously, I didn't hurt her feelings that bad for her to retaliate so quickly. The challenge sparkling in her eyes conjures up something inside me. Something like … need. The old Cade would have snatched the controller out of her hand and put her on her knees for a proper apology. The old Cade would want the new Cade to flip her over his knee and blister her ass until her laughter turns into moans.

But the new Cade wins out and faces forward, trying to reclaim his man card by intercepting her quarterback's pass.

"Suck on that!" I shout.

It occurs to me then that I don't even know her last name. Around here, and in the military, we refer to each other by last name more often than first name.

"What's your last name?" I ask her, never taking my eyes off the screen as my guy weaves through her safeties.

Breck pauses the game, and I whine.

"Why?" She looks oddly nervous about answering the question. It's just her last name, not her social security number.

"Uh, because I don't know it. I think most employers know their employees' last names. The bank prefers both names, usually."

Breck lets out a fake laugh and fiddles with her controller. "It's Bennett."

Bennett.

The name pierces my chest as if she had just stabbed me.

His name still haunts my dreams. Right alongside Drew, Parker, Lewis, and Kyle.

"Are you giving up?" she taunts me, shoving her elbow into my side, pulling me from thoughts of the past.

I swallow down the memory of the nineteen-year-old kid I once knew and shove her back. "No one is quitting, Bennett. Let's finish this."

It's Breck's turn to be quiet as she studies her controller, digesting my comment. Is it from calling her by her last name or from being too candid? I'm so off and on with her she probably has whiplash trying to keep up with my mood swings.

Ignoring her has proven difficult. Each day she draws me in and chips away at the wall I've worked on building for the past five and a half years. I try so hard to keep her out but she keeps at me with her soft curves and smiles that could literally join warring nations.

This woman is my kryptonite.

The jelly to my peanut butter.

And I'm fucked.

Because as often as I deny myself of her presence, I still feel her. When she's in bed at night, typing away on her laptop, I fantasize about what those fingers would feel like drifting under my sweats, across the swell of my boxers. I want to know what she tastes likes when she dances to some ridiculous song while she cooks, dipping her finger in the food when she thinks no one is looking. When she gazes at me like she knows all my secrets and still stands beside me, I want to take it all.

Everything.

I want everything she's willing to give and everything she's going to make me work for.

For the first time in years, I want to be greedy and take what I've been denying myself.

"Better move that ass, Jameson. Your guy is going down in three, two ..."

Breck takes a cheap shot and un-pauses the game, immediately intercepting my guy from the ten-yard line and wins the fucking game with a touchdown of her own.

She springs from the sofa and tosses her controller beside me like she made the touchdown instead of the animated character on the screen. Like a siren, she sways in front of me, grinning.

"Looks like I'm the winner, Major Jameson."

The air conditioner must be out because it's hot in this living room. And it gets even hotter when she laughs and pokes my chest with her pink-coated fingernail.

"Are you going to congratulate—"

I blame it on the heat and her scent. Thick and sweet, it invaded my senses and I couldn't take it. I launch myself from the sofa, clutching that taunting finger in my hand, and yank her flush against my chest.

I'm fucking panting, she's got me so worked up.

"What are you doing?" she asks.

I'm going to hell on the express train.

Instead of answering her breathy question, I grind the steel fucking rod in my pants along her stomach. She gasps and I don't miss the opening.

My mouth descends on her, my tongue sweeping in and silencing any further bullshit remarks she might have made. Her bottom lip rubs against the stubble along my face and I hold her still, palming the back of her head. I suck that pouty bottom lip, savoring the unique taste of Breck. Her free hand goes to my shoulder and squeezes down the side of my arm, gripping my bicep. My dick throbs painfully in my pants, and I can't get enough, exploring every crevice that makes up the smart-ass mouth of hers.

I taste it all.

Until the front door slams.

I jump back first, pushing her away and scanning the room for any prying eyes.

"I'm sorry," Breck mumbles out quickly like it was her damn fault. Her eyes dart to the floor as if she is ashamed.

She shouldn't be.

I'm the one who should be tied up to a tree for a good lashing. This beautifully sweet woman wanted to kiss me and I freaked the fuck out, pushing her away like she was a virus.

I need my ass beat. Hard.

Inhaling, I try calming the fuck down so I can focus on not acting like a dickhead, but it's too late.

The new Cade buries the protests of the old Cade and I do the right thing by this girl. She deserves better than me. She deserves someone able to love her. Not me, who can't even love himself.

With a strength I don't want to use, I meet Breck's pleading eyes and beg for the last time. "Please let me take you home."

She doesn't flip me off like I expect her to. Instead, she makes a small noise and nods. "Okay." She sighs and gives me a fake smile. "I think it's time. Give me thirty minutes to pack?"

My Adam's apple bobs but I stick to my decision. "Sure."

Her lip quivers and it's the first time I've ever wanted to beat my own ass. She turns and heads up the stairs to her room when Hayes pokes his head around the wall.

It's hard to tell if he wants to punch me in the face or hold me down for Breck to do it.

Honestly, I would let either of them do it.

I'm a cold-hearted bastard.

chapter fifteen

Cade

It's been two days since I took her home.

I tried asking Hayes if he's heard from her, but he's pissed and won't tell me if he's spoken with her. I want to know if she's okay. I haven't slept since she left, replaying our kiss over and over. I'm having a nagging sensation I fucked up royally, keeping me from resting more than usual.

Breck wouldn't even speak on the way to the orchard. She sprang from the passenger side of the truck so fast I couldn't even open the door for her. With a half-assed wave, she hopped in the bed of the truck and struggled to toss her suitcase to the ground.

I tried to help.

Insisted even.

But she made up some bullshit about me doing too much for her already.

So I stood at my truck like a douche, watching as she dragged her heavy suitcase along the gravel, waving a hand behind her shoulder and then flipping me off as she closed the door behind her.

She was officially done with me.

I should feel happy, but I don't. I feel like I have the flu.

My head hurts and my body aches. The only bright side to this shit-tastic morning is that Anniston and Theo are coming home. Thank God. I could use a few days to not think. To be told what to do and when. My brain needs something to think about, other than Breck.

★ ★ ★

"So how did it go with Breck?"

Anniston is snuggled in one of the patio chairs with her legs tucked under her and a cup of decaf coffee, wasting no time getting to the inquisition. After she cried and hugged us all, making sure we were all in one piece, she made a pot of coffee and asked me to join her outside.

"It went okay," I say, taking a seat in the chair next to her.

"Just okay? You didn't pick up any cooking skills you want to show me?"

My brow arches and I hope she can see the bullshit look I give her. Her intent with Breck was not to teach me how to cook. I know as much as the next man.

Anniston meets my expression, her forehead wrinkled with how high her brows are arched. She knows I'm not being forthcoming with her.

"What did you do?" she asks, sighing after a moment, leaning back in her chair as if she's settling in for a long story.

I pop up out of my chair, my temper igniting from all the pent-up frustration over the last forty-eight hours.

"I was an asshole, okay! Is that what you want to hear?"

I pace around the patio, ten seconds from a meltdown, pulling at my hair before kicking the football Vic left out. I go through a myriad of sounds but none of them makes me feel any better.

It's quiet when I finally turn around and face Anniston who has a stupid ass smile on her face.

It pisses me off.

"Why are you fucking smiling?" I grit out, fighting to keep from yelling and acting like an even bigger asshole than I already am.

My question only makes her smile bigger.

"Commander!" I yell, not able to hold it any longer.

Anniston chuckles. "Why, Major, I believe this girl has gotten in your head."

I shake my head adamantly. "No." There is no fucking way Breck is in my head. On my nerves maybe, but not in my head.

Anniston continues to smile at me like she knows something I don't. "Huh," she muses.

What the fuck is "huh" supposed to mean?

We're silent after that, Anniston sipping on her coffee, staring out into the night, me pacing ruts in the grass. The cicadas are out, humming their rhythm. It's peaceful in a world full of chaos. I pace for a few more minutes, willing myself to settle down and find neutral ground with Anniston.

"Where's Theo?"

"He and Hayes are having dinner with a new prospect."

I only saw Theo long enough for him to say, "I see you didn't get laid. How pathetic." After that, he and Hayes holed up in my office and then disappeared. I assumed it had something to do with their latest prospect for the Atlanta A's.

"Hmm." I say, not sure where I was heading with the conversation. I flop down onto the chair next to Anniston, huffing out a breath. "I kissed her," I admit into the darkness.

I don't see Anniston turn in her chair but I *hear* her.

"Oh?" she breathes.

I nod, not sure if I want to reveal any more.

"And was it good?"

I inhale another deep breath, readying myself for the tongue-lashing coming my way.

"I freaked out afterwards," I say, shame coating every word like a dirty blanket over pristine sheets. "I pushed her away."

"Well, maybe she's into guys that play hard to get." Anniston's teasing tone snaps my head up from its pity party.

"Don't joke," I scold her. "This is serious, Commander. She may never come back."

Anniston snorts out a laugh. "She'll be back."

My blood pressure rises and my face flames with embarrassment. "You don't know that," I say rudely, way more pissed at the idea of Breck never returning than I should be.

Anniston stares at me with a glint in her eyes, a smile peeking over her coffee mug. It's the same smile she gives me when I do something that makes her proud. The question is, why is she giving it now?

"I *know*. She'll be back. Then you'll grovel and beg for forgiveness," she says.

I stare at her, open-mouthed.

"What freaked you out, Gorgeous?" she continues like she didn't just rock my world with her assuredness.

I shrug and swipe a hand through my hair. Sighing, I admit, "I don't know. It caught me by surprise, I think."

Anniston nods before grabbing her book off the side table and standing up. "Well, now you won't be surprised." She pinches my cheek before placing a kiss over the sting. "Goodnight, Cade."

She leaves through the sliding glass doors, and I'm left alone in the dark to deal with my demons and lies. Kissing Breck didn't catch me off-guard. What caught me off-guard was that I wanted more. I would have taken more had someone not opened the door.

The truth is, I *need* Breck.

And that scares the fuck out of me.

I'm an asshole, I text Breck.

Within a minute she responds, *I agree*.

After my talk with Anniston, I felt like I needed to apologize to Breck, not grovel as Anniston suggested. I disagree with that approach wholeheartedly. Apologizing seems a little less pussy than groveling. But maybe girls like it? I wouldn't know. I've never even apologized to a woman other than Anniston.

I've never had a girlfriend.

The military was my girl. I lived for the adrenaline. For the adventure. For the honor. My dick was the only one with a weakness for a woman. Okay fine, I admit I enjoyed the hell out of it, too, but it was only ever sex for me. I never wanted to get to know them or meet their parents. I just wanted a wet hole, and I didn't even care what hole it was.

I was simple like that.

I text her back, *I'm sorry. I shouldn't have kissed you. It was inappropriate.*

Are you serious? I kissed you back! We're adults. It wasn't inappropriate, she fires back.

I'm not sure that texting her was the right course of action, given her curt responses. *I won't admit that I'm good with women. I never have been.*

Why do you hate me so much? she asks.

Oh God. Is that how she feels? That I hate her? I don't hate her. Far from it. I want her so much that I hate myself. *I don't hate you.*

Three dots appear, showing she's typing. Why is my stomach cramping? Am I nervous?

Then why did you ask me to leave every day?

Because I'm an asshole and don't express myself very well is what I should say. But I go with a slight variation of the truth. *You make me nervous.*

Why? Is her only response.

My hand cramps from texting, something I'm definitely not used to doing for so long. *Can we talk? In person? Tomorrow?*

I want to talk to her about as much as I want to talk to the psychologist Ans makes me go to a few times a year. But I'm not a dick and I like Breck. Probably too much, and I don't want her to think the reason for my behavior is her. It's definitely me.

She still hasn't texted back, and it's probably for the best. It's easier for her to think that I hate her and not that I really like her but won't allow myself to form an attachment.

Anniston was the only exception.

She saved my life.

After waiting a few minutes without a response, I turn on the TV and find myself watching one of the movies Breck recorded—*Kickass*. I laugh out loud at a few scenes, and before I realize it, I've watched the entire thing. It's well past midnight and I need sleep. Theo will be up and ready for a run in a few hours. Most of the time, I can fall asleep to the TV, but for some reason, what I crave tonight is the sound of Breck typing on her laptop. The repetition of her nightly blogging lulls me to sleep better than anything I've ever tried.

And I fucking need it desperately.

I roll over and check my phone to see if she's texted back. She hasn't, and knowing she had to think about meeting me hurts more than it should.

Great job, Cade. Now you'll have to explain to Hayes and the rest of the guys why she won't ever come around again.

My shoulders tense up and my body craves a run due to the anxiety coursing through me. I should sleep. Try to keep my body in a normal rhythm. Most nights, I force myself to sleep early and then I can stay awake if I need to in the wee hours of the morning, but at least I will have gotten some rest.

I pull the covers over my legs and punch my pillow a few good times before I lie back and stare at the ceiling. It's going to be a long night.

I try remembering the way the key strokes sound but it doesn't do the trick. Counting sheep or bullets doesn't either. I'm definitely not going to go ask Ans for a sleeping pill, but honestly, I could use one right now.

After an hour of counting the blade rotations on the fan, frustration gets the better of me. I roll over with a groan, and when my phone chimes, I yell into the pillow. I spring out of bed as if my life depended on it, grabbing my phone.

Sure.

Fucking sure. I can deal with sure. I get back in bed with a grin on my face that I'll never admit to and debate what to text back or if I should text back at all.

I'm going to text her back. It's not like I'm sleeping.

Are you writing a review right now?

Her response is almost immediate. *Yeahhhh …why?*

I feel like a giddy teenager. *I watched* Kickass *tonight. I give it four stars.*

You low-balled it. I gave it five.

I smile. *You see the best in everybody.* Fuck. *I mean you see the best in everything. The movie had opportunities for improvement.*

I'm fucking sweating. Did I really type that shit? Where were you on that one, autocorrect?

Every movie is a five for someone, even if it has areas for improvement. Some reviewers will still view it as perfection.

I swallow, rereading her text repeatedly. Does she mean me or are we still talking about *Kickass*?

Some movies aren't worth your time, I text.

That's not your decision to make.

And now I know we aren't talking about the movie. *I'll save you the time and spoil it for you. My script doesn't end with a happily ever after.*

She takes a minute to respond. *I've always been more of a fan of the alternate endings.*

Why must she be so goddamn stubborn? Why can't she be quiet and complacent and find her a nice guy with some mental stability? Why must she keep feeding my addiction?

Why are you still up? I ask her.

Why are YOU still up?

And this is why my dick is hard. Arguing with her is like foreplay. It's in my nature to respond to commands and not being able to shut that sass up has me rock fucking hard.

I can't sleep. I text her.

Take something.

I scoff. *No.*

She sends me an annoyed emoji that makes me laugh. I admit, *I'm used to hearing you type at night. It's too quiet without you here.*

It's not a lie. I can hear Ans moaning in the next room and Hayes' headboard is chipping away at the sheetrock across the hall. It's like a pay-by-the-hour motel in here at the moment.

If you want, you can call me. I won't talk and you can listen to my keystrokes. She responds.

I'm shocked at her offer. I really want to listen to her but I feel like if I take her up on this, I'm crossing a line. A big red line. I stare at the ceiling, hearing Anniston's cries and Hayes' grunts, and I realize for the first time how alone I feel. When she was here, I didn't.

I press on her contact and listen to it ring. She picks up on the third one and doesn't say a word. And then she starts to type, and my eyes drift closed. The only sound is her breathing and the tapping on her laptop.

And it sounds like home.

★ ★ ★

"I don't understand what you're saying, Jameson. It sounds like you're saying a hot-ass chick—who can actually tolerate your broody ass—let you kiss her, and you…" His eyebrows shoot up his forehead, encouraging me to repeat what I told him. "I just need to hear you say it again so I'm clear what happened," he clarifies, totally lying. All he's doing with that shitty grin plastered on his face is aggravating me, but I give in and play his game because I need advice from another guy, and unfortunately today it's Theo.

"I pushed her away afterwards," I say again for his sick sense of humor.

Theo's grin morphs into a look of horror. "How dare she! That bitch! Doesn't she know she's supposed to kiss your dick first?" His tongue goes to his cheek as his hand makes a back-and-forth motion at his mouth. "You're right, Jameson. I would have pushed her away, too. A kiss on the mouth is a cardinal sin. You're better off with a girl who knows what she's doing."

Deep breaths, Cade. You knew talking to him would be rough. Exhaling, I mutter, "How did you ever find a woman?"

Theo smirks and tosses me the football. "Jameson, your commander gets off on my mouth. Generally, it's between her lips. Which lips, depends on how filthy I get."

I am not surprised in the least.

I rocket the football back to him, completely choosing to ignore his comments about Anniston. I don't want to know all the crude, sexual things they do when I'm not having to witness it firsthand.

"Look, Jameson, I don't know why we're out here in the heat talking about feelings. I don't know if all this celibacy shit has increased your estrogen or what." He tosses the ball back—in terrible form, I might add—and I snag it before it veers too far right and out of my reach. "But listen to me very closely. Fuck. This. Girl. Just fuck her. What is the worst that can happen? She realizes you're a big vagina and never calls you again?" He grins, teasing me, and I throw the ball as hard as I can, hitting his left shoulder. He laughs, unfazed. "That would solve your problem, right? Her leaving you alone? Isn't that what you want?"

Maybe.

I'm not sure now. I know I kept giving Breck a hard time about going home, but the last week was pretty good. I'd gotten to know her better and I actually grew to like her a little bit. Granted, her fuzzy socks and constant dancing and overall optimistic outlook on life got on my nerves, but overall, she's beau—nice. She's nice. And too good for a man like me.

"Geez, Jameson. Lighten the fuck up. It's just sex. You don't have to promise her a white picket fence and three kids. Just a good time—or bad. It's been a while since you've given it a go, but either way, you can knock the rust off Jameson Jr. and stop depriving him of some action just because you're being emotional and all of a sudden in touch with your feelings."

"Talking to you is pointless," I observe, slipping an earbud in one ear, intent on zoning out and going for a run to clear my head. I need to think. All this shit with Breck is stressing me out. Do I want to fuck her? Yes. Does she deserve to be fucked by a mess like me who can't commit and can't love because he doesn't even love himself? No, she doesn't. Do I want to be selfish and do it anyway? One hundred percent.

"Ugh, now I feel guilty, like I should run with you or something," he says, tossing the football out into the yard.

I shake my head, already trotting down the hill. "Please don't. I'm good."

Theo chuckles, ignoring my request for solitude, and sprints past me. "Come on, Jameson, let that testosterone loose and race me. Winner buys drinks tonight."

Damn it.

I take off behind him, pushing hard to catch up. I never turn down a competition with Theo. It's what we've always done; push each other to our limits. He's pushing me out of my head, and whether I want to admit it or not, it's working. We race past the barn, not laughing, not hearing the music pounding in our ears with each step. We go balls-to-the-fucking-wall with each stride until the only thing I can think about is winning.

★ ★ ★

What was supposed to be a simple race turned into an Olympic trial through the pastures. I don't know how Theo has so much endurance. He has less mass to haul around than I do, making him significantly faster than me. I kept pace until the last quarter mile when he sprinted faster than a gazelle to the house, making it look as if he was playing with me the whole time. Now I'm in a worse mood than before.

Hands on my hips, my lungs are on fire when we make it to the backyard. The sight before me is comforting, a smile tugging at my lips before Theo ruins it with a shitty remark.

"Thank God you needed a girl chat and we didn't have to suffer her wrath."

We both stand, me catching my breath and Theo eyeing Anniston's tits as she lays horizontally over Hayes and Mason as they do pushups. She's casually filing her nails and barking out reps while the guys groan, their arms shaking from the weight of the up and down motion.

I send Theo an eat-shit look. "I did not need a girl chat. I simply asked for your advice, which was terrible by the way."

Theo shrugs and starts toward Anniston but not before throwing back, "Terrible or not, you know it's the truth."

Ugh. Fucking Breck is a bad idea.

Entertaining *anything* with Breck is a bad idea.

Falling asleep with her on the phone was an even *worse* idea.

"Speak of the siren herself." Theo chuckles, kneeling on the ground by Anniston's head. "Showtime, playboy," he says before biting Anniston's nipple through her shirt and making her squeal.

For a second, I consider throwing a deck chair at his face. But the crunching of a van flying down the driveway stops me.

She came.

Like she said she would. And now I owe her an explanation for my behavior.

I rake in a few ragged breaths and wipe the sweat from my forehead as Theo shouts, "We're back here."

He laughs when I flip him off, knowing good and damn well he could have given me an extra minute. Breck appears around the corner in cut-offs and a Flash t-shirt, her high-top Converse shoes tying together her sloppy, yet incredibly cute outfit. She's like my very own comic book nerd. Sexy and cute, just begging for me to prove how much bigger my hammer is than Thor's.

"Hey, Breck. What's up?" Anniston greets her first since her head is hanging off Hayes' back.

"Hi. I'm sorry to interrupt. Cade—"

Hayes interrupts her as he pulls his head up and flashes her his trademark wink. I feel a growl bubble up but I hold it in so as not to embarrass myself more than I already have. Hayes wants his ass beat.

Fucking with Breck in front of me is a death sentence at this point. I've all but pissed on her leg to claim her. Hayes annoying me after two days of hell is bordering on a murder charge.

"You're looking scrumptious this morning, darlin. You got a hot date or something?"

Pink spreads across Breck's cheeks, making her look sun-kissed. "Uh, no. It's laundry day," she blurts out, looking at me from under her long eyelashes.

I flash her an apologetic smile, refraining from making contact with Hayes, and nod to the back door. We need to talk and not out here with an audience.

Breck holds up a finger, asking me to hold on. "Anniston, can I speak with you for a minute?"

I feel sucker-punched when Anniston pulls up and looks between me and Breck, and says, "Sure."

chapter sixteen

Breck

B,

The mood is somber in the tent tonight. Kyle's wife sent him a letter that she was leaving him—something like she couldn't take being alone all the time. It has me thinking. Guys like us have a hard time maintaining relationships. The military seems to be our girl. Maybe I shouldn't pursue Jess. She deserves someone who can be there for her all the time. How's class going? Any new man in your life that I need to order a hit on? Miss you, weirdo.

#milosacedthesupermanreview #yoursandjesswasmediocretohis #boysrulegirlsdrool

Ben

"Come over here and tell me what's going on." Anniston motions with her nail file for me to come closer. I do. And when I'm standing awkwardly at the guys' heels as they push up and down she says, "Have a seat. You can take their ass."

The guys choke out a laugh at the possibility of a double meaning.

If they could see the look of disbelief on my face, they would tease me for days about it. It seems to be their thing with me. Teasing. Anniston pats Hayes' butt, encouraging me to sit.

"Stop, boys. Let her sit." They both groan but do as she requests. She gets up and motions for me to take her spot. Slowly, I lower myself down and lay across their behinds. I hate to admit it but knowing these two strong men raise and lower their bodies with my weight makes my girl parts tingle.

"Twenty more, marines," Anniston barks out with a chuckle while Hayes and Mason grunt and lower to the ground. I struggle to figure out what to do with my hands. The motion feels strange, but I try to relax and focus on how the muscles in their glutes and lower back flex between the reps.

"Are they in trouble?" I ask Anniston who is smirking down at Hayes for some reason. I don't know if this is part of their daily training or some kind of punishment.

"Oh no. They aren't in trouble. Well, Hayes probably has done something shitty, but no, this is just part of their daily workout regimen. Since I've been gone so much, I wanted to work out with them." She chuckles when Hayes makes a disbelieving sound.

"Don't let her lie to you, B. She went on that honeymoon and binge ate so much she thinks the extra ten pounds she put on is equivalent to us moving up a weight class."

I suck in a breath. Did he say Anniston gained weight?

Anniston throws her head back and laughs. "You're a liar, Connor Hayes! Give me ten more just for being a pain in my ass today."

Both guys bark out a "ooh-rah," but it's laced with humor. It's obvious they are happy to have their commander back.

"So, tell me what brings you by, Breck?"

Right. Why am I here again? Because I am a stupid and naive girl, and I feel terrible thinking I've set Cade back by kissing him.

"I …" *Get your shit together, B. Just tell her. She knows Cade. Maybe she can share some insight on how to get through to him.* "I came to apologize to Cade."

Her head lifts to look me in the eye. This is one of those moments where instinct demands you not look away from the predator or it may attack you. That's how her stare feels right now. She likes me, but she will kill me if I've hurt Cade in any way. If I've learned anything from living here and being around this family for two weeks, it's that they take care of one another, no matter what.

"Oh?" Eyebrows arched and a hard look on her face, she encourages me to continue.

This was a bad idea. I should have just called him. What the hell was I thinking? Oh, that's right. I was thinking I would toss on some clothes, breeze in here, and say, "Cade, I'm sorry for kissing your kissable face. I'm sorry you're so damn hot that I want to have your babies. And I'm sorry that I'm a liar, and now we have this complicated and fucked up relationship." Yeah, not so smart.

I swallow and lift my head. "Can we, uh, speak in private?"

Anniston nods curtly, her face one in deep thought. "We're done for the day, boys. Go shower and hydrate."

Both guys collapse on the ground with me still on their back. They groan and I spring up. "I'm sorry!" I say. "I didn't mean to stay on you."

Anniston laughs, dusting imaginary lint off her spandex shorts, and waves away my comment. "They can take it. They bench twice your weight on a daily basis. They're groaning because it probably makes them horny. Well, Hayes anyway."

Hayes stands, sweat dripping down his jaw, and winks at me, adjusting himself right in front of me and walking away as if nothing happened.

My mouth gapes open, caught between a laugh and shock, and I snap it shut.

Anniston taps me on the shoulder, reading into my look as more shock than humor. "Don't worry about it. The doorbell ringing gets him hard. You'll get used to it."

I'm not going to correct her and tell her I'm already used to it. Hayes is my friend. My partner in crime. My horny compadre.

I know—not from experience—that the slightest breeze hardens him in seconds flat. But for some reason, I keep mine and the guys' relationship a secret. I know it's stupid. After all, Anniston invited me to help out which led to this friendship with the guys, but I want to be stingy with them and not tell her I love them like brothers.

Anniston pulls me from my thoughts, lightly touching my arm. "Come on. Let's go talk in the kitchen."

Anniston made us something to drink, and we've been chatting about how things went during my two-week stay. She didn't push me to get down to the nitty gritty reason I'm here. Instead, she had me tell her of my adventures with the guys. She laughed with me and genuinely seemed thrilled that we had bonded.

It was her love and selflessness for the guys that had me wanting to speak up and be truthful. This woman was not my enemy. Yeah, she makes me feel insecure, but so what?

Hence my random confession.

"I pushed Cade when he wasn't ready. I shouldn't have kissed him," I blurt out like someone with zero social skills.

Anniston eyes me thoughtfully and takes a sip of her water. "Why don't you think he's ready? Did he tell you he wasn't?" My mouth slams shut as she drills me with questions. "Did he not kiss you first?"

Okay, she's making this seem super simple, and it's not. Cade has issues, and I didn't consider them when I shoved my tongue down his throat two days ago.

"He did kiss me first. But that's not the point."

Anniston adjusts in the chair and cocks her head to the side. "Is it because you're getting close to him and he still doesn't know about Bennett?"

My stomach takes a swan dive right out of my ass. I blink back at the woman who is Cade's most trusted confidant. She knows. This whole time she knew who I was.

"Does he know?" I swallow and pull my knees under me.

She makes a soft noise, her lips going tight at the corners. "I was hoping *you* would have told him by now."

And now I feel like the shittiest human on the planet.

The vein in my forehead throbs, and I know it's only a matter of time before my eyes will burn with tears. "I'm going to," I whisper, unable to meet her eyes. "But he's still so angry about the past that I'm afraid he won't receive it well."

Anniston looks thoughtful as she twirls a strand of hair around her finger. "He probably won't, you're right." The burning sensation arrives as predicted, and the first swell of tears accumulate at the corner. Anniston, unbeknownst to my imminent sobfest, forges on. "But that doesn't mean he should be kept in the dark. It's not good for his healing."

She's right. Keeping this secret from him will only make things worse.

"But he just started to warm up to me," I plead, a lonely tear plummeting to its death onto my bare leg. Anniston eyes the wet spot and gives me a look like she may want to hug me.

"He'll come back around," is all she says. The fact that she didn't deny my guess at Cade's reaction gives my heart palpitations like it's already bracing for the inevitable heartbreak. Another tear slips out, and this time it accompanies a noise that sounds a lot like a cry.

"Oh, B." Anniston is out of her chair and has her arms around me in seconds. Her voice is comforting, and honest to God, she smells so good for someone who was just working out. Her flawlessness only adds insult to my already insecure state and I cry into her sports bra.

"I'm so sorry," I tell her before pulling back.

She chuckles and rubs my back. "Sometimes, Breck, people surprise you. I'm not saying Cade will swallow that you're Bennett's sister easily—he's for sure going to act like shit when he finds out." If her speech is supposed to make me feel better, it isn't working. "All I'm saying is that Cade may surprise you with how resilient he is. He's come a long way the past year and a half." Anniston's smile as she looks out the window at the guys almost seems reverent.

"Do you love him?" I ask her, my insecurity knowing no bounds, and apparently neither does my filter. "I mean—"

Anniston's throaty laugh cuts off the rest of my explanation. "What you really mean is, do I love him enough to want to fuck him?"

I choke. Full on, hacking up a lung kind of choking. "No …"

Anniston's bubbly laughter wanes ever so slightly before she sucks in a breath and wipes at her eyes, leveling me with a stern look. "No, Breck. I don't want to fuck him."

Was that a sigh of relief I let out?

"Do I want him to get fucked in the near future? Absolutely. But you see, Breck, my taste in dick is aggressive and smartass." Her eyes go to the window again and she smiles at Theo who is giving Cade hell about something we can't hear. "And a whole lot of asshole." She pats me on the leg. "I love Cade. I always will." My pulse races and I want to stop her before she shares any more with me but I also don't because whatever she is going to say, I need to hear it. "But I love Theo more. More than anything or anyone. That may sound shitty, but it doesn't make it any less true. Mine and Cade's relationship differs from that of mine and Theo's. I love Cade like a brother—like my best friend. I can't ever imagine sleeping with him. Just because we're friends and business partners does not mean I want to jump his bones. Cade deserves someone special. Someone who won't command him, but who will support him and give him the confidence to take control of his life and command himself. I'm not that person, Breck. You are. You are the selfless one for Cade. Not me. I've loved one man my whole life, and now that I have him, Von Bremen will always come first," she admits softly.

"I know it's difficult understanding my relationship with all the guys. The best way I can explain it is, think of them as my brothers. My family. I joke and carry on with them but I'll be the first one to come to their rescue if they need it. I'm not your enemy. I won't stand in your way. All I ask is that you don't hurt him. Or any of them. The others seemed to have taken to you as well."

I can see her point. After having lived with them for two weeks,

I've taken to them, too. I want the same for them as she does. "I understand," I tell her softly. "It's just …" I clear my throat. "The way he looks at you…"

Anniston breathes deeply, her face softening ever so slightly. "You only see what you want to see," she tells me.

So now we're being cryptic.

"I don't understand what you mean." She gazes out the window once more, Cade and Theo catching us this time. Anniston crooks her finger, motioning for them to come inside. I guess our chat is over.

"The way Cade looks at me doesn't hold a candle to how he looks at you," she says absently before standing to face me just as the screen door slams. "Open your eyes, sweetheart, and take hold of what you want." She swipes the pad of her thumb along my eyes, catching any of the remaining tears just as both guys lumber into the kitchen.

"Good thing you called us in here. I was just about to kick Cade's ass." Theo tosses a smile over his shoulder but Cade just looks bored.

"He wishes," is all he responds, holding my gaze like he can read my mind.

Anniston chuckles but instead of responding to their mess, she shocks the shit out of us all by saying, "B's agreed to go with Cade to the gala next week. She'll need a dress."

Cade and I both choke at the same time. What the hell is a gala and why did she tell Cade that I needed a dress? Or shit, that I even agreed to go?

"I, uh …" I let out another cough. "I have dresses I could wear."

Anniston waves me off. "Oh no, this is black-tie. Cade can take you to the place we use."

Cade shoots her an incredulous look, his eyes wide and, is that a hint of fear I detect?

"Won't you, Cade?" Her face is stern with a no-bullshit look and I fidget before Theo breaks the tension.

"Congratulations, Jameson. Welcome to the world of torture. Upgrade your data package to unlimited so you can stream a game while she tries on every dress in the shop, including the ones that are too small." Theo smirks, a hint of a smile directed at Anniston like he's remembering something fun. "Spoiler alert. Those require you to pry them off." He shakes his head at Cade. "I can't tell you how many I had to buy because I said, 'fuck it,' and ripped the shit down the seam."

Cade swallows and nods slowly. "Are you guys going, too?"

Theo's face scrunches up like his gum turned sour. "Fuck no. You're on your own. Have fun with that shit."

Cade shoves at his shoulder, and not lightly.

"I already have my dress," Anniston explains, "and Theo will wear what the fuck I tell him to wear." She glances over her shoulder at Theo, smiling. He rolls his eyes and throws open the fridge, rooting around like he doesn't care one way or another what he wears as long as Anniston is the one to take it off him. "Cade needs a new tux," she says. "He's outgrown the one he has."

I only feel a little annoyed that she knows he has outgrown his clothes.

"And since you agreed to go" —she cuts me a look that I interpret as *deny it and I will cut off your hair while you're sleeping*—"You'll need a dress, too. Luckily, Cade had already planned to go this afternoon. You can go with him and kill two birds with one stone." She shrugs her shoulders like she didn't just sentence Cade and I to awkward hell for the rest of the day.

"I don't think I can afford a new dress," I mutter, embarrassed about my financial situation for the first time.

Anniston waves me off. "Please. Cade will take care of it. Right, Gorgeous?"

Cade's glare looks the opposite of pleased to take care of it. He looks like he would rather punch something instead of flashing Anniston a fake smile and gritting, "I'd love to."

Theo slips behind Anniston, bending down so his chin rests on her shoulder, and flashes Cade and I a cocky wink with a clear underlying meaning. "You kids behave in those dressing rooms."

"I'm sorry Anniston roped you into going to this gala," Cade says. I've been staring out the window while he drives, playing an old sign game Ben and I used to play on road trips. It was obvious this was not how we planned to discuss what happened the other day.

The smile I give him is weak. "It's okay. Sue will be excited. Being seen more in the community is good for business." Total lie. I'm actually pretty excited to be Cade's date. I can only imagine how edible he looks in a tux. Cade drums his fingers on the steering wheel, seeming nervous. "I can make something up if you don't want me to go," I offer.

Cade veers off the road at my suggestion before correcting, "No, that's not it. I want you to go." He rakes his hand through his hair and sighs. "I know how she can be when she wants something. I don't want you to feel like you have to go if *you* don't want to."

We're going with awkward, I see.

I place a hand on Cade's jean-clad thigh. The muscle twitches under my touch, and God I want to squeeze it. "I want to go with you," I say, my voice seeming loud in the quiet cab.

Briefly, Cade eyes our connection—my pink painted nails on his dark-wash denim—and then … he smiles and covers my hand with his big one. My lungs decide that now is the prime opportunity to stop working. I swallow, staring out at the open road. I'm at a loss for what I'm supposed to say. We still have much to discuss. Cade's hot and cold attitude with me is still an issue. He either likes me or he doesn't. I can't take much more of this push and pull we've been doing.

My hand twitches under his, and after a minute, I break the silence, my big girl panties firmly in place. "About that kiss."

Cade lets out a harsh breath. "I'm sorry," says the man who checked for vampires outside my window just a few days ago. "It's difficult for me to be around women."

I pause, blinking at his hardened jaw. "You seem okay around Anniston."

That snaps his head around. "She's different."

Of course she is. "Why?"

Cade scoffs at my question, and for a minute I think he's not going to answer me. But then the truck slows, and he pulls off onto the shoulder. He presses the button, and the windows lower before he flips off the ignition.

Suddenly, the granola with milk I had this morning seems like a bad idea. I should have gone with something more substantial. Then maybe it wouldn't feel like there is a churning vat of nerves in my stomach right now. Cade unbuckles his seatbelt and turns his body to face me.

I press the button on my own seatbelt. "I guess you want to talk." I make a show of looking out the window at the deserted road leading to the only highway in Madison, not a car in sight. As a matter of fact, I don't recall passing one on our way either.

"You deserve my full attention."

Hello, soaked panties.

The fabric makes a sound when my bare thighs slide along the seat cushion to face Cade. If he's giving me his full attention, the least I can do is give him mine.

"I … uh." His confession starts out rough, his voice shy with a hint of a raspy quality to it. "I like you," he tries again, the words spilling out in one breath.

To say I am completely shocked would be a lie. I knew he liked me in his own way. That's not the issue. The issue is whether he likes me *and* my vagina, because there's a distinct difference. One is called the friend zone and the other is called a boyfriend. Or fuckbuddy. I wouldn't be opposed to either.

"I like you, too." I say, watching his hands twist together in his lap. He's nervous. And it's causing me to have word vomit. "I *really* fucking like you."

Cade's laugh is low and rumbly. "I really fucking like you, too …" I feel a *but* coming on. "But I can't be with you." I feel my cheeks pull down into a frown as Cade hurries out, "Not that I don't want to, because I do." His tongue slips out, wetting his bottom lip before he bites down and releases it slowly, the motion looking incredibly sexy. "I really fucking do, Breck. I want you to know that."

I nod like I understand, but I still don't. What's the issue? He wants to take my panties off, and I … well, I want to rip his boxers off with my teeth like a rabid dog.

"I'm sorry. I keep leading you on," he says.

And now I want to attack him for another reason entirely. "Don't talk to me like I'm some love-struck teenager."

Cade's jaw tics and his eyes narrow at my abruptness. Yeah, motherfucker, I have balls, too. Well, sort of. Never mind. You know what I mean. I straighten, allowing all the frustration of the past two weeks to bubble to the surface. I'm nobody's plaything. "Look Cade, I get it. You have issues. Who doesn't?" One of his eyebrows quirks up almost like he's amused. "But you either want to fuck me or you don't. It's as simple as that. But all the closeness, hair washing, and subtle breathing down my neck is getting old." The other eyebrow jumps. "I expect a man to know what he wants and go after it. Maybe that's not you but—"

I don't have time to brace myself before Cade's hard body slams into mine. Hot and unyielding, he pushes me against the door, the handle digging into my back as his mouth attacks my neck first. Nipping and sucking, the mouth that has commanded dozens of men, growls against me. "You make me crazy," he admits, placing open-mouthed kisses along my jaw, toward my lips but never getting close enough. "Every damn day, I've watched you. I can't even tell you how many times I've imagined shutting you up with something other than words."

Huh. Coincidentally, that doesn't offend me at all. I think I might like being silenced with some D.

His breathing turns harsher, and the hand on my hip tightens before unceremoniously yanking me underneath him. If his truck was a manual, I would swear the shifter was digging into my leg, but it's not, and that's totally his dick. I may have come from a pretentious family, but an uppity girl I am not. I grind into that steel rod between his legs like our lives depend on it. I claw at this man like I'm plummeting to my death and my nails against his sweat slicked t-shirt are my only hope. Basically, I am shameless as I dry hump this mountain of a man on the side of the road and I couldn't give two shits what anyone thinks about it.

"We can't do this here," he pants out above me.

I'm not so fancy. "Sure we can," I argue, pushing my opening along his length. His groan sounds utterly pained.

"You deserve better," he manages. Honestly, I don't care if he hits it in a dirty-ass bathroom, but I can't necessarily say that, now can I?

"I don't mind." That doesn't sound too whore-ish.

Cade takes a few breaths and lifts himself up, prying my hands off his shoulders. "We can pick it up at home."

For the record, I only frown. I don't kick or holler, "This is bull-shit." I simply turn the previous open-mouthed smile I had going into a hardcore frown and say, "Okay."

Cade nods a few times like he's trying to convince himself that this is the best idea. But inevitably, he starts the truck, turns the air on full-blast, and gives me his trademark chin jerk. "Put your seatbelt on."

It's good to know that, unlike most men, Cade can still think with the head on his shoulders when all the blood flow is mucking around in the head stuffed into his jeans. I do as he asks, and when I'm secure, he pulls onto the roadway in the opposite direction.

"What about the tux?" I don't mention the dress because serious-ly, I have one I could wear.

"Fuck the tux," he growls, gripping the steering wheel for support. I'm, if nothing else, a team player. So what do I respond with that has Cade stepping on the gas harder?

"Ooh-rah, Major."

chapter seventeen

Breck

B,

 I finally did it. I asked Jess out. I know I told you about Kyle's wife which had me thinking Jess deserved better, but I overheard major telling Kyle that we deserve happiness, whatever that may be. Then Drew added that he should fuck anything that moves for the next month and get over it but that's beside the point. The point is: Jess makes me happy. She hasn't responded. Maybe help your brother out and tell her how awesome I am?

 #youoweme #kindof #twentymoredaysuntilleave

 Bennett Brannon

No one is around when Cade and I come hauling ass down the gravel driveway as if Satan himself was behind us the whole ten miles back. Cade doesn't speak to me the entire ride. He *does* have to adjust himself several times, and that makes me pretty fucking happy.

 I made him hard.

 The girly giggle I let out only makes him scowl. He doesn't like that I make him crazy, but karma's a queen, and for once, she's giving me what I deserve.

Major Jameson.

Before I can stare at the rod in his pants any longer, Cade throws the truck in park, comes around the front of the truck—I've learned not to open it—and opens my door with pent-up aggression. Placing my feet on the running boards, I reach up and lock my fingers around his scruffy chin, and place a chaste kiss on his scowling lips. It shocks him for a moment, but then he smiles, shakes his head, and kisses me sweetly against the truck.

"Come on before someone sees us." He pulls back, swiping his knuckles along my jaw, and I seriously think I could do him on the gravel. Obviously, I don't offer it, that would be slutty. Instead, I take his hand and jump down from the truck, letting him pull me through the door and up the steps before locking us behind his bedroom door.

For a moment we just stand there and stare at his bed made up all nice and military-like with the corners tucked. Too bad we're about to make it look like a tornado tore through the room, sparing it no mercy.

"Do you need a minute?" Cade asks me with a hint of nerves.

Be a hero, B. Take hold of what you want. And what you want, right now, is this beautiful man. And maybe his dick. Okay, especially his dick.

I take a step forward in Cade's space, and he tosses his keys onto the dresser. "No, Major Jameson, I don't need a minute."

I knew calling him Major Jameson would do it.

Before I can even digest what's happening, Cade tosses me onto his bed, his enormous body following suit. I laugh once we've stopped bouncing and slowly move his hands between my legs. The heat there is obvious through my shorts, and Cade needs no further direction. His deft fingers pop open the button, and I unzip them as he lifts himself up, balancing on one muscled arm, and tells me to, "Take them off."

And for shits and giggles, I add fuel to his fire and respond with, "Yes, sir."

I don't have to worry about my shirt—or his for that

matter—because he removes them with speed the Flash could only dream of. Cade is in beast mode as he growls low in his chest, pushing me into the mattress. His heavy body grinds down on my bra-clad nipples, and I've never hated it as much as I do now.

Cade's hands roam over my arms, my shoulders, never stopping in one spot for long. His tongue leaves a trail of goosebumps as he works from my shoulder, stopping to suck my poor neglected nipple through my bra.

"Take it off," I whine. The girls want to be free. But I stop my crying when he pulls the cup down, massaging the entirety of my breast in one hand. The first twinge shoots straight to my core, my body so alight with warmth that my scalp tingles. "Keep going," I tell him, but he doesn't listen. His mouth moves down my chest, to my stomach, placing soft kisses there.

I want his mouth somewhere else but I don't want to be too greedy. That would not be ladylike at all. But the whore on my shoulder says a little nudge in the right direction wouldn't hurt. I've never been easy, but Cade's mouth, the weight of his body on mine, is like fat-free cake. I want it all. So I push his head a little lower, and wouldn't you know, he goes down without a fight.

He starts with just breathing against me, and then his nose buries into my wetness and I nearly come from the action alone.

"Oh, God. Please take off my panties."

Cade grunts, his hold on my open thighs, his grip tightening almost uncomfortably. I shift, trying to find a better position without being a whiny bitch but Cade holds me still, his mouth leaving my center.

"Cade?"

I lean up on an elbow and rub down his back. His muscles are rigid and tense underneath my fingertips. I move to his face and lift his chin with my finger, noticing that his eyes are dilated, his stare bordering on vacant. "Cade? Are you okay?" He doesn't answer me. The only response is squeezing my thigh harder in a punishing hold. Vaguely, I think of his PTSD but since I've never seen it happen, I'm not sure if he's just being aggressive in bed or what.

I try again, my tone calm, hoping he'll speak to me. "Cade. You're hurting me. Look at me." He doesn't. All he does is squeeze the non-existent muscles in my leg, and I nearly cry out from the pain. "Cade, please," I beg, as tears prick at my eyes. I don't want it to be this way. I've never been hurt or had rough sex, but this—this vacant stare—as he pins me down with the weight of his body, silent like the marine he is, has me fucking scared.

"Cade, please let me up. I don't want to do this anymore." A sob builds in my throat, and I try pushing at his bare chest. "Cade!" I scream as the first tear falls. "Get off of me!" The first tear is followed by about fifty more before instinct kicks in and I scream for help. Someone will see me in my underwear, but I can't deal with whatever is going on in Cade's head. Obviously he is somewhere far away from here, and to be honest, the look in his eyes and the power of his body bearing down on me has me fearful for my safety.

"Help me!" I scream to anyone who can hear me. Surely someone will hear unless they're all outside.

Oh, God.

What if they left?

Panicked, I kick and scratch at Cade, pleading for him to let me go, but he holds me steady, only grunting in response to my hits.

"Please." Tears drop onto my chest. "Please stop, Cade."

But he doesn't. His gaze remains far away before he starts to rock, squeezing me so hard that I scream out from more than fear. "Help me! Someone, please!"

The door flies open seconds later, and I have never been happier to see Theo's scowling face.

"Something is wrong," I cry out to him, sucking back the tears and God knows what else on my face. "Something is wrong with Cade."

Theo's brows lower, and then it seems to dawn on him what's happening. He hollers for Anniston and then rushes to us, trying to pry Cade's hands from my legs.

"Jameson," he whispers softly, his voice smooth and confident like he's done this a million times before. "Listen to my voice, Jameson." Theo tugs on his hand again, but it doesn't loosen. I try not to cry anymore, pushing through the pain. Cade is suffering from something I will never understand, and I ... a hiccup escapes me. I caused this. I pushed him when he wasn't ready. I never thought the reason he hasn't slept with anyone in years is because it's a trigger for him.

My chest feels like I've swallowed fire. It hurts. This beautiful and kind man, who was doing great here with Anniston ... all his progress ... I've set him back. Shame overrides my embarrassment as Anniston and Hayes run into Cade's bedroom, Anniston with a syringe in her hand.

"What happened?" she asks, rushing to Cade's side. Immediately, she starts talking to him like Theo is, low and calm. She doesn't even bother waiting for an explanation from me. She knows what's going on and what needs to be done.

"Gorgeous," she soothes, stroking her hand along his cheek, "I need you to look at me." She turns his chin, and he lets her. "Good job," she praises, handing Theo the syringe and placing both hands on his cheeks, forcing him to see only her. "Where are you, Cade?"

Cade breathes harshly into her face but she holds him still as Hayes comes over and joins me on the bed, reaching for my hand, interlacing our fingers and putting his index finger of his other hand to his lips, telling me to stay quiet.

I want to scream. I want to break down in front of all these people because Cade still has me pinned and my leg is throbbing. I'm just fucking ashamed and embarrassed at the whole situation.

I want to go home.

But then I hear Cade grunt before loosening his grip and rasping out to Anniston, "Make it stop. Make it go away." His voice is pained like whatever he's reliving in his head is the equivalent to torture.

I stay quiet, letting the hot tears trail down my face as Anniston motions for Theo to hand her the syringe. "I'll make it go away," Anniston promises. I barely make out his nod when Anniston says, "I need you to let go of Breck, okay?"

For a moment everything is just dead silent and then Cade jumps back like he's seeing me for the first time. "Get her out of here!" he roars, trying to push up from the bed, but Theo holds him there, whispering calmly into his ear. I reach out, wanting to comfort Cade but Hayes scoops me up and shakes his head.

"Let's get you out of here, darlin." Hayes carries me to the door, allowing me one more glance at the mess I made. Theo squeezes Cade's shoulders and holds him steady while Anniston injects him with what I guess to be a sedative. The last thing I see before Hayes carries me out the door is Anniston touching Cade's face and asking, "You still with me?"

And when he answers, "I'm always with you, Commander," a part of me dies inside.

He doesn't need me.

I'm crazy for thinking he needed saving. I'm no hero. Everything he needs he has right here. As Hayes carries me across the hall to his room, I finally let go and just fucking cry.

I cry big, fat, ugly tears into his olive-green t-shirt. I cry because I've left everyone and everything behind for a cause I thought I was meant for. I cry because I wasn't there for Bennett when he passed from this world. I cry because I freaked out and couldn't bring his mentor back from a horrific flashback today. A flashback I caused.

And then I cry for me again because now I love this family like my own but I don't belong here.

Hayes rocks me back and forth on his bed, quietly shushing me to his solid chest. "Let me get you some clothes, darlin."

Oh God.

He's so fucking sweet that I sob louder. Hayes squeezes me tight and kisses the top of my head before sliding me off his lap. Immediately, I roll over on my stomach so he doesn't see my face. His pillow smells like him, all clean and earthy, and goddammit, the tears keep coming.

After a few minutes the door clicks closed and Hayes sits alongside me, stroking my back calmly. "I grabbed you something from

Anniston's closet. Y'all look to be about the same size."

I mumble a thank you into his pillow, refusing to look at him. He only chuckles and smacks my ass hard, startling a gasp out of me. Which coincidentally stops my crying.

"Come on, darlin. I need a drink, and from the look of it, so do you. Get up and get dressed. I'll get us a bottled water before we go."

Does his offer make me cry more? You betcha. Do I really want to go? Not really, but I nod my consent. I'm not going to let my partner in crime down, so I sit up to face him. There's no point in worrying about what he thinks about me at this point. He's seen me in my underwear, pinned down by his commanding officer, and carried me to his room while letting me snot and cry into his shirt which looks like he's been in a wet t-shirt contest.

"I'm sorry about your shirt," I say distractedly.

Hayes laughs and claps me on the shoulder, standing up. "Don't worry about it, honey. Girls cry on me all the time." And then he rips off his t-shirt and tosses it to the floor. Suddenly my tears are all dried up. Why does he have to be so damn fine? Why are they all so good looking? I mean, I have a hard time finding dates that look even half as good as Hayes, and here is Anniston, living with six hot-as-sin men.

She's my hero.

And unfortunately, she's Cade's, too.

★ ★ ★

The bar Hayes pulls into reminds me of a horror movie Ben and I used to watch when our parents left us with the nanny while they hobnobbed with the elite of NYC. Tara, the struggling law student by day and nanny by night, never cared what we were doing as long as we didn't interrupt her study time. Bennett loved horror films. Me, I loved superhero movies. *Spiderman. Fantastic Four.* Comics. Anything other than a fairytale. Disney movies made me nauseous. Never once, in my ten years did my animals sing or help me clean my room. Nope, when I cried, I cried alone until my big brother could wrap his arms around me and lull me to sleep with his terrible knock-knock jokes.

So, as I take Hayes' hand and let him pull me through the doors of the bar that should be named Titty Twister from that Tarantino film instead of the simple and unassuming name, Patty's, I feel a bit nostalgic. I miss Ben. He would have loved this place.

"Patty's has the best beer," Hayes says, walking backwards, pulling me with one arm. "You like beer? Or do you prefer those girly drinks?"

I'm about to tell him that over a year ago I was a college student, doing keg stands—okay, so that's an exaggeration—but I can drink beer, even the cheap stuff. But Hayes never lets me get a word in, though, as he continues to weave through the crowd. "I mean, I'm not judging. A drink is a drink. I'm just saying that the beer here is good."

Finally, he takes a breath and stops at the bar. And smiles at me. Stark white teeth gleam in the dingy overhead lighting, confirming that Hayes never misses a whitening schedule. I stare at the hair sticking to his forehead in the crowded bar. In this light it almost looks brown. His cheekbones aren't as defined as Cade's, but they're prominent enough for you to drag your finger across them and end at the treasure that is his pouty lips. Not that I would do it. But *someone* could. It's a shame those lips belong to a man. I would kill for lips like his. Kylie could suck a bottle for hours and not achieve that kind of pout. His bottom lip significantly fuller than the top one, would be so easy to suck—

"You know, if you keep looking at my mouth like that, darlin, we might end up making some bad decisions tonight."

Heat scalds my cheeks, but instead of denying that I was staring, I go with honesty. "I've made enough bad decisions for one night."

The towheaded hottie dips his chin in acknowledgement before lifting his sapphire eyes to meet mine. They sparkle with something I can't quite put my finger on. "If it weren't for bad decisions, Breck, no one would be certain of anything." I must look confused because he laughs and nudges me toward the bar. "I'll take a boilermaker," he yells to the bartender who lifts one finger in acknowledgement. "What'll it be, darlin?" I glance around at the other women, eyeing their confidence.

I did not come to Madison thinking helping Cade would be an easy feat.

I came here with the intention of helping Cade, but I don't seem to have much of an impact other than making matters worse. I want to honor my brother and fulfill his duty to the brotherhood, but I think it may be time to move on.

Cade is doing well with Anniston and the guys. He doesn't need me. It's time I go home.

Pulling my shoulders back, I look at Hayes with new resolve. If I'm leaving, I'm going to go out with a bang.

"I'll have what you're having." Those pouty lips tip just slightly at the corners. "Ooh-rah," he whispers, mischief dancing in his eyes. I'm not sure what I just agreed to, but I have a feeling my one bad decision tonight will soon have company.

★ ★ ★

"Seriously?" Spittle flies out of my mouth in a very unladylike way. "Poison Ivy?" Another fit of laughter doubles me over as Hayes continues to give me a play-by-play of how he screwed this girl in a bed of poison ivy, suffering its wrath on his nether regions. We've been at Patty's for well over two hours and I've lost count of how many boilermakers I've had. Drunk is not the word I would use for the state we are in right now. Shitfaced would be the more accurate term.

"Hell yeah. In the beginning, commander discouraged us from having" —he waggles his eyebrows—"relations with anyone until we sorted out our lives." He shrugs, taking another swig of beer.

"And you didn't agree?"

He scoffs. "Hell no. Just because I was homeless doesn't mean I didn't have needs." I wait, hoping he'll say more. I'm more than curious about their unconventional relationship with Anniston. "I may not have known where my next meal was coming from or what I wanted to do for a living, but I knew my balls still felt blue at the end of the day. And after so many years of using sex as an outlet, I couldn't give it up. Not even after Ans took us in."

The greasy fry I shove in my mouth tastes like cardboard, or maybe that's because my tongue is numb. Regardless, it doesn't have a chance in hell of absorbing all the alcohol churning around in my stomach. At least it's kept my mouth from asking too many prying questions, like the one that escapes me now. "And, Cade? Is that why he doesn't date? Because of Anniston and the rules?"

Like I've asked the most ridiculous question on the planet, Hayes belts out a laugh, sliding down in the booth so he can put his feet on my bench. "You could say that," he starts, taking another swig of his beer. He gives me a serious look. "We all have demons, Breck. We're all fucked up, but Cade …" He sighs, running his hand through his hair. It almost looks as though he's in pain. His forehead is creased and his mouth is turned down in a frown. And then he blows out a breath and crushes me with one sentence. "Cade will never be capable of a relationship, darlin."

Who would have thought I could feel anything with all the whiskey and beer coursing through my veins, but here I am, in a bar slamming shots with a fine piece of man candy, and all I can do is *feel*. My heart aches and a feverish sensation spreads through my body like I'm coming down with something. I want to cry. Hard, ugly tears that can only end with Tylenol and Rocky Road ice cream.

"Look at me, darlin."

I don't. I can't believe I'm such an idiot. I should have never come here. I should have listened to Jess. She's right, Cade doesn't know me. He will never need me. This past year of working for minimum wage, barely getting by, has all been for nothing. Absolutely, nothing. What a loser I am, chasing a man that doesn't want to be found.

"Breck." Before I can answer, Hayes slides into the booth next to me and takes my hand, massaging it with slow, methodic circles. "I want you to understand something." A tear drips onto our hands and he squeezes tighter. "We're not the picket fence kind of guys. We've watched life drain from the eyes of our enemy by our own bare hands. We've killed women and children with one order. We are Marines,

Breck. We don't know how to be anything else. We don't know how to love. We're a mess, and I think it's better if you see this for what it is. I'm not saying Cade doesn't like you or could love you, eventually. I think he could. But he won't allow himself. The only reason he sticks around is because he feels like he's indebted to Anniston. She saved his life. Does that mean he's healed and ready to settle down and pop out two-point-five kids? No. Guys like us don't deserve a girl like you or a happy ending. Someone has to pay for what we've done. And well ..." He trails off, leaving me to fill in the blanks.

Atonement.

They feel like this is what they deserve, but I don't understand why. Other Marines live happy and healthy lives. Why does this group feel differently? I can understand some of why Cade feels responsible, but Hayes ... I realize that I know nothing. What was I thinking coming here? I'm an idiot. Tomorrow, I'll talk to Sue and Jess. It's time I move on and start thinking about Breck. This is not my home.

Hayes squeezes my hand again before wrapping his arm around my shoulder. I let him pull me into his hard body, wrapping my arms around his chest. I'm essentially hugging this man who believes he's not worth the ground I walk on after sacrificing his life for my freedom.

It's fucked up.

Would this be Bennett? If he had lived through the explosion, would he have shunned me? Taken to the streets and believed he was serving his penance for killing an eight-year-old who was seconds from blowing up his team's Humvee? The thought has tears stinging my eyes. "Is that how you feel, too?" I ask, because I have a feeling his speech is not all about Cade. "Do you think you deserve to be punished for the things you've done?"

Hayes grunts, making a soft noise. His breath smells of whiskey and beer when he forces out an answer I wasn't expecting. "Don't go mistaking me for a good guy, darlin'." He unfolds out of the tiny booth, pulling me out after him. "You're killing my buzz, Breck. I think it's only proper you make up for it with a dance." His pupils are dilated from all the liquor, and by the way he sways his hips in a silly motion, I know those bad decisions have come to fruition.

But fuck it. I have nothing to lose. Hayes said so himself. Cade won't ever love me.

I've been a fool, but not anymore. I'm going home.

I'm so sorry, Ben.

With tears in my eyes, I let Hayes pull me to the middle of the dance floor, where we drink.

And dance.

And drink some more until we feel nothing at all.

chapter eighteen

Cade

The first thing that occurs to me is that my eyelids feel like some-one sewed weights into them while I was knocked out. My blinks are painful and heavy when I finally manage to open my eyes long enough to see the light coming in from the window. Clearly, I slept through the night, and by the sounds of the nuisance woodpecker outside, well into mid-morning.

Last night seems like a dream. A bad fucking dream.

I remember the mascara streaked down Breck's swollen face the most. Fear and pity were the dominant emotions that stared back at me from those reddened eyes. I wanted the pain to go away so badly that even those tears didn't stop me from letting Anniston inject me with a sedative.

I'm a coward.

I should have endured.

I should have overcome the demons in my head.

I should have comforted her, but I didn't.

Instead, I let Hayes carry my girl out of the room and do it for me. But no matter how bad I beat myself up about it, the fact remains the same. I couldn't ease her pain when I couldn't even ease my own.

All I saw was *her* face.

All I could hear were *his* cries as he held my hand and gurgled out what an honor it was to serve by my side as he took his last breath.

Because of me. Because of *her*, my team lost their lives.

And I'll have to live with that fact for the rest of my life. I blow out several deep breaths and attempt to scrub away the memories before pushing up on my elbows to look around. My bedroom is clean—not that I keep it dirty—but my discarded clothes and the sports drink I left on my nightstand have all been picked up. The only thing out of place is the green detox drink sitting on my bedside table, letting me know Anniston has recently been in here.

I'm already dreading the seaweed-like cleansing drink. It's supposed to help clear the after-effects of the sedatives from your system. I don't believe it. The taste is unlike anything I have ever tasted. It's putrid and reminds me of when my mom used to make Drew and I eat the cold zucchini we'd leave on our plates.

Chugging this beast of a drink down first thing in the morning seems like a punishment, but it isn't. Anniston just wants me feeling better as quickly as possible, and for her, I'll drink it, as much as it pains me to do so.

The muscles in my legs ache when I drape them over the edge of the bed, a side effect of having a flashback. I've been told I clench and stay locked in a position until I'm able to pull out of it. I'm grateful for the help but I'm also not, all at the same time. I deserve to suffer for being a murderer, not get a free pass of a good night's sleep.

But like every other time I've been sedated, I tell myself that today is another day. Another start to be better. So I grab my puke-like drink and drag my tired, sad ass downstairs toward the kitchen.

Theo is perched on a chair in the breakfast nook when I lumber stiffly into the kitchen. A tablet in one hand and coffee in the other, he watches the screen intently. "Morning," I greet him gruffly.

He pulls his gaze from the screen and says flatly, "This prick is going to make me a fuck-ton of money."

I pull out the chair next to him, leaning over to see what he's talking about. It's scouting footage of a college kid, pitching a no-hitter game. "Is that the kid that propositioned you for Ans?"

Theo called me over his honeymoon ranting about some brazen kid who had the audacity to ask him, as a condition of his signing, for one night with Anniston. I don't know all the details, but I can assume he did not let that happen since the kid is still alive.

"Yep. The devil himself," he mutters.

"You got him to sign?"

Theo makes an offended noise that makes me smile. "Of course I fucking did, Jameson. Who do you think you're talking to?"

I take a long pull of my detox drink, only gagging slightly. "Gross. Ans making you drink that poison?"

I nod, swiping my hand across my mouth, checking for any spills. "Yep."

Theo's face screws up in disgust. "Pour that shit down the drain. I'll be your witness that you drank it all." I give him side eye and he laughs, correcting his statement. "I'll be your witness until it benefits me to rat you out."

"That's better. For a minute there I thought you were going soft," I observe, taking another sip, trying to empty my cup quickly so I can wash it down with some coffee. "You run yet?"

Theo, back to watching his new rookie, shakes his head at me. "No."

Any other time I would give him shit about waiting to run with me, but this morning, I'm feeling gracious. I heard him last night, sought out his voice, like an anchor to my new life, trying to pull me out the madness. It's not the first time he's talked me through an episode. He and Ans have both become instrumental in my recovery. Theo and I never speak of it, though, because Theo doesn't do thanks or sentimental chats. So when he does something like waiting to run with me after a rough night, it reminds me of what a great guy he is underneath all the sarcasm and rude commentary.

I push down the emerging emotions and ask him, "Wanna go in a little bit? I need to find Breck first and apologize, make sure she's okay after last night."

Theo looks up from his screen, a knowing smile tugging at his dimple. "I wouldn't sweat it. She handled it like a lady."

I'm confused with his reassurance, and the way he says it sounds like he knows something I don't. "What do you mean, 'handled it like a lady?'"

Theo snorts, pressing the button on his tablet and laying it down on the table. "I mean, she handled it like a woman scorned." He draws out the explanation, watching me, waiting patiently for the reaction he wants. I don't give it to him though. I wait him out until his grin morphs into a wide, beaming smile before he makes my world explode. "She and Hayes got shitfaced at the bar. I heard her snoring from his room this morning."

I see red.

Blood. Fucking. Red.

"Come again?" I ask very calmly, clenching the revolting drink in my hands.

Theo chuckles and stands, walking over to put his empty mug in the sink.

"Holler when you finish spanking some sense into her and we'll go run."

I chug the rest of my drink, not even tasting the putrid liquid sliding down my throat, and toss my cup to Theo who catches it easily. I charge out of the kitchen, intent on kicking Hayes' ass. I throw open the door to his room and find the sweet beauty asleep against, more than likely, his filthy sheets. Alone.

Breck's hair is fanned out across his pillow, her lips parted ever so slightly, her soft breathing calming down the rage I was just feeling. The mattress indents and she rolls toward me when I sit down next to her. My fingers itch to touch her, but I refrain. She looks so peaceful as she breathes evenly, her eyes fluttering like she's dreaming.

I'm being a total stalker hovering over her, Hayes' beer t-shirt askew, showing her flat stomach ever so slightly.

"Oh." Hayes pokes his head through the door, sweaty and a little green from his run with Anniston. "I came to check on B."

I swear Breck woke up on her own accord and not because I literally growled an animalistic sound at Hayes that had him backing out the door, closing it, and yelling, "Theo picked us up. I slept on the couch and Anniston helped her to bed. I kept my hands to myself, I swear."

He better fucking had.

And of course, Von Bremen spared me no mercy by jerking my chain this morning just to see me get worked up. Fucker.

"Hey," Breck drawls, all groggy from sleep, pulling me from my thoughts. God, I want to touch her. Kissing her would be even better. Honestly, I'm seconds from just groveling at her feet with different renditions of an apology.

Instead, I go with, "Hey."

Her lip twitches and I think she's going to smile but then it goes flat. "How are you feeling?" she asks, pulling the blankets up so I can't see her body. All the air feels like it rushes out of the room.

I did it.

I finally broke her.

I should feel relief but that's not the emotion I'm currently dealing with. This emotion feels foreign and I'm not quite sure what to do with it.

My hand moves on its own accord, caressing her face, my thumb lingering on her lips. "I know I keep having to apologize for my behavior," I start, pulling my hand away. "I can't lie and say I won't behave poorly again—"

She cuts me off. "You couldn't help it."

A ghost of a smile tugs at my lips and I drop my head in shame. She's right, I couldn't control it, but fuck if I don't wish I could.

"I'm sorry you had to see that." I really am. I thought maybe I had gotten better—that I wouldn't be triggered by intimacy.

I was wrong. Being with Anniston these past eighteen months have changed nothing in that regard. I'm still as fucked up as before.

Breck closes her hand around mine. "Cade."

I stare at her hand draped over mine, tiny and breakable, just like her heart. "You deserve better than me," I whisper down at our hands. Out of the corner of my eye, I see her rise up to her knees, pulling her hand off to place it around my waist, her head resting on my shoulder.

"We'll agree to disagree," she mutters. "I want you, Cade. Not just the sex. All of you. You're stubborn and annoying ..." I scoff and she squeezes tighter. "But I kind of like you. Every broken piece. I want the whole enchilada."

I laugh at her ridiculous food reference and then I go still before admitting my issues. "It's been five years since I've tried being with a woman. I don't know if I'm capable of giving you the 'whole enchilada.'"

Breck's breath falters against my neck. "Did the same thing happen then?"

I want to lie.

I want to feel like a normal man who can run through an entire town of pussy without getting emotionally attached to any of them, not a man who can't make love to a woman without having flashbacks of his gutted team. She deserves the truth even if the truth paints me as a monster. "Yes. It happens every time. I can't control it."

Breck's quick intake of air is the only indication she heard my confession. Hayes' bedroom stinks, the air feeling stagnant as Breck and I stay quiet.

And then she asks the question that everyone who tries to help me wants to know. "Will you tell me what happened to your team?"

It's none of her business what happened to my team, but if I ever want to form some kind of relationship with her, I need to be honest. Anniston says purging is the first step to healing. I don't know if that's true, but I guess I'm about to find out.

"Take a walk with me?"

The air is sticky, but that's not why sweat is beading along the back of my neck. I'm nervous—first-date-teenage-boy kind of nervous.

"I was supposed to be giving an interview that day," I start, clasping her hand in comfort as we trek through the blistering heat, another seaweed drink in my hand, Breck with one as well. Anniston insisted we both needed some detoxifying—for obvious reasons. Me from the sedative, Breck from the unknown amounts of alcohol she consumed last night.

My gaze, locked on the pear tree ahead of us, stays steady as I continue with my story. "She was an embedded observer, more commonly known to civilians as an American journalist. She was doing a piece on humanitarian efforts in Afghanistan." By my side, Breck stays quiet, giving me time to put my thoughts together. My breathing is choppy and harsh when I finally pull in a cleansing breath and start again. "But instead of interviewing me, we decided our time would be better spent engaging in other oral activities." Breck's face flinches. "I can stop," I tell her, knowing no girl likes to hear about past conquests.

She shakes her head. "No, keep going."

I wish she would tell me to go to hell and never talk to me again. She's crazy for even entertaining my story. "Well, I'll spare you the details, but my team, this kid Brannon to be exact, called me saying they had a lead and wanted to know if they should proceed or wait on me." Bringing up Brannon and Drew always sends my blood pressure through the roof, but I know she needs to hear it. Relationships have to be built on trust, and although I've never cared to have one in the past, I do now. I want to do things right by Breck.

Breck's steps falter for a second but we keep walking toward the barn. "I wasn't finished with the journalist, but Brannon said they needed to move quick before they lost their guide." I cough to relieve the tightness in my chest. "I sent them on without me. Drew was their captain, and would have taken over the team after our tour ended. I was being groomed to become a colonel. It was my last field assignment before I would join my fellow commissioned officers behind a desk."

A tear falls down Breck's face and I squeeze her hand. "My past is not an easy one to digest," I tell her. "Men would line the streets of Madison for a chance to date you. You don't have to settle for me. I'm fucked up and I can't promise I'll ever be normal."

Breck shrugs a shoulder, trying to soak up the tear with her shirt. "I know what I'm getting into, Cade. Please continue with your story."

I don't really think she does. I think she believes there is something in me that can be saved. It's like trying to salvage moldy cheese. You can cut off the bad spots and it looks normal, but it's still rotten cheese.

But I indulge her, allowing my demons their platform. "For an hour, I entertained my American companion—work seemed like a foreign concept until the sun set. I had almost forgotten that I sent them, but then my radio chimed out a broken sound—it was a call for help." My voice turns gravelly and Breck now has a steady stream of tears running down her face.

I spare her the gruesome scene of finding Drew with his eye hanging out of its socket, his leg completely detached from his body. I leave out that I couldn't even recognize Kyle, Parker, and Lewis. Their bodies were mangled, the IED obliterating everything that was caught in its path. "I heard the explosion while I was en route."

Breck sucks in a sob and I pray she doesn't run screaming after this. "By the time I got to them, my brother and the three others were dead. The only one alive was the kid, Brannon." Breck releases my hand to cover her face, her cries becoming almost uncontrollable. "I sat with him, amongst the rubble, my dead brother staring at me. I sat there …"

A memory tugs at me. One I've pushed down for years. I swallow, my brain purging the last memory I have of Brannon. "I sat there while this kid told me a story of his little sister who had this amazing spirit, selfless and free. He proclaimed how he had always admired her but was pissed that she was more fearless than he was."

Breck whimpers beside me but I keep going, unable to stop the memories. "He said he knew she would be okay without him because she had the heart of a warrior." I swipe at my eyes, surprised that I'm showing emotion in front of Breck when I've smothered it down every time before. "He pulled a letter out of his pocket—some guys keep a letter on them in case they don't make it back home—and told me that when I delivered it to tell her that when it rains, the heavens would open and he would be watching her."

I take a breath, his request sending painful spasms through my chest. "I was supposed to hand deliver the letter with his message." Shame churns in my gut. "I tried once, but no one was home, so I passed it on to another officer to handle. I couldn't bear to face Brannon's family or the sister he spoke about so reverently."

Breck looks away from me, swiping at her face. "I'm sure she knew," she says, her voice meeker than I've ever heard. "I'm sorry, Cade. I don't feel so well. The alcohol is finally catching up with me. Would you mind if we continue this conversation later?"

Disappointment settles around me, thick and stagnant, just like the weather. "Sure. I'll walk you back."

"Actually, I think I would like a ride home, if that's okay."

This time, the last thing I want to do is take her home.

chapter nineteen

Breck

Dear B,

Not much to report. The days are long and the nights are lonely. The good news is that Jess sent me a letter, and she signed it with XOXO. That's hugs and kisses, right? We talked about going out once I get back. (Insert fist bump.) Knowing she's willing to give me a chance makes counting down these last couple of weeks more manageable. Are you still killing it in class? Major mentioned your cookies again. Don't be stingy, you don't need the calories. Send us more. We're starving.

#theyaresodamngood#bigbroisgoingtoscore#jennett#yepImadejess-sandIashipname

Ben

Cade's rendition of the night my brother died had me curled into the fetal position while the shower pelted me until the water ran cold. Sue tried coaxing me out of the room with promises of pound cake, but even the sugary sweetness couldn't pry me from the bathroom floor.

Cade answered the questions I've always wondered. Did Bennett think of me? Did he die alone?

The answers both warmed me and crushed my soul at the same time. In his final moments, Bennett thought of me. Cade thinks he killed my brother by not going on the mission with them, but in reality it was his purpose to comfort a dying man, to be by his side, providing him strength to let go. Cade will never know the debt I owe him. Out of everyone, it was Cade who found Bennett. His hero. His mentor. His big brother. If it couldn't have been me, I'm glad it was him even though he suffers so painfully from the incident.

The thought that my brother and his brother's death triggers his PTSD causes this insane feeling of guilt within me. I wanted to come clean and tell him that the kid he referred to as Brannon was my brother. The girl with a heart of a warrior was me, except I don't feel like I have a warrior's heart right now. It feels shattered like glass, bleeding me from the inside out.

I freaked when he shared Bennett's final moments. I couldn't even breathe let alone muster up the courage to disclose my secret. I'm terrified once I tell him all the progress we've made will be obliterated. Cade won't have anything to do with me once he finds out who I really am. I know Anniston said he may surprise me, but I'm not so sure. I think he's more resilient with her than any other person. But maybe it's for the best. Maybe that will help me leave and go back home. Cade trying to talk to me, to form a relationship with me by disclosing his demons, has me on the fence again. If he's willing to try for us then I want to try, too.

My phone chimes beside me where I currently lay, wrapped only in a towel, staring at the popcorn ceiling in my bedroom. Sue finally gave up on me and let me self-destruct alone. Tomorrow I will have to apologize and hug her for trying to console me. Any other time, I probably would have let her, but not today. Today has too many issues for me to deal with and Sue need not witness my fallout firsthand.

The chime alerts me again, and I'm second guessing my decision not to turn it off. Groaning, I flop over to my stomach, grace and poise not on my mind at all, and grab the noise maker.

It's Jess. *I know something is wrong, bitch. Answer your phone. You don't send me a text saying, 'not today Satan', when all I asked was if you were done with your* Ant-Man *review. Answer. Your. Phone.*

Then Milos joins in. *Jess is threatening to fly to Georgia, and I quote, "To massacre every motherfucker in that teeny tiny town until she finds you." What's going on? We're here for you.*

I almost smile. I love my friends. Jess texts, *Cade is dead. And that fucker Hayes, too. Unless he's hot. I'll fuck him first before I smother him with the gigantic boobs I've yet to pay off.*

I read the next one and stop short when I see it's from Cade. *I didn't want to give you a ride home. I never did.*

I knew that and the fact that he's worried pains me. But I continue, reading the next text from Jess. *What's this Anniston bitch's last name? Van Helsing? Apparently, the airlines don't allow weapons on the plane. I'll have to drive. B!!!*

The final text from Milos does me in. *The best heroes are the ones who hide in the shadows. Their resilience is always the deadliest.*

Each text, in their own way, make me cry harder. I miss Jess. And though I've never met Milos, I miss his ass too. He's right, though. Resilience is the best superpower, and I have it in spades.

I am a motherfucking warrior.

My brother would kick my ass if he saw me wallowing on the floor like an idiot. I may have lost him to the war, but he's never left my side. He's been with me this whole time.

And like karma and Thor threw me a bone, thunder rattles the window in the old farmhouse and I find myself throwing on clothes like it's a sport, grabbing my phone and rushing outside.

I run through the orchards, swiping at the leaves, a euphoric tingling zipping beneath my skin. Lightning flashes and the heavens open, the rain pouring down in sheets. I fall to my knees with a cry that I'm not sure is happy or sad. I soak up every ounce of love I feel from those rain drops before staring up, blinking through the wetness, and saying to the boy who believed I was a hero, "I see you, Bennett Brannon, and I can feel you, too."

✯ ✯ ✯

Have you ever had a moment where you feel like you're in a dream?

I remember my mom calling me when Bennett died, the indifference as she told me what had happened, like she was talking about the weather or one of Dad's new companies, not that my only brother was killed overseas, his remains coming back on a plane the following week.

I don't remember feeling the pain until I laid down that same night and tried Skyping him. He needed to know that our mother had officially lost it … but he never answered. His account was later shut down, and I remember the tears that turned into hysterics.

The silence was horrific, but being alone was the worst.

Not even Jess could soothe me. Alcohol. Doughnuts. You name it, and I tried it. Nothing relieved the overwhelming feeling of being all alone in the world. I lost my brother and my entire family with him. After we buried Bennett, my parents didn't check to see if I was in need of support. Oh no. My mother had a new audience to coddle when she realized she could open a charity in his memory.

I was an orphan. Abandoned in a world I no longer loved.

Until I found cooking.

And then Cade.

Suddenly, the void I was feeding dried up. Hope bloomed, and so did I.

To make a long story short, I've only ever felt like I've been in a dream once.

Today makes twice.

I turn in front of the mirror. The strapless crimson dress clings to my breasts, the incredible bra Anniston bought me pushing my girls skyward, convincing any man that I have way more than I'm working with. The tulle skirt flares at my waist, and I feel like a real-life princess. My hair is styled into a classic updo, and my makeup looks like I've never seen a day of sun in my life.

I'm not being a conceited bitch when I say I look fucking hot tonight.

Luckily Anniston has great taste and bought this without me since Cade and I never made it to the dress shop. It's been five days since Cade confessed. After the night in the rain, I dragged my soaked body back into the house and cried into Sue's lap for a couple of hours, accepting not one, but two pieces of pound cake before returning all of my messages.

Luckily Jess had calmed down, locating Mason's number somehow, and he bravely talked her down. She said she's saving it in case this happens again, but I know her and she's saving his number for R-rated reasons.

My text to Milos was filled with crying emojis, and being the gentleman he is, he changed the subject and talked about the new *Infinity Wars* movie we are both excited to see.

I saved Cade for last, knowing our conversation would take longer. He asked if I ever wanted to see him again, and duh. I totally did. It was awkward, but then he asked if we could watch a movie together over the phone. I obviously went for *Thor*, the first one. Cade had never seen it, and well, I needed some Chris to perk me up. We found ourselves discussing strategy, Cade letting his military training bleed through. He was so cute trying to figure out how Thor didn't realize his brother was betraying him. He seemed genuinely upset. When it was over, a heavy silence fell around us and I told him I needed to go. I had a review to write.

He just went for it with no hesitation, no embarrassment.

"Can I listen to you type it?" I melted. I could barely complete my review, but I did, knowing he needed the rest after the day he'd had.

We've talked every night on the phone since then, ending with him listening to my keystrokes every night. Today will be the second time I've seen him in the flesh since he told me about what happened to his team. I brought some pies—and jelly—over yesterday, and he kissed me goodbye, but otherwise we've been hands—and eyes—off, starting over like teenagers, getting to know each other over the phone.

A soft knock comes from outside the door, and I know it's him waiting on the other side.

"Are you ready?" I say to the woman in the mirror. She is going to slay tonight. I blow myself a kiss. One, because I'm lame, and two, because I've never felt more beautiful than I do right now.

"Can I come in?" Cade asks. I'm only a wee bit nervous at him seeing me in the gown after our detox from each other. Anniston said he was going to be a walking erection all night. I may have fallen in love with her a little.

With one more quick inspection, and the deepest breath I can manage in this tight dress, I go to the door and pull it open.

"I'm sorry I was taking so long," I tell him, looking down at his shoes. I don't know why I started there. Maybe seeing him in a tux would be too much for these sheer panties. Or maybe it's because I'm a chicken.

We'll never know because Cade's finger slides under my chin and lifts it slowly until we're eye to eye. He swallows, his gaze lazy as it roams over every inch of me. "You look stunning." The flush spreading across his neck tells me he thinks I'm more than just stunning. His gaze is that of a starving man who just found a buffet. He wants to devour me.

And let me admit, before you think I'm some kind of badass, I want to eat him up too.

This man in a tux is deadly.

Why is he deadly?

Because I may cut a bitch if she puts her hands on him.

This man. This aggravating man, is all mine tonight, and I plan on wrecking him.

"You look like a stripper," I blurt out.

I never said I was good at dirty talk.

Cade laughs. "A stripper?" He looks down his front, probably checking for a thong hanging out of his pocket or something.

"I just mean, you look like a wet dream."

That really makes him laugh. He tugs me closer, his arm slipping around my waist, his hand palming my ass. "Are you saying you have wet dreams about me, Brecklyn?"

There he goes again with calling me by my full name.

I pull back and make a show of rolling my eyes. "I didn't say *my* wet dream. Just *someone's*."

"Uh huh." He chuckles, pulling me in closer so his face is in my neck. "Keep telling yourself that." The air from his breath tickles the back of my neck, and I shiver.

"You're being overconfident again," I remind him.

His tongue is suddenly against my neck, sucking, tasting when he hums, "And you're being fucking tempting again."

"Damn it." Theo's raised voice pulls Cade's head up, and the heat on my face is now from more than Cade's incredible tongue. "Anniston, put condoms in your purse. We'll need to be the responsible ones tonight."

Cade chuckles when Theo scowls like we ruined his fucking night. "That's right, Von Bremen. You owe me for all the times I've covered for you," Cade jokes over the top of my head before separating, placing a soft kiss on my cheek, and asking, "Are you ready to go?"

I nod, and Theo makes a pained noise, leading us down the stairs where Anniston is waiting, looking like Holiday Barbie. "B! You look stunning. A beautiful siren." She winks at Cade and says, "Better hurry and put her in the car. The guys won't hesitate to whack off to the image of her in this dress."

I freeze, Anniston's comment too similar to the one Cade said to me through the computer all those years ago. Holding my breath, I wait for Cade to put it all together and shove me away, but when he laughs over the top of my head, squeezing my hip firmly, I realize I'm just being paranoid. And probably guilty. Maybe I can tell him after the gala tonight. There's no sense in ruining his evening now.

"I think you might be right, Commander." The man who asked me a zillion questions on the phone over the past five days, getting to know me in every way possible, agrees with his commander's assessment. Gently, he nudges my hip in the direction of the front door. "We should be going before we're late."

★ ★ ★

Three hours into the gala and I've concluded that I never want to do this again. It reminds me of my parents' stuffy garden parties. Okay, saying it's stuffy is rude. Most of the people are nice. I've only encountered a couple of assholes who obviously have more money than sense and need a tax write-off before the year's end. They can go fuck themselves. Even Cade groaned before having to speak with them.

The highlight of the event has been hanging back with Theo while Anniston and Cade work the room, making connections and selling their mission statement. Theo, although rich himself, has a distinct dislike for most of the people and their plus-ones.

"The woman to your right spends her afternoons in 'book club' which we all know is really the woman to your left's cunt," he says flatly, downing the last of his champagne. I haven't been drinking since the fiasco with Hayes, but Theo seems to be having more fun with less of a filter after downing a couple glasses.

"Are you saying they are having an affair with each other?" I don't know why it seems so scandalous, but I was fully prepared that he was going to say with another man. "Yup. The First Wives' Club of Madison."

"No way do they call it that," I argue. Theo shrugs, his line of sight moving from the dainty thirty-ish woman to Anniston. She and Cade are talking to a couple men dressed in tuxes like all the rest. Their body language is comfortable, laughing at something one of the suits has said. I watch Cade scratch a spot along his scruff, nodding as if he's fully invested in the conversation. Anniston's simple black gown pools at her feet, and her voice carries toward us when she laughs. She takes a step back, nearly falling over her dress. Cade snags her elbow and she flashes him a smile of thanks, leaving her hand tucked there. It's a simple move. It's kind—chivalrous even. But this nasty taste creeps into my mouth, making me frown while my eyes narrow at the two beautiful people in front of me.

I chance a look at Theo. He's not showing any outward signs of jealousy. Having him storm through the two men and yank his wife off my man is not asking too much, is it?

I ask him the question I really need the answer to. "How do you deal with it?"

His stare never leaves Anniston when he responds, "How do I deal with what?"

Ugh. Why couldn't he have known what I was talking about? Having to spell it out is awkward. And sad. But I've already opened my big mouth, so I may as well get what I need.

I fumble with the bracelet on my wrist, sliding it up and down my arm. "How do you deal with their relationship … their love?"

This time he does look at me, and it's the strangest expression I've ever seen on his face. He's not offended or pissed, or about to cuss me out in front of hundreds of people. Instead, his cheek twitches and the hint of a smile emerges. "Is Cade's jelly girl jealous?"

Yes. But I'm not about to own it at this moment. I shrug like maybe I give a fuck about Cade. A little.

Theo's chuckle is low and laced with amusement. "I'm going to be real with you, okay?"

I nod. I can handle real.

"At first it bothered me."

Thank you. I knew it had to.

"I hated Cade." He glances at the two still locked in conversation. "Even now, good friends as we are, I still think mine and Anniston's relationship would be easier without having to share her attention with five other guys. But how shitty of me to demand she leave them just because I get a little insecure occasionally." He shrugs like admitting this is awkward to him.

"Do you ever think one day she may wake up and realize she and Cade are more than just friends?"

There's a pregnant pause before Theo answers. "Sure. But isn't that the risk you take in any relationship? Maybe she falls in love with the bag boy in the checkout line? Or, maybe she decides that she wants Martha's killer cunt?" I laugh. "The thing is, relationships aren't guaranteed. It's up to each one of us to fight to keep what we have alive. Cade may be a pain in my ass, but he's part of what makes Anniston so incredible. Before Cade, she wasn't the girl who fought for what she wanted. She followed me from game to game, unhappy. She wasn't the bright and vibrant woman I see today." He sighs, taking a moment before he continues, "I guess what I'm saying is, the Cade you know now is not the Cade from nearly two years ago. Would you have loved him at his lowest? At his filthiest?"

I interrupt because I know the answer. "Yes, I'd like to think I would have."

Theo nods his head slowly like he's just getting to know the real me. He lets out an amused breath. "You know what? I actually believe you would have."

I feel a smile tug at my lips. Hell yeah, I would have. I gave up my life for him. I've watched him for a year, praying to see the Cade my brother spoke of, waiting for him to notice me again. I can't be sure I would have been able to pull him back from the brink of death like Anniston did when she found him. She is a doctor after all. But even if I could have handled the mental and physical issues he had back then, I don't know that I would have pushed him like Anniston did, commanding him when he wanted to give up.

I'd like to think I would have, but I'm not positive.

I'm grateful to Anniston for saving Cade's life when no one was there for him, but it's hard to digest their relationship. I think Theo's point is simple, though. Cade is who he is because of Anniston and vice versa. Who are we to ask them to give up something so precious just because we get jealous?

"Has it gotten easier for you?" I ask him. His lip pokes out in thought, his eyes becoming brighter as he catches movement from Cade and Anniston. Anniston is stroking Cade's upper arm, her playful eyes locked on Theo. She's fucking with him. I look at Cade, and he's grinning, too. Apparently, they're bored with the conversation and have decided to play, *'Let's see how pissed we can make Theo.'* But Theo doesn't look pissed. He looks the opposite—eager, bouncing on his heels like he's ready to sprint in their direction. A man in a suit steps in front of him, blocking his view, and I swear he growls beside me.

Theo snags another glass of champagne from the waiter as he passes, downing it in one gulp. "Look, B," he drawls, taking a step behind me. "You and I have something that Cade and Anniston don't." His breath dances along my bare shoulder, the muscles along my neck tensing under the warmth.

"What are you doing?" I ask him, a little breathless. I'm naïve, I'll admit, but this conversation took a wild turn and I'm not sure how to handle it.

Theo rumbles out low laughter. "Trust me, B. Let me show you what we have that they don't."

I stare back at Cade whose smile is waning with Theo's head bent at my shoulder. Anniston's bright blue eyes are narrowed, too, and it seems their stroking has stopped altogether.

Huh. "Okay," I tell Theo, eager now to see what he's about to do. "Show me."

He huffs out a, "Good girl," in my ear, dragging his fingers up my bare arm, stopping as he reaches the curve of my neck. "Watch his face." I don't need for him to tell me that he means Cade because that's the only person I'm watching.

Replacing his finger, Theo blows along my neck, inadvertently creating chills. "Do you see it?" he whispers. I chance another look at Cade. His jaw is clenched, the muscles in his neck straining.

"What am I looking for?" I ask Theo.

He chuckles. "For the moment when he realizes he now has a weakness."

I catalog every movement Cade makes as he grips Anniston's arm. He's not paying attention to the guy in front of him, or Anniston, even. He's watching Theo.

And me.

Those dark eyebrows are furrowed, and his lips have thinned into a tight line.

I grin. "I see," I tell Theo almost too excitedly.

The friend breathing on my neck laughs. "Atta girl. Now look at Anniston."

I'm a little nervous to look at Anniston, but I do because for the first time since moving to Madison and helping Cade, I feel hope bubble up. Anniston is conversing with a suit, but it's her eyes that give her away. They keep flashing up from her associate to Theo, and it's obvious she's not happy. Her body is rigid, her back straight. The fake smile she's sporting strains as if it begs to turn into a frown. "I see her," I tell Theo, who is still nuzzling my neck.

"Good. Now, can you tell me what we have that they don't?"

I take one more look at Cade and Anniston. They may be upset and slightly jealous, but I still don't know what he means. "I don't know," I mutter.

"Put your arm around my neck," he instructs me. Any other time, I would be hesitant to engage in such games with Theo but I'm desperate for insight into Cade Jameson. I lift my arm, holding Cade's angry eyes in my mind the whole time I slip it over Theo's neck. It takes all I can do not to smile. "Do you see how Jameson just took a step forward?"

I nod into Theo's hair that is seriously close to my face. "Yes."

"Do you see him do that when I nuzzle Anniston?"

The smile hits me hard. "No, I don't."

Giddy doesn't even begin to describe the elation coursing through me. Theo just showed me that I mean something to Cade. Something more than Anniston. "That's because what you have, sweetheart, is *power*. You're this man's kryptonite. Not his commander, but something else. Something deeper where he's willing to ruin his professional image to keep my lips from creeping up—"

Lost in a sea of Cade-likes-me feelings, I miss Cade moving through the crowd until I'm yanked away from Theo abruptly.

"Von Bremen."

"Jameson. Nice of you to join us. B and I were just getting acquainted."

Cade shuffles me to his hip, wrapping an arm around me in a secure hold. "A little too acquainted, if you ask me."

Theo shrugs, glancing at Anniston who is still locked in a business conversation she's apparently unable to get out of. "Good thing no one asked you." He chuckles, shoving Cade's shoulder. "If you'll excuse me, I have a girl who needs a good fucking in the alley. Appreciate you getting her all warmed up for me." He flashes me a wink. "Don't forget what I said, B."

I have power.

Power over Cade.

Cade fucking likes me.

My grin is wide when I put my fist out and bump it with Theo's. This man is my damn friend for life. If he ever wants to trade down, I'm game.

I'm teasing! But if Cade ever dumps my ass, I would totally consider it.

Theo punches Cade's shoulder. "You forget, Jameson, you're now playing a game you won't ever win. Checkmate, bitch."

Cade stands still beside me, his fingers gripping my side like he's trying to keep me from running into Theo's arms. Theo doesn't miss it, laughing at Cade's expense. "Don't hurry home, kids. Mommy's been a bad girl." He tosses Cade a *fuck-you* smile and turns his back on us, laughing as he pushes through the suits unapologetically, snagging a glaring Anniston by the waist. He nods, saying a few words to the suits, hands his empty glass to one, and then excuses himself and Anniston while pulling her down the hall by the arm until the darkness conceals them.

The sound of a stinging slap echoes down the empty hallway.

Mommy apparently just got spanked.

Theo has power, and Anniston has a weakness.

Theo.

Cade has a weakness, too.

Me.

Something like a rush of power zips through my veins,

empowering me to take Cade's hand, his fingers instinctively lacing through mine.

This new information is making my stomach do somersaults, and I don't hate it.

"You want to go?" Cade interrupts my girl-power thoughts with his sexy voice, the champagne bringing out the southerner in him.

I turn, giving him a thorough once-over, an idea already forming. "Absolutely."

Cade Jameson isn't going to know what hit him.

chapter twenty

Breck

B!

    Major Jameson pulled me to the side today and said he thought I had a future in the Corps. Like I could make something of myself here! Can you believe it? Your big brother is a badass! LOL.

    #istilldonthaveasixpackthough #butIstillrunfasterthanyou

    Love,

    Your awesome fucking brother

Cade pushes through the bedroom door, already loosening the bowtie from around his neck. "That was painful. I can't believe I'm about to say this, but Theo wasn't the most obnoxious person in the room tonight."

He huffs out a breath with a half-smile, like he's amused by his own admission. On the way back he was unnaturally quiet. It's plausible that he was thinking of excuses to take me home. But that would be unlike him. A month ago, he would have asked me if he could give me a ride home. Not now, though. Not after getting so jealous of Theo only an hour ago.

I'm being paranoid.

Cade's gone silent on me again, and I look up and see he's staring me down, a brow arched in what may be aggravation. Was it not a rhetorical question? Did he want me to agree that the fundraiser this evening was like a trip to the gynecologist, irritating and dreadful?

"It was rather stuffy." I offer with a soft chuckle.

Nose scrunched, Cade shakes off whatever he was about to say and undoes the buttons that secure the only barrier between me and his beautifully marred chest. A chest that has seen battle. A chest that displays his courage and honor. A chest that has made sacrifices. A chest that feels like home.

Memories of the first time I saw him on the Skype call flood my brain as I step into him, crowding his personal space.

His hands stop.

Whispering, I place my fingers over his, taking over unbuttoning his shirt. "I got it."

He swallows thickly, nodding only once.

Methodically, I push each button through its hole, inch by inch, revealing his scars. Purple, pink, red, and tan. They display a rainbow of colors like a Picasso hung in the most prestigious museum.

Cade's breaths have become shallow, and I keep going for fear he may stop me and suggest something else we could do.

Once completely bared, I meet his murky-mint eyes, watching him as he watches me lower myself, placing a soft kiss to one of the more ragged scars.

He shivers. "What are you doing, Breck?"

I'm not going to answer his ridiculous question, because clearly I want him naked. I hum, pushing him back toward the bed. Whatever turmoil is going on in his head his body doesn't seem to agree because it puts up no resistance. In fact, his body almost seems eager.

When the backs of his legs hit the edge of the mattress, I smile, sweet and innocent. "Let's get you out of these clothes, yeah?"

Another swallow.

Realizing he's waging some unknown battle in his head, I answer for him, sliding his shirt down his shoulders, taking his tie with it. I leave the cufflinks, creating a makeshift restraint by tying his sleeves together.

"Breck. Take off my cufflinks."

Knotting the bowtie through his shirt to his bedpost, I kiss up his straining forearms. "I think I like you just like this, Major Jameson." I flash him a cocky smile and add, "At my mercy."

Cade grunts, yanking against the knotted bowtie. "Don't play with me. You know we can't do this."

My feet ache from the four-inch heels but I keep them on, feeling powerful over this giant of a man, and take a few steps back, admiring my handiwork. I smile victoriously at Cade, testing the resistance of the restraint. It's good. He won't get out too quickly.

"Breck. We can't do this," he repeats, but his tone is weak. He wants this just as much as I do.

Theo's speech plays on repeat in my head. I need to find my place in Cade's life and take control of what I want. And right now, I want to suck Cade off. I want to blow him so hard that he never thinks of that journalist again. He needs to let go of this fear that he's going to hurt me. But most of all, I need him to see me. Not *her*. Just me.

My plan is to start slow and ease him into intimacy, hoping that one day soon he'll be able to make love to me like I've dreamed of. He does not understand the lengths I would go for him. To be exactly what he needs. And right now, tied to his bed, he needs a release.

I take a seductive step forward.

"You know I can get out of this. And when I do…" He trails off, his eyes glowing with carnal need.

His threat only fuels my flame. "I'm sure you can, but you won't."

His head cocks to the side, measuring my words. "I won't?"

Trailing a nail down his chest, I confirm, "No, you won't. Do you want to know why?"

He tips his chin in my direction, eyes blazing with excitement. "Why?"

With a harsh yank to his pants, I unfasten his belt, leaving it open. The button is next. And when I ease down the zipper, I lean in, breathing my answer along his neck. "Because you want me too bad."

Cade growls, testing the knot on his restraint but he doesn't argue which tells me I was right on the money. He wants me. Enough that he's willing to try again. Restraining him wasn't such a bad idea.

I nip at his ear, grinning. "You do, don't you?" Another bite. This time he pulls with enough power to move the bed. "Tsk, tsk, Major. Commander will be upset if you scratch the floors."

"Fuck you, Breck." His words aren't intended to be mean because his eyes relay the simple clarity that he does indeed want to fuck me.

My laugh is bordering on irrational when I pull back, our eyes locked in a lustful stare. "I'm going to fuck her out of you, Major, until you only see my face."

I push his trousers down in one motion, freeing his rock-hard length. It bounces against my stomach, eager to play. Caressing eight phenomenal inches of man, I stroke up and down, his hips moving against me. Cade groans, his head falling back in surrender.

"Watch me, Cade." His neck snaps to attention, his breaths labored and shallow, his dick pulsing in my hand. "You're a liar, Breck." He inhales a ragged breath, his anger palpable. "You want me to think you're meek, but you aren't, are you?"

A devilish smile tugs at my lips as I ease off my underwear, slipping them over my black pumps. "No, Major. I am not meek, I'm powerful. I'm your kryptonite."

Someone has to love him, and I've waited a year to do it. "That's enough talking for tonight," I chide. He groans, turning his head back and forth. My hand drops to his middle, taking hold of his balls. He stops moving, giving me the opportunity to stuff my panties in his mouth.

His eyes go wide with surprise.

"When I suck you off, you will only taste me, Major."

Cade's chest is rising and falling harshly as I shove my panties further in his mouth, gagging him. Forcing him to taste what he did to me all night long. Tense all over, he holds perfectly still, allowing me to bind him, tasting me on my panties.

I cup him gently, easing down onto my knees, my tongue tracing along the lines of his swollen sack. Slow, torturous, swipes have him on the brink, his muffled moans seeping through the lace of my panties wedged between his teeth.

"You want in my mouth, Cade? You want me to take you deep? You want to gag me, Major?"

His knees buckle at my filthy mouth, encouraging me further. Deep as I can go, I swallow him whole, pursing my lips around each vein, sucking harshly at the valley of sensitive skin between the shaft and head. Faster, my sucks become pulls, swallowing every inch of muscle I can take in. Wanting all of him, I fasten my hands around him, grabbing his ass, forcing him down my throat, gagging myself until my eyes water.

All Cade can do is go with my pulls. Thrust after thrust, I swallow his head, summoning moan after moan from his beautiful face. His eyes are waging a war between closing in pleasure and watching in fascination as I take his punishing thrusts.

He's panting when I moan around him, reaching down to pleasure myself. Frustrated, he tugs against his restraints, trying to speak. I shush the indecipherable words, releasing him from my mouth and raking my teeth softly against his velvet shaft. "Do you see me dripping, Cade?" Sheathing my teeth, I suck sweetly before doing it again. "Do you see my face as I bring you to the cusp of pleasure? Why do you fight us?" Another suck. "Why do you fight this attraction? Be with me, Cade. Take a chance. I won't let you down."

Cade grunts, yanking at his restraints.

My smile ratchets upward as he proves unsuccessful. "I can wait. I can be patient."

Another rake of my teeth has him bowing forward. "But in the meantime, I plan on shattering you. You'll never see another face but mine when someone kneels at your feet." I suck hard at his head, yanking his weakened body forward, allowing him to gag me. Talking around his pulsing length, I vow, "I'm going to destroy every single memory you have of that woman until you can't even remember the color of her hair."

With one final pull, I slam his hipbones over and over into my chest, choke after choke until he finally roars behind his gag, coming down my throat in hot, creamy spurts. I swallow every last drop from his satiated body until he goes limp inside me.

Gently, I release him, his body jumping at the sensitive touch of cool air. I rise, steady, and clutch the back of his neck, pulling the underwear from his mouth.

Cade's eyes are fierce when I claim, "Now I bet you won't envision some journalist."

I push away from him, turning my back to his flushed face. He needs some time to digest that he just came and didn't have a flashback. Score one for Breck.

Situating my dress and snagging my clutch from the nightstand, I head for the door. "See ya later, darling."

His voice is dangerously raspy when he calls to me, inches from the hallway, "Breck. Let me take you home."

As much as I would like to climb in the bed and sleep the night away with him, I honestly think we need to take this slow. I disrupted his entire thought process by tying him up and sucking him off. He needs space. And shit, I need time with my vibrator. He may have gotten off, but I'm still pent-up as fuck.

Feeling stronger than I am, I square up my shoulders, flash him a flirty smile, and wrench open the door. "Another time." And then I slam the door behind me.

"Breck!" Shouts of fury and the scraping of furniture is all I can hear as I hustle down the hallway. I can ask one of the guys for a ride home. I wouldn't dare piss Cade off by walking, and I think my feet would stage a protest in these heels. I smile stupidly, very pleased with myself. I brought Cade Jameson to his fucking knees.

I run into something or someone rather hard. "Looks like you took my advice." Theo.

His eyes are alight with playful curiosity. I shrug, not wanting to give anything away. "Eh, he lost a game we were playing."

Theo chuckles. "I know all about those types of games. Pussy is always a killer." He turns away, chuckling to himself and going on about *motherfucking pussy voodoo*. I don't know what that means, but whatever.

I hear stomping and yelling coming from Cade's room.

Before I can think through it, I dart down the steps, almost giggling until my feet disappear out from under me, and I yell. The pissed off Marine grabs me by the arm, lacing his other arm behind my knees, tossing me over his shoulder easily.

"Put me down. I need to go home!" Well, not really, but he seems pretty mad, and survival instinct tells me I need to seek refuge and *not* at the McAllister Jameson Foundation.

"Oh no. You're not going anywhere." Cade slaps my ass hard, and the shocked gasp I make isn't missed by Theo who smothers a laugh down below me. Traitor. "You started this, and you will finish it," Cade growls, readjusting me on his massive shoulder.

"I thought I already did," I pop off, damn proud of my quick comeback. It's short-lived, though, because Cade delivers another stinging slap to my ass cheek before he growls, digging his fingers into my thigh.

"Ow! Theo!" I yell, seeing the traitor who I thought was my partner in crime smiling below me. "You said…" I trail off, not wanting to give away his advice. He said I was powerful.

Another sting as Cade clomps up the stairs. I'm sure my ass is going to swell up. I flip Theo off. This is not funny.

"I never said he wouldn't retaliate. Hang in there, B. Looks like you're in for a rough night." He salutes me before disappearing out of sight with shaking shoulders as Cade takes a slight turn into his bedroom and deposits me onto the bed without even trying to be gentle.

I flop across his sheets, legs spread, hair in my mouth and eyes like some kind of ratchet ragdoll. Totally sexy. "What was that for?" I whisper-yell, a little pissed off. Righting my gown, I huff out my annoyance at this caveman attitude I'm witnessing tonight, and inch up the bed until I reach the headboard.

The man whose body looks like a Greek sculpture sits down in his chair and just stares at me, jaw clenched. His shirt is torn and draped open like the curtains to his soul, allowing me only a glimpse of the scars he wears on his skin. His chest rises and falls in a harsh rhythm while his enchanting jade colored eyes hold me in captive silence.

"You want to be mine, Brecklyn?" The deep gravelly tone of his voice is like I've never heard before. Sure, I've heard it raspy, but never like this. He sounds almost predatory, like he's about to interrogate a man instead of asking me a loaded-ass question.

I swallow. I'm not sure if he's finished scaring the shit out of me or not. He slides the pad of his finger along the seam of his lips before he breathes against it and asks, "You want to shatter me?" I was a little caught up in the moment when I said that. "Answer me, Brecklyn."

Ah, hell. He used my full name again. I'm guessing a joke would be received negatively at this point in the conversation. Clutching the soft sheets in my hand, I answer him honestly for once. Theo was right about one thing: Whether Cade wants to admit it or not, I mean something to him.

So I decide to be brave. "Yes."

Simple and to the point.

Honest and truthful.

I want him.

Every single scar.

Hooded eyes narrow on me, unblinking, and then he picks up his phone, tapping the screen before filling the darkened bedroom with a hypnotic beat. "Then dance for me like you're mine."

Holy shit.

"I, uh … I only dance for fun." I wave my hand around. "You know, when I'm cooking."

He breathes along his fist, slow and careful, like he's measuring me up. "I know. You've made me more than uncomfortable at a few breakfasts."

I did? Huh. Who knew?

I suddenly feel like Wonder Woman has nothing on me. I ease myself off the bed, bending to take off my shoes.

"Leave them on."

Oookay. What's a few more minutes of pain?

Standing, my hips sway to the beat, feeling unnatural since I'm usually just bullshitting, doing random dance moves I've seen on YouTube. Cade beckons me toward him and eases me onto his lap, pulling my dress up around my hips to accommodate my spread position. He breathes me in, reaching around my back and unzipping my dress at a lazy pace. The fabric peels away from my body as if he's parting the sea with his fingertips, and my skin tingles.

"Keep moving," he whispers into my shoulder, his fingers drifting lower.

Let's be honest here. I am not dancing. I am dry humping this man to the beat of the music. Okay, well, they do that in clubs, too.

His hand disappears under my dress and immediately my stomach clenches. Please touch me. Please slide those long fingers—

"I need you to talk to me. Like before," he mumbles, his finger grazing the elastic of my panties.

I don't want to ruin this moment and act like an idiot, but I have no clue what he's talking about. "What do you mean, talk to you like I did before?"

Cade breathes harshly into my chest, the hand not under my dress unfastening my strapless bra. "Talk dirty. I need you to talk dirty to me. I think with you restraining me and the commanding tone, it kept me out of my head." He flashes me a scolding look. "I would prefer not to be restrained every time, so let's see if that filthy mouth of yours will be enough."

Well how about that? Mister I Can't Be With You wants me to be a dirty girl. I can do that. I can *so* do that.

"Put your fingers inside me, Major Jameson."

Cade pushes my panties aside. His pace is slow, hesitant, as he moves closer to my center, taking care to stroke along the thin strip of hair.

"I want to ride your fingers," I admit, moving my hips over his hardened cock. "I want you to shove them in one by one until you can't fit any more without ripping me in two." Cade's chest is rising and falling, his breathing erratic and strained. "Now, Major."

Saying that may have been the wrong thing to say because I swear Cade damn near fists me, sending me doubling over into his shoulder.

"Fuck my fingers, Brecklyn." Is that his fingers or his goddamned fist? I can't tell. The biting pain countering the fullness is distorting my perception. "Take what you need."

Slowly and carefully, I move over his fingers. Clockwise and then counter clockwise, I manipulate this man's fingers like a chiropractor until the magical spot comes alive. Gasping, my mouth gaped open, I chase the tingling sensation until I explode, a rush of wetness dripping down my leg. Exhausted, I lay on Cade's chest. His arms wrap around me so we're chest to chest. Heartbeat to heartbeat.

We come down slowly, our breathing returning to normal when I try to lift off of him. His arms tighten, his sweaty mane still pressed against my cheek.

"Stay with me tonight," he mutters.

Yeah, I didn't say no.

chapter twenty-one

Breck

B,

   We actually had some downtime this week. You would be so proud of your big brother. I used that trick you taught me in Madden and kicked both Jameson brothers' asses. It was like taking candy from two sore losers. Jess told me about your internship! I knew you would get it. You're going to be famous one day and I'll be able to tell everyone I know that I knew you when you nearly caught the house on fire toasting a Pop Tart.

   #icantwaittoseeyou #nottoomuchlonger

   Bennett Brannon

The wheat bread pops up in the toaster after what seems like half an hour of being in there. The guys' eggs are just about cold from waiting on its slow ass. When I checked with Anniston, she said they were wrapping up their morning workout and that I was good to get started on breakfast.

   That was twenty minutes ago.

For the past twenty minutes, I have watched her through the window barking at Mason about something I can't make out. Tim and Vic are out there with them and trying hard to look anywhere but at where Mason and Anniston are arguing. I don't know what Mason did or didn't do, but the stubborn set of his jaw says he doesn't give a fuck about whatever Anniston is raving about.

The awkwardness that surrounds them makes me grateful I'm in here and not in Tim and Vic's place. Actually, I would rather be nestled in Cade's bed where I was earlier before he woke me, slipping out of bed to run with Theo.

I glance through the French doors one more time and, yep, Mason is still locked in a staredown with his commander. The food will just have to get cold. I am certainly not going to interrupt whatever is going on out there. The avocado shouldn't brown unless they stay outside for hours, but still, who wants to eat warm, mushy slices of avocado?

Fuck it.

I'll just let Cade know breakfast is ready and he can go intervene if he wants. Or they can eat a cold breakfast. I did my part, either way.

The gym is nestled in the back of the house where there were probably a couple spare bedrooms years ago. The wall between the two rooms has been knocked out, creating one huge room that houses state-of-the-art machines that tone those ridiculous bodies. I knock before I enter. I don't know why. Maybe it's Cade's quiet space or something. It just feels intimate for some reason.

Or maybe I'm just feeling awkward after last night. After riding Cade's finger like a tried-and-true pro, we showered together in silence, Cade washing my hair for me. We dried, neither of us putting on pajamas, and crawled into bed, him sliding behind me, a protective arm around my waist. I was a little worried he would have a nightmare and wake up confused with me in his bed, but he didn't. He slept soundlessly and was up at five to go run with Theo, who I heard make a crack about celebrating tonight for finally popping his cherry. The thing about staying here is that there is zero privacy. If you don't want them to find out, then don't date any of them.

I push open the door to the gym and call out hesitantly, "Cade." He grunts out a response from somewhere and I have no idea what he said. "Breakfast is ready," I say anyway, stepping into the lighted room with rubber floors. If I was a person who enjoyed such things as exercise, I would be in here all the time. Unlike most gyms, this one doesn't stink like nasty balls but rather like cleaner. Taking in the treadmills, weight benches, and some other torturous-looking machines, I finally find Cade.

And I can't even prepare my vagina.

Hanging with his knees over something that looks similar to monkey bars, Cade raises his upper body to his knees, lowering back down and then repeating the movement.

Heaven help me, I wasn't prepared to witness the beauty of those square blocks of hardened muscle straining under the weight of his body. I wasn't prepared to see the glistening sweat on his bare chest as he blows out hard breaths with each repetition. And I certainly was not prepared to see his solid jaw, flexing and clenching while he grits out numbers until he stops, calling out, "Forty."

Mouth open, I stand there staring, and I can only think one thing: Cade could totally kick Thor's ass.

"Brecklyn." Low and deep, Cade calls out from his current upside down position.

Stop staring at his abs, weirdo, and answer him. "I …" Clearing my throat, I start over, attempting not to squeak when I repeat, "Breakfast is ready."

Cade lets his arms dangle past his head and tips his head in my direction. "Good. I'm famished." His eyes rake over the tiny pink sundress I'm wearing, his assessment making me feel as though I'm standing in front of him naked. "Move the stool closer," he demands, pointing to where it's parked.

I get it and place it underneath his head. "Right here, or do you want me to move it over more?" He tells me to shift over so it's just slightly parallel to his head. "Do you need anything else?" I ask stupidly. I mean, he is hanging from a bar.

"Yeah. Take off your panties and hand them to me."

I choke. "I'm sorry? Did you say my panties?"

Cade licks his lips and raises his head so he can see me better. "You heard me. Now go lock the door."

I stand there, staring at him like a goober before he barks out, "Now, Breck. Don't make me repeat myself."

I dart to the door, flipping the lock, and hustle back to Cade, sliding off my oh-so-sexy cotton hipsters. He holds his hand out and I place my worn-out clearance panties in his hand.

"What are you going to do with them?" I ask, completely surprised at his behavior.

"Stand on the stool."

Oh my God.

I hesitate for just a second when that damn eyebrow of his cocks up, pretty much daring me to defy him. I really could just bolt out of here. But I'm no idiot, and whatever kinky shit he's up to, I'm willing to play along.

I step on the stool, and before I can even situate myself, he orders, "Place your feet at the sides." My eyes widen at what he's asking me to do. My vagina, bless her wet little soul, will be front and center. "Don't make me repeat myself," he says.

This motherfucker is in a mood today. I make an annoyed face but do as he asks and spread my legs to the width of the step stool.

"Now, since you've interrupted my workout" —I cut him another look, and he winks at me upside down, his face not even red from hanging for so long—"you're going to count out the rest of my reps until we reach fifty."

Oh. Well that was not what I was expecting.

"You understand?"

I nod, and he tosses my panties to the ground. What the hell?

"Grab my thighs."

Grab his …"What?"

His voice goes low and his eyes hood with something wicked.

"Grab my thighs, B."

Holy fucking shit.

A sixty-nine position?

Reaching forward, with my feet planted on the stool, I grab hold of Cade's thighs. Oh God. They feel like boulders underneath my fingertips. I'm reveling in the fine smatters of dark hair against the rolling hills of muscles when he says, "Count from forty."

I gaze down between our bodies, Cade's chest rising and falling slowly, unlike mine which is seconds from hyperventilating.

"Your face is going to be in my—"

He cuts me off. "Count."

You got this, B. Who cares if your pussy is directly in his face?

Inhaling, I count out his first rep. "Forty."

Underneath my fingertips, his thighs flex and his upper body rises until his head is between my—oh God. Cade swipes his tongue along the seam of my entrance, holding himself in an inverted sit up position. His arms stay crossed at his chest, the only movement being his tongue as it flicks my clit.

"Holy shit," I breathe against his legs, my head coming to rest on his knees.

Removing his face from my dripping whore of a vagina, he chides me with a cocky grin, "Count."

I groan. This is going to be the longest fucking workout in history.

I rasp out, "Forty-one," and Cade relaxes into his vertical position and then pulls up again, his tongue swiping across my seam, this time seeking entrance. He licks along the edge slowly and methodically like it's summer and I'm melting ice cream. "Forty-two," I whisper, on the verge of crying with his torturous lick against my clit.

"Good girl," he rumbles, the vibration from his voice better than my vibrator.

"I don't think I can handle any more of this," I whine, my fingers squeezing his delicious thighs like someone is trying to steal him from me.

He shifts his body and adjusts his grip, pulling my hips closer to his face, responding in a tone that takes me from annoyed to needy in one breath. "You will handle it, Brecklyn. For interrupting my work-out, you're going to come all over my face."

Cade's dirty talk is hot, but I'm not going to wave my white flag yet. One thing I know is that Cade enjoys when I fuck with him.

"You know, I'm thinking this 'interrupting your study time and your workouts' is all bullshit. As a matter of fact …" Leaning over, I shove my face into his manhood, the motion stealing his breath. His hands grip my outer thighs tighter. Yeah, I know what the major likes. "I think you like having an excuse to stop whatever you're doing," I say, my nose running down the length of his thickening cock. I nip at his thigh and the muscle jumps. "You know what else I think?" Cade waits for me to continue, Jameson Jr. growing harder under my ad-vances. "That you're being lazy. I mean really, my Ken doll had better abs."

Cade's rumbly laughter spills out between my legs and it makes me smile. The man with abs that could actually rival the best body builders returns with, "Oh, he did, did he?"

I hum against his thigh, inching my way back down to his dick. "Mm-hm." He chuckles one more time, fully aware that I'm lying my ass off right now.

"Hey, B?"

"Yeah?" My voice is strained, attempting to keep my amusement under wraps. "Count," he demands before he shoves his tongue right through my entrance, sucking up any remaining laughter from me. "I can't hear you," the asshole says from underneath me.

"Forty-three," I mutter out, my neck feeling like the sun is beat-ing down on top of it even though we're indoors. Cade's licks are slow and methodic like he's disarming a bomb and not eating me out. His tongue circles my opening, creeping up at an annoying pace to where I want him most.

"Now see, Brecklyn, this is lazy." Excruciatingly slow, Cade circles my clit. Smartass.

Knees that have only ever run when something was chasing me

buckle, and I have to grab his thighs of steel for support.

"Did your Ken doll do that better, too?"

Now he's just being petty.

"No, but my vibrator does," I manage between pants. Cade hums a disbelieving sound against me, and then … oh God. My knees give when he drags the scruff of his face against my sensitive flesh. It tickles but hurts in a way I can't quite explain other than it feels fucking incredible. His bottom lip drags along, the wetness of his mouth soothing the burn.

"I'm gonna come," I whimper against his cock. His dick jumps against my cheek but I don't even have it in me to love on it. Cade has me reduced to a sweaty noodle.

"No you aren't. Count."

This time, I really am whiny when I respond, "You're not even doing the exercise properly anymore." Really, he hasn't pulled up since rep forty-one.

"That's because you aren't counting," he says, his breath feathery against me. This is not playing fair.

"I was—" My argument is cut short with a cry of pain? Pleasure? I can't tell because a bright light flashes behind my eyes and I swear I've died. When I come to, Cade's teeth are squeezing my swollen bundle while he sucks furiously. He sucks so hard that my clit will be shredded and unusable by the time he's done with it.

Cade Jameson is fucking wrecking me.

I cry out against him, my eyes watering, my mouth dropping open from how fucking crazy good this feels.

The man who was just laughing seconds ago shifts and removes his head from between my legs. His face is glossy, and I'm not ashamed at all. I do, however, want to yell, "What the fuck?" I was so not finished. But I back off and stay quiet since … well, you know what happened last time.

Cade makes a movement like he wants to get up. I let go of his legs, straightening my body back into an upright position.

"Are you okay?" I ask him. He doesn't say anything, only drawing up to the bar, pulling his legs through his arms and dropping down on the mat below.

I stand in awe of his masculine power when he lunges, startling me. I let out this girly squeal when he growls. But instead of shoving me to the ground, he loops my legs around his waist and carries me to a bench, laying me down.

"What are you doing?"

Cade flips up my dress and parts my legs. The air is frosty against my feverish skin. I swear he would only have to blow on me and I would come.

"I'm more than okay," he mumbles, answering my earlier question while placing soft kisses to my restrained thigh. Thank God I shaved this morning. His head moves toward my center, leaving a wake of sweat down my leg. I'm not ashamed to say that at this point, I could lick the sweat off his face if he would let me. This man brings my inner whore right out.

I fist a handful of those wavy curls, and he takes that as his cue, burying his face right into my center. Moans fill the dead space, and it takes me a second to realize it's me. Cade's hand snakes up my dress, squeezing my breast, cupping it firmly and silencing me.

I close my eyes and focus on the warmth, the vibration of his throat as his tongue swirls my clit. I'm sweating, feeling like my blood sugar is low when someone bangs on the door, causing Cade and I both to jump.

I sit up and look down at him between my legs, his lips covered in my arousal. God, he looks so sexy on his knees.

But then we hear, "Finish her," in a Mortal Kombat voice as someone passes by, and we both laugh.

"I'm sorry," he says, chuckling against my leg. "Nothing is ever private in this house."

I shrug off his apology. I really don't care how many people hear us or know what we're doing. I'll take Cade Jameson any way I can get him. And besides, I could pick Hayes' voice out of a line-up. He was probably coming to work out and heard us. Little shit.

"I know what I'm getting into, Major. Now, where were we again?"

The smile that tugs at his bottom lip should be memorialized. Bright and happy Cade Jameson smiles over the top of my pussy, and what he says against my clit has me coming on his pretty face.

"Yes, ma'am."

"We're going to the lake tomorrow," Cade says, wiping off the bench where I shamelessly came not once, but twice. Guess Cade and I can now say we've added to the jizz in this room.

"Okay," I say, sliding my underwear back on, a sinking feeling in my stomach. He's letting me down easily. "Sue and I have a ton of orders to fill. Soak up some sunshine for me." That didn't sound clingy, did it?

Cade stops wiping down the bench and gives me a funny look. "I was hoping you would come with us."

He was? Well, color me surprised. "You mean, you don't want to offer me a ride home?" I tease with a smile. He rolls his eyes, tossing the towel into a nearby hamper before swaggering his fine ass up to me.

"No, smartass. I don't want to take you home. I want to take you to our lake house. It's my birthday."

This motherfucker. My eyebrows battle with my hairline when I look at him like I might smack him. "Your birthday?"

He's lucky he looks ashamed. Otherwise, I think I might have kneed him in the balls.

"Cade! Why didn't you tell me?"

He shrugs almost boyishly. "It's not a big deal. I would rather not celebrate it, but Anniston insists on it."

"Well, duh. It's your birthday, not just another Saturday," I argue with the idiot.

"Does that mean you'll go with me?"

The blood must still be pumping below because he must be crazy to think I would turn down going anywhere with him when he's asked me so earnestly. I press against him, my hand cradling the back of his neck, communicating what I need. He complies. At first, it's just a peck, a sweet kiss meant to imply that I'm a sure thing, but when he hums, like he is actually worried I may say no to him, that is when I go for it. My tongue pushes at his lips, shocking them open. My hand holds his head to mine, my free hand yanking at the elastic on his shorts so hard he grunts. I'm about to plow this man right here on the floor.

Cade takes control, grabbing my wrist and halting any further molestation of his nether regions. "Soon," he pants against me, his forehead resting on mine.

Soon. I can do soon.

If we're being technical, I could wait years for Cade, but I don't want to. I know we haven't had long since the PTSD incident which will now be referred to as the night we never speak of, but things seem different since Cade admitted what happened with his team that night. He seems lighter. Less burdened by guilt. I can't say for sure but he seems better than before. Happier even.

"Okay," is all I respond with while stroking up and down his back in a soothing motion.

And that is that.

Cade's birthday is this weekend, and I'm going to bang the hell out of him thirty-three times. One for each year and one to grow on.

Something tells me he won't mind.

chapter twenty-two

Cade

The next morning we all load up in our respective vehicles, Theo bitching more than anyone else. "I don't understand why Killer and Tim both have to ride with us. Why can't they ride with Mason?"

Hayes, perched on his motorcycle, hollers across the driveway, "Because we couldn't fit all your crowns in one vehicle, princess."

"All the luggage is Anniston's," he argues, turning around to glare at Anniston in the passenger seat of her SUV, casually doing something on her phone like no one is yelling next to her. "I told you we didn't have to bring half the house. Put some of that shit back so Tim can ride with Mason and Vic."

Everyone laughs, knowing good and damn well he planned on pulling over and christening every gas station they stopped at. Anniston and Theo revel in being exhibitionists. Having Tim and Killer in the car shoots that plan to hell.

Anniston barely graces him with a look before Hayes barks out, "Get in the car, Von Bremen. It's only an hour and a half drive."

Theo, irritated from shit not going his way this morning, flips off Hayes, turns on his heel, and flops down in the driver seat. His window inches down slowly and he turns his head in my direction. I laugh before he even says anything. "Jameson. I will ram your ass if you drive like a chick. I'm serious. I'm not in the mood for your Sunday driving. Keep your foot on the gas."

Breck snickers next to me, all buckled in like she should be. "I'm gonna put my foot on something else if you keep running your mouth," I promise, only slightly joking. The asshole in the car next to me rolls his window up, cutting off anything else I would say, and revs his vehicle before speeding off, sending gravel flying up behind his tires.

"Why is he so upset this morning?" Breck asks, the mint of her breath prominent in the small cab. "I heard him and Ans in the kitchen this morning. He can't be pent-up already."

I eye Breck curiously. "Did you watch them?"

She scoffs. "No." But her hands fidget in her lap, telling a different story.

"You little liar," I tease, not offended in the slightest.

"They were on the island!" she exclaims in a hurry, thinking it would upset me. "Right in front of the stairs." Her face is flushed from embarrassment.

I throw the truck in drive and follow behind Mason and Hayes. "Don't worry about it. We've all watched them at some point. They aren't discreet with their sex life."

Breck nods, her face still pink. "Do you like public sex?" she asks with a hint of curiosity.

"No," I tell her honestly. "I don't. No one gets to see what's mine."

My answer seems to put her at ease, her shoulders loosening as she leans back against the seat. "Good, because I get stage fright."

Her simple and honest answer puts a stupid grin on my face. "So you're saying you aren't able to come on demand?"

She frowns. "Can you come on demand?"

No, but I would be willing to try it with her. "I'm afraid not, but if you blow on me the right way and talk dirty, I might get really close to it."

Her face turns crimson again and the tips of her ears match. I've embarrassed her. "Don't be embarrassed. I like it when you talk dirty." I reach over and grab her hand, interlacing our fingers. "No one has ever talked to me that way. I like it."

That admission has her meeting my eyes with a hint of a smile. "Oh yeah?"

"Yeah," I tell the girl who I lied to every weekend about why I was at the Farmers' Market. For fifty-two weeks, I traveled into town and made up this bullshit excuse that we were out of jam. And every week, I would come home and put yet another jar of jam in the jam-packed cabinet.

Breck turns on the radio, filling the cab with soft country music. I try hard not to grin. "You like country?"

She shrugs her dainty shoulders, kicking her foot up on the dash. I cut her a look, and she glances back, raising her foot higher with a devilish grin. "I like classic country. None of the new pop country everyone seems to be coming out with."

My foot slips off the gas. She likes the classics? She is never getting away from me now. The guys like to talk shit about my taste in music, which is eclectic really, but there's something about driving that makes me want to blast the sounds of the south. Call me a good ole boy if you must, but a southerner I will always be. It reminds me of home, my dad taking me and my brother down old back roads, teaching us to drive with Willie Nelson blaring through the speakers. It was a time when I felt free and careless. Nothing could touch me in that truck.

Until it did.

Until I drove away from the only family that had ever loved me. I killed their son. Their true son. I let them down. I let Drew down, the best friend I ever had.

"Cade?"

The concern in Breck's voice pulls me back from the thoughts of my parents. I swallow, clearing any emotion from my throat before turning and answering her. "Yeah?"

"You okay?"

Her hand moves underneath mine, and it occurs to me that I was probably squeezing the hell out of it. "Did I hurt you? I uh …" I stroke the soft skin of her arm, giving her hand a break. "I zoned out for a moment. I'm sorry."

Gray eyes blink back at me, measuring my words thoughtfully. When she seems satisfied, she undoes her seatbelt and slides to the middle of the bench. I tap the brake. "What are you doing? Put your seatbelt on." I'm not joking around. The last thing my soul can handle is scraping her off the road after she's flown through the windshield.

"I am. Hold your horses."

Hold my horses? I give her a look. I am not amused.

"Five. Four." I count down, tapping the brake, and it dawns on her I'm fucking serious.

She scrambles, locking her buckle together before I can get to three. "There. Nice and secure. Are you happy now?"

No. Because now I'm distracted as fuck with her curvy body next to me. Just thinking about yesterday in the gym has me rock hard.

"I didn't realize The Foundation owned a lake house," she says, changing the subject, easing the tension in my jeans.

"We don't. It's Theo's. Well, I guess it's Theo and Anniston's." Breck smiles, waiting for me to continue. "After he quit professional baseball, he sold his apartment in Atlanta and bought the lake house."

"Why?" she asks.

"Because he has more money than he knows what to do with?" I say, taking a guess. "I don't know why he bought it, but the place is huge with five bedrooms and a separate apartment atop the boathouse. It easily sleeps all—" The reasoning hits me all at once. It sleeps *all* of us. Us. Not just him and Anniston. We've been coming here once a month for a year now. Fishing. Boating. Skiing. Grilling. We've had some really great times over the course of the year. As a matter of fact, it's my favorite place to go. The serenity, the calm amongst the chaos.

That motherfucker.

I make an amused sound. Von Bremen likes to play the villain, but this goes to show he is anything but. In his own way, he has made contributions to this Foundation right under our nose.

"It sleeps?" Breck questions. Right. I stopped mid-sentence. "It sleeps all of us." I don't elaborate, allowing Theo his secrets.

Breck smiles. "You like it there?" she asks, hearing the fondness in my tone.

I nod. "Yeah. I love to fish and the atmosphere is so peaceful."

"It's been years since I've been to a lake. My parents preferred the beach." Her voice seems sad.

"Do you miss having a relationship with your parents?" I ask. I'm curious because lately I find myself wondering if my parents are okay. They are getting older now and I wonder if they are in good health.

Breck sighs like it pains her to admit it. "Yeah. I do. We didn't have the best relationship but I remember good times before Ben—" She stops mid-sentence, her eyes misting. "Cade, I need—"

"I'm adopted," I blurt out like an idiot, cutting off whatever she was about to say. "I'm sorry," I quickly add. "You first."

A tear forms in the corner of those eyes that remind me of the mountaintops as they reach the heavens, and she swipes it away. "You first. I was just rambling."

But it doesn't feel like rambling. It feels like I interrupted something important. "Mine can wait. Please ... go ahead."

She waves me off with a forced smile. "It was nothing. Tell me about your family. You were adopted?" Her prompting is all I need to purge the other tragedy in my life.

"I am. My real mother was a surrogate for this rich couple." I take a breath and Breck squeezes my hand in comfort. "They wanted a child, but the wife was infertile. So, my mom agreed to donate her egg and body for the couple to conceive, but when I was born ..." My chest spasms and I have to rub the increasing knot there. "When I was born, the wife of the couple couldn't bear to look at me. Said she was wrong and wouldn't ever be able to love a child that wasn't hers. My biological father signed over his rights, and I was left with my mother, who already had three children of her own. I was the outcast. My stepfather couldn't bear to raise me because I wasn't his. They fought all the time. And then he left. My mother was so angry—blamed me for her ruining her life. It wasn't until I met Drew in fifth grade that things turned around. His parents were wonderful and welcomed me with open arms. I found myself sleeping over at their house more than my own. Eventually, Anne, Drew's mother, asked me about my parents. By this time, I loved her more than I loved my own mother. I remember crying in her arms begging for her please not to send me back, and she shushed me, telling me everything would be fine."

I sigh, chancing a look at B. Her eyes are watery. "She adopted you?" she guesses.

I nod. "Yeah. She went to see my mother. She never would tell me what happened but then she asked me if I would like to live with them forever." I chuckle, remembering my reaction. "She couldn't get the words out of her mouth before I was saying yes. I remember Drew being the happiest out of all of us. He said he had always wanted another sibling but something happened and his parents never could have any more children."

My eyes feel heavy and itchy. Am I about to cry?

"Anyway," I say, clearing my throat. "I became a Jameson after that. I was no longer a Davis, and I felt like I was reborn. The world was my oyster. So when Drew wanted to become a commissioned officer after college and travel the world, I was all over it. We decided on the Marines, and although I think I could have gone into the Air Force and become a pilot, Drew had dreams of becoming special forces. I had grown protective of him even though he was a few months younger than me, but he was wild and free spirited. Much like Theo." Huh. Almost exactly like Theo.

"I wouldn't leave him so I joined the Marines too. We were in this together."

Breck shuffles, her hand squeezing mine tighter before she asks, "Is that why you don't speak to them anymore? You feel you killed their real son?"

My throat constricts as she hits the proverbial nail on the head.

"Yes. He was all they had, and I failed them."

"Oh, Cade."

I flinch. I don't want her pity. I deserve the agony of being alone. I killed their son. My best friend. I took the only thing they had left in the world.

Breck unlatches her seatbelt, her hands going to my face in a gentle caress.

"What are you doing?" I ask. My foot eases off the gas, and I pull onto the shoulder. I refuse to drive with her unrestrained.

"Put your seatbelt back on," I admonish, throwing my truck in park. Breck ignores my demand, placing a soft kiss on my cheek. Her lips feel warm and soft against my face. Her hands go to my hair, running through the strands, giving them a gentle tug. Another kiss to my temple has me reaching for her, pulling her body into me.

She drags her lips from my temple to my mouth, and I give in.

I want her.

I want her to make the images of Drew disappear.

I want her to make my parents disappointment in me disappear.

I want to lose myself in her until I can't think of anything other than her warmth.

I'm kissing her hungrily when she goes for my jeans, her small hands flipping open the fly. Immediately, I'm pulled back to reality. What the fuck am I doing? We can't do this. Not out here. What if I hurt her? I push at her hands, pulling away, and catch my breath.

"We can't do this," I tell her, the pain in my voice matching the pain in my jeans. Breck ignores me, unbuckling my seatbelt, and shoves at my chest, pulling my legs onto the seat so I'm reclined against the window.

"No," I tell her, stopping her fingers with my hand. Her face, splotchy with unshed tears, falls even further. "I want to. I do. But last time …" I remind her. With what I can only describe as determination, she takes my hand and slips it under her shirt, placing my palm over her heart. It thumps rapidly underneath my touch.

And then she tugs my jeans down.

"No dirty talk this time," she tells me, pulling me out of my boxers, her fingertip rubbing over my swollen head. "Listen here," she continues, pushing my hand more flush against her chest. "Stay with *me*, Cade." And then she slides off her cotton shorts, moving over me, straddling me the best she can in our cramped space. She rises on her knees, her face searching mine for any signs of distress. With one hand, she cups my cheek, her soft skin against my rough one, and with her other hand, grips me hard, lining up with her entrance.

"Be with me, Cade. *Just me.*"

I don't know what finally makes me give in. Maybe it's the determination in her eyes, or maybe it's because I feel stronger when she's around. Maybe it's because I love her and I want to make her proud. Either way, I take a breath and guide her down, sheathing me inside her. The warmth is what I notice first. Then the squeezing as though something is massaging the tension from within.

It's been five long years since I've been inside of a woman. And being bare … nothing compares to the feeling of her hot skin on mine. Deep within her body, my dick slides along, grazing her innermost parts. She's perfect. So fucking perfect. My eyes are heavy and threaten to close while my head falls back to the window. Breck's grip is firm though, and she pulls it up, coaxing me out of my head with her breathy voice. "Look at me, Cade."

I do. I look at her with every neuron I have. I look at the moisture dotting her makeup-free forehead. I look at her lips, parted ever so slightly as she chases her ecstasy. I take in the curve of her earlobe, the tiny cupcake earring nestled within it. I watch her naturally long lashes flutter as she struggles to keep her eyes open.

And when she looks down, her hand taking my head with her, I take in the sight of us becoming one. My length disappearing into her body. Her taking all of me. Every. Broken. Piece. Profound and beautiful, I watch the girl who pushed at me, tempting and charming as she chipped away the armor of my heart right up under my nose. I watch her hand clutch mine to her chest as she comes undone, crying out, her rhythm slowing and her heart rate slowing. "Don't be scared," she says, still moving on top of me. "I've got you."

The way she's looking at me is like she alone has enough willpower to keep my head here. This beautiful woman is offering her silent strength. She's fighting the demons alongside of me, and it's with another squeeze of her hand that I know there's no way I won't stay in this moment with her.

This woman is my partner.

My stubborn-as-fuck woman.

The girl who has wormed her way into my heart with her sweet tone and sassy mouth.

The woman who loves me despite my sins and without judgement.

This woman. This incredible woman is a motherfucking hero.

And I am so done running from her.

With both hands, I reach up and bring her face down to mine. I kiss her hard, our teeth clashing against one another. I take her hand pressing mine to her chest, and I move it to mine, allowing her to feel my heartbeat instead. She makes a small sound that undoes me right then and there. I grasp her hips and drive into her from below, chasing my everything until it erupts out of me with a roar, doubling me over into her chest.

Our bodies are slick with sweat, our breathing erratic and fast when she manages out, "Happy Birthday, Cade."

I kiss her hard until she has to pull back for air.

This woman is mine.

I stare, taking in Breck's disheveled appearance. Her mouth quirks and turns rather smug. "I thought you didn't do public sex."

I laugh and kiss the side of her neck, reveling in the smell of apples coming from her. "I thought you got stage fright?"

She pulls back, shrugging, a naughty gleam in her eye. "Maybe I can see the appeal."

★ ★ ★

We arrive two-and-a-half hours later than everyone else. One step into the modern lake house, and we're greeted by all the guys with a standing ovation, led by Theo.

"It's about fucking time. Pay up, bitches! I won," he says to the four men behind him. He holds his hand up for a high five and I ignore him and pass by, pulling Breck behind me. I sure hope she isn't embarrassed because if she decides to stay with me, this is a common occurrence. I've been guilty of teasing Theo more than once.

"I'm sorry," I tell her, pulling her down the hall toward the back exit to the boathouse apartment where we'll be staying. "Unfortunately, it probably won't be the last time he says something shitty this weekend."

Breck laughs softly. "It doesn't bother me. It's like you have five brothers."

I pause, my hand on the door to the boathouse. Brothers. "Huh. I guess it kind of is."

A sincere smile tugs at my lips as I open the door for Breck to step inside. The apartment is small with only one bedroom and one bathroom. It's pretty much a glamorized hotel room. But at least it's away from the guys and their incessant teasing.

"This is beautiful," Breck mumbles, running the pad of her finger along the driftwood furniture Anniston picked out.

"Anniston decorated," I add. "And Theo and I—well mostly me—redid the floors and painted."

Breck makes an amused sound at Theo's lack of help and pokes her head into the bathroom, taking in the upgraded space with fresh paint and tile on the floors. "You guys did a great job. It looks like something out of a magazine." I never thought about it like that, but yeah, I guess it does. "Do you mind if I freshen up?" She nods toward the bathroom.

"Sure. There are clean towels in the cabinet. Take your time. I'll go get our bags."

She stands on her toes, arching her back for a kiss. I indulge her, tasting the salty taste along her top lip. "Mmm … I take it back. Hurry." I give her a little slap on the ass and she moans, disappearing behind the door while I head outside to get our bags.

Like most women, Breck takes forever in the shower. I've already re-trieved our bags from the car and have been playing pool with Theo on an app on my phone. I'm winning and I know it's killing him. He sinks the eight ball and ends the game. I'm typing out a text to rub it in when a buzzing sounds from Breck's overnight bag.

It's got to be her phone. Should I answer? What if it's Sue?

The buzzing starts up again. I'll just get it and take it to her.

Unzipping her bag and rooting around way too many clothes for a weekend, I finally locate her phone and pull it out, a necklace wound around it.

I bring the phone up to eye level and unwind the necklace. It's not a necklace.

It's dog tags.

I'm frozen, my body literally locked in one position when Breck opens the bathroom door, steam billowing out behind her like stage art. "Sorry I took so long—"

She gasps at the sight of me, the air whooshing from her lungs. I'm crouched over her bag, Bennett's dog tags clutched in my hands.

"Your phone was ringing," I mutter in a low, robotic tone. She looks confused for a moment like my statement wasn't what she was expecting. Should I have said his full name? Called out his birth-day? His blood type? Did she think I wouldn't recognize his name? Everything about this kid is ingrained in me.

I was his brother.

His superior.

I held his hand as the life drained from his eyes.

My forearm tenses, thinking about his face, the last time I saw him, bloody and trying to smile through the pain. Through the fear. He was staying strong. For me.

I haul off and punch Breck's overnight bag with a sound that is almost animalistic. Rage is coursing through my veins, and my heart pounds in my ears, deafening any other sounds. My chest heaves like I'm suffocating but that can't be true.

Another sound escapes my chest. It sounds like I've been

possessed by a demon. I raise my head slowly, my lip twitching into a snarl when Breck takes a cautious step toward the front door.

The movement snaps me out of the rage. I spring to my feet like I weigh nothing. Hell, I can't even feel my legs—the endorphins have taken over. "You're a liar, Brecklyn Brannon," I grit out, taking a calculated step toward her.

A cry bubbles out of her throat and I want so bad to go to her but I don't. She's a traitor.

"I'm not a liar," she pleads, her eyes searching my cold, closed off ones. "I was going to tell you. Please let me explain."

My head goes back and an evil sounding laugh erupts out of me. "So you wanted to confront your brother's killer. Is that it?"

I don't give her the chance to explain. Instead, I take another step toward her so we're toe to toe. "Well, here I am, sweetheart. Let me make it easy for you."

Tears are streaking down her face at a rapid pace, but she can't seem to form any words when I produce a knife from my pocket. I press the button and it makes a clicking sound when it extends.

Breck cries out, the words garbled. "Cade," she pleads with me, her small hands reaching for me.

My face is blank, detached even, when I grab her wrist and place her hand around the handle, pushing the blade against my neck. Her hands tremble beneath mine and it only makes me increase the pressure, driving the knife farther into my neck.

"Please don't do this," she begs, trying to break my hold. But I'm stronger, and I increase the pressure until I feel the sting of the blade breaking skin.

"Stop this!" the girl who just made love to me in the car demands.

I laugh at her fake tears. "This is what you came here for, right? Vengeance?"

She's shaking her head, her free hand pushing against my chest. "No," she denies vehemently, the tears masking the smoke color I love so much. "I came here for you. To help you."

A growl erupts out of me, the pressure from our hands becoming increasingly difficult to talk through. "Lies. It's all lies. Everything about you is a lie," I yell.

Her knees give way and she collapses, but I'm well past giving a fuck at this point. I make a tsking noise, yanking her back up. "Finish what you started. Tell me how much you hate me. Tell me what a coward I am. Tell me I'm a killer."

Sobs rack through her entire body and my chest aches to comfort her, but I don't because what we had was a lie.

A covert mission.

"No," she argues, seemingly drawing strength from somewhere. "You will not do this to us."

Us. There is no us.

"I killed him," I grit out slowly so she understands. "You want to know how great of a hero I am, Brecklyn?" I spit her name like it's poison. "While I was fucking the journalist, your brother was gasping for air."

I let out a bitter laugh that doesn't sound borderline crazy, and Breck sobs a painful sound. "I fucked her right where you saw me getting blown that day on the computer." As soon as I saw his name on the dog tags, I remembered her. "I can't even remember the journalist's name. But I remember you. Your eyes, as you watched me come apart in her mouth. I wanted you. I wanted to see the blush on your cheeks glisten under my sweat. I wanted to wreck you." I chuckle dryly, fingering a piece of her hair, the pain in her eyes gripping my heart. "But instead, you wrecked me."

With the knife still at my throat, I continue on. "He" —I can't even get the words out—"he called out to me in the rubble. Want to know what his last words were?" Now I'm just being mean. Bleeding my pain onto her innocence. "He said …"

A tear falls from my eye, and even though I'm being a total asshole, Breck still reaches for me with her free hand and says, "No matter what you say, I'm still with you. I'm strong enough for the both of us."

The guilt eats at me as she stands in front of me, strong and defiant just like her damn brother. Relentless. "He said it was an honor to serve with you, Major." She only lets one tear fall, and it pisses me off. "An honor?" I shout. "I sent my team on without me. I sent your brother, *my brother*, to their deaths, Breck. All because I wanted pussy."

She still doesn't budge, her chin straight, her face strained. "You would have died, too," she argues like she isn't arguing with her brother's killer.

I yank her closer, and she gasps from the shock. "I would have known to check the cabinets! It should have been me!" I yell to the senseless woman in front of me.

She whimpers but she doesn't back down. "Don't do this," she begs. "I'm so sorry. I should have told you who I was."

"You should have killed me when you had a chance," I tell her, seconds from spiraling into a full-blown attack. My hands tremble over hers and I know if I don't get out here right now, I will end up hurting someone.

"I won't let you do this," she challenges, trying to pull my hand from hers but failing.

I yank her closer. "Do it," I beg. "Put me out of my misery. I killed your brother. I killed the only family you had."

She cries out, shocking me out of the rage. "Help me!" she yells, her voice echoing in the small space. "Help me!" she calls out again.

I grit my teeth, the rage dissipating at her tears and cries for help. No matter how angry I am, I'm not for scaring women. Even the ones who lied and finally broke through my armor. "No one is coming, B. You had them all convinced that you loved me. They won't bother us until the morning." My voice is resigned, quiet even, as I let her hand go, flipping the blade back into the handle of the knife. "I'm sorry," I tell her for the millionth time that I've known her. "You and your brother deserved so much better than me."

Sighing, I place the dog tags in her hand, closing each of her fingers around them, honorably.

Her tears fall at a steady stream as she secures them in her palm.

"Please don't do this to us. I'm sorry for not telling you the truth."

I swipe at the tears falling down her face, memorializing her. "I'm sorry, too," I whisper with all the regret in the world.

I deserve this.

Falling in love with Brannon's sister.

His warrior.

I turn and head out the door, not even turning around when she sobs, "I love you. I loved you before I even saw you. His letters. He spoke so highly of you."

Does it feel like my chest is on fire? Absolutely, but even the pain doesn't make me turn around.

I'm letting her go.

I head straight for my truck, my keys a comforting escape in my pocket.

"Cade!"

Anniston's voice stops me. I turn and see her on the dock, her eyes going between me and Breck standing outside the boathouse. I give them both one final glance and then I turn around, done with everything, and continue up the hill to where my truck is parked.

"Cade!" Anniston's shout draws a crowd, and before I know it, all five of my brothers are on the front deck with matching concerned expressions. I give them a nod, silently asking for them to watch over the girls, but I keep heading to my truck.

Theo hops the bannister and takes off in a jog, catching up easily. "Where you headed?"

I don't spare him a glance. "Look after them for me," I tell him, fishing my keys out of my pocket, my truck just a few steps away.

Theo scoffs. "Fuck no. I'm done taking care of strays. You brought Breck into our lives, she's your responsibility."

I ignore the stray comment and unlock the door, Theo appearing in the passenger seat. I sigh. "Go back to the house, Von Bremen. The girls are upset."

He buckles his seatbelt, clearly not going anywhere. "It looks like the girls are more than upset. I'll be damned if I stay in that mess.

Where we headed? I hope it's not the streets because I can't deal without a shower every day."

I start the engine with one more companion than I want, and look over at the pain in my ass already changing my preset radio stations. "Von Bremen?"

"Hmm?"

"Shut up or I'll stab you."

chapter twenty-three

Cade

Three hours of driving and I'm still a fucking mess. I can't tell if I'm sad or pissed off.

Theo's phone has been chiming nonstop from a steady stream of texts. I don't have to think hard at who could be texting him. Anniston is freaking out and I feel slightly guilty for leaving the way I did. She doesn't deserve my wrath.

Breck does.

Lying, scheming Breck.

At first, I couldn't put it together. The dog tags in her bag … I thought maybe they were the designer necklaces that imitated dog tags, but then I saw the engraving. The name.

Bennett Brannon.

The greenie I took under my wing. The youngster that admired me more than he should have.

His sister.

His sexy fucking sister has been in my bed this entire time. How did I not put two and two together?

Because you blocked out everything that reminded you of your past, asshole.

She said she came for me. To help me. The lie sounded beautiful slipping out of her mouth. I wanted to believe her. I wanted to wrap her in my arms and listen to her teary explanation, but I knew better. I know what I did—who I am.

I'm a killer.

A disgrace to my country—to my men.

She didn't come for me. She came to stare into the eyes of her brother's killer.

I just can't figure out why she stayed so long. Why befriend the other guys? They had no part in what I did all those years ago.

"I have to take a leak."

Theo's voice loosens my grip on the steering wheel. He's been silent until now. And had it not been for his phone chiming every thirty seconds, I would have forgotten he was in the truck.

"Too bad," I tell him, forcing my eyes on the horizon. The sun is setting and I still have another hour and a half before I reach my destination. I don't remember making the conscious decision or where I was heading. It was like my truck just knew what I needed to do.

Theo smacks my free arm off the console, takes the bottled water from the cup holder, and chugs the last of it before unzipping his pants.

"What are you doing?" I ask, my foot easing off the gas in case I need to make an emergency stop.

"I'm about to piss in this bottle since you won't stop." Theo shoots me a questionable look, waiting for me to agree. Fucking with Theo usually puts me in a better mood but his stupid look does nothing for me today.

I shrug, glancing at the bottle in his hand, and then look back to the road. "Go ahead. Don't make a mess."

It wasn't the answer he was expecting, and he throws the bottle, hitting me on the side of the head. "Pull over, Jameson. You've had enough whiny-bitch time. I'm hungry and need food to endure any more of this self-loathing."

Grunting, I ignore him, keeping my eyes on the road. I'm not self-loathing. Much.

"Are you going to let me look at your neck?" he asks out the blue, shocking me.

"No."

"So you enjoy looking like a crazy person, then?"

I let out a sigh, knowing he isn't going to shut up about it. "I'll clean it up in the bathroom when we stop."

Theo eyes me with something like concern. "Will you give me the knife?"

I jerk back the tiniest bit. "I'm not suicidal," I clarify.

His brows arch high up his forehead. "No?" He fingers the dried blood on my neck, and I swat his hand away.

"I was caught up in the moment," I lie. I really wanted her to hurt me, to punish me for taking away her brother. Her family. Maybe I didn't want her to kill me, but I wanted the pain I carry on the inside to match the pain on the outside. I wanted to bleed for her.

Theo makes an exasperated sound. "I think you're full of shit. Hand over the knife, Jameson."

For the first time in the almost two years I have known Theo, he looks like he might actually beat my ass. He's serious. No jokes, no ploys, no comments.

"I promise, I'm not suicidal," I tell him again, my tone becoming softer.

He nods. "I believe you, but just in case, how 'bout you give it to me anyway?"

I deserve to be treated like a baby. It was a stupid thing to do. I scared Anniston and apparently Theo. After everything they've done for me, they don't deserve this behavior. I make a show of being annoyed, and fish the knife out of my pocket, slapping it into Theo's palm.

"Happy now?"

Theo turns the knife over in his hand and then looks at me. "No, Jameson. I'm not happy." Then he tosses my knife out the window.

"What the fuck?" I shout.

"What the fuck?" he bellows back at me. "The *fuck* is that you've come a long way, Jameson, and the girl tells you she's your dead teammate's sister and you go all *Carrie* on her ass. Drama queen much?"

My breathing falters. "You and Anniston knew who she was?"

Theo shrugs, clearly not guilty about keeping the secret from me.

"I oughta beat your ass," I tell him, tapping the brakes, ready to pull over and take out some anger on his pretty face. "Why wouldn't you tell me?" I roar.

Theo throws me a side glance. "Do you remember when Lou had Anniston at gunpoint in the barn?" I nod, not seeing how this is relevant. "Well, if I recall correctly, you wouldn't allow me to know your plans on getting her out." I go to argue and he holds a finger up. "I specifically recall you having Tim babysit me so I wouldn't, and I quote, 'Do something stupid.'" His eyebrows raise, indicating that he would like for me to acknowledge that his recollection is accurate.

"That was different," I argue.

"No, it wasn't. Anniston noticed you stalking the poor girl every weekend so she had me ask Thor to check her out. The report came back with a lot more than we expected. Including your parents."

Thor, Theo's retired security, dug into my past? My head drops to my chest. "Anniston knows about my parents?"

Theo laughs. "Of course she does."

"Why didn't she bring it up?"

Theo shrugs one of his massive shoulders. "She wanted you to *want* to tell her yourself."

Fuck. "That still doesn't make it right that you both kept who Breck really was from me," I argue fruitlessly at this point.

Theo eyes me curiously. "Are you sure? Because I think we all knew how you would react. Anniston simply wanted to make sure she wasn't some kind of psycho for your sake and for the sake of the rest of the house. Do we regret keeping it from you?" His lip quirks. "No, we don't. You would have never given Breck a chance. You would have shut down and ran just like you did all those years ago. Am I right?"

I want to say no. I want to argue and say they didn't know me at all, but the truth is, he's right. I would have kicked Breck to the curb without hesitation. Like I just did.

"You shouldn't have taken the option away from me," I say, sighing.

Theo's eyes blaze for a minute. "Didn't you ask me to put my girl's life in your hands two years ago? Didn't you take the option away from me? For my own good?"

I swallow, remembering the statement clearly. "Yes."

Theo nods. "I returned the favor. Except I saved you from yourself. Maybe it wasn't the best decision I've ever made, but Anniston and I only had good intentions. And it wasn't our secret to tell. Breck deserved a chance."

"Did she tell you why she was here?"

"No. We assumed it had something to do with Bennett, but we weren't sure."

I flash him a smirk. "What if she was trying to kill me?"

Theo snorts. "We thought you could take her."

I laugh, the sound foreign to my own ears. "I hate you sometimes," I lie to the bastard who has become one of my best friends.

"The feeling is mutual, Jameson. Now can we please stop for food? I'm fucking dying over here."

"Yeah, yeah," I tell him, pulling off the exit. "Where do you want to stop?"

Theo doesn't look at me when he says, "You pick since it's your birthday."

Well, I'll be damned. "Don't go getting soft on me now, Von Bremen."

He flips me off but stays silent until I choose the place, pulling into a burger joint. I head to the bathroom first, cleaning up the exaggerated scratch on my neck before meeting Von Bremen at the counter to order food. He glances at my neck briefly, and I cut him a bland look. It's not that bad. I got caught up in the moment. I won't allow it to happen again. Theo chooses not to engage in conversation, but when he pays for our food, I can't help but break the awkwardness. "I think this is the most romantic birthday date I've ever had, Von Bremen. I hope you don't expect head after it."

The lady manning the counter clears her throat, her eyes growing wide as she hands Theo his change.

"Jameson, I expect head after I *text* you. If I buy you *dinner*, I expect you on all fours." His tone is flat and serious, and the poor girl at the counter is blushing.

"He's joking," I tell her with a laugh. Theo grabs our cups off the counter and slams mine into my chest so hard it flattens in half before tossing over his shoulder, "I'm glad to see you have your sense of humor back. I was wondering if you were gonna act like a pussy all night."

He brushes past me, filling his cup with ice and hopefully nothing with sugar in it. I don't know if I can handle him being overly hyper tonight. I'm slightly embarrassed and highly amused when I approach the same cashier and ask her for another cup. She nods her head quickly and hands me another.

"Thank you," I tell her. "Sorry about all that."

She smiles, and when I turn to get myself something to drink I hear, "Holy shit, they're hot."

The compliment momentarily brightens my day. It used to only piss me off if a woman thought I was hot, but now, after Breck, something has changed. I find it sweet.

"Why are you smiling? That girl call you an asshole or something?" Theo is lounging at a table in the corner, his feet on my bench. I shove them off, the impact of them hitting the floor echoing in the sparse fast-food joint.

"You know they don't bring the food out to you, right?"

The look Theo gives me says one thing: Wanna bet?

A few minutes later, the same girl at the counter brings our food out with a bounce in her step. "Here you are, gentlemen," she says.

Theo quirks his lips and actually thanks her. "Thank you, sweetheart."

I chuckle. This motherfucker. "Sweetheart?" I ask him in disbelief after she leaves. "You never say sweetheart."

"Well, one of us has to be the gentleman, Jameson, and you're too busy being the whiny bitch today so I took one for the team."

He took one for the team. The simple statement hits me straight in the soul.

My team.

Not the one that died, but the one in front of me.

The one in Madison, Georgia.

My family.

Breck.

"Do you believe her?" I ask him after a minute, my tone solemn.

Mid-bite, Theo looks up from his burger and fries, swallowing down a massive amount of food. "Who? B?"

I give him a terse chin jerk. "Yeah, B. Do you believe she came here to help me?"

Theo takes a second, chewing his food carefully after taking another huge bite. "It doesn't matter what I believe, Jameson. It matters what you believe. But for the record, I don't think she came here seeking revenge."

I pick up my burger after that, both of us eating dinner in silence until his phone rings, vibrating the table. He looks at it and then looks at me.

"Ans?" I ask.

He shakes his head. "B." My gut churns as we watch his phone vibrate on the table, going unanswered. When it finally stops, he sighs. "You should call her."

"She deserves better," is all I can manage to say.

★ ★ ★

My parents' house sits in a quiet neighborhood surrounded by large oaks and Spanish moss along the Georgia coast. Jekyll Island, known for its peaceful atmosphere, was known as Satan's time-out corner to Drew and I. In other words, it was boring as fuck.

But it was home.

The sulfuric smell pulls me right back to the most epic years of my childhood.

Bike rides to Driftwood beach, pretending we were Navy Seals rescuing some hot chick who had been captured by evil villains, walkie talkies and camp-outs underneath the canopy of stars. The break of the waves against the retaining wall lulling us to sleep was better than any lullaby Anne had ever sang to us. We were boys pretending to be men. Rebels in a quiet neighborhood made up of mostly retirees. Friends turned brothers over the course of the summer.

The American flag waves at me from their front yard. It still stands, never falling, never surrendering. The light underneath shines bright as a lighthouse, like a beacon calling us home.

"She still has it flying," I murmur under my breath to Theo, who over the course of thirty minutes has become increasingly antsy.

"Hmm …" is all he says, texting something on his phone.

I feel my lips pull into a half frown. "What's your deal? You've been acting weird since we got back on the road." His gaze is slow to meet mine when I put the truck in park, right behind a sedan in my parents' driveway.

"I don't know, Jameson, you tell me. You upset the girls. Took off without a word to anyone, and now we're hours away from home at your parents' house who you didn't call to tell you were coming and who you haven't spoken to in five years." He gives me a flat look. "Oh no, I'm fine. Everything is fucking peachy."

If I were to shove him, I think I could do it without breaking my truck window. "You didn't have to—"

The front door opens and the woman who accepted me into her home with no hesitation appears at the door with a confused expression on her face. The sun sets behind her, making her look like an angel.

Theo sighs before stepping out of the truck and mumbling, "Just know this was all Anniston's idea. They just happened to like me."

What? What the fuck does that mean? Before I can ask him, Theo jumps out of the truck and sprints to my mom hollering, "Mama Jameson!" Her entire face lights up, wrapping Theo's ass in her arms and kissing him on the cheek like they have known each other forever. Like he's her son.

You have got to be fucking kidding me.

His words sink in. It was all Anniston's idea. She's been keeping tabs on my parents. I can only assume when my dad steps out, shaking Theo's hand and showing him something on the porch that has Theo nodding, that I realize they've been taking care of them, too.

My stomach flips, but it's not nerves. It's guilt. I've been so fucking selfish in my self-loathing that my friends, my family, had to step up and take care of my parents for me. I hate myself. I don't deserve the Jameson name given to me by these people. I deserve to be called a Davis. *They* were selfish. *They* are the family I deserve, not the ones standing on the porch, staring back at me, waiting.

"Come on, Jameson." Theo hollers from the steps. "Mama Jameson made peanut butter cookies and I don't care how traumatic your birthday has been. I will eat every single one of them without remorse."

She made my cookies.

She knew we were coming.

Fucking Theo.

He knew where I was heading because he's been here before, and from the relaxed stance he's sporting, he's been here many, many times.

A spark hits me in my soul. Like flicking a lighter, Anniston and Theo, even Breck, have been trying to spark it within me. Waiting. Hoping. Praying for the old Cade to return. And in the driveway of my childhood home, I finally catch flame.

Whatever I've done, whatever sins I've committed, it's time to own them. It's time to make amends.

It's time to live up to his name.

My name.

The Jameson name.

I take out my phone and pull up Anniston's number, typing the only thing I can manage. *Thank you. We'll be home soon.* She'll know what it means.

And then I send one more before I get out, to Breck. *I'm sorry.*

I toss my phone in the cup holder and get out of the truck. I stand awkwardly with my hands in my pockets until my father takes a step down the stairs. With weighted steps, I follow the path of the driveway, my father matching me step for step until we meet in the middle.

The man who looks nothing like me, with his gray hair and blue eyes, slightly shorter by a few inches, stands tall in front of me. His chin quivers as he takes me in, his tired eyes roaming over all of me as if checking that I'm in one piece. I straighten, waiting for the anger, the backlash, the pain of killing his only son when he holds his hand out for me to shake. "Welcome home, son."

An ache I feel on a daily basis spreads along my chest, up my forehead, and I know without a single doubt that this man in front of me is not blaming me. His eyes are glassy, his cheeks puffy, his arm slightly trembles in front of me as I take him in one more time before I clasp his hand in a firm grip like he taught me. "Dad."

The man that taught me how to be a good man yanks me to him, enveloping me in a tight hug, his chest silently heaving against my own. We stand there for a minute, me savoring his strength, and him … well, I don't know what he's savoring but he stands there and allows us to get it together before he pulls back and looks me in the eye. "Now go hug your mother. We've been worried sick."

He steps back and salutes me, and it's all I can do to keep my composure. With less than perfect form, I return his salute, and bark out, "Yes, sir," which puts a smile on his face.

We turn and walk quietly to my mother. Theo went inside at some point and got a cookie, because he's shoving the majority of it in his mouth with a smug smile on his face, but I don't charge him or flip him off like usual. Instead, I have eyes for only one person. And she's standing there, holding her chest with tears streaming down her face.

"My boy," she says softly, her hands twitching like she wants to reach out and touch me but isn't sure if she should.

"Mama," I return, a sad smile forming. I hope she knows how sorry I am for being such a bastard. I swallow when I'm within her reach. "Mama, I'm so sorry—"

Anne Jameson snatches me by the collar and pulls me to her chest, nearly knocking the breath out of me. "Happy Birthday, baby," she cries into my neck, my arms flexing around this woman for the first time in five years. After a few pinches, like she's checking to be sure I'm really in her arms, she pulls away, swiping at her eyes. "Come inside before Theo eats all your cookies."

Laughter bubbles out of me as my mom disappears through the front door with my dad. I place a hand on Theo's shoulder and stop him before we go in. I don't know what I want to say to him, this whole day being a clusterfuck of emotions. "I, uh …"

Theo blinks and then arches a brow, shoving the last of the cookie in his mouth with a shitty grin. "The porn collection in your closet is rather eclectic. Tell me, did you try the one where she sixty-nines you from—"

I punch him hard in the shoulder, cutting off the rest of what he would have said. The bad part is I knew exactly what he was referring to which means he's definitely been rooting around in my room. But instead of being angry, I feel peaceful. I feel complete. Like for once, the hollowness that usually embeds itself in my chest is full.

I push past Theo, stepping foot in the house I never thought I would see again, and throw behind me to my brother, "Stay out of my fucking room, Von Bremen."

★ ★ ★

After spending the night at my parents' and enduring a small birthday celebration with all my favorite foods, Theo retired up to my room—probably having phone sex with Anniston—and gave my parents and me some much-needed privacy. To talk. To cry.

In the living room, in the comfort of my mother's arms, I finally come clean to my parents about what happened to their son, minus the journalist part. Some things you just don't admit.

My father is the one who inevitably does me in. He comes to me on the couch and kneels at my feet, raising my chin with his strong fingertips. "He would be appalled that you think *you* would have saved *him*."

His statement makes me chuckle because it's absolutely true. Drew never needed saving. He blazed in situations with the soul of a true badass. He was fearless. And a damn fine Marine.

"True. But at least we could have been together," I say, regret spilling out of me one breath at a time.

My father makes this exasperated noise and my mother whimpers. "Is that what he would have wanted, Cade? For you to have died with him? For us to have been left without either of you?"

I swallow, staring at my father's hard eyes. I've been a dumbass thinking they never wanted to see me again. "I thought you hated me," I tell him quietly.

My mother pinches my side, causing me to flinch. "You better not say what I think you're trying to say. Are kidding me, Cade? All this time … all the waiting…" She cries, and I pull her to me, ashamed of myself for never facing the truth. I should have given them their moment of rage or forgiveness. I took the choice from them by running.

"I'm sorry, Mama. I was an idiot."

My mama pinches me and sniffles. "You sure were. We suffered for four years until Anniston contacted us. Four years, Cade!"

Only four years? I've been gone five and a half years. That would have meant Anniston and Theo knew about my parents long before Breck came along. "If it hadn't been for Anniston sending us updates on you, we would have gone insane with worry."

And now I know that's what Anniston was doing. But honestly, I'm not even mad about it. I'm glad she and Theo took care of them when I couldn't, when I could barely take care of myself. "I'm sorry. I couldn't bear to face you after what I had done to Drew."

Tears leak from my mother's eyes but she doesn't make a noise. "We wanted to come to you," she sniffles softly. "But Anniston asked us to wait until you were ready. She said you would come to us."

I scoff at her true statement. "Anniston tends to get what she wants one way or another." In this case, predicting that I would eventually find my way back home.

My mother smiles. "She's a sweet girl. She and Theo have been so nice to us."

A grunt of disappointment in myself is the only sound I can respond with until my father gets up, his old knees popping with the motion. "We talked with Theo, and he thought it was time we gave you this." Andrew Senior pulls a tattered letter from his pocket, and with great reverence, places it into my palm. "They delivered it with his things, when you were on the street." He drops his head, willing the emotion back before continuing, "We couldn't contact you, otherwise we would have. But then you were doing better at the Foundation and Theo thought it was best we wait."

Fucking Theo.

Emotion sits thick in my chest like a bad cold when I clutch the dirty letter in my hand. I know what it is, and there is a part of me that doesn't want to know what's in it, and yet, a part of me craves to read his final words. "Thank you," I mumble, staring at the letter like it holds the key to my sanity. "I'm so sorry," I plead with my father, hugging my mother closer. "I'm so sorry for everything I put you through."

My mother squeezes me, placing a kiss on my forehead, taking my father's hand. "You're home now. And that's all that matters to us."

My father claps me on the back. "You're a Jameson. Nothing in the world would change that, Cade."

My face feels damp. Is that …?

A tear.

Goddammit.

I swipe it away, holding my parents' gaze as they stand in front of me. "I understand that now, sir."

My father claps me on the back, my mother stroking my face once more like she's memorializing it. "Get some sleep," he says. "We'll see you in the morning." It wasn't a question. Andrew Sr. quite literally gave me a look of death like if he doesn't see my ass bright and early in the morning, he will hunt me down.

"Yes, sir."

When they retire upstairs, I take several deep breaths. I think about waking up Theo and having a drink, but ultimately, I stay where I am on the sofa. I unfold the note and read until the words blur in front of my face.

Cade,

Can you believe the heat out here? Motherfucker, man. I will never be able to knock up a girl and force her to marry me with all my swimmers burnt the fuck up.

I know I'm dead when you're reading this and it's supposed to be some kind of sad, heartfelt goodbye note—I'm sure yours is very ass-kissing and will make our parents proud—but I'm not going to go out in a ball of mush.

So here it is.

My final words to you.

1) You suck.

2) I don't know who you blew to make major because you definitely didn't make it on your skills alone.

3) Sleeping next to you while you jerk off is still awkward. No, I wasn't asleep, asshole.

4) Meghan, that chick from down the street, said I was a better lay than you were, so ha! She also said she was into girls so she might not be my best example. I was going through a dry spell.

5) You still suck at video games and your deadlifts lack the correct form.

But I guess if I'm dead, I can be honest with you. You weren't too terrible to have around. You built some great forts and made Mom happy eating all her apple pies. You didn't snore and you kicked Micah's ass for me in the sixth grade. I still say I could have taken him.

It's been an honor to be your brother.

Take care of Mom and Dad and find a girl to marry you. Bribe her if you need to. You aren't getting any prettier.
Take care of yourself.
I'm watching you, motherfucker.
Drew

I empty the bottle of whiskey my dad keeps stashed away until I pass out.

Theo wakes me in the morning with a smug ass smile and a cup of coffee. It takes me a while to say goodbye to my parents, promising I will return soon and stay longer. They are eager to meet all the guys, and the new lady in my life Anniston has been telling them about.

Breck.

Another wrong I need to right.

But before I prepare to grovel, I ask Theo to make one more stop with me.

★ ★ ★

"This place looks like it's crawling with incurable diseases, Jameson. Are you sure it's reputable?"

Theo is chewing at his fingernail all wide-eyed, giving everything in this hole-in-the-wall tattoo parlor a thorough once-over. I almost want to make fun of him for it, but honestly, I'm a little nervous too—it does look a little rough.

The walls are covered in laminated drawings—a shrine to the artists' work. From dragons to Betty Boop, gang signs to praying hands, not an inch of sheetrock shows through this thousand-square-foot building. It's clean, though, housing two open chairs for piercings and non-private tattoos. Three other chairs are in back rooms with a shower curtain pulled across, improvising as a door.

The overall feel of the place is one hundred percent Drew. I didn't tell Theo my brother has a history with this place. I just asked with a clogged throat if he would make one more stop with me. He nodded only once, buckled in, and turned on the radio. Now, though, after sensing I'm okay and not on the brink of a meltdown, his friend game is on.

"Chad is an old friend. I trust his word," I answer, vaguely tracing over one of the sketched doves on the wall.

Theo's face scrunches up, the lines in his forehead creasing in concentration like he's trying to read into my words and extract the truth from them.

"What? Why are you looking at me like that?" I ask, tracing another image in the hope he'll get distracted and move on. My friend, Chad, is bullshit. I don't have a friend named Chad, but Theo doesn't know that and I'm not in the mood to explain it to him in the middle of this questionable tattoo parlor.

"Now I know for sure I'll have to get a tetanus shot when we get home." He rubs his arm in a grimace before morphing it into a lazy smile. "I'm not stupid, Jameson. You have zero friends. You found this place online and read the hell out of the Yelp reviews before making an appointment. Chad is a reviewer. Am I right?"

I'm struggling to keep a straight face. Bastard. "Why did I bring you, again?" I ask with a chuckle.

Theo's smile is a full-on grin by this point. "Because I'm the only friend you have, and in a few hours when Hep C sets in, you'll need me to take you to the ER and convince Breck you weren't getting a fifty-dollar quickie on Moreland Avenue by some STD-ridden hooker."

I punch him in the arm, my throaty laugh taking the sting out of my hit. Theo stumbles back, rubbing his bicep furiously with a semi-scowl. "Come on, Jameson! That's gonna leave a bruise."

"For once in your life, shut up," I tell him, glancing over another one of the laminated pages. Drew's note burns in my pocket. *Make them proud.* His words echo around in my head. I haven't made anyone proud of me. I've disappointed everyone in my life at the way I've dealt with my grief.

After firing off an email to the therapist Anniston requires me to see on occasion, I feel better knowing I am one step toward getting my shit together. If I ever want to get Breck back, I have to start with making room in my head for her. I can't afford to be selfish anymore. There are too many people who deserve my devotion.

"Cade." A guy, presumed to be in his late fifties, steps out behind the curtain. I've never met him before so I don't quite know what to expect but I do know who he is.

He's the artist that tattooed nearly my brother's entire body.

"Chris?" I call, catching Theo's questioning brow.

Chris charges over to me, a huge smile poking out through a facial tattoo of a skull. "Man," he says while clasping my hand, "it's good to finally meet you. Your brother talked about you often." He gives me a quizzical look though, stepping back a little. "Although he said you were much smaller."

I snort. Fucking Drew and his bullshit. "He wished," is all I can respond with, the comment not causing pain like it used to.

"You know what you want?" The man with almost one hundred percent of his body covered in tattoos asks me.

I nod, pulling the napkin from my pocket. I scribbled out something rough last night and I'm hoping he can make it look a shit ton better than I drew it. "Obviously something better than this, but essentially this is what I want."

Chris studies the drawing and then looks at me. "This is big. Gonna be painful."

I tip my chin, my gaze floating over to Theo who is totally eavesdropping on our conversation. "I can handle it," I say, flipping Theo off with my hand down at my side.

"Alright then, come on."

★ ★ ★

Four painful hours later, I'm standing in front of a full-length mirror, flesh raw and swollen, the entire left side of my torso covered in a barren tree. The branches are engulfed in flames, turning to ash as a fiery phoenix rises from the dirt, consuming it with its blaze. The roots hold the tree strong as the crows fly from its branches.

The tree is my body.

The roots are my family.

The phoenix, my rebirth, burning away the demons that haunt my soul.

I'm starting over.

I'm rising from the ashes.

I'm letting go.

And I'm going to make all of them proud.

Starting with my jelly girl.

chapter twenty-four

Breck

Dear B,

Shame is a crazy thing. I did something today that I'm embarrassed to even tell you about, but I'm going to anyway because the guilt eats at me like a virus. I failed one of the simplest exercises today. I thought I would be discharged from the program it was that bad. There was no way I could come home and face Mom and Dad. I'll save you from the worst of it, but later that evening after the major did barrack checks, I slipped into the jon, took my razor blade, and sliced open a vein on my wrist. As the blood pooled in the sink, I panicked. I couldn't leave you alone with our parents. I instantly regretted my decision and tried to stop the bleeding when someone banged on the door. I knew I would be out of the program once they found me like this with a blade in my hand. When I didn't answer the knock, the door flew open and Major Jameson stood there, nostrils flaring, looking very pissed off. He snatched my wrist, held pressure with his hand, and pulled me out of the bathroom. We went to his private quarters where he stayed silent, fury being the only emotion radiating from his person. He told me I better not make a fucking sound, and then doused my wrist in something that felt like liquid fire. I felt like I was burning from the inside out but I held it in. He wrapped my wrist and then sat across from me and said, "Even when you die you don't leave this brotherhood." I didn't know what he meant until he kept on, "My blood is your blood. In your darkest hour, call on me, and we'll fight together. Semper Fi, brother." It finally hit me that I didn't just take a job in the military. I entered a family. A family is only as strong as its weakest link. Major made me swear to never do this again, which is against protocol, and then every night, he showed up after everyone was asleep, and we trained. I'm so sorry, B. I never wanted to leave you. Please know that. I'm just so scared of being a failure to you.

I need to go.

Don't worry about me. I'm okay. I finally feel like I've found my place.

I'm finally home, B.

#iwishiwasastrongasyou#wonderwomandoesnthaveshiton-you#youstillsuckthough

Private Bennett Brannon

"Even in death you don't leave this brotherhood. In your darkest hour you can call on me and we'll fight together. My blood is your blood." I stare at one of Bennett's first letters to me.

I'd like to think the reason I packed up everything to come for Cade was because Bennett would have wanted me to. Because even in death, he couldn't leave the brotherhood. The duty passed to me, and in Cade's darkest hour, he needed someone to fight with him. But after crying over all Bennett's old letters, I realized that the reason I felt so compelled to come here was not because I owed it to Bennett, or owed Cade a debt. It's because each letter my brother sent made me fall in love with this hero. This man he respected. The man who saved his life and was there for him when no one else was.

His brotherhood.

I loved Cade Jameson before I ever laid eyes on him that day on

Skype. I missed the letters my brother sent, giving me a glimpse into Cade's life. I had to see him. I had to make sure he was okay. My heart hurt knowing he was alone and had no one to fight alongside him. He needed an ally, and although grief and sadness were mixed in with my initial reasons to set out on this journey, my intent was solid.

He needed the brotherhood, and I would be it.

But that was wrong.

Cade had a brotherhood. He found a family. What he needed was something else entirely. He needed a partner.

And I blew it.

"Breck? Darling?" The sound of Sue's muffled voice carries through the door, drying up a few tears that have been steadily falling down my face for almost an hour now. Cade hasn't responded to any of my messages. I stayed with Anniston for the first two days he was gone, but then I thought he may come home if I wasn't there. It wasn't fair to the guys—or Anniston—for him not to return home because of me. Jess begged me to come home, and my suitcase is out and ready to go.

But I need closure before I can leave. If Cade Jameson wants nothing to do with me then I want to hear it from his mouth.

"Breck?" Sue calls again. I tuck Ben's letter away in the shoebox I keep them in and go to the door, sucking in a deep breath before I open it to find a frowning Sue. "You have a visitor," she says, her cheeks puffy like she, too, has been crying. I rush her, hugging her closely. This woman has been my rock, my family for the past year when I came to Madison. I can't imagine not having her in my life.

"Are you okay?" I hug her, feeling like a shitty friend for not spending time with her lately. She strokes my hair, before pulling back. "I'll be fine. I'll just miss you is all."

What? I haven't decided if I'm going back home to New York. Like I said, I need closure before I can leave. "I'm not going anywhere," I answer her. Not yet, anyway.

She gives me a knowing smile and pulls me from my room, pushing me down the hall. "Your guest is waiting."

Right. My guest.

It's probably Hayes or Anniston. They've come to check on me a few times since my blowout with Cade a week ago. I know he's come home. Anniston texted me when he returned. To say my feelings weren't hurt is an understatement, but I guess I deserve his silence.

I trudge down the hall, my bare feet slapping against the wood. Then I come to a halt.

"What are you doing here?" I ask from my position in the hall.

Cade turns around at my question, his jaw hard and stubborn as he looks me over. "I came to offer you a ride home."

Fuuuck. Why, God? Why does his voice have to sound so damn sexy? Why couldn't he have a laugh that sounded like a chipmunk and annoyed me to the point of packing my shit and heading home? Why does it hit me right in the nipple?

I cock a hip out and narrow my eyes. Oh no, Mr. Jameson, I'm not going that easily.

"I am home." I state the obvious.

His steps are predatory when he eats up the space between us, a cocky grin tugging at his mouth. "I beg to differ," he says, snatching the hand off my hip, and turning me upside down on his shoulder. I make a sound that I will never own up to. It's loud. And between a squeal and a moan.

"You see, Brecklyn, I've been doing some soul searching this past week." He opens the front door, stepping outside before demanding, "Close the door. Sue doesn't appreciate bugs coming in." I make a face behind his back, pulling the door shut behind us, and then I smack his ass.

I've been waiting to do that for a long time now. Someone had to do it with this new, devil-may-care attitude he's rocking, and that someone was going to be me. He owes me after everything I've been through this week.

My hand stings after slapping the literal buns of steel, and he laughs, continuing his pace like he didn't feel it at all. He opens the passenger side of his truck and deposits me onto the seat like I'm a bag of groceries. The seatbelt comes next before he shuts the door and saunters off to the driver's side.

When he shuts the door behind him, sliding the key into the ignition, he looks at me and lets out a sigh that sounds exhausted. I wonder if he's been sleeping.

"I'm an asshole."

My forehead wrinkles. "And?"

He chuckles, turning sideways, placing his hand along my cheek. "And I'm sorry. I know that doesn't make up for the awful way I behaved toward you, but I hope it's a start." He blows out a breath, his emerald eyes serious as they bore into mine. "I was so angry about you keeping who you were from me."

I cut him off. "I know. Understand that I never meant to hurt you. I just …" For the millionth time this week, my eyes well with tears. It's miraculous that I'm not dehydrated. "I wanted to be there for you like you were for Bennett. It was wrong to not tell you who I really was."

Cade's head nods once in understanding. "You were right, though. I would have never given you a chance knowing you were his sister." His hand strokes down my face. "For so long, I blamed myself for his death. For all of their deaths. It's not something I can easily let go of." My heart plummets like maybe this is a goodbye speech and not a *Pretty Woman* moment. "But I'm trying. I've made weekly appointments with my therapist and have agreed to take the PTSD meds when I need them."

Are you there, heart? I can't feel you beating. Did he say he's trying?

Don't get excited. He may not be willing to try with you.

"That's great, Cade. I'm so proud of you."

And I mean it.

Cade flashes me an annoyed look, his frown looking extremely kissable. "Be quiet and listen," he scolds me. "What I'm trying to say is that I'm asking for a do-over. A clean slate. I'll be real with you and you be real with me. No more lying. No more hiding."

I swallow, blinking back at the face that has come to mean so much to me.

"Are you saying you forgive me? For not being honest with you about Bennett?"

Cade unbuckles my seatbelt and slides me to him. "I'm saying I love you, Brecklyn Brannon, and I'm asking if you can give me another chance to be the man your brother knew."

I kiss his lips, the wetness of my tears smearing his face. "I don't want the man my brother knew. I want the man who brushes marshmallows out of my hair. The man who walks on the outside of me so I don't get hit by oncoming traffic. I want the stubborn pain in the ass that asks me to talk dirty to him." I push at his chest, wanting him to lay back. I'm about to blow this man in Sue's driveway. Yeah, shit is about to get classy in here. But Cade hisses as if he's in pain, and I stop my near assault. "Oh my gosh. Did I hurt you?"

Cade grimaces, tugging his shirt up for me to see. Half of his chest is covered in a tattoo, covering his scars. The other half is bare, his scars evident in the sunlight. I trace the angry skin, irritated by the new ink.

"I didn't want to look like the old Cade," he mumbles, watching my face for a reaction. Gently, my fingertips graze his skin, over the burning tree, tracing the wings of the fleeing birds.

"It's beautiful," I tell him before placing a kiss on the bare scars on his chest, making sure this side of him doesn't get forgotten in the newness of the ink. He is who he is because of what he endured.

"Let me take you home, B." His question is hesitant like he's scared I might turn him down. I drag his shirt back down, kissing him lightly along his stubbled jaw.

"Okay, Major Jameson. Let's go home."

★ ★ ★

This isn't a movie and therefore we didn't drive off with the wind in our hair and smiles on our faces. I went back inside and cried and snotted in Sue's shirt while Cade stood awkwardly off to the side. He then had the pleasure of mercilessly teasing me while he helped me pack up my room.

Everyone has period panties, okay? Do not lie and say you don't.

"Those are Sue's. Put them down," I say flatly.

Cade laughs, holding the worst pair of panties up for me to see. "These are not Sue's," the idiot argues.

I snatch them from his shaking hands and shove him toward the closet. "How about you carry the boxes out to the truck so I can give these panties back to Sue?"

He doesn't buy it, but he picks up two boxes and carries them outside, his laughter carrying down the hallway.

Men.

A few hours later, all I could pack up is loaded in the back of Cade's truck. I kiss Sue goodbye and tell her I'll be back Monday morning.

Homegirl still needs a day job.

And besides, Sue is like family, and baking with her has become a constant in my life. Cade said Anniston offered me a job at the Foundation, cooking for the house since they anticipate more veterans, but I told her I would do that for free. Cooking is something I enjoy doing for my family.

Twenty minutes later, as the truck pulls into the driveway, all five guys and their commander stand on the porch holding *Welcome Home* signs and smiles.

It's then that I know exactly what Bennett was feeling in his letter to me.

I've finally found my place.

I'm finally home.

epilogue

Cade

"**R**ise and shine, Jameson! It's moving day."

Theo seems obnoxiously loud this morning. I have no idea what time it is, and I refuse to look. Exhaustion is real. Groaning, I roll over, feeling for the warm body next to me, and hook an arm around her naked torso, pulling her into me. My cock greets her first, jumping against her ass with the mere possibility of being inside her again. Granted, this is why I'm so tired in the first place.

I realized right off the bat that sleeping next to Breck was a far better solution than sleeping pills. It's not often that the nightmares strike anymore. Talking to the therapist, and to the families of my fallen team, has brought me some peace, at least where their deaths are concerned.

I still suffer from flashbacks, but instead of Drew standing there accusing me, I see him next to me, in the trenches, both of us fighting alongside each other. I still wake up sweating and needing to run out the memories, but instead, Breck holds my face and counts down from ten, pushes me back down, and then loves me until the last thing that's on my mind is leaving the bed.

"Two strays down. Four to go."

Ugh. I forgot he was still here. "Go away, Theo. I'm not running this morning."

His scoff sounds closer than I was expecting. Is he by the bed? I don't look because it will only encourage him.

"Just because you have a girlfriend now, Jameson, does not mean you can abandon the routine. Bros before hoes or whatever military slogan you guys like to use."

Silent laughter shakes the bed, and I realize Breck is laughing. The fact that she isn't pissed at Theo's intrusion makes me love her even more. She's adapted so well to living here.

"You mean dicks before chicks, Theo?"

Have I mentioned how incredibly sexy I find it that Breck gives Theo shit? By the way my dick is poking along the seam of her ass, she knows exactly what it does to me.

"Sure. Yeah. Whatever, B. Let's go, Jameson. My coffee is getting cold."

Breck pushes her bottom against me, drying humping the hell out of me.

"Go run with Killer. I'm not going this morning." I let out a moan when Breck opens her legs slightly to accommodate my extremely impatient cock. The wetness that greets me only solidifies my decision. "Out, Von Bremen!"

I should have known better when he doesn't move and the bed dips. "Go ahead. I'll wait while you give B a mediocre orgasm. It shouldn't take long. What did you tell me the other night, B? Four minutes tops?"

Breck smothers a laugh under the covers all the while taunting me with the back-and-forth movement of her hips.

"Don't laugh at him. It'll only incentivize him to keep on," I growl into her ear, and halt those mesmerizing hips with the firm grip of my hands.

"Go run with him. He's right. It's your thing."

I cut her off with a small thrust between her legs. Fuck me, she's even wetter now. "No, he'll live."

"I won't live."

"Go away, Theo!"

"Give us twenty minutes, Theo, and I promise to have him in a better mood for your run."

I groan when Theo's weight shifts off the bed. "I like that you're a negotiating woman, B. You could learn something from her, Jameson."

"Go!" I damn near roar. I am already lining up with the entrance to the promised land when I hear a low chuckle and the door clicks shut.

"I thought he would never leave," I say, rolling over and tossing the covers off after taking a quick look around. Knowing Theo, he's probably lurking in the corner or some shit, trying to get in a free show.

"You're gonna put me in a better mood, yeah?" I tease Breck as I tug her closer, encouraging her to straddle me. She needs no direction and slowly drags her legs over mine, spreading her arousal along my dick until she stills. Her hair is all mussed from sleep, but she has never looked sexier in this moment, sitting on top of me all confident and commanding, her pink nipples standing at attention just waiting for an order.

"Major Jameson, I think it's time you shut up and let me fulfill my promise."

With a fake huff of annoyance, I lay back against the pillows and stretch my arms out wide before tucking them behind my head.

"Show me what you got, babe."

She grins, and in the darkened room it almost looks predatory. And then she moves my arms from behind my head and places them on the slats of the headboard.

"Don't move them. Do you understand me?"

Aw, hell. She seriously is about to make Theo right and have me coming in four minutes flat. "Come o—"

Words fail me, and I can't seem to breathe when she slams down on top of me. Soft hands brace themselves on my chest, one at my

heart where the phoenix tree I had tattooed six months ago memori-
alizes my fallen family. Her fingers trace the lines of the leafless tree,
through the birds that fly for freedom, until she finds the burning
phoenix that rises from the ashes of the roots that define him. She
clutches my chest, no longer worried about hurting me. Alternating
between slow circles and hard thrusts, Breck loves every inch of me.
My hands stay put and let her have her moment even though I want
to grip her hard and shove every inch I can into her until she screams.

I relish the moment of being loved.

Of being cherished.

And when she lowers her mouth to my chest and kisses the scars,
I explode inside her as she sucks the very soul from my body.

"Merry Christmas, Cade."

"Merry Christmas, B."

"Who did this?"

Everyone struggles to contain their laughter while Anniston
points at the two Elf on the Shelfs placed in a precarious position atop
the decorated mantel. Amongst all the stockings, Alpha, the female
elf—no surprise there—is on her knees, her face planted in Omega's,
the male elf's, crotch. If that weren't funny enough, the white, milky
substance all over her face has my stomach cramping from holding in
my laughter.

"Aww, Ans," Theo starts, undeterred by the hate glare Anniston
is rocking. It's probably the twitch and the slight upturn of her mouth
that makes him continue on without a care. "She's just giving him a
Christmas blowjob. After all, it's the season of giving."

Breck's body shakes next to mine. She's become very comfortable in this unconventional family of ours, but even she knows to
hold in her laughter until Ans breaks first. This being our first official
Christmas together—last time Theo was rehabbing from a gunshot
wound—Anniston went all out. We tried to protest all the decorating
and gift giving, but Anniston wouldn't hear of it. So this whole Elf on

the Shelf idea has been our way of participating.

For the entire thirty days of Alpha and Omega's presence, they have been caught doing naughty—mostly pornographic—things. No one knows who does it each night, but I have to admit, after the first week, Breck and I joined in and participated in a few. And by the smile on Anniston's face, I'm betting some of the elf shenanigans were her and Theo's doing. The *only* reason she is making a stink about it today is because we are having guests. And well, some people may not find our humor as amusing as we do.

Finally, Anniston breaks with heaves of laughter. "Get this cleaned up or stash them somewhere. People will be here soon."

Theo strides over to the elves and swipes them off the mantel with one arm, right into Lawson's stocking. Anniston insisted on him having one even though he and Nicole have been moved out for over a year now. "All clean. What's next on this nightmarish morning, boss?"

Eyes narrowed, Anniston pinches Theo's arm. "Get—"

The doorbell rings, and we all groan.

"Breck. Help me in the kitchen?" Anniston calls out. Breck kisses me on the cheek and pulls away to follow Ans. Have I mentioned the love I have for a woman who can cook? The old saying that a way to a man's heart is through his stomach is not one hundred percent correct, but it holds some hard truth. Some days, Breck will text me what's on the menu for dinner, and my stomach is growling before I can even hit reply. But when she texts me what's on the menu for dessert—it's not food—I am rushing her like a linebacker just so I can have a little taste before everyone gets home.

Life is good.

No, scratch that.

Life is great.

Having Breck in my life has been life altering. She has the patience of a saint, bless her heart, when dealing with my PTSD. She gives just as good as she gets from Theo, and that makes me happier than it should. She's no longer insecure about Anniston but has developed a tight-knit friendship with her. Together they are an unstoppable force.

"Get the door, dipshit." Theo is shoving me toward the front.

"You get it," I argue for no other reason than to annoy him.

He scoffs. "I'm not getting it. It may be someone I have to speak to."

Oh, for fuck's sake.

"I'll get it, you fucking pussies." Mason pushes past us with annoyance and Theo winks, holding his fist out for a bump. Grinning, I bump it back.

"Cade!" Ugh. What now? "It's for you." For me? I didn't invite anyone over for Christmas.

I push past Mason and approach the door. There, standing amongst all the lights and potted Christmas trees, are my parents.

"Merry Christmas, Cade."

Something hot and prickly spreads under my skin. I try to swallow back the feeling but it keeps coming until my mom throws her arms around me, hugging me until it gets difficult to breathe. "I hope you don't mind," she sniffles, the tears dampening my shirt. "Anniston invited us to spend Christmas with you."

Damn Anniston. Never taking no for an answer. She asked me if I wanted to invite my parents but I told her they were probably busy, and not to worry about it. She obviously didn't give a fuck.

"I'm glad you could make it," I manage through the tight squeeze and lack of oxygen my mother is creating.

Even though I made amends with my parents over Drew's death, it still feels a little strained between us. Mostly on my end. I'm still a work in progress.

"Come inside," I say, pulling away.

My mom places a kiss on my cheek and moves inside the house. I hear, "Mama Jameson!" and then she's hugging Theo, squealing as he spins her around. I want to be annoyed that Theo has a better relationship with my parents than I do, but I can't. All I can do is smile at the best friend who's managed to penetrate through my defenses and become my brother.

"Son." Dad's touch draws my attention away from Mom and Theo.

"Dad." Extending my hand for a gentlemanly greeting, he takes it and pulls me in for a hug, clapping me on the back a few times. "Good to see you again, Cade. You look ... happy."

I nod, staying silent. I'm afraid my voice may come out gravelly and well, less manly. So I go with a nod over his shoulder.

I am happy. Happier than I've been in a very long time.

Hours pass with several more guest arrivals. Lawson and Nicole are huddled close on the couch, laughing at the bullshit coming out of the guys' mouths but more noticeably are the two newcomers that come to see Breck. Another Christmas gift from Anniston, Jess and Milos both flew out here to spend Christmas with Breck. The only family she claims. I never realized how much Breck relied on their friendship until seeing her with them, her face lit up, a gorgeous smile stretched from dimple to dimple ... she's absolutely stunning.

And happy.

"So, all of you guys are single, right?"

Jess is hilarious. She's given Hayes a run for his money in smack talking. I think I even saw him blush at one of her crass remarks. Milos is calmer, and I nearly made a mockery of myself when I growled as he greeted Breck with a hug. He took it in stride, said something in Croatian I didn't understand, but apparently Breck did because they both laughed and patted me on the back like it was a good try or something. I'm still not a huge fan of Milos, but so far his hands have kept to himself. A safe route for him.

A glass clinks several times in a row, drawing our attention to the heart of our family.

Anniston.

"I just wanted to say thank you all for being here today and celebrating our first real Christmas together as a family. Our lives have changed tremendously in two years. It hasn't always been easy, but we've persevered together." Anniston catches my eye. "Just like we always have. Theo and I are so grateful to call you family—"

"Speak for yourself, Ans." Anniston cuts Theo a look of promised death if he says shit like that again. "Fine, I like you assholes a little bit," he amends.

With a sigh, Anniston picks up where she left off. "As I was say-ing, we are so grateful to be sharing this day with all of you since …" She looks at Theo. For support? Surely not. When has Ans ever need-ed moral support? My stomach clenches with a sense of doom. I knew being happy would not last long. "Since we are opening the new quar-ters to house more guys today."

Whew.

We all clap and give a few dog-like barks in honor of the new space.

"I am happy to announce that even though I'll be sad to not see his face every morning" —she flashes me a teary smile—"I'm honored that he's agreed to take over the new barracks. Congratulations, Major Jameson, you have been promoted to commander."

Everyone claps and whistles while Breck squeezes my hand in celebration. Breck and I are moving out today. It's only into anoth-er building on the property, but it seems monumental. I've struggled with the idea for months, but Anniston pushed, like she always does, and gave me the encouragement I needed to do it.

I'm ready to lead another team.

I'm ready to give back to others. I owe it to Drew and Bennett and the rest of my fallen team.

I owe it to Anniston.

I owe it to myself.

"Quiet down."

Everyone shushes and gives Anniston the floor once more. "I couldn't be prouder of you, Cade." She takes a deep breath and looks around the room. "I have one more announcement to make before we open gifts." A tear falls down her cheek, and Theo stands, wrapping her in his arms. "We're gonna have a baby."

Silence.

"I'm pregnant," she tries again.

Silence.

"Congratulate us, fuckheads!" We all clap after Theo's demand,

Breck and my parents more excited than anyone. But for me and the guys … we're all terrified. Is this the end for us? Will Anniston want to get out of the lifestyle we have to raise the baby in a more normal environment? The thought has me nauseated.

Anniston breaks the awkward congratulations. "I know what you're thinking."

I highly doubt it, but damn if it doesn't make me feel shittier for being selfish and not wanting her to move on and have a life without us.

"You're thinking this poor girl will never have a date because no boy will be crazy enough to walk onto the plantation with five uncles who know how to snipe him from the driveway."

Did my heart start beating again? I think it did.

Breck squeezes my hand, feeling the tension coiling in my body and the sigh of relief I let out. Anniston wants to stay and raise this little one with all of us.

"I don't know about y'all, but I'm thinking now when Theo hears *Daddy* it won't quite have the same kind of appeal."

We all laugh as Theo lunges at Hayes and they exchange playful blows.

"Wait." It's just occurred to me what Anniston said. "It's a girl?"

Her lips tip up with blatant satisfaction when she nods and says, "Theo doesn't stand a chance."

I look at Theo, at the glare he's sending my way, and double over with laughter. "That's karma for you, Von Bremen." He flips me off. "Two women bossing you around …"

We all join in this time, laughing at Theo's expense. He takes it good-naturedly by throwing the ice from his drink. He still has an arm, so it hurts like a bitch when he pelts me square in the chest.

After our laughter dies down, and everyone gets a turn rubbing the small baby bump on Anniston's stomach, we open gifts and enjoy the love and laughter of each other's company.

"Cade. Can I see you outside for a moment?" I shift Breck off my leg and nod to my mom.

On the porch, I gesture to the swing for my mom to sit. "What's up?" I ask, sitting down next to her. A small wrapped package is clutched in her hand. I want to get up and go back into the house. Whatever she is about to give me will be a game changer. I can feel it, but I show respect and keep my ass planted on the swing.

"I wanted you to have this."

I don't know if I can take any more surprises today. I swallow hard and nod, reaching for the square gift wrapped in basic red wrapping paper. Slowly, I unwrap it and reveal a black, velvet box.

"It was my mother's. I want you to have it."

That hot, prickly feeling rushes along my skin again, this time making it up to my eyes. I already know what it is. Tradition is important to my mom's family. Clutched in my hand is my grandmother's ring that would have been for my brother. It's tradition to pass down a family heirloom to the firstborn. I can't open and look at it. Instead, I hand it back to her.

"I can't accept this."

She pushes back. "You can."

Another push. "I insist."

She shoves the box at me. She's done asking. "I know you think you don't deserve this, Cade, but like it or not, you are my son. I may not have birthed you but I've loved you as my own. I still love you. I have prayed for you every day." Tears flow freely from her eyes, making me feel like a total jackass. "You are my son. Honor me by taking this ring and continuing my family's legacy."

Fuck. With my finger, I swipe away her tears and pull her into a hug. She sniffles, squeezing me tight.

"It will be my honor, Mama."

As my mother cries silently into my chest, purging all the pent-up pain and anguish, I open the box and see an old, handcrafted setting with brilliant diamonds, and I know one thing.

This ring was made for Breck.

epilogue

Breck

Winding down the mountain roads with the windows down in Cade's truck feels a lot like riding a roller coaster, except Cade is driving so slowly that we may never reach our destination—a big fat secret he won't tell me. All I know is we're headed into the North Georgia Mountains, this horrifically long road the only route there.

"You know, babe, if you went over twenty-five miles an hour we may actually get there this weekend."

Cade clutches the steering wheel like at any moment a bear will dart out in front of us and he'll have to *fast and furious it* out of the way. I'm not complaining because the motion causes the muscles in his forearms to flex, and well, I can appreciate that view for the next few hours.

"How about you get your feet off the dash and let me drive?" He cuts his eyes to my freshly painted toes wiggling against his leather-wrapped dash.

"Why do I have to put my feet down? Do my feet stink?"

His jaw tics as he tries to hold back a grin. The three-day scruff he's rocking is so sexy when he pairs it with an annoyed facial expression. If I have to piss him off this entire ride to ensure that jaw and scruff are between my legs upon arrival, then so be it. I'll take one for the team.

"No, your feet do not stink. However, if I were to have a wreck, your legs would be obliterated."

Ugh. Sometimes I find his protectiveness cute. Right now, not so much. I did not shave my legs and paint my toes this awesome shade of pink to match my lip gloss for him not to notice. At this angle, I totally look like I could have a thigh gap.

"I'll take my chances, Commander."

"I wasn't asking, Private Brannon."

Fine. He's going to be a hard-ass today. I can already feel it.

"I hope you're not going to be grouchy this weekend. It's our first trip together. Get excited, Cade!"

"I am excited. I just want you to arrive in one piece." He trails a cursory glance down my legs which don't look nearly as sexy on the floorboard. "Sexy-ass legs and all."

Okay, so that comment made it worth the two hours in the bathroom this morning.

"Since you put it like that, I guess I can behave for another forty-eight hours."

A laugh bubbles out of him. "I am not driving *that* slow. We should be there in another hour." Immediately, I call him on his bullshit estimation by arching a brow. He shakes his head with a chuckle and amends, "Hour and a half. Tops." By some miracle, he takes one hand off the wheel and makes the sign of the cross on his chest, bumping his dog tags in the process.

About three months ago, he walked out of the bathroom with them hanging around his neck. I didn't acknowledge them at the time because I knew he didn't want me to. Instead, I ran to Anniston and shared the news. Together, on the floor of her office, we cried tears of joy. And that night, when Cade and I crawled into bed, I wrapped them in my hands and moved on top of him until he heard every silent word through the movement of my hips.

I loved him.

And I was so very proud of him.

"Well, at least let me find something better to listen to on the radio," I argue, already pressing buttons on the stereo before he can object.

"What? So now you don't like the classics?"

"No, I just want to listen to something a little more upbeat and happy. *This classic country*, as you call it, is wearing me down with all the whining. Do they ever end up happily ever after?"

Cade purses his lips as I find a local pop station. The Lumineers bang out a catchy tune I've heard a million times so I immediately start to sing it. The music pulses through the speakers and my body sways as I clap along with song.

"Sing with me, Jameson!"

I try pulling at his hand, but Mr. Responsible is not having it, and keeps them secured on the wheel. He gives me a raspy, "Ho Hey," along with the song and it goes straight to my nether regions, making me feel like I want to be very naughty on this back road to nowhere. Unbuckling my seatbelt, I shuffle across the bench seat, sliding up next to his cool body, where he has the air conditioning vent blowing directly on him, which makes no sense with the windows down. I close it because I have on shorts, and no one told him to dress in cargo pants and a t-shirt in ninety-eight-degree weather. Mountains or not, it's still hotter than the seventh circle of hell with Georgia's humidity.

"Don't even play. Get back to your side and put your seatbelt on."

I'm going to tell you my secret to get what you want with Commander Jameson.

Defiance.

"Make me."

The low growl he emits carries over the tambourines of the happy song and immediately takes the atmosphere from carefree to intense. Just like I'd hoped. My fingers work at his zipper, pulling and tugging. He's not even helping me a little bit, but that's okay. I'm a pro at pulling

Jameson Jr. out of his cargo pants. I've had tons of practice since we've moved in together.

"You're going to make me wreck."

Bull. I've done this before. For some reason, he's playing hard to get today.

"Then I suggest you focus."

His voice cracks when I slide his hardened length past my teeth. "Come on, B. Just wait until we get to the cabin," he pleads.

So we're headed to a cabin. He's been tighter than a frog's ass about where we're going for the weekend. Hell, they all have. I tried bribing Theo with chocolate chip cookies, his favorite, but he wouldn't budge. This is going down in the Jameson manual under information extraction.

Tongue flat against the prominent vein, I force every bit I can take of him down my throat until the tears prick my eyes. And then I suck. Up and down, I pull random grunts and groans until the truck veers off the road and comes to a stop.

Uh oh.

I'm trying to keep the rhythm, but when he reaches between us and unlatches his seatbelt, I falter. The victorious grin I've tried to keep under wraps emerges triumphantly.

"Apparently, you need something to settle down." Cade pulls me up, my lips making a popping sound as I release him.

"I have no idea what you're talking about." Countering him when I lick my lips may have been the final straw because before I know it, he shoves me to my back, pops the button on my shorts, and pulls them down, leaving them dangling on one leg. Too tall to lie on top of me, Cade settles on one knee and then with a jerk that steals my breath, he lines up with my entrance.

"I'm going to fuck you hard and fast," he warns, giving himself a few strokes.

"Good," I taunt him further, locking gazes with those emerald eyes. "I like it when you're rough."

His nostrils flare, and I'm ready when he pushes forward, never warning me again.

True to his word, he fucks me fast and hard on some back road in the middle of nowhere. Sweat drips down his forehead, running along the hard lines of his neck until they reach his t-shirt and stop. His dog tags jingle with every thrust, almost like they're part of the music still playing on the radio. Sitting up, I wrap my legs around him and pull him closer, encouraging him to go harder. The strain in his face is evident. He's close. So am I, for that matter, but I want to hear it before I take him with me.

Between pants, I whisper, "Ask me."

His eyes close and his breathing turns shallow until he opens his eyes again. Green eyes that have witnessed death and destruction look at me with reverence as he says, "Can I offer you a ride home?"

For all the women who think the only declaration of love is in the form of three words, let me tell you that knowing someone loves you comes in many forms. I may not be normal. Cade may not be normal. But what we have is real, and him asking me if he can give me a ride home says everything it needs to say. He loves me.

"I am home," I return before everything clenches inside me, and we both tip over the edge of sanity, clutched in each other's arms.

We're cleaned up and back on the road in no time. Cade seems a little more relaxed than he was so I'll take that as a win. As for me, I'm secured in a seatbelt, far enough away from Cade that I won't be too much a distraction for the duration of the trip.

"Are we there yet?" I tease.

"Hush. Listen to your boy bands."

Scowling, I rifle through my purse and find my phone for something to do. My hand grazes the bottle of meds Anniston gave me for an emergency. I have to admit I'm nervous about being alone with Cade during the fourth of July. I know fireworks bother him even though he says he will be fine. Anniston gave me a rundown on what to do if he has an episode, along with some sedatives. I tried to argue that we should take this trip at another time so he's in a place he's comfortable, but he wouldn't hear it.

I place my thumb on the phone and bring up the home screen—a picture of Cade and me. I'm covering his eyes as I lead him into the house which was insanely decorated for his birthday we did several weeks after the fact. But what's so memorable about that moment was his smile. It was the brightest I had ever seen it. That day, surrounded by his friends and family, he was genuinely happy.

Two texts messages flash on the screen, one from Anniston and one from Theo.

Ans: Have fun! I can't wait to hear all about it.

Gah, I love her. I know I was hellbent on hating her, but after getting to know her, I fell for her just like the guys. Once I got past her layers, she's become a really great friend to me.

Theo's text makes me laugh. Obviously, it was intended more for Cade so I read it aloud.

"Theo texted." Cade rolls his eyes but is already grinning. "He says, and I quote, 'Tell Jameson I noticed he didn't pack enough condoms so I put an extra box in his bag. I'll be disappointed if he doesn't use them all. I didn't raise a quitter! You know I always got your back, B. You're welcome.'"

We both laugh out loud into the cab of the truck, now that Cade rolled the windows up, claiming we needed to cool off before we ended up just going back home and fucking all weekend. Honestly, that doesn't sound like a bad idea at all.

Laying my head back, the cool air blowing through my hair—it probably looks a mess but I don't care—along this winding road, feels like heaven with Cade by my side.

Apparently heaven also felt like sleep because when I wake up, Cade is poking me in the side. "Now she's quiet," he says, all cute and taunting. "Come on. I want to show you something."

I check for drool and climb out when he opens the door. "What year is it?" I tease.

"Ha ha. You're hilarious." He tugs me to his side and wraps one of those beefy arms around my shoulders. "Have you ever went panning for gold?"

I hope the look on my face does not reflect what I'm thinking, because what the fuck? What does he take me for—a coal miner's daughter? "No, I can't say that I have."

He chuckles, clearly reading into my meaning. "Well, you can't come to Dahlonega without trying it."

Where the hell is Dahlonega?

"Whatever floats your boat, Jameson."

Inside the cabin-like building along the river, Cade buys us a few bags of dirt which seems silly but whatever. "I thought we would be digging for gold. What is this?" I flip the bag of dirt over in my hand, trying to see if I have anything more than mud in it.

"Do you want to dig in the dirt?" He points to my nails. "I hear it's great for the cuticles."

I scowl at his awful sense of humor and follow a troll-like man to what looks like a huge trough. "Smartass."

Cade shrugs, grabbing my hand before the guy tells us what to do. Basically, pour your bag of dirt into this thing that looks like a sand strainer, and see what you get. I'm sure it's rigged but I have to admit, I've never done anything like this before and it's kind of exciting.

"Let me know if you need anything," troll-man says, slinking off behind his counter.

Cade thanks him and opens one of our bags of dirt. "So, you know what to do, right?"

I nod. "Pour, sift, and scream if I find gold."

He makes this soft noise and corrects me. "Maybe not scream. You don't want to scare the other guests."

My face scrunches as I look around the empty cabin, "What other patrons? It's just us."

Cade looks around too and shrugs. "Maybe it's the off season?" It's Fourth of July weekend. I would think they would be busy, but what do I know, I'm no travel agent. I let it go and focus on finding gold. Cade seems intently focused on his dirt, so I try to get to work, carefully sifting out the dirt in the trough water for any gems that may be hiding underneath.

When I turn up empty-handed and Cade has three flakes of gold, I'm pissed. "I got a bad batch," I pout.

He chuckles and hands over his sifter. "Try mine. I seem to be having good luck today."

He comes around and stands behind me, placing his hands on the sifter, helping me sift the dirt.

I'm combing through every grain of dirt when I spot gold. "Gold! I found gold!" Acting like I just struck oil, I bounce up and down as Cade chuckles behind me. Carefully, I clean off the mud. I see more, and it's in the shape of … "Oh my gosh."

Cade lets go of me, taking the ring from the sifter, and eases down to a knee. "I've made a lot of mistakes in my life." He pulls in a ragged breath and gives me a gentle smile. "You will not be one of them, Brecklyn Brannon."

There's no point in stopping the tears. They're coming whether I want them to or not.

"I don't know why you have no self-preservation and love me."

Oh hell. I drop to my knees, against his protests, and place my hands on each side of his face. I want to remember every single second of this moment. I want to remember the almost tears that well along the bottom of his eyes. I want to remember his hands shaking on mine. And most of all, I want to remember the way he is looking at me. Like he can't imagine ever loving me as much as he does right now.

"I love you with everything that I am and everything I hope to be. I'm not perfect, Breck. I'm flawed and damaged beyond what is repairable. I'm going to piss you off and probably let you down eventually, but Breck …"

With his thumb, he wipes away the tears along my cheek. "I will never betray you or forsake you. I promise to love you and protect you until my very last breath."

A hiccup escapes me as he seals our fate with one last declaration. "I feel like I should tell you that you could do so much better than me, but I'm selfish and I'm begging you to marry me instead so I'll never have to live a day without you."

I silence the rest of his proposal by kissing the ever-loving shit out of this man. I kiss him so hard he loses his balance and has to stick his hands out behind him so we don't fall on our asses. I kiss him like there's not a weird looking little man watching us.

I kiss him like it's our forever.

Back at the cabin Cade rented for the weekend, we're naked—of course—under a blanket, staring at the night sky. Fireworks are going off every few seconds, lighting up the sky in vivid colors of the rainbow. I tried to get Cade to go inside when the first one went off and he tensed up behind me, but he refused, claiming the mountains have the most beautiful skies. So we stayed, wrapped in each other's arms as the rest of the country celebrates.

"How are you feeling?" I ask.

He slides his mother's ring back and forth on my finger, and then places the softest kiss to my cheek and says, "Like I'm free."

other books

Commander

Gorgeous

Drifter

Pitcher

Join my **reader** group, Kristy's Commanders, on Facebook.
www.facebook.com/groups/147968202596232

Sign up to receive updates on all my new releases.
Check out my website and purchase signed copies of your favorite
paperback.
www.authorkristymarie.com

Follow me!

Amazon
www.amazon.com/author/mariekristy

BookBub
www.bookbub.com/authors/kristy-marie

Instagram
www.instagram.com/authorkristymarie

Facebook
www.facebook.com/authorkristymarie

Twitter
www.twitter.com/authorkristym

Goodreads
www.goodreads.com/author/show/17166029.Kristy_Marie

acknowledgements

To the best readers in the world, I wrote this book for you. Never in a million years did I think Cade would draw as many fans as he did. I hope I did him justice and gave him the happily ever after you envisioned. Thank you for all your kind words and wonderful reviews. You are the reason I continue to write these crazy stories. If you loved, Gorgeous, please consider leaving an honest review. Each review means the world to a new author.

Thank you to my reader group, Kristy's Commanders, for your enthusiasm and support through this whole process. You guys are like family to me and I couldn't have done it without you.

To my beta readers, Sue, Candece, Laura, Misha, and Audrey. Thank you for encouraging me and reading this book so many times that you could quote it. For talking me down when I thought the material was destined for the trash. I pray I didn't scar you for life with all those rough drafts.

Thank you to Nikita, Andrea, Vanessa, Stefanie, Cee Cee, Nicci, Ange and Cynthia for taking my mess and looking over it. It's a hard job but someone has to do it. I'm honored it's you.

Jessica. Each time I have to write something to you, it never feels like it will be enough. I won't ever be able to thank you like you deserve. For pulling me up and dusting me off when I had meltdown after meltdown. You're the reason I'm still standing. You're the constant in my life. Whether we're just talking shit or discussing real world issues, you always put a smile on my face. I love you more than words.

Ajee. Whatever I did to deserve your friendship, I need to do it more often. Thank you for staying up and plotting with me. For believing in me even when I didn't. For being the powerhouse behind my brand and creating the brilliant graphics for Cade. You are one of the most amazing women I have ever met and it's been an honor to call you my friend. Please never leave me. I will have to stalk you and shit will get awkward.

Thank you to Sonja, one of the greatest readers ever, for coming up with Cade's phoenix tattoo. I hope you love it.

To my sister, thank you for being my biggest fan and lying to me when I sent you first draft crap to read. I know it was garbage but the fact that you always made me feel like I just wrote a Pulitzer Prize winning piece means the world to me.

To my team that made this book decent. Letitia Hasser of RBA Designs. You amaze me how you can take my scattered ideas and turn it into something amazing. Stacey of Champagne Formats. Every time I think you've out done yourself, you go and be incredible again. Thank you for being so kind to me and teaching me your bookish ways. I heart you. And to Kara of Great Imaginations Editing. Thank you for taking a million typos and turning them into actual words.

And to my family that will never read this book. I'll tell you *thank you* in the kitchen. I just wrote a fucking book and I'm tired of typing.

about the author

Kristy Marie lives in Georgia with her husband and three children. When she isn't reading or writing, you can find her at SunTrust Field cheering on the Atlanta Braves. Commander in Briefs is her first series but definitely not her last.